Old News

An Edna Ferber Mystery

Ed Ifkovic

Poisoned Pen Press

Poisoned Pen Press
6962 E. First Ave., Ste. 103
Scottsdale, AZ 85251
www.poisonedpenpress.com
info@poisonedpenpress.com

Printed in the United States of America

For Bob and Ginny

Chapter One

"Murderer! The nerve!"

My mother's icy words startled me. I stopped walking, baffled, as she pinched her face into a tight, hard mask, her dark eyes glassy with fury. Yet she was staring straight ahead, taking in the busy hot July sidewalk. Nearby, in front of a four-story apartment building, a boy in grimy knickers and slough boy cap was batting a baseball with a hickory stick while another boy, crouched down on the opposite sidewalk, yelled to him. "C'mon, Izzy. Learn to hit the ball. C'mon." Hearing my mother's loud voice, the boy with the bat froze, stepped onto a stoop, tucked his bat between his legs, his eyes wide.

"Mother." I reached out and touched her elbow, but she flicked me away. "What?"

She darted ahead. "That brazen woman," she was mumbling. "How dare she!"

For a split second, almost involuntarily, she turned her head to the left, resting her glacial gaze on the woman tucked into an old Adirondack chair on a shadowy front porch. Throwing back her head in a display of disgust—a gesture I'd long endured—my mother let out a harrumph. I found myself smiling in spite of myself. My little mother, like a fussy yet feisty stepmother out of a child's fairy tale, appeared a stick-figure vaudeville dowager, all indignation and bile.

"*Khutspedik*!" She slipped into Yiddish. "Brazen! Some folks have no shame, Edna."

"What?" I adjusted the package I was carrying.

My mother unfroze her mask, striding ahead so quickly she left me standing there, the bewildered daughter, watching the old woman on that porch.

Suddenly, horribly, our eyes locked.

What I saw in that woman's withered face was a troubling mix of fear and sadness, a woman folded into that big chair. She wrapped her chubby arms around her chest and suddenly dipped her head so that her abundant ivory white hair shielded a haunted face. I gasped, so stark was that fleeting meeting of eyes.

My mother had already climbed the steps of the sprawling Victorian home next door, pausing on the landing to look back and yell out my name—"Edna, really!"

I said again, "What?" She responded with a loud clearing of her throat.

When I looked back at the porch, the old woman had disappeared. A screen door slammed. Then an unseen hand closed the heavy oak door behind it.

I couldn't move.

"Edna, would you become the talk of the street?" my mother hissed. "What is the matter with you?" Her waving became frantic.

I followed her up the steps, but glanced over at the empty front porch. The two houses were similar in style, three-story homes with wraparound porches, floor-to-ceiling windows, though the one we were visiting had ledges with boxes of ivy and phlox. Glorious houses with arabesque trim and gingerbread scalloping. They were anomalies on Monroe Street, now dotted by four-story wood-framed apartment houses, the first floors occupied by storefront dentists, tobacco shops, kosher bakeries, and tailors. The long block began at Maxwell Street, that roaring, cluttered open-air marketplace. My mother and I had stepped off the Jefferson trolley, skirted around pushcart peddlers and hawkers, and headed down Monroe. The soot-blackened apartment houses were ramshackle, unpainted, with faded green asphalt shingles and tarpaper roofs. At the corner little girls played hopscotch, giggling and speaking in broken English. Despite the heat, two bearded men argued in a doorway, both dressed in *kapotes*, those long black coats, and wide-brimmed Russian hats pulled low over shiny foreheads. They spoke rapid-pace Yiddish, pointing at each other, speaking over the other.

Every time we walked along Monroe, my mother grumbled. Today an itinerant scissor- grinder, his rickety contraption braced to his back, had jostled her, and was rewarded with a verbal comeuppance. The same with a shifty young man who pulled up his sleeve to reveal his arm covered with used watches as he whispered of a deal he'd give her. Only look, please.

When she entered the foyer of the home we were visiting for two weeks, she let out a sigh of relief: the grisly gauntlet survived, pesky street rabble avoided, precious refuge won. My mother wasn't happy visiting on Monroe Street.

"I really have no choice," she'd whispered to me when the invitation was offered. "Old friends. My dear Esther. We have no choice."

Now my mother dropped her packages onto a little oak table near the front door, then grasped her throat, a gesture that mimicked someone strangling her—in case I missed the point. She faced me. "I will go to bed knowing a murderer sleeps steps away."

Again, my feeble question. "What?"

"We will be murdered in our beds."

"Mother…"

She lost patience with me. "Lord's sake, Edna. For a writer you certainly have no memory for…important events." She nodded toward the unseen home next door. "Leah Brenner. That dreadful woman stabbed her poor husband Ivan to death. A knife to the neck. A decent man, hard-working, stabbed." She pointed. "Right there in that parlor. Feet from us. Next door." She shivered and walked away. "There is so little justice left in Chicago."

"I remember now," I called after her.

She narrowed her eyes. "I should hope so, Edna. I talked of nothing else for days. Frankly, it was the murder none of us will ever forget."

• • ● • •

I did remember, of course, though I'd not thought about the scandal for years. In fact, I never knew Leah Brenner years back, and probably had glimpsed her only a few times. But I did have a vague memory, one time, of seeing an attractive woman standing on that very porch. True, I'd only visited my mother's old friend, Esther, one other time, back in the summer of 1905, another sweltering, heat-wave summer, two blurred weeks when I was nineteen years old and working as a reporter for the *Milwaukee Tribune*. That was eighteen years back now, a lifetime ago. I'd never said a word to Leah Brenner, though I kept that image of a beautiful woman in her forties, out of place on that porch in a dress no one else on Monroe Street would dare to wear, a daffodil-yellow taffeta go-to-meeting dress.

Now one image came back to me: she stood there, immobile, her dark hair covered by a black lace scarf—despite the steamy heat—as she watched the street with a cold stare. It was the coldness that made me notice her. A colorful Goya portrait—a voluptuous woman in yellow and black.

I was a young woman then, impatient with that mandatory visit to my mother's old friends, Esther Newmann and her family. Esther was a kind, overflowing woman, round as a plump hen, someone my mother, Julia, sometimes claimed was a distant cousin. Other times she said Esther was simply an old friend of the family, part of a close-knit neighborhood back in Germany. Kindred spirits, these families, bound with a loyalty to the Old World left behind. But the story shifted every so often.

During that short visit, Leah Brenner stood on her porch dressed in that elegant tea dress and muttered as some errant boys took a shortcut to the next street by running through her yard, slingshots in back pockets and huckleberry grins on their beet-red faces. That was the sole image I held of her—not one of heinous murder.

At that time I had a schoolgirl crush on her son, Jacob—slender Jacob with the shaggy hair and careful moustache and those mooncalf mink-brown eyes in a long, gaunt face—twenty-five or -six, a vagabond poet who once idly flirted with me. I, horrified and sputtering, turned my back on him—not because I was rejecting the handsome man but because I was afraid he'd see me blushing, trembling. He wasn't happy with my cavalier dismissal. His cruel ditty spread up and down the street that week, words that others happily hurled at me as I walked there:

Edna, Edna, sugar and spice,
An orchid locked in frozen ice.
Edna, Edna,
Not nice—

The rhyme did nothing to squelch my foolish ardor. I'd watch him saunter down Monroe, headed to Maxwell Street, whistling, his coal-black hair glistening with oil, black polished high-button shoes, and a rakish cap on his head. He'd wink at the girls, do a half-bow, and his matinee-hero moustache would shift seductively. I dreamed about him, felt my heart flutter when he appeared, but so did my sister, Fannie. So did most of the girls on Monroe Street.

Three years later, another brutally hot Chicago summer, August 2, 1908, his mother plunged a knife into the neck of her ailing husband, Ivan, the local butcher. A marital spat, ferocious, in the family parlor, and then—an impossible act. Or so it was said. The police dragged her in, but she'd seemed in a coma, unresponsive or icy, stoic, so the gossipmongers variously reported. According to my mother, she had to be carried to the Harrison Street Station lockup. She nodded her head at their questions, closed her eyes, and waited. Everyone believed she was guilty because she never fought back. Even, I heard, her children—including my beloved Jacob. Everyone talked about it…that long hot summer in South Chicago, a word-of-mouth court of law, a rag-tag gossip mill of Homeric sweep. Did you hear how Leah Brenner, that beautiful woman, went mad and killed her husband? A pity, such a stunning woman.

My mother had whispered. "And a Jewish mother, can you

believe? Such things don't happen." Then, a sigh. "A curse on that family, always."

I hadn't thought of that murder for years, though I still thought, rarely, of Jacob.

We'd all read the sheaf of news clippings Esther sent to us in Appleton, Wisconsin, the blow-by-blow account in the *Chicago Tribune* and the *Herald & Examiner*. My mother devoured them as though reading a yellow-backed potboiler from Bertha M. Clay. Leah Brenner a murderer? It never worked for me: that juxtaposition of the attractive matron in yellow who struck me as so composed, a beautiful woman eyeing the hardscrabble boys slinking past. Then the story disappeared from the press and from our conversations.

My own world was unraveling then—my disaffection with my grueling reporting job in Milwaukee, my sudden and unwelcome nervous breakdown, my sheepish return to Appleton, my…my beloved father dying…

Now, fifteen years after the sensational murder of a simple Jewish butcher by his devoted wife, I was back on Monroe Street for two weeks—and Leah Brenner sat on her front porch. She probably was in her late fifties or early sixties now, but she looked older—the abundant white hair, the tiny body. She startled me. Worse, I'd caught the woman's eye and was immediately enveloped by a stunning loneliness that covered her like a shroud.

The knife-wielding murderer back on her porch, her hands folded decorously into her lap, her woeful stare taking in the helter-skelter street.

Leah Brenner had come home.

Chapter Two

My mother raised her voice and wagged a finger like a hectoring schoolmarm. "For God's sake, why didn't you tell me, Esther?"

Rattled, Esther mumbled an apology.

"We'll be murdered in our beds." My mother pointed to the ceiling, doubtless imagining her unprotected bed at the end of the upstairs hallway. She shivered.

Esther's voice faltered. "Well, Julia, really…I think…you…I didn't think you…" She stopped, helpless. "*Nu*, I'm sorry."

My mother was muttering something.

"What?" I asked.

"That woman was always too pretty. Such women are dangerous. There ought to be a law against…excessive beauty."

I smiled at her. "Mother, hardly a crime."

Her glance was unfriendly. "Thank God we in this family never had to worry about such a problem."

Esther's eyes softened. "It's all right, Julia. Leah is harmless. She's been back for a few years now. No one says anything. Life is…normal now. Nothing bad…"

My mother started to say something, but stopped.

In the steamy, large kitchen, I caught my breath. Sweat dripped into my eyes. My dress stuck to my body. A dreadfully hot day. A loaf of bread was rising in the oven, a pot of water boiled on the stove, and Esther chased after a pesky fly with a swatter. The two women seemed oblivious to the sauna. Instead, they chatted away, merrily, peculiarly content in the room, while I patted my forehead with a handkerchief.

This was the heart of the house, the pulse, safe haven for the women of the home, *di kikh*: cozy, with the tantalizing aromas of a meal in preparation. The heart and soul of the rollicking, loving Jewish family, a room where conversations and confidences among women took place. The thick oak round claw-foot table was covered with stained oilcloth, the walls had been painted too many times—now lush green and white, with traces of old red and black seeping through—and on the walls hung homiletic mottoes encased in glass and blunt black frames, an oversized calendar by the doorway, Hebrew letters advertising Nate's Delicatessen on Maxwell above a grainy black-and-white photograph of the popular storefront. The air was thick with the battling scents of cinnamon, of vanilla, of diced peppers and onions, of sour cream. Every afternoon the inviting, rich tang of yeast as bread dough swelled in a white enamel bowl on the sink counter, stacks of freshly laundered dish towels covering the top. Comforting as a baby's breath, the heartbeat here took you back to storied villages happily, if mournfully, left behind in the Old Country. *Unsere leite.* Our people. Sit. Please. Make yourself to home. *Kum areyn.* Come in.

Esther had been rolling out dough for strudel, and the wafer-thin dough covered most of the table, even lapping precariously over one edge. Motes of white flour drifted into the air, and a slant of afternoon sunlight streamed in from a side window, illuminating a ghost-like shaft across the room. She'd started to cut the dough, but had paused, knife in hand, as my mother thundered the news of Leah sitting on her own porch. I saw momentary confusion in Esther's face, her eyes blinking, but also something else: a desire that Julia leave the subject alone. Esther liked an even, serene life, daily routines that allowed her peaceful nights of undisturbed rest.

"Well…" she stammered, glancing away.

"Well, nothing, Esther dear."

Sighing, Esther put down the knife and wiped her flour-white hands with a dishtowel. She turned to me with a feeble smile. "Edna, some lemonade. Fresh. For you." She hurried to the icebox and poured me a glass. Icy cold, tart, and robust. I remembered it from eighteen years before. Esther's summertime elixir. A cure-all.

But not today.

Both women stared at each other, a curious standoff, these two childhood friends. Esther sighed, but my mother was not in the mood for peace. A contrast, indeed, these two women, though both were short. Esther, early sixties now, happily round, ringlets of fat around her neck, her middle, even her forearms, her moonlike face unblemished and pink, the old woman beginning to look like the baby she was more than a half-century before. She'd stuffed herself into a flowered housedress that had seen too many washings, the crimson tea roses now bleeding pink; she ignored a burst seam at one hip, the unraveled hem of the dress that sagged at her ankles, these days an old-fashioned look in a post-war decade in which hemlines had begun to shoot upward. A stained white apron, much like a butcher's apron, thick and severe, was tied at the back and dropped to her shins. With her iron-gray hair pulled back from her forehead and sloppily tied with a frayed ribbon, she looked the aged family servant, the Tuesday washerwoman who spoke no English and wept in Yiddish.

A contrast to cosmopolitan Julia Ferber, the same age, born into the same comfortable North Side Chicago neighborhood, this woman who left the rigidity and coziness of the German Jewish home to marry the handsome Hungarian immigrant with dreams and nothing else. Julia, a slender slip of a woman, always in fashionable dress of frilly lace brocade or creamy burgundy silk or summery white linen—Julia, whose narrow, tight face you never forgot because her deep-set eyes held you, shadowy, so much anger there, so much resentment, so much judgment, so much…unforgiveness. A woman who never let her two daughters forget her failed marriage to a quiet, scholarly man who wouldn't fight back. A dynamo, always here, then there, and never happy anywhere. A husband dead now after years of illness and blindness, her life spent six months in New York, six months in Chicago, dependent on a daughter who made bags of money from her popular short stories sold to *Everybody's* and *Good Housekeeping.*

She never thanked me.

Both woman sat down in the hard-backed chairs pulled from the table, and I joined them, all three of us quietly sipping lemonade. Julia faced her friend, waiting.

"Nearly one hundred in the shade today," I commented slowly. "Three days in a row." No one answered me. Beads of sweat glistened on our faces. Another housefly buzzed by, and Esther absently followed its progress. She was too tired to swat it. She sat there without talking.

Avoiding Julia's stare, Esther finally broke the silence, her fingertips playing with the edge of the strudel dough, already turning brown. "You gotta feel sorry for her."

Julia bit her lip and put down the glass with a thud. Flour wafted into the air, a small white cloud. "Esther, you were always the easygoing, soft-hearted sad sack." A thin smile, kind. "I grant you that. A *mensch*, truly. What can I say? A little girl hugging stray cats who always scratched you. Giving away your last piece of candy." Then her voice hardened. "But surely you cannot allow…"

Esther held up her hand. "Allow? Julia, a woman can live in her own house. What say do I have? Any of us? No laws broken… she has children…"

My mother returned the hand gesture, traffic-sign style. "In the name of God, Esther. Do you hear the words that come from you? There are young children on this street. Families. Respectable folks."

Helpless, Esther turned to me. "Edna, what do you think?"

I deliberated. "Esther, I have one brief image of Leah Brenner from eighteen years ago. Before the murder, of course. She is standing on her porch dressed for a party in a bright yellow dress. I remember thinking—what a beautiful woman. Jacob's mother. That memory—which I know is not helping here." I drew in my breath. "Well, to be truthful, today she's a little old lady, harmless, still an eye-catching woman, I grant you—but lost-looking, sad."

My mother tapped my wrist with her fingertips, her familiar Morse code that communicated my failure to grasp even basic human behavior. "Edna, really. You're always ready to forgive the worst of humanity."

I narrowed my eyes. "And you sometimes condemn the best of humanity."

She drew her lips into a thin line. "That makes no sense, Edna."

I shrugged, imitating her, and spoke to Esther. "It was so long ago. All I recall are bits of information from the clippings you sent us. I remember that she was sent away, no? But not to prison, if I remember correctly. Some home? So now she is living back at her home? Was she found guilty?" My mother visited Esther three or four times over the long span of years, the last perhaps five years earlier, but she never mentioned Leah to me.

Both women glanced at each other, conspiratorially, as though considering how to shield a pesky child from grownup indiscretion and scandal. My mother's crooked mouth suggested disgust—and disbelief.

Esther peered up at the copper-plated ceiling, disturbed by a wispy dust web hanging off the overhead light. She whispered a word. "Guilty." She shook her head sadly. "The whole story…I mean, it's the only story that this street cared about. But there are not many old-timers still living on the street nowadays. When it happened back then, she…froze. They found her bending over Ivan's body, quiet, quiet. Like…dead. She never said a word… even when they charged her with murder. The whole time— quiet. Only this moaning from deep inside her. She wouldn't answer. Like she just *lost* her voice."

Julia interrupted. "They never found the knife. I remember that."

Esther had a faraway look in her eyes. "I never understood that. They said she probably washed it off, put it back in the kitchen. You know, there were knives everywhere. The wife of a butcher." She actually smiled wistfully.

"And they believe she had the presence of mind to do that?" I wondered. "A crime the result of an argument. That strikes me as impossible."

Esther shrugged. "So who knows? What can I say? They took her away. Everything happened so fast."

"She confessed?"

"No. Stony silence. What I know is what Jacob tells my Adolph. They are very close, those two…even afterwards. Especially afterwards. Adolph the jokester can't tolerate nobody talking about that family. Jacob took it real hard. After all, his mama was taken away. So close to his mama, that boy. Always. He's a young man then, a boy really, crying, crying. Some whispered her silence covered her son's guilt. A mother will not let a son be taken away. So who knows? So my Adolph he followed Jacob around, the protector always, even as boys. Everyone pointed at Jacob. So sad, the young boy whose mama slices his father…" She squinted. "And Adolph tells me that Jacob says to the police, 'She didn't kill Papa.' Over and over, like a chant, he says. Jacob almost arrested, fighting the police. He wants to rip his mama from the arms of the police. Yet the police don't believe it. 'Yes,' they say, 'simple story. Wife kills husband. It happens all the time.'"

I interrupted, peeved. "And the whole street believes it."

My mother whispered, "They'd had a big fight that morning, Leah and Ivan. A horrible fight, bloody. Everyone talked about it."

"Married folks fight," I offered.

A slap of sarcasm from my mother. "So how would you know?"

A familiar barb. Me, unmarried at thirty-eight, the spinster novelist who drifted from Chicago to New York, suitcases and mother at her side. My sister, Fannie, happily married now with daughters. Though my mother harped on my unmarried state, I also knew—as she knew, deep down and resolutely—that she demanded this spinster daughter remain so, and stationed at her side.

I pursed my lips. "Because that's all I used to see."

My mother and I both tried to look sorry—a tired skirmish, that one.

"Anyway," Esther went on, "I guess they decided she was crazy, like she'd lost her mind in a fit of anger—she'd have to be, Jacob told Adolph, so the judge or someone put her away. Not jail but…"

Julia burst out, "Not over to Dunning, the asylum for women, but to Jacksonville, an asylum hundreds of miles away from here. A seven-by-eight cell, I heard."

Esther concluded, "The family told everyone she went to stay with cousins in New York. Down Hester Street. We just nodded at them. What could we say?"

"Good God," my mother cried, "a bed in Bedlam for her. A murderer, after all."

"But life went on. You gotta go on. So Jacob and Leah's older sister, Sarah, lived in the house, along with her twins, Ella and Emma. The older son, Herman, got married right away, ordered everybody around. He makes a lot of money and moves away." She shrugged her shoulders. "Rich and more rich, that man. *Gelt geyt tsu gelt.*" Money goes to money. "After a while people stopped talking about Leah Brenner, the butcher's crazy wife. Now and then someone babbled something and Rabbi Kurtz would knock on the door. Silence, please. A little respect. A family shattered. My Adolph, then so religious—the Talmudic scholar, would you believe?—he quotes, 'One shouldn't open his mouth to Satan.' Like evil talk brings the devil into the house. So Adolph shut the gossipers up."

"But now she's back on her porch." My mother pointed through a kitchen wall, her bony finger trembling. "A dreadful reminder. When you romp with the devil, you infect the neighborhood." Again, the shudder. "This cannot end well."

Esther shrugged as she moved to refill the lemonade glasses. "Now you sound like my Adolph quoting Scripture." She went on. "Around three years ago we heard she was back. Maybe less. No one knows exactly when. She was let out for some reason.

I don't know the facts. But one day, casual-like and without warning, Jacob tells my Adolph his mother was back at home, but hidden inside. He seemed…happy, my Adolph said, but he didn't know how to talk to her. We never seen her, maybe a fleeting glimpse through a window…if you were passing by and glanced over there. The summers went by, and she never came outside. You knew she was inside that house. Like a shadow on the wall. It was a little…scary or something."

"What about her family?" I asked.

"You'd see Sarah heading to Maxwell Street to shop, you'd see some strangers knocking on the door and disappearing inside, you'd see Herman in his Chesterfield topcoat and silk hat and cigars parking the town car at the curb and going inside to see his mother. But never with his wife and little children. You never saw Leah outside, gossiping over the back fence like the old days. Or hoeing in the vegetable garden like she always liked to do." She sighed. "Leah and I used to share coffee at this very table…so many mornings. She was my friend." She touched the strudel dough gingerly. "Then Jacob stopped talking about it. Adolph had nothing to tell me." She stressed, "And I *did* ask. What can I say?"

I ran a finger down the sweaty glass I sipped from, puzzled. "But today she's on her porch. She's outside."

Esther whispered. "Well, maybe she got a little crazy inside that house. Wouldn't you? Like, go crazy? A world outside and you can't go to it. No air to breathe, you know. This hot, hot summer, so brutal. Maybe she got tired of staring at those walls. How many cages do a woman gotta live in? Yes, I've seen her out there one other time, a week ago. It made my heart race. I even nodded at her as I passed to market. She turned away."

My mother was impatient. "Esther, you were always too forgiving."

A surprisingly sharp look from Esther. "Leave the woman in peace, I say. Please, Julia dear. The woman's been through hell."

"She created her…"

Esther stood. "I feel sorry for her."

"She ruined her family, Esther."

For a second Esther closed her eyes, then popped them open. Her eyes were bright. "I sometimes wonder if that's true. We sit in this kitchen and have all the answers." She grinned now. "Enough talk, this sadness. A short visit, Julia, you and dear Edna. After all these years. And Edna getting real famous, too." She smiled affectionately at me, a twinkle in her eye. "Who'd have believed it? The short stories in the magazines that come in the mail. The novel *The Girls*. Your picture in the *Tribune*, no less. Everyone talking about the Ferber girl who is a New York wonder. A writer. And when I heard you were writing a new book on Chicago—about the Dutch truck farmers outside the city, High Prairie, the marketplace Haymarket, maybe even Maxwell Street, what do you call it? *Selina*? Or *So Big*?—I don't know, I remember you told me, Julia—I says to my Sol that an invitation is overdue. She can visit the marketplace so close by, a block away, the peddlers, the hot dog stands..." She stopped.

A throat cleared, a rheumy grunt. We stared into the doorway. Esther's mother-in-law, Molly, unseen, listening from the hallway.

Julia was mumbling, "Dear Esther, we *do* have rooms being readied in the Windermere at Hyde Park in a couple weeks—the painting will be done then. Edna likes to be in Chicago in the summer—to write. The energy, she says."

"I do *love* it," I added. "To walk to the stores off the Loop, a block from Lake Michigan with the soft breezes, up and down State Street, lazing in Jackson Park, the theaters on Randolph and..."

"It ain't this old neighborhood," Esther broke in. "Here"— and now she smiled at me—"you come for atmosphere."

"And your cooking." I laughed and patted her on the wrist. "Your pot roast makes me slobber like a family dog. So succulent, so perfect."

Esther spoke to my mother. "But I don't know how Edna can finish her book in this scorching heat. Is it the hottest Chicago summer ever? Such a life we live here in Chicago. Every day in the nineties."

"I think 1923 will go on record as…"

We stopped, all of us turning. *Tap tap tap.* The loud banging of a cane on the hardwood floor of the hallway, purposely, deliberately, Molly stood there, her wrinkled face set in a censorious glare. While we watched, she emphatically banged the cane. *Tap tap tap.*

"Molly," Esther faltered, "you were napping?"

A quivering voice, laced with iron. "What napping can an old lady do with the three of you yammering out here about stuff you got no business talking of?" She stepped into the room but didn't sit, staring at us.

The tall, thin woman was slightly stooped now, one shoulder lower than the other, the slight hint of a sagging cheek. Molly Newmann, family matriarch, redoubtable, the fierce head of this household, a woman who stymied conversation in a room and then, begrudgingly, would permit it to resume. Molly Newmann, felled by a piddling stroke last year that did nothing to temper her power, save for her reluctant reliance on a thick black walnut cane and too much peach-tinted rouge on that failed cheek. Brilliant white hair maneuvered into an incongruous French pompadour, always impeccable, a face ravaged by wrinkles I didn't remember, the martinet in her late eighties. A face dusted each morning as though flouring a table for strudel. Long, stringy arms, liver-spotted, arthritic in the fingertips, but awesome in their power to demand. Once she'd been famous for her aristocratic mien, the erect spine, the absolute pronouncements, that unyielding stare that made her daughter-in-law quake and sputter; now, crippled, she refused to believe she was mortal.

I'd heard Esther whisper to my mother that she was dying, the doctors warned them, but Esther added that no one, especially Molly the near-nonagenarian, accepted the inevitable. "She'll bury us all."

Molly adored my mother—a kindred dictator—and tolerated me, but was notoriously indifferent to her son, Sol. Yet she doted crazily on her forty-year-old grandson, Adolph, affectionately called Ad by everyone but his mother and grandmother, unmarried and living upstairs, a gadabout bachelor who spent most of his free time flattering the old woman when he wasn't promising to marry Minna, his adoring girlfriend of ten years. A Jewish patient Griselda, long-suffering.

"Molly," Esther reported, "Leah is on her porch again."

I spoke up. "We were surprised, my mother and I. We'd gone to pick up some things at Marshal Field's and…"

Molly tapped her cane, lethal punctuation. *Tap tap tap.* "So what?"

"I guess the old reporter in me…you know…it's a intriguing story, that murder, filled with…"

Molly drew in her parched cheeks, and the multitude of deep-ground wrinkles shifted like some sudden seismic upheaval of landscape. "We will not discuss that woman in this house. That harridan. Poor Ivan, a good man, stabbed." Her words leaked out of her barely open lips.

"I caught her eye and…" I stopped.

Again, the rhythmic tapping of that cane. Fierce, demanding. *Tap tap tap.* One hand gripped the table, her fingers carelessly squishing the hardening strudel dough. "Old news. That's all it is. Over now. Lord, we lived though it *once*. Next door to report-ers and noisy folks and prying idiots and weeping children and pathetic Jacob hiding out upstairs here with Adolph when he wasn't baying at the moon…I'll not have it in my home." Her voice bounced off the ceiling. "I won't."

With that she turned, nearly toppling, stabilized the cane, and left the room.

Esther picked up the knife and gazed at the table. "My God, I've ruined the strudel."

Chapter Three

On Friday night and on Saturday till sundown, Monroe Street was quiet. The reverential shade of Shabbas, the suspended breath and the intoxication of prayer. You could hear the long wail of the Illinois Central trains. Sometimes you could hear the wind off Lake Michigan. You heard the low hum of soft voices as folks strolled to temple, a murmur that lulled me, especially after the roar of New York City on a brilliant Saturday morning. I lingered on the front porch, waved off invitations to attend services, and fiddled with the pad in my lap, sketching out the midnight scene at Chicago's rough-and-tumble Haymarket, my heroine, Selina, loading her vegetables onto a two-horse wagon and venturing with her little boy, Dirk, into man's territory.

It didn't work, that scene—not here, not under a blazing sun and an Old World tableau of black-clad congregants, men with beards and bewigged women, a line of bedraggled children behind them. A street now home to Russian Jews, devoutly Orthodox, who eyed the old guard worldly Germans with suspicion and sometimes anger. The Newmanns were nominally religious, German Reform, the men and women sitting together and the men without kippahs outside shul. Years back, a previous owner of the Newmann home had nailed mezuzahs on the entrances, though no one in the family ever touched them as they passed in or out. An occasional service, on the High Holy Days, of course, or to hear Rabbi Emil Hirsh speak at Temple

Sinai on Grand Boulevard. But everyone went to hear that august man who inspired even the lackadaisical believer.

But on Saturday night Shabbos was over. The street began to percolate, children streaming outdoors, folks gathering on sidewalks, on stoops. And on Sunday morning, early, the sun peeping out, Monroe Street came gloriously alive. I rose at dawn to the distant *who-wah who-wah* of auto horns and excited sidewalk chatter and children yelling. Outside of my second-story bedroom—Mother across the hall, snoring contentedly, with Sol and Esther one door away, quiet—I saw the street bustling and jumping as souls headed to Maxwell Street, baskets over arms, canvas bags slung over shoulders, carts dragged behind them, little children tucked into sides.

Hurriedly, I dressed, intent on being in that swell of people, lost in that robust spirit, believing it would make my Selina come alive, my prose sing. When I came alive, my heroines did, too. A quick cup of strong black coffee in a chipped mug, a chunk of homemade, butter-slathered pumpernickel, a hard-boiled egg, and a glass of fresh-squeezed orange juice—and I was out the door.

Walking by the Brenner household, I noted its shabby respectability, the chalky white paint peeling off the sagging clapboards, a pale green shutter slipping from a hinge, a few missing roof tiles, the untrimmed boxwood hedges lining the cracked walkway. It was a house the inhabitants forgot about, and so different from its twin next door. There, proudly, Sol Newmann manicured the hedges, edged the sidewalk with an artist's eye, slapped on a fresh coat of sunny yellow paint to the clapboards at the end of winter, accented the shutters with a dark green tint. And Esther doubtless was responsible for the glittering windows, so hard-polished they seemed not even there. Rows of petunias and larkspurs and marigolds banked the sidewalk, a wash of brilliant color. English ivy dripped from boxes positioned on the porch railings. A showplace, really. In front of the Brenner home was a yellowing parched lawn. A large fallen tree limb rested in a clump of evergreens—an ugly remnant from the harsh, icy Chicago winter.

But as I passed by, the front door suddenly opened and for a brief second Leah Brenner stepped out, pushing against the screen door. She was juggling a cup of coffee and a napkin that held pastry or a roll, cradling both to her chest, so she didn't see me gawking there, the pesky intruder on her solitude. Then, spotting me, she backed into the screen door that had closed behind her, turning away, almost frightened.

Apologetically, I yelled, "Good morning, I'm…"

She was gone, scrambling back into the house, the heavy oak front door slamming behind her.

Feeling a little foolish now, I scurried down the block, past the apartment houses, and turned onto storied Maxwell Street. For a moment, breathless, I was overwhelmed by the spectacle before me, this cluttered, frantic Jewish marketplace, a cacophony of whistling and yelling and hectoring—a flow of mangled English, rapid-fire Yiddish, and a Babel of greenhorn Russian, German, Spanish, Polish, what have you. What really hit me were the pungent smells—frying onions, hot dogs boiling in bubbly oil, roasted garlic, overripe apples and pears, hot peanuts, roasting meats sputtering on grills, unwashed bodies, tattered clothing— stale, fetid aromas, both appealing and disgusting, so intense as to make me dizzy. On Sunday this "Poor Jewish Quarter," as the locals called it, at the intersection of Maxwell and Halsted, in the shadow of the Loop, pulsated, thrived, swelled, exploded. From dawn to dusk, an unbroken rhythm. "Jewtown."

Yet, even as I walked through the crowds of shoppers and vendors, Leah's riveting image stayed with me—I couldn't escape that face.

For an hour I wandered, enthralled by the spectacle that made me conjure up old market days in Eastern Europe: pushcarts with squealing wheels lumbered by, vendors hawked notions, old shoes, tobacco, watches, baubles, bits and pieces of jewelry, pocket knives. Women in shawls haggled over the price of tomatoes. Or beans. Or toothbrushes. A rug with the fringe coming undone. Under signs in Hebrew the pullers cajoled, beckoned—the fancy young men, slick and cheeky, who attempted to pull passersby into shops.

The first customer of the day—that needed sale that guaranteed good luck. *For you, sir, a deal. A bargain.* A skirmish between two bearded peddlers. *Mach mores, Judi.* Mind your manners, Jew! People in and out of shops—pawnbrokers, haberdashers, money lenders, kosher meats, bath houses, dry-goods emporiums, tailors, tobacco stands. *Your son, he should go to Izzy the shakhans. A marriage arranged. Easy. Such girls he knows, dutiful daughters.* Long johns, worn once, almost new. Chickens squawking, then eerily silent. For a kosher home. Look inside. I. Klein. Bremmer Cookie Factory. Nathan's Ice Cream Parlor. Phillipson's Clothes. Wittenberg Matzoh. Nate's Delicatessen. Mackevich's Notions. Magic potions. Jezibel Root.

The streetcar emptied peddlers carrying packed burlap sacks on their backs. Haggle, haggle. *Such a bargain, you wouldn't believe, yes?* Or: *Today only, for you alone, your name on it.* Or: *New today, and only slightly worn, a winter coat from a rich lady.* In the middle of a heat wave, stultifying, the puller draped the wool coat over his shoulders. *A bargain. Today.* Mottled phrases mixed with Yiddish. *Trog Es Gezunterheyd.* Wear it in good health. *Such a hat will make you look like a Hollywood beauty. Five cents. A nickel. Is nothing. Truly. A bargain.*

Who's the big shot, oy? Such a Macher! Bertha's Rummage Store. Myer's Cigars. *A few cents. We're all poor. With God's help, we starved regularly,* the writer says. *Gypsies everywhere today. Watch out!*

Exhilarating madness, though uplifting.

I munched on a salty soft pretzel I bought for a penny, a smear of brown mustard gracing it for free. *For you alone, my dear…*

Fruit ice for you. Cherry. Pineapple. Lemon. An organ grinder. *Roszhinkes mit Mandlen.*

But my mind kept wandering back to that quick glimpse of Leah Brenner in her doorway—her hurried retreat. Worse, yesterday's sudden eye contact: all that naked loneliness there, that haunted emptiness.

Leah the murderer.

A knife in the neck.

I imagined I saw her on Maxwell Street. On Twelfth Street. On Halsted Street. The white-haired woman pushing doilies at me, her small eyes weepy. Another old woman with a gaunt face—could an old woman still be that beautiful after all the years? Like Leah? The gnarled, bent woman, her head wrapped in a black babushka, dipping her withered fingers into hot water to extract a hot dog. Her, too. All the old women. *Mein Yiddische Mame. For you, my dear, a special treat, the best wiener. Today. The sun is shining*…Even the beggar on Des Plaines. The *schnorrer* with the melancholy eyes. Him, too.

Leah Brenner, touching all my moments on the teeming street. Hand-shaking, back-slapping, laughter, grunting. The puff of tobacco. *Menshlikhkeit*. Communion. The Jew in the blood.

Finally, spent, I turned off Maxwell back onto Monroe and stopped dead. On the corner was the old kosher butcher shop once owned by Ivan Brenner and his partner, Morrie Wolfsy. I'd walked by it before, and often during my visit, but now considered it. The two old friends ran Nathan's Meat Market for years, the market named for Morrie's grandfather and Ivan's father, a happy compromise. Both their names still on the shadowy window, though Ivan was long murdered and Morrie had closed up shop a short time after the murder.

An unlikely partnership from the start, ill-fated: Ivan the German Jew who liked to sleep all day Saturday when the shop was closed for *Shabbos*, and Morrie, the craggy Russian Jew who criticized him for it, though he was hardly devout himself. *Ah, my friend Ivan, becoming a goy, he is.* They'd met years before at a bathhouse on Halsted, and became friendly. Each with so little cash. A partnership of shared monies that began to unravel almost at once, though they stayed in business for years and years. The bickering, the name-calling. Threats to leave.

Threats…

And then the murder.

The store sat empty now, not rented because Morrie refused to rent it for reasons no one understood, and the front plate-glass windows were smudged and grimy, ignored. Peering in, I saw empty counters, sagging shelves, thick dark sawdust still covering the floor. A light dangled off a loosened fixture. An abandoned store. Last night Esther told me that Morrie had operated the left side of the store—the meats—and Ivan the right side—the poultry. A line down the middle. Hours spent late on Saturday night and all day Sunday. Morrie hopped the Halsted Street streetcar, headed to the stockyards, returned with a slaughtered cow strapped to his hunched back, the carcass wrapped in waxed paper, staring at the floor as he ignored the other riders. Ivan lined up crates of squawking chickens and other fowl in the back room, where, once chosen by a finicky customer, they were summarily dispatched.

"Such fabulous duck breast, succulent, the lines for it on Sunday," Esther rhapsodized.

That compatible arrangement ended with Ivan's death. Morrie gave up the business.

But I was surprised to see a long table pulled into the center of the room, covered now with heaps of old clothing, bunched rags tied with string, battered shoes, crumpled hats. *Shmatte*. A rag picker's trove. As I stood there, an old man hobbled from a back room and spotted me, my face pressed against the window. I jumped back, embarrassed, but I realized he'd shown no surprise, no interest, not even an iota of curiosity. He simply *looked* at me. An ancient man with an ill-kept yellowish beard and a nearly bald head, dressed in a rumpled black suit with fringed black-and-white *tsitsis* under his black vest, a yarmulke precariously on his head. Then, eyes narrowed, he motioned me away.

I had no idea why I became so rattled, so easily.

I read his lips: Go away. *Oy*. You.

Stunned, I rushed to Esther's house.

Chapter Four

Leah Brenner was sitting on her porch.

I stopped walking. Glancing up, I half raised my arm, a tentative greeting that was awkward—and probably intrusive. I wasn't sure why I did so, but at that moment I flashed to my mother's blatant condemnation, Molly's fierce disapproval, and Esther's kind regard. There was something wrong with that picture, though I had no idea why I felt so. I didn't move, planted on the sidewalk. Heat waves rippled off the pavement. The leaves on the towering maple tree on her front lawn wilted, drooped. The sun hurt my eyes.

Her response took a moment, a swallowed "Hello." As though she'd not spoken in decades and was unsure she had any voice left. And that one muted word exacted an awful toll because she folded into herself, shoulders dropping, arms loose, her head dipping like a bird burying its head into its feathery chest.

"I'm sorry, Mrs. Brenner," I stammered, uncertain. "Do you remember me?"

A pause, then a scratchy voice, metallic. "No, but I know who you are now."

"I'm Edna Ferber, visiting next door. At the Newmanns'."

"I know all about your visit. You're the writer."

"Yes." I squirmed. "How do you know…?"

"Jacob told me you're next door. My son. He tells me the news of the street. Then my daughter mentioned *The Girls*. My daughter, Ella. They were talking about you. You know, I read one of your short stories…once."

"Once?"

"A while back." She leaned forward. "I loved it."

An awkward pause as we watched each other.

"I met Jacob eighteen years ago. One summer. I was here for a week or so. A vacation. My last time here. Visiting. I remember your son."

An unfunny laugh. "Of course. Everyone remembers Jacob. Every *girl* remembers him, I should say. The Yiddishe Romeo, himself." She clicked her tongue. "It's just that he never stopped running long enough for any of them to catch him."

A strange remark, a little bitter.

I raised my voice, glancing toward the Newmann porch. "I remember you standing on this same porch, Mrs. Brenner. One hot afternoon. Just that one time. In a beautiful yellow dress."

"Really? I don't remember that dress." A heartbeat, too long. "That was another lifetime."

I started to walk away, but she spoke quickly. "You arrived a few days ago."

I nodded and took another step. "Yes…"

She rushed her words. "I saw you yesterday." Now she glanced toward the Newmann home. "With your mother. I remember Julia Ferber…from years ago."

Yesterday: the sudden locking of our eyes, that moment when something was communicated in a bizarre flash, and then was gone.

Boldly, surprising myself, I said, "Do you mind if I come up on your porch?"

She hesitated, and then, once again, glanced toward the Newmann house, closed tight again the day's growing heat. She nodded, her hand waving to me slowly, a butterfly's gentle fluttering. As I stepped onto the porch, I imagined my mother peering out the upstairs window, wondering about her overdue daughter, and then, horrified and sputtering, sinking into an unlovely swoon on Esther's oriental carpet.

On the porch, facing me, Mrs. Brenner seemed at a loss.

"Would you like some iced tea?" she asked, and I nodded. A noise from the street jarred her—two girls passing, giggling, tickling each other. Her eyes searched the street. A boy kicked a ball down the sidewalk. "Inside," she mumbled. "Please."

The air in the parlor was stifling, the windows sealed tight, heavy dark blue damask curtains drawn, an overstuffed sofa and two bulky armchairs blocked by scattered tables cluttered with plaster-of-Paris figurines, gaudily painted cheap tchotchkes, crystal bells, a porcelain planter with wilting ivy growing from the body of a garish French shepherdess. Disquieting, this rummage-sale collection, though every piece of bric-a-brac seemed shellacked and spit-polished. A gigantic menorah on a sideboard dominated the still room. A dreadful room, airless, a coffin, dimly lit by a light in the hallway.

Leah saw me eying the cheap carnival collection. "My sister, Sarah." She pointed at a particularly egregious paperweight— Niagara Falls at night, painted-on glitter stars, a tourist's unfortunate souvenir. "She insists that it's art." A bit of sarcasm in her voice. "I spend most of every day fighting the dust." A quick smile. "Although I insist the dust softens the ugliness of the pieces."

"You live with Sarah?"

Steely-eyed, unblinking, she said, "She lives with me. This is my house. My husband's and mine. Back then."

"I didn't know."

"Because I haven't been here doesn't mean it's not my home."

"True."

She took a step toward the stairwell to the second floor. "Sarah is unhappy that I decided to open the front door and breathe in the fresh air. To sit outside. In front."

I grinned. "It *is* your house."

No humor in her voice. "It is, indeed." She pointed to a chair. "Please sit…Edna." A heavy sigh. "I forget how to invite people into my life." A shrug of her shoulders.

"Frankly, sometimes it's better *not* to."

She ran her tongue over her lower lip. "How cynical you young people are today."

I headed to one of the armchairs. "When you've been a girl reporter in Milwaukee…"

"I hate reporters." She drew back. "Oh, I don't mean…"

"Oh, I don't care…Mrs. Brenner."

"Leah. My name's Leah."

"All right, Leah."

"Let me get you a cold drink. Sit. Please."

She bustled about, bumping into a table, stepped back, deliberated, then swirled around, a maddened dervish, before heading into the kitchen. Unable to settle, frantic to please, her hands fluttered around her face.

I said to her back, "I'm glad you've made it to the front porch."

Gazing straight ahead, she answered, "I watch a street that most days says nothing at all." A pause. "I like it that way."

When she sat back down opposite me after placing a pitcher on the table, she pointed at a glass. "Help yourself. It's not very good."

"A tempting offer, then." I smiled at her.

She drank nothing but watched me quietly.

Finally, breathing in, she began talking in a low voice, almost difficult for me to hear. "When Jacob told me you were next door, I was thrilled. I don't remember you from years ago—no reason to, I suppose, so many young people on the street then—but I did read your short story 'The Homely Heroine' in *Everybody's* when I was away. I realized who it was, who wrote it, I mean—you know, Appleton and all. Your mother visiting next door years ago. We'd talked once or twice. I was so…thrilled. I remember the story because it was so…so sad. One line I memorized: 'Pearlie Schultz used to sit on the front porch summer evenings to watch the couples stroll by, and weep in her heart.' I can't forget that line, Edna. 'Weep in her heart.' I told myself you understood something about me—about others—like me. And so…I waited to see you walk by. I hoped I'd have the courage to *talk* to you."

A beautiful woman, Leah was, even now at sixty, a face that held you, yet she was a woman who'd seen herself in my homely heroine, the sad Pearlie, fat, unwanted, morose…

"I'm glad you did."

A quizzical look. "Why?"

That jarred. I had no answer. "I don't know. I…"

A wispy smile. "I'm the neighborhood woman with a past. You shouldn't be talking to me."

"I suppose so."

But she was speaking over my swallowed words. "Edna, I was so hungry to get back home. I got sick to my stomach thinking about it. I've been back now for nearly three years… but in solitary confinement. For a woman like me, every place becomes a jail. Every space has four walls. The cage makes you crazy, though." She reached for a glass, then changed her mind. "Yet, I've accepted my place as the town leper. What choice do I have? Madness—or acceptance." She shrugged. "It sort of makes it easy, finally. Others tell you what you are—define you. You know how the world sees you."

"You don't know how I see you."

That surprised her. "Tell me."

I waited a bit, carefully chose my words. "Simply, a woman tired of isolation."

I watched her. Such a small woman, though soft at the edges, a little plump, pale as if sheltered from sunlight, but with dark, flickering nut-brown eyes, a woman who struck me as years older than her sixty or so years, her face drawn, a puffiness around those alert, brilliant eyes. Yet something about her…no homely heroine, this one, truly…a real beauty, exotic, foreign, the forbidden gypsy on the outskirts of town. You could see that she'd once been stunning because, in some way, she still was: the alabaster complexion and the dark eyes, that regal chin with the cupid's-bow mouth. But it was more than simple beauty— her slight movements were the instinctive moves of a sensual woman. A regal Cleopatra sitting with me, the Jewish slave girl on the Nile.

"That's so, I guess." She echoed the word. "Isolation. Yes." Suddenly she locked eyes with me again. "You know what they say I did."

I started. "Yes."

"Tell me what I did."

My throat went dry, my vision blurred. I sputtered, "You stabbed your husband to death."

She watched me carefully, her eyes faraway. "That's what they say I did. But I don't remember *that*. What I do remember is bending over him as he slumped on the sofa and seeing my fingertips dark with blood and wondering where it came from."

My voice was a squeak. "You don't remember a knife?"

She shook her head back and forth slowly, a sleepwalker's rhythm. "No. Nothing. Nothing but my…wonder at that dark blood. Then I forgot how to talk. Strangers were talking at me and I was nodding, nodding, nodding. Staring at them, just staring at them. A moan from deep inside me. I don't remember anything after that, though they tell me they asked me questions. But I simply stared. Nothing. It was like I forgot how to talk—or *couldn't* talk. A blur, all of it, the days that followed. Echoes in my head. They told me that I killed Ivan, washed the knife, hid it back in the kitchen, then stooped over his body on the sofa to make certain he was dead. Over and over they said that to me. They said I kept nodding: yes yes yes yes. And then, I don't know how much later—a blur, everything a blur—some man tells me I'm going away. A home for crazy women, a cell, a cot, food I can't eat. Food I spit out." She stopped talking. Her fingers trembled as she touched her cheek. Her face was flushed.

"But now you've come home."

She was looking over my shoulder. "One day they tell me—you can go now. I have conversations with the doctor, and he says, 'You can be around people now. You can walk outside. Everything is all right now.' My Herman comes to pick me up in a car that scares me…so far away. Another planet. Herman, the only one who visited but then stopped because I couldn't speak. For years I didn't talk—I stared at people. *Who are you? What do you want me to say?* And then, one day, like that, I found my voice again. Words came tumbling out. I couldn't *stop* talking." She smiled wistfully. "Like now—with you here. I can breathe again—at that moment. And they say, you can go home now."

She stopped talking for a moment.

"Home," I echoed.

She waved her hands around the room. "I wanted to be home. Back here." She shot me a look. "But now that I have my voice back, Sarah tells me to keep still—don't talk to anyone. People will *hurt* me. Be still. Stay inside. People don't want to see you— know that you're back on Monroe Street. She gets nervous when I talk to Jacob, who watches me too closely. To my daughters who are afraid of me. My son, Herman, who thinks I embarrass him. Embarrass! No, a mother who gossips embarrasses her children. A mother who kills…what word is there that fits? 'Quiet,' Sarah tells me. 'Lower your voice. The neighbors!' My biggest sin was opening the screen door and sitting on that porch."

I sat up, spine rigid. "They took your life from you."

She stood and touched a figurine on a side table, held it up to her face. Her fingers squeezed it tightly.

Suddenly, her voice rising, "You don't think I killed Ivan?"

Irrationally, I blurted out, "No, of course not."

A bitter grunt. "Ah, a majority of one." A shrug. "Maybe two. You and me. Who can believe that?" A long sigh as she tilted her head to the side. "*Gey red tsu der vant.*" Go tell it to the wall.

But at that moment I knew, to my soul, that my instincts were true and just. Something was wrong with that faded photograph. "No," I repeated firmly. "When you found your voice again, you would have remembered."

She put down the figurine, too close to the edge of the table, but then walked to the front window, stared into the street. She faced me. "It doesn't matter now. I can't shift the axis of the Earth, right the wind currents, turn back the tides. And, I suppose, I *am* to blame somehow. I *caused* my world to turn upside down."

"What?" This was making little sense.

"I wasn't a good wife." Another bitter smile. "Ivan and I fought for weeks. My fault, I tell you now, Edna. Yes, Ivan was a cruel, hard man. He could be nasty, controlling. Not at first—not when we first married. They never are, their words lovely and assuring. Then they change. He'd be mean to me—to the children. Especially my Jacob." She shivered. "Such cruelty to that boy. The world's sweetest boy, that one. Impossible—despite my pleading. Of course, the more I defended Jacob, the worse the cruelty."

"But how did *you* hurt him?"

Slowly she left the window and settled into a chair, facing me. "I *hurt* him bad. We hurt him, me and Morrie, his partner. One stupid, idle flirtation, weak and silly, a lapse of judgment on my part, regretted immediately. And confessed at once. I brought shame on Ivan's head—and he rightly accused me. My wife—Jezebel. He *told* everyone. I suppose he had to because he was so mortified, embarrassed—what will folks think of *him*? The proud man with the wanton wife. And I sat on that front porch with a scarlet letter on my chest for the neighbors to gaze at. For Morrie's angry wife to spit on me. For old Molly Newmann, happy to slight me as we passed."

I'd not expected such candid revelation, nor, frankly, wanted it. "Leah, I don't think that I…" I sipped the last of my tea and reached for the pitcher. Her eyes followed my movements.

She spat out her words. "I courted disaster, Edna. Men always watched at me. Lovely, they'd whisper. A beauty, they'd whisper. Look at Ivan, dumpy, a *lumpen*, the fool with the ravishing bride. Men followed me, got silly, said things they never thought they'd ever say to a woman. But Ivan spent long hours in the back room of the butcher shop where the men hung out. The butcher's cave, they called it. They talked about me. He said they found me…I don't know…attractive. So it started to bother him. Pride gave way to fear…to a lack of trust in me. What did I unconsciously tell them when I strutted in? What did those men see when they watched me walk by? Why did it *please* me so?" For a second she closed her eyes and didn't move. "All those times Morrie flirted—frivolous, dumb, a ladies' man behind his wife's back. A reputation, he had, that man. Ivan laughed but I knew it bothered him. He'd married a wife everyone said was beautiful, and that meant trouble. When we got married, it pleased Ivan, me on his arm. You know, Ivan *reveled* in it—at first. Drunk with it. But then he got mean, accused me, shut me out. Screamed at me—made me cry. Never tempted by those dreadful men, I was always faithful. The wolf whistles. The leering." She shuddered. "But I let myself—once—with Morrie—a hug, a kiss. Stupid, stupid. So…stupid of me. Nothing more. A kiss in a doorway. One minute of a nun's life. I confessed—I had to, because I loved Ivan. But how we fought. And that morning, Ivan home sick and fighting, fighting…"

Here she was now, weary, drawn, but I imagined her years back, a woman in her middle forties, vibrant, those dancing eyes, the Rubenesque flesh, the sinuous flow of a woman's body that drew men closer, Circe's siren song. Some magic other women couldn't understand, only sense, but men couldn't resist. Leah, the impossible temptress, all the more lethal because she did nothing to foster it—indeed, didn't *want* it.

"Leah, I don't know what to say."

Suddenly she leaned forward, poured tea into a glass, and drank half of it. When she put the glass down, her hand trembled. "I brought about Ivan's death. I believe that. That night I let Morrie touch me. That opened the door to all the chaos to follow."

"But you didn't kill him."

She shrugged and interlaced her fingers, spreading them before her face. Only those brilliant eyes were visible. "What can I say?"

A shrill voice erupted from the hallway. "Leah, who are you talking to?"

A woman stepped into the room, a frightened look on her face. She actually pointed at me.

"Sarah, this is Edna. We talked of her staying next door with Esther Newmann. Edna Ferber. Ella gave you her book and…"

A phony laugh that became a cackle. "We really are not ready for guests, Leah."

She stood with her arms folded across her chest, a humorless schoolmarm momentarily taken off guard.

Leah said in a soft voice, "We're just talking, the two of us." She pointed to the pitcher of iced tea. "A cold glass of…" She stopped.

Sarah pivoted on her heels, glanced toward the kitchen, unsure of her next move. From the back of her throat came a slippery rasp that reminded me of a baby's sudden regurgitation. "That may be…" she began, but stopped, indecisive. Her eyes caught the figurine Leah had picked up. Nervously she moved it—positioned it next to another. She scowled at Leah.

Like a failed negative of her sister, Sarah had a similar small face, narrow chin, high forehead, with the same abundant white hair, but there the comparisons ceased: Sarah was skinny, wiry, the bird on the wire, twittering, while the alluring songbird luxuriated nearby. Brittle arms, breakable. Her eyes were not Leah's vibrant, deep brown that hinted at the voluptuous siren of days gone by—rather, Sarah's were dull, the washed-out eyes of a woman who had lost all interest in life—who, in fact, was indifferent to a world she'd never cared for.

That revelation bothered me because her attitude toward Leah made it clear she found Leah's return home a nuisance. Routines shifted, the workings of a household realigned—plaster-of-Paris figurines in regimented positions—nothing demanded from Leah but nonetheless her presence monumentally annoying. The spinster forced to share her coveted space.

She spoke to her sister as though I weren't there. "Jacob didn't come home last night—again."

Quietly. "I know."

A darting glance at me, lips pursed. "Is that why you were sitting on the porch? Waiting?"

"I was sitting on the porch because these rooms are a prison."

Sarah glanced back at me and shook her head slowly, letting out a tinny laugh. "The years away have allowed dear Leah to cultivate sarcasm."

Leah clicked her tongue. "Not sarcasm. Realism."

"No matter." She turned away, but at that moment the front door opened.

Jacob Brenner strolled in, pausing in the entrance, one hand balancing himself against the doorjamb. "What?" he stammered.

"Jacob," his mother said. "I was worried."

A slight, wistful smile covered his face. "My mother loves me."

"Really, now," Sarah barked.

Jacob was nearly forty but still resembled some romantic hero on a vaudeville stage, the aging juvenile, though one now tarnished and a bit dissolute. With those dark brown eyes, half-closed, and that shock of coal-black hair in need of a trim, he struck me as a Semite Heathcliff—dangerous because of his beauty and brooding. He'd inherited his mother's once-in-a-lifetime beauty. Eighteen years back, at twenty or so, he was dashing and smooth. I would watch him move down the sidewalk—that casual saunter or strut, the shoulders high, the head rocking as though to a tune only he heard. He owned the street, that boy—the pavement seemed to dance underneath him. Now, sadly, the long face with the square Leyendecker jaw and the elegant Roman nose seemed puffy, loose, but when he turned to stare into my face I still saw the young, erstwhile matinee heartthrob, the man who gave me sleepless nights.

"A fellow gotta have some fun."

His mother nodded toward me. "Jacob, do you remember Edna Ferber? We talked about her visiting the Newmanns. The novelist."

He smiled, trying to charm me, the old instincts taking over. Turning, his foot slipped. "A pleasure."

I didn't know how much pleasure he was having at the moment—his Aunt Sarah frumpy and grunting beside him—but he half-bowed and reached for my hand. I refused to offer it.

Edna, not sugar and spice.

Edna, not nice—

For a second, in a practiced, uncalculated manner, he stared into my face, wooing, trying to claim my attention. But I was invisible—me, the dowdy, unloved thirtyish spinster with the bushel-barrel hair and the sallow complexion.

"You don't remember me?" I asked pointedly, really too sharply.

In his boozy state he tried to focus. A man not skilled at lying. "Of course. I do. I…" He stammered and, of course, he said the wrong thing. "I remember every girl I ever met."

Sarah grumbled. "For God's sake, Jacob."

Jacob, confused, turned away with that chivalrous half-bow, and left the room. I could hear his sloppy footfall on the stairs.

Leah burst out laughing, a little out of control. Sarah watched her, as did I, but Sarah's look was harsh and spiteful, mixed with nervousness. I was filled with wonder. Leah's laugh sounded rusty, jagged, The musical instrument you haven't played since high school.

Leah sputtered, "Lovely, Edna. Lovely. My Jacob doesn't listen to himself." Then, through her girlish giggles, "You know, I haven't laughed in fifteen years. I haven't…laughed. Really." She was observing me with affection, and I realized how much I liked the woman. A ripple in her voice, the laughter rose again.

Then, like a slammed door, she stopped, her face closed up. It was as though she'd been slapped in the face. She trembled. I thought she'd cry because her lips quivered, but she said in a cool, deliberate voice, "I won't allow myself to cry…ever again."

She looked lost, helpless.

I stood up. "I need to leave. I'm expected back."

Neither sister moved as I stood up. As I opened the front door, sighing deeply, I heard the rush of clipped steps behind me. Suddenly, Leah stood near me—too near, almost on top of me—as if, because of those horrible, confined years, she'd forgotten about the civility of space. Her face so close to mine, eyes moist, nose running. she was still smiling. Impulsively, she reached out, not to grab my hand, but simply to touch my shoulder. So sudden a gesture, so charged. Like a numbing shock from an electric current.

"Thank you, Edna."

She backed away.

Outside, stumbling down the wooden steps, I realized I was crying.

Chapter Five

My mother lay on the sofa with a cold compress plastered to her forehead. Sarah Bernhardt, rehearsing. As I walked past her, headed upstairs to my room, she let out the choked death rattle she'd employed many times, always with me, the errant daughter. A moan, a whimper, an alley cat's meow. This was the plaintive anthem of aggrieved Jewish motherhood, doubtless carried over to America in an immigrant's heart and soul, in the red blood, the one precious item not declared at Ellis Island.

"My own daughter!"

I stopped walking because I knew my part in this seasoned melodrama.

"What?" I asked with little patience.

My mother struggled to sit, letting the compress slip into her lap, unnoticed. Her face was ashen. "My nosy daughter…of course, you talk to the one person *no one* talks to. You choose…" She fell back into the cushions.

"Ah, spies in the house of Newmann."

Sitting up, smoothing her dress, my mother leaned in to me, confidentially. "Molly is a snoop, truth to tell. That old woman doesn't miss a trick. A real *kokhlefel*." A busybody. "She may be an old lady hobbling around with that noisy cane, but her eagle eye covers the street. She can out-walk me to Maxwell, amazingly." But then, remembering my misdeed and the reason for her taking to the couch, she whispered, "I was in the kitchen

with Esther, the two of us sipping lemonade and chatting of…
of…nothing, you know, the way old friends talk of nothing. And
Molly yells from the back of the house, 'Your Edna is walking
up the steps of the Brenner porch.' I was flabbergasted."

"Mother, it's no big deal. A conversation."

Leah's voice echoed in my head. *Thank you, Edna.*

My tears as I stumbled on the sidewalk.

A conversation.

Slowly, my mother stood up. Huffing, she walked by me, close
enough so I could see the pain in her eyes, though she ignored
me. In the kitchen, in seconds, I heard the overlapping titter
of excited voices—a strident Molly, a hesitant Esther, and the
tumultuous Julia Ferber, who apologized for my behavior. "What
can I say?" said Julia, fatalistically. "A mother does her best." My
mind slid maliciously from the idea of the Three Fates—mythic
and magnificent—to the dour witches of Macbeth stirring a pot
of chicken soup (with just the right amount of black pepper,
really) and cursing the heavens that allowed the dutiful daughter
her unfortunate lapse in common sense.

Furious, I made a decision. I stood in the doorway, arms folded
across my chest, and glowered. All three women paused—all three
had been speaking at once, a waterfall of babble—and waited.

"Leah Brenner did not kill her husband, Ivan, fifteen years
ago."

That wonderful line echoed off the copperplate ceiling.

My mother gasped, grabbed for her throat, though she probably wished it were mine she reached for. "Edna, really. We are
guests here."

I repeated the line, louder now, spacing out the words, adding,
"I believe she's been railroaded."

A good exit line, worthy of Ethel Barrymore as the curtain
fell. I turned and began walking upstairs, although I missed the
first step, banging into the wall, a clumsy move that somehow
diminished the impact of my purposeful declaration.

Silence in the kitchen, and then, as expected, a thunderous
roar of indignation, disbelief, and shock.

"Julia, what in the world…?" From Esther.

"Craziness, this child of yours. *Meshuga.*" From Molly. *Tap tap tap.*

• • ● • •

That evening, headed downstairs for the Newmann Sunday supper, I dreaded what awaited me. Throughout the afternoon I fiddled with my notes for my novel, even pecking away on my typewriter, a *click click click click ping* that battled with the *tap tap tap* of Molly's cane in the hallway. My mother had purposely avoided me, except for a guttural grunt as she passed my room. Our first Sunday supper at the Newmanns', an anticipated one: Esther Newmann's suppers were legendary. This night's, especially, due to my mother's prodigal visit after so many years, my own return after eighteen years—me, the feted novelist, a matter of pride, that invitation. Right now, however, I expected silence, recrimination—I expected a collective cold shoulder or marrow-deep wail.

What I found was a drifting conversation that skirted the taboo subject of neighborhood murder. Instead, the chatter was of food: the first course of soup, hearty beef barley soup with marrow balls, with hand-rolled hair-fine noodles, served in a tureen so ornate it seemed a relic from a Roman bacchanal. Esther's roast chicken, a gigantic bird glistening brown, juices running, the aroma of generous paprika and bay leaf. A stuffing of chestnuts and apples and a hint of red onion, a nutty confection that made my mouth water. Mashed potatoes so fluffy, laced with diced parsley, they seemed cotton candy at the fair, pats of sweet butter melting in the white canyons. A salad of tart brine-soaked dandelion greens mixed with bits of sliced oranges and sugared strawberries, and slathered with a vinegar glaze that seemed lit by fire. A robust feast, a triumph, and my mother discussed all parts of it, a culinary autopsy, praising, celebrating, worshipping. And rightly so, because I relished Esther's domestic art, her magic touch, that deft reach of spice and invention and love.

We sat around the heavy mahogany dining room table on chairs covered in deep-crimson plush fabric. I faced a fireplace fronted with a fire screen of vaguely oriental design—humming-birds flitting on bamboo stems. An antique grandfather clock stood across from a built-in china cabinet. Over the mantel was a spread of family photographs in black-walnut frames, sepia-tinted—a formal wedding photograph of Esther and Sol, young and slender, unsmiling, he in an ill-fitting suit with a boutonniere (a sprig of lilac) and she in lace, with wraparound filigreed train, a bouquet of calla lilies held tightly.

So animated was the conversation about food, so heady and almost comical, such a purposeful skirting of what occupied our minds: darling little Edna's mammoth transgression. Each time I began to say something, one of the women spoke over me. "Such a copper pickle you find at Lyon's Delicatessen," Molly blurted out. "I mean, it looks painted green. I swear."

"A blouse I found on the bargain table at Goldblatt's—only a small tear I can fix." From Esther.

I didn't care.

I wanted to talk about Leah Brenner.

Once, opening my mouth to mention something about my morning stroll through the Maxwell Street marketplace, old Molly, bent over her plate, brightened and shared an anecdote that had no end. In fact, it really had neither beginning nor middle, some ramble about a greenhorn peasant trying to buy a *shiffcart*, a steamship ticket, at a drug store off Union. It was blather—and welcomed at the table. We waited for a punch line, but none came. Molly was upbeat and sparkling, yet it was forced and deliberate. It tickled me, I had to admit, that chaotic story, because I liked the old woman. She believed it was her job to give direction to her undemonstrative family. Esther, a soft-focus sentimentalist, beamed over her food, and her husband, Sol, a generous man who cultivated serenity, often struck me as asleep when you spoke to him. A little balding man with a scaly scalp and bushy white eyebrows on a blotchy face, he responded to most questions by checking first with his much-adored wife, as though begging her to answer for him. They were as wonderful a couple as God chose to send to this Earth. Old Molly, ancient now and opinionated and fiery, was the bandleader of that family.

"Where's Adolph?" my mother asked.

Esther pointed to the grandfather clock. "He's late. That job at Feinstein's Hardware, I suppose. Some afternoons he works, some mornings..." She waved her hand in the air. "Who knows? He's picking up Minna."

Molly addressed me. "Adolph's intended. A lovely girl, a grade-school teacher."

Sol spoke up. "Yeah, he's been *intending* for ten years now." He stressed the word, but with affection. "I keep telling him—a little bungalow like they're building now. Come May One I'll borrow Sy's truck." The first of May, when all of Chicago chose to move, whether they planned to or not.

Molly smiled at her son. "Now, now, Sol. He's just a boy."

Sol grunted. "He's forty, for God's sake. He hasn't been a boy since I had hair." He touched the top of his bald head. "A *batten*." A lazy boy.

No one laughed.

Sol was perplexed. "I seen him up on Clark. At Bob's Quick Lunch. Early this afternoon. He was walking out of there with Jacob. They..." He stopped. "What?"

Apologetically, Esther explained to Molly, "They *are* old friends, you know."

Molly wasn't happy with the direction the talk was going. "A bad influence, that Jacob."

"Two drifters," Sol added.

Molly turned to me. "A drinker at the taxi-dance halls, that Jacob, I tell you. People tell me things. Adolph tells me but makes excuses for him." She smirked. "Jacob calls himself a poet. What kind of money can a poet make?"

"A poet?" I asked.

"Yes, Jacob Brenner, the idler, he tells everyone he's a poet. A...wastrel, he is." Molly raised her voice.

Esther's voice was hurried. "Jacob is always so polite to me."

"Only to women," Molly grumbled.

I cleared my throat. "Not *every* woman."

"Edna, really," my mother sniped.

Esther was chuckling. "Our Monroe Street Romeo without a balcony."

Sol muttered, "And his sidekick is our Ad. The two running off to the movies at the Biograph. I seen them. Even at the Tivoli on College Grove, fancy-spancy, one dollar a ticket. Crazy. Throwing away money neither one got."

Molly breathed in. "Now you leave Adolph alone, Sol. A good boy with a big heart."

"Two playboys with polished shoes and flashy spats," Sol added. "Ad and Jacob. The Katzenjammer Kids up there on the stage. One jumps left, the other jumps right."

A vaudeville cue, it seemed, because the front door opened and Adolph strolled in, unhurried, trailed by a wisp of a woman, a nervous grin on her face.

"I'm late, I know," Ad said with no apology in his voice, a wide grin on his face. "It's Minna's fault." He bowed toward the woman, still grinning but now red-faced.

"Don't believe him," she said softly.

"We never do," Sol said.

"C'mon, Papa." Ad swirled around clumsily, the loose-jawed clown.

He'd changed since my fleeting acquaintance with him eighteen years before. Then he was a gangling young man, early twenties, prominent Adam's apple and cowlick, though attractive in a farm boy way—an ah-shucks goofiness. Of course, he was no dashing Jacob, his next-door buddy and ne'er-do-well wanderer in the streets. But Ad Newmann had a shyness that made you like him, smile at him—as though he was genuinely surprised when someone noticed him and—*liked* him. I liked him because of his breezy manner, the way he seemed tickled to find himself drifting somewhere in the solar system. When Jacob said something vaguely risqué, though out of earshot of his parents, Ad blushed. He was Sir Galahad, a shining knight that no one needed.

He grabbed his father from behind and squeezed him. "You love me, Papa."

"Only on rainy days."

Everyone laughed.

"You know I'm your favorite son, Papa."

"Ah, clever—my only son."

Ad had added flesh to those long stringy bones, and the effect was pleasing: a hail-fare-thee-well soul, a little beefy but still appealing, if slick and smooth in his rumpled summer linen suit. Another perennial bachelor, Esther insisted, though his endless engagement to the doe-eyed Minna Pittman, a teacher out in Lawndale, occupied much of the suppertime talk when Ad was absent. Ad once played with the notion of becoming a rabbi, caught up in Talmudic studies for what seemed a wasted year—his family holding its breath—but since then he'd had too many jobs. He worked as a puller on Maxwell Street, wooing customers into Wittenberg's Clothiers; but, painfully honest, he pointed out the faulty seams in the pants he peddled. So he did this, then did that, and nothing for very long.

The atmosphere of the dining room shifted when Ad and Minna sat down. Ad's smart-aleck affection for his family caused Esther to *tsk tsk* at his rolling nonsense and Sol to betray his impatience with the son who liked to stay in bed most mornings. But everyone seemed to *relax*. Because, most times, the conversation of the dowager Molly and her son and daughter-in-law, though friendly, was peculiarly formal. Ad was the yeast that bubbled the surface of things. He even got my mother to smile when he described his battle with a peddler on Maxwell.

"So he says to me, '*Gay avek, nudnik,*' and I say back, 'You're *a gantser kener,*' and he says, 'You call that English?'"

I struggled a little with the translation. *Get out of here, you pest. You're a know-it-all.*

Minna Pittman said little and seemed thrilled with Ad's performance. The Ben Franklin eyeglasses on the small, tight oval face gave her face a pinched look, with a worrywart's nervous habit of darting eyes and twitching nose. She was dressed in a prim summer smock with too many girlish blue periwinkles dotting the fabric, the woeful look of an older maiden aunt, one good for darning one's socks and embroidering a frilly parlor antimacassar. A mean-spirited depiction, I admit, but Minna Pittman kept staring at Ad Newmann with the unadulterated adoration of a frenzied girl gaping at a Saturday-afternoon matinee idol. A little disconcerting, and wholly delusional.

Ad monopolized the supper, as I suspected he often did—a rollicking, if insipid, spiel of zany stories from the marketplace. At one point he began an anecdote about a friend and his battle with chopped liver—"So a pan of *gehakte leber* slips into her lap and…and…and the man says"—which suddenly veered dangerously into the risqué, though, I realized, Ad was oblivious of the double entendre he was executing, which made it all the more delightful. But his father, rolling his eyes, grumbled, "This from the sad rabbinical student."

That failed vocation was a sore spot with his father. Ad, I knew from his mother's long in-kitchen catalogue of her son's occupations, had especially disappointed his father when he'd abandoned his studies. Ad's yearlong fevered fascination with a religion he'd paid scant attention to most of his life had resulted from an old man who sat for hours at the butcher shop, the cracker-box Talmudist in the back room. Ad lingered there with Jacob, a scoffer at the strictures of his own religion. But not so Ad, enthralled by the old man's devotion to storytelling…the ancient and mysterious lore of Judaism. Jacob had little patience with Ad's new passion.

The result, unfortunately, was that Ad reinforced his image among the men as a moralistic prig, tinged now with a bit of the mystical medieval Jew, a scholarly diversion at odds with his fly-by-the-seat-of-his-pants life. When that ended, Ad worked as a handyman, a pushcart vendor of hot dogs, a helper at Nathan's Meat Market after Morrie Wolfsy went it alone for a few months after Ivan's murder. "That was so short a time," Esther told me. "The spine-chilling squawk of a chicken beheaded sent him out the door." An encyclopedia salesman, a shoe salesman, a pretzel maker, and now, a jack-of-all-trades gadabout at Feinstein's Hardware up on Halsted.

Perhaps Sol was resigned to his son's wanderlust, though his impatience seeped through his love for his son. But the cult of adoration was not the sole province of Minna, at that moment picking gingerly at a chicken wing. No, the charter member of that familial club was old Molly herself. Severe and crotchety though she might be, and a magpie of neighborhood gossip, she doted on her only grandson.

"She always has," Esther told my mother and me earlier. "Her special boy. She blames Jacob Brenner for Ad's lack of… of focus, you can say. She doesn't *like* Jacob."

Sol and Esther's other child, a younger daughter named Harriet, lost in the shadows created by Ad's sunshine, married young and retreated to Cleveland with a husband and three children, returning only for the High Holy Days. And only sometimes, at that.

Molly left the room for something, beating that cane on the hardwood floor, *tap tap tap*, forcing us to stop talking, and, as she passed Ad's chair, her gnarled fingertips caressed the back of his neck. He smiled up at her, a little boy's grateful glance. It was, frankly, a loving gesture that communicated to the rest of us that there should only be two people at the dining room table. I caught my mother's eye. Her glance said, emphatically, *This is how devotion is supposed to look. Pay attention, Edna.*

I supposed it was hard to dislike the scattered Ad because, well, we tend naturally to *like* children.

I'd been watching him, lost in thought, enjoying his schoolboy banter, so I'd missed something. I wasn't paying attention to what was said, but the air in the room got heavy. Sudden stillness at the table, every head turned to Ad. Molly, returning to the room, had stopped walking, teetering there on her cane. No *tap tap tap* now. She swayed, then fell into a chair, her face grim.

"What?" Ad asked, puzzled. "You all crazy? All I said was that we met Jacob sitting on his porch as we were walking here tonight. He told us Edna stopped in to see his mother earlier today." He glanced at me. "They had iced tea or…or something. And…" His voice trailed off.

"This afternoon," Minna finished. "I think."

Now every eye centered on me. At that moment I realized—how had I not?—that my visit to Leah Brenner, which had devastated my mother and infuriated Molly, the unspoken topic of conversation at supper—had surfaced. The lethal river sloughing under our pleasantries and bonhomie had burst to the surface. Edna, the trespasser in the Garden of Eden.

Esther sighed. "Adolph, we know all about that."

Ad was perplexed. "Well, what's the problem? Jacob was downright *happy* about it. He…he was happy. And Jacob ain't happy very often. It's strange, that household. His mother hides away, and nobody knows what to do with her. I stop in, but I know I shouldn't. I gotta meet Jacob…elsewhere. Jacob said Edna, here"—he nodded at me, smiling—"Edna, here, made his mother…you know…"—fumbling, fumbling—"happy."

Molly smiled without any humor. "This is not suppertime conversation, Adolph dear."

Helpless, faltering, with a trace of anger, he replied, "She is our neighbor."

"I know who is my neighbor," Molly snarled.

Baffled, he spoke to his father. "Papa?" But Sol was focused on his plate.

Of course, it was the only topic I was interested in, and so I began. "How is Jacob dealing with his mother, Ad? I'm sure, after the years away, and now back at home, he…"

My mother's scream broke in. "Edna, really!"

"You must admit it's an interesting household. A woman accused, sent away, deemed mad, returned, a killing that remains a mystery."

Ad was watching me, a hint of a smile on his lips. "Edna, we don't talk about Leah Brenner in this house. Or Ivan. Or that horrible day. The dark blot on the street."

His grandmother sighed. "Adolph, dear, we're not monsters.

The way you paint us. It's just best to bury the past. Such sadness then…that woman…"

I spoke up. "But clearly you haven't buried anything. That wound is still open, frankly, if it's a taboo subject here and the merest mention raises everything to the level of high drama."

"Edna." My mother barely squawked out the word. Only Julia Ferber could make my drab, unlovely name seem a curse. "Edna!" She'd been cutting a piece of chicken and she held the knife in mid-air as we all stared at it.

Ad answered my question. "He says his mother is quiet. Lonely. By herself. Waiting for visits from her children. He skirts around her because he doesn't understand what's going on. There are days he's real depressed…like he doesn't know what to do. You can't talk to him those days."

"So he hasn't made peace with her return."

Ad nodded. "She's his mother but, you know…"

Molly hissed, "She killed a good man."

"A mean man. Rotten." But then Ad was sorry for the remark. Molly frowned at him.

I went on. "Does Jacob believe his mother killed his father?"

My mother rose, dropped her napkin to the floor. She still held out the knife, menacingly, but, spotting it gripped in her fingers, let it drop onto her plate. It clanged and slid onto the lace tablecloth. At that moment the grandfather clock chimed the hour and she yelped, like a shaken child. "My Lord, Edna, are there no boundaries?"

Ad was enjoying this, the smile still there. "He's happy she can talk to someone like you. A writer like you. She likes you. He's glad." A glance at his grandmother and then at his mother. "I'm glad, too. The Talmud says"—he winked at his father—"if I can remember from my scholarly days, 'It is fitting for a great God to forgive a great sinner.' Maybe we should obey."

"Obey!" thundered Molly. "We're not God, sorry to say." A wry smile. "The Talmud also says, 'Let yourself be killed but do not kill.'" She banged the table. "All right, enough. Let's clear the dishes. Esther made strudel to die for."

Minna, who'd been swiveling her head back and forth, panicked, jumped up and grabbed a platter. "Shhh, Ad," she whispered to him. "*Sha*! Quiet! You know how this will end up."

I laughed nervously. "It's the reporter in me, I suppose. A curiosity. Back in Appleton the great Houdini and I solved a murder, the two of us a team. I covered a gruesome murder and trial in Milwaukee and…" I stopped.

My mother's look was venomous. "An unmarried girl on the streets of that beer-besotted hellhole. Thank God for Prohibition." She faltered a bit, observing the bottle of Manischewitz on the sideboard. "My daughter, the *alte moyd*." The old maid.

I would have none of it. "I'm sorry. I don't believe Leah Brenner killed her husband. Not one bit. Where was the knife? A dazed woman wouldn't plan…" Again I stopped.

An explosion in the room. Sol let out an unintended belch, immediately frowned upon by a decorous Minna standing near him, still holding that platter. My mother, uncertain, sat down and then stood back up, though she never took her eyes off the ponderous grandfather clock, as though she coveted the power to turn back time. Molly gasped for breath as Esther reached for her glass of lemonade, an involuntary sob coming from the back of her throat.

I was growing nervous now, aware of my impolite behavior and suspect talk. After all, I *was* a guest—at least for the remainder of the next week. Short story writer for the national weeklies be damned: I was simply the pushy daughter of an old friend, and not a nice one at that. Edna Ferber, ace reporter, once again ruining one more suppertime. I thought of Jacob's cruel doggerel. *Edna Edna not nice…*

But still…"She seems so…lost. A dark Rebecca on that porch, watching…" I breathed in. "I kept thinking of the beautiful woman in a Walter Scott romance…*Ivanhoe*, you know…And what evidence? Really! You know, they never found the knife. Not in that room. Not in the kitchen. Not in the body. Wouldn't the knife be in the body? In the neck? Strange, no? Given her paralyzed stare when they found her, leaning over the body, speechless, and for years afterwards, how could she have had the presence of mind to…?" I stopped. Enough.

Esther was sobbing quietly. "Ever since she got back—like three years ago now—we *avoid* her. We don't see her, but we know she's there in that house. It's like a huge boulder fell onto the street. It's ruined everything. Leah was a friend of mine. We shopped together. We visited in each other's kitchens, had coffee. Picked *kirshen* from the tree out back…cherries for pie. Yes, she was a little…different. I don't know what word to use…"

"I do," said Molly, her ragged voice breaking. "A Jezebel. A harlot. A temptress. Take your pick."

"Mama," Sol began. "Not again. Please."

She silenced him with a ferocious glare. "That…that sickening moment with Morrie, that horrid butcher. Yeah. The men always gaping at her, joking, the improper wink. What kind of decent Jewish mother, that woman?" She turned to Ad, who avoided her face. "You remember how the men talked about her, sitting in that grimy back room of Nathan's, that *fleyshmark*, the meat market I never went into, refused to, those groups of strange men, tongues out, yammering on and on. That dark hole. And she loved it, don't tell me she didn't, I could see—the attention of stupid, stupid men. Ivan was a hard-working slob with a wife who moved like a courtesan. Yeah, the man could be hard. How could he not be?" A rasp from the back of her throat. "She brought Sodom and Gomorrah onto this quiet street."

Esther sobbed into her plate and Sol gently touched her shoulder, let his fingers rest there. It was, I thought, as loving a gesture as any old married couple could share.

"I'm sorry to ruffle everyone's feathers," I went on. "But"—a nod at Ad—"what does Scripture say about love? Ah—'God wants the heart.' Right? Doesn't Leah deserve *that*?"

Ad was still smiling, but a quiet, mischievous boy's smile. Though I liked him, it dawned on me then that Ad thought me a frivolous woman, a silly meddler, one not to be taken seriously. I was a rabble-rouser who at the moment was amusing him. That rankled, surely, and I wondered how shallow he really was. His knee-jerk sympathy for the marooned—and maybe railroaded—Leah had the depth of oilcloth. Maybe I shouldn't like him so much.

Molly was trying to stand, grasping the edge of the table and gripping her cane. Her voice trembled. "A supper ruined." Eyeing me sharply, she stepped away from the table.

"I'm sorry," I said, though I wasn't.

My mother spoke to the clock. "A lifetime of 'I'm sorry' from a daughter who digs the hole for my early grave."

"I'm…" I began again, penitent, but stopped. I wasn't sorry.

Molly began her slow move away from the table, *tap tap tap*, but she paused, and I watched her teeth chatter in the hot, hot room. She faced me. "A lifetime lived here," she whispered, "and that woman changed everything." She slammed the floor with her cane.

She turned to her son, Sol, who seemed baffled by her fierce stare. Then, quietly, she repeated her awful line: "That woman changed everything."

Now her eyes were on me.

Chapter Six

The next morning I hailed a taxi on Halsted and headed downtown toward the Loop, and finally, refreshed with coffee at Moe's, walked into the *Chicago Tribune* building. Using the name of an old friend, Tim Boyden, a features editor now living in New York—and employing my own current celebrity—I managed to get hold of a small stack of clippings in a manila folder at the *Tribune* morgue. The meagerness of the file surprised me because I'd expected a wealth of newsprint spilling out. After all, this was a Chicago murder story, one that happened in the safe and quiet Jewish neighborhood off Maxwell—not like the recent whoop-it-up gangland murders Chicago was beginning to wrestle with since Prohibition became the law of the land.

But there was so little information, and contradictory at that, most facts repeated day after day, then spottily, until a month later a small paragraph buried deep in the paper chronicled Leah's quiet removal to an asylum. Hardly splashy news, this domestic murder, not newsworthy. A woman—with a rumored sub-rosa reputation, wink wink wink—kills her loyal and faithful husband in a blind rage after a violent argument, then sinks into silence and solitude, and is finally defined as mad. What amazed me was the cavalier tone of the reportage—Leah cattily recalled by neighborhood women and even some men as notoriously flirtatious, sometimes irreverent, non-observant, this Jewish mother—a woman with a flippant remark, a reckless laugh. A woman already talked about, and not nicely.

So little about the actual murder.

Such a paucity of facts. The investigative detectives located no knife, no bloodied clothing, and there was no confession. A man slumped over, a cruel gash on the right side of his neck, dead from choking on his own blood. Nothing, save a woman paralyzed over the dead form of her husband. Her fingertips smeared with his blood. Blood splattered on his shirt collar, on the sofa cushions, on the floor.

The very first news account accused her. As the first patrolman on the scene noted, "She looked like she did it."

That said it all. Case closed. Hang her. Stone her.

I raced through the clippings, my fury growing. A glib, skewered portrait of a woman with questionable character. Innuendo, suspicion. One cagey reporter shared cigars with a bunch of men gathered in the back room of Nathan's Meat Market, cracker-barrel philosophers all, the wisdom of Solomon at the ready, men who praised Ivan as sweet and friendly and Leah as—a vamp.

"She never fit into the neighborhood," one man told the reporter.

Murder in a fit of anger, a burst of sudden madness, a marrow-deep depression, and a slow descent into the dark corners of the irrational mind.

Leah, by all accounts glass-eyed and frightened, said nothing, a piece of beautiful clay moved from one spot to the next. The Chicago House of Corrections. The Cook County Hospital. She answered no questions.

The judge quietly signed papers to commit her.

No one, I realized, got her to talk about what happened.

When Detective Tom O'Reilly was asked by a noisome reporter about the whereabouts of the knife, he blithely remarked, "A butcher's wife's kitchen. Come on. *Her* kitchen."

Not really an answer at all.

So my morning at the news morgue did little to answer my questions, though the hour there firmed up my initial sense of Leah's innocence. Detectives entertained no other suspects. The case had been simply too *easy* to wrap up, to file away. The same way Leah was conveniently filed away in a small cell far from home, like Hester Prynne with her nagging inner thoughts and mournful reflection. A woman sat alone, forgotten, until one day she decided she'd had enough of silence and found her voice again.

She came home.

• ● ●

I left the *Chicago Tribune* and wandered, window shopping, making the mistake of boarding the slow-moving, jam-packed streetcar on Indiana Avenue, hopping off, buying ice cream, but finally ended up back on Halsted Street, that long, long street everyone ended up on sooner or later. Tired, my mind back at the news morgue, I ambled down Maynard, off Maxwell, a poor stretch of wooden shanties, soot-blackened tenements, dark basement apartments without baths or light. The world of sweatshops, rows of skinny boys in black-brimmed caps and *tzitzis* hunched over tables, boys who never saw daylight.

Here on this bright afternoon the East European *shtetl* emptied out into tenements that once housed German Jews, who were now abandoning the area for the green lawns and pristine boulevards of West Chicago. And yet—not everyone. Esther and Sol and Molly, and Leah and Ivan—they stayed on, wanting the old neighborhood. The children left, but they remained. I wondered why.

Once again, turning toward the Newmanns' house, I stood in front of Nathan's Meat Market, that touchstone to the past. Empty now, abandoned, the interior dark.

"Edna." A sweet voice from behind.

Jacob Brenner stood near me, a loaf of bread cradled to his chest.

"Jacob, you startled me."

"You seemed lost in thought." He pointed at the butcher shop. "The only kosher butcher on this block. *Der kosherer katser.* You know, Morrie Wolfsy kept it going for half a year after Papa died, though he seemed to lose interest. He'd forget to open some days."

"It sits empty?"

Both of us peered through the dark front window. Someone had left a light on in the back room.

"He owns the building. He keeps an apartment upstairs, but his wife hates the neighborhood, sticks up her nose at it. Too *poor* now. They got a grand house out in Lawndale, a la-di-dah place with a concrete fountain in front like it's Versailles, but Morrie wanders back here, stays in his old apartment upstairs or sits in his back room where all the guys used to spend useless hours. Me included. The boys' club. Forbidden poker. French postcards even. Craps. Sometimes." He laughed. "Chickens beheaded and the politics of America argued over and over."

"You'd think he'd rent the store."

"He won't. Won't give a reason. But he owns a couple of the apartment houses on Monroe. He comes back here once a month to collect the rents. He lives on that money now—the butcher shop is history. He runs his rental properties from the upstairs apartment. That's the only time we see him in the neighborhood. He's old, tired. Hey, Morrie's not a bad sort. Sometimes, back then, a spell of religion would overtake him—the result of old Levi the ragpicker thumping his fist at the infidels—and Morrie'd boot us all out. When Papa died, some folks blamed him."

He stared into my eyes. "There was even a rumor that he killed Papa. No one believed *that*, even though they didn't get along. But afterwards, though, he just went through the motions at work. Like his soul died. Like his heart was pierced. He stopped being friendly, snubbed folks. Customers drifted away."

"Did you think he murdered your father?" I asked bluntly.

Jacob didn't flinch at my words. Nor did he answer me. He shrugged as if I were discussing the ongoing heat spell.

"Wanna look inside?"

He stepped to the front door and turned the knob. It opened.

"Morrie never locks it. Nothing inside of value anymore, really." He lowered his voice. "I think he hopes the old gang will stop back in, especially those times he's upstairs counting his money. But there is no old gang left. He knows I sit by myself here at night. Alone." Then he grinned. "I used to slip in to write my poetry at night—when I did that sort of thing. Waiting for inspiration that never arrived. It's quiet here."

He stepped inside but I didn't follow him into the shadowy dark room. "No, Jacob. No." A violation, I felt, trespassing. I walked away from the shop but glanced back at Jacob in the doorway, as he shut the door.

He joined me. "You shouldn't ask me that question, Edna. I still have...nightmares. I still..." Then, a helpless shrug. "Well, I guess everyone was a suspect." A hint of a smile. "Even me. I was upstairs that day."

He started to move away. "Jacob," I called to him, and he stopped.

His melodious voice, always so cooing and seductive, suddenly got brittle, harsh. "I don't want to talk about *that*. Not anymore."

"I'm sorry."

He stepped back, in his eyes a flash of—not anger, but pain. "No, you're not, Edna. I can see this...that horrible event fascinates you."

I nodded. "True, but I don't want to *hurt* you—or your mother."

A sad smile. "Me—you can't hurt. At least *most* days. I don't care about most things these days. I get morbid, curl up inside. Too many years have passed me by. After the murder, I got depressed. Before that, I was the rah-rah playboy of the neighborhood. Me and Ad all night at the Booster Club on the roof of the Morrison Hotel. Everyone wanted me *there*. Bert Kelly's band struck up a song when I walked in. I was *popular* then. The girls circled me like I was gold in the street. I thought I'd be young forever. Lord, Edna, I'm gonna be forty years old this year. I make my money running numbers in a speakeasy on Clark Street."

"But you're a poet."

Now he laughed long and hard. "Edna, Edna, I don't think you realize how funny you can be." He got a faraway look in his eyes. "I do wish I could remember you from…what? Eighteen years ago, right?"

"Why?"

"Because, after all these years, I think you still like me." A sheepish grin.

"And others don't?"

He frowned, his eyes darkening. "When everyone wants to be around you 'cause you're good-looking, you keep waiting for them to get tired of begging for your attention. You end up…" He trailed off.

"You end up feeling sorry for yourself." I paused. "Or despising yourself."

He chuckled. "God, you don't let a soul get away with anything, Edna."

"No reason to."

Suddenly he put his face close to mine. "I don't want my mother hurt."

I waited a heartbeat. "Jacob, I think your mother has found her own way. Maybe, like you, she can't be hurt anymore. She's found a peace she can live with." I paused. "But I don't know if I believe you. I think you *can* be hurt. You lie to the world, Jacob. You've been hurt—badly so."

He sidestepped that. "You know, I'm real glad you talked to Mama. Maybe you're right—she's made her peace with the world, but it doesn't help that the other women on the street shun her."

"I know. Molly Newmann, for one."

A fake shiver. "An unforgiving woman, that one. But she didn't like Mama from the start. When I was real small, I remember she snubbed her—gossiped. Mama was just too…pretty." But then he sighed. "Esther was the only one who was friendly. I mean, Esther invited Mama into her kitchen for coffee. They went shopping." He frowned. "The women of Monroe Street have made a devil's pact to make certain my mother never is happy again."

"Horrible,"

"You're not like that."

"Jacob, I don't think your mother murdered your father."

That statement stopped him cold, and for a second he flinched, turned his head away as though afraid our talk might be heard by eavesdroppers. Sweat covered his brow. Finally, he said, "I think you're wrong, but, as I say, I don't care anymore. Papa was a tough man, brutal."

I was indignant. "I can't believe you'd say that. You'd accuse your mother?"

He tried to look apologetic. "Look, Edna. It's got nothing to do with my love for Mama. That's *there*. Always. She and I… always close. We had—have—a special bond, the two of us. But…who *else*? The police told me…"

"I wish I knew." Then, turning my head, "Yes, the police had all the answers."

He walked away but turned back. "Please don't, Edna. Don't make things messy again. That was an awful time for all of us. Let sleeping dogs lie."

"Yes, especially for your mother."

"C'mon, Edna. Really."

I fumed. "Jacob, you're not very attractive when you're so… callow."

His eyes popped. "You think I don't know that?" A bow. "I gotta go. Get back to the old fortress."

"The fortress?"

"Me and my buddy, Ad, the two bumble brothers, each barricaded in our bedroom caves in the old homestead, fending off the Amazon women warriors. Me—my Aunt Sarah, who hates me 'cause I'm still there. Ad, smothered to death by a *bubbe* who wanted him to be the golden child, the revered rabbi, the heir to the covenant of the ark…" Another bow. "Hey, we hide away and dream of being little boys all over again. Goodbye, dear Edna from eighteen years ago."

But then he changed his mind, circling around me like a bratty child.

"What?"

"I just remembered something. Speaking of women warriors, you may have heard of my twin sisters, Ella and Emma." He laughed. "Or is it Emma and Ella? I can never tell them apart." I glared at him, and he fumbled. "It's an old joke. I never tire of it."

"Perhaps you should. I already have. Yes, I know you have two younger sisters. In fact, I have a dim memory of two wide, startled faces peering out a second-story window as I stood on the sidewalk—this, of course, eighteen years ago. They had to be seventeen or eighteen back then."

"Four years younger, unmarried, spinsters now, identical except for one important fact."

"And that is?"

"One won't visit our mother nowadays, the other one does, grudgingly."

"Interesting. And they have what to do with me?"

He chuckled. "Ella—the bossy one who visits once a month like clockwork, the one with the hickory stick, the one who orders meek and trembling Emma around like a dumb house servant—gave my mother your novel *The Girls* when she heard you were visiting next door. She loved it—three generations of women in Chicago or, as I overheard her tell Mama, a story of how insufferable dominating mothers can be." His eyes flashed wide. "A message to Mama, perhaps?"

I laughed. "Not *quite*, that storyline." But of course it *was*—a fact that my own mother pointed out and fussed over. "Have you read it?" I asked Jacob now.

He rolled his eyes, purposely exaggerating the gesture. "A book about unmarried women? Spinsters? You don't know much about me, do you, Edna?"

Wryly, my tongue in the corner of my mouth: "What I know is actually too much. Men—young men in particular—spend their time winning battles in wars no one else has heard of."

"What does that mean?"

"Men love to walk in their own victory parades down imaginary streets."

He grinned. "You lose me, lovely Edna. Anyway, Ella and Emma—or is it Emma and Ella?—lived with me and Sadistic Sarah all the years of Mama's absence. Our own prison sentence. Once Mama returned, Ella and Emma skedaddled, though I'm not sure why. My brother, Herman, who pays all the bills and keeps us all out of debtor's prison, thought it was a good idea. Clear out. Vamoose. Get out of Dodge. Especially Emma, who was *afraid* to be there."

"Afraid of what?"

"Dunno." A heartbeat. "Maybe the nightmares will return—the ones that made her wake up screaming. So Ella won't allow Emma to visit now. Afraid she'll upset Mama."

"And your point is what, Jacob? You do trot around a story."

"They want to meet you. I told Ella how close you and I once were…"

I walked away. "Good day."

He got serious, ran after me and touched my elbow. "No, no, wait. Please, Edna. I'm a fool. They want me to bring you to tea some afternoon. They share a room—genteel as all get out, them being unmarried and possibly prey to ne'er-do-wells and bounders—the other side of Maxwell on Canal, a rooming house run by Mrs. Goldberg, as scary a woman as God decided to send to torment other souls on Earth. For single women only, guard dogs at the front entrance." He turned his head to one side, coyly. "Please. I promised them."

"Only if you read my novel, Jacob."

"I promise."

"You are lying to me again."

A hiccough. "Yes, I am. I lie to all women. They *expect* it."

"You're…impossible." I paused. "But all right. You arrange it."

• • ● ● •

That night, meeting Ad in the hallway, he whispered to me that Jacob would meet me on the sidewalk the following afternoon at half-past two. "Be discreet." He leaned in, a goofy smile on his face. "Hide behind the hedges."

"Ad, what?"

"Jacob, though my best friend, is not welcome here since his mother came home and soured the peaceful life of Monroe Street." He gazed over my shoulder. "If he telephones here, asking for me, he's told no one is home. Even, I suppose, the person answering the telephone."

"And you allow that?"

He bit the tip of a fingernail. "Does it look like I set the rules here, Edna?"

The next afternoon, dressed in a light cerise polka-dot sundress with a brimmed straw summer hat with paper roses, I met Jacob, who was planted dramatically and conspicuously in front of the Newmann house. As always, he greeted me with the gentlemanly half-bow, and off he sailed, two or three jaunty paces ahead of me.

I rushed to keep up with his long strides. "Are we in a foot race, Jacob?"

He slowed down. "I just assumed you'd naturally fall in at my side."

"And I just assumed you had some common courtesy."

"I guess we were both wrong." A wide grin, infectious.

From Maxwell, we turned down Canal, and stopped before a four-story brick building, squat and ugly, soot-blackened red brick and unpainted wrought-iron fence. A small sign said: "Mrs. Goldberg's Rooms. Single Women Only." And then in some bowdlerized German or Yiddish or God-knows-what: *Hier wir the Englisch sprech*. In sloppy black paint, some passing wag had added the words "Only If" at the end of that sentence, perhaps a bit of sarcasm.

We met the two sisters in the stuffy parlor at the front of the house. They stood side by side, bodies touching, arms hanging stiffly at their sides, both with ridiculous red bows in their hair. Introduced first to an obese Mrs. Goldberg in a black Victorian smock, obviously the moral sentry and resident custodian of maidenly virtue, we then stood in the cramped, overstuffed room among the velveteen-covered armchairs and tuffed settees covered with intricate antimacassars. Embroidered quotations from Scripture hung haphazardly on faded rose-printed wallpaper. Mrs. Goldberg seemed unimpressed by my local celebrity, barely suppressed a belch when one of the twins gushed about *The Girls* and my picture (with interview) last year in the *Chicago Tribune*, and then led us to the small dining area at the back of the house, off the kitchen, where a table covered in slick oilcloth held a dangerously lopsided chocolate cake and bargain teacups from Marshall Field's basement sale. I thought I'd been bizarrely ushered into a failed rehearsal for *Alice in Wonderland*. No matter: seated, tea poured decorously by one of the twins, cake sliced but vaguely moldy on a plate, the twins began to speak at the same time, their voices overlapping as in an echo chamber. They sang of the delight—the wonder, thrill, pleasure, surprise, fear, panic—of actually meeting me again.

"Again?" I managed to get out.

They laughed. "Not *again*," one said, in a solo performance now. "We do remember you and your sister, Fannie, following Jacob down the sidewalk…"

"Please," Jacob broke in, "I'm blushing."

"I never did such a thing," I lied. Outright. I refused to look at Jacob.

Ella and Emma giggled like schoolgirls on holiday.

So the minutes passed in inane blather. Yet, perversely, the more we spoke of Chicago and childhood and Maxwell Street and the World's Fair of 1893—which neither of the twins went to, though Jacob said he and Ad had seen Buffalo Bill's Wild West Show there, and, an improper wink, exotic Little Egypt— the more my mind kept darting back to their mother's arrest for murder. That was my only interest here. Yet Emma and Ella seemed not to have a care in the world, save the collection of tourist postcards from Europe that one of them (Ella?) babbled about and the watercolor landscapes the other (Emma?) threatened to show me.

Both were tiny, pencil-thin women with parchment complexions and spit-curl hairdos from another century, though the huge red bows struck me as affectations borrowed from a children's storybook. Both were wearing heavy black patent-leather shoes, square-toed, that I associated with nurses in military hospitals. Both leaned back and forth, bumping into each other like elastic bands that kept snapping back into place. They had the maddening habit of talking as one or, worse, finishing each other's sentences. It was evident, finally, that one of them—Ella—controlled the other by severe looks, by abrupt words, by touching her sleeve when it was time for her sister to shut up. Emma was the meek one, though she never seemed to shut up. Ella ordered her around ("Emma, pour more tea, please" or "Emma, sit back, you're blocking my view of Edna"), and Emma complied, tittering nervously.

"When Ad told Jacob you and your mother were…"

"…visiting, we said, it's hard to…"

"…believe. After…"

"…all these years."

They were Dickensian parlor maids, dithering and bleating.

But I wasn't ready to leave. The one story never touched on—Leah Brenner back in her old kitchen—kept me still.

"It's amazing how much Jacob looks like your mother," I began, staring past everyone at a faded chromolithograph hanging crookedly on the wall.

A moment of silence, palpable, but one woman managed, "Jacob got the good looks, you know."

More silence, awkward now. Ella fingered the crumbs on her plate.

Jacob cleared his throat. "Ella, Mama wondered why you skipped Thursday. You said you would come to visit but…"

No one paid attention to me, Jacob purposely shifting his body away.

"I forgot the time. We were shopping and the time passed. You know how it is." She arched her shoulders and sat back. "Cake," she mumbled, directing my attention to the table.

"I enjoyed visiting your mother," I said to her. "She told me she looks forward to your visits." I was making that up but felt safe fabricating the line. After all, I assumed Leah *did* want visits from Ella.

Jacob leaned forward. "You know, Emma, you need to visit Mama, too."

Emma turned away from us, facing the door. For a moment her face closed up, eyes half-shut. The color rose in her neck, a muscle throbbed. A hand trembled.

Ella fussed but said loudly, "I won't allow Emma to go." A sickly smile. "You *know* that, Jacob."

"What?" From me, stupefied.

She spoke in a clipped, artificial voice, "She'll get too emotional and say the wrong thing. I've forgiven Mama, of course, but she won't. She *can't*. It'll be awkward."

Emma was on the verge of tears.

Jacob spoke again, "She misses you, Emma."

What she said next stunned me. "She murdered Papa."

So bold the line, said so innocently, a throwaway comment as if about the heat of the day or the price of butter at a market stall.

Ella nodded, a half smile on her face. "See what I mean?" she said to no one in particular. Then, a sidelong glance at me, "She doesn't have a forgiving heart."

Emma was ready to say something, perhaps to counter that notion, but she shook her head and looked down into her lap.

Jacob, flustered, nodded at me. "Edna, do you see how this matching set of humanity has found one subject to disagree on?"

Ella spoke up, nonplussed. "We don't talk about it, Jacob. Emma has her own views."

Which, I thought, you so emphatically reinforce. Emma, browbeaten, servile. Her story squelched.

Yet Ella was smiling at her brother, and even Emma assumed an adoring look as she gazed at him. They loved him dearly, I realized, doted on the gadabout wag, loving his teasing—even, I supposed, his indifference.

"I found your mother delightful," I forced myself to say again. The teacup rattled in my hand. And then, with cool deliberation,

I added, "A woman wronged, frankly. I don't believe she killed your father."

Emma yelped and said too loudly, "The police told us…"

I interrupted, "A peculiar case, uninvestigated, a belief that your mother's silence and fright constituted confession. Frankly, that was the conclusion of some vainglorious police sergeant or detective who never thought of what your mother was going through."

Emma was anxious. "But the captain told me…" She breathed in. "He said…definitely…"

"And you listened." I answered in a biting tone. "Men tell me things all the time, and I ignore most of it." Quietly, I sipped lukewarm tea and sat back.

"You're confusing me." Emma was nearly in tears.

"I don't mean to. But, truthfully, all of you were willing conspirators in the easy condemnation of your mother."

Ella cleared her throat. "Well, I never believed it. She just never seemed *capable* of it. I mean, she always ran away from fights with Papa. But the police…" A helpless shrug. "We had to listen to someone. We were all…drifting."

Jacob was squirming in his seat, uncomfortable, mumbling about leaving. "I have to be somewhere."

I eyed him cautiously. "No, you don't."

Startled, he grinned. "Yeah, that's true, but this place gives me the willies."

Yet the visit was an opportunity I'd not have again, so setting down my teacup and pushing away my untouched slab of congealed cake, I said, "You were all there that day. In the house. Didn't you *see* anything?"

Silence, heads turned toward the doorway. Finally Ella whispered, "Emma and I were up in the room we shared. Papa was home sick that day." She squinted, ignoring Emma's short audible breaths. "In the morning he and Mama fought, yelling so loud it scared us. We hid behind our closed door." Her voice was mournful. "We've told this story over and over. I mean—years ago we did. I went to the attic to get some fabric and when I stepped into the hallway, I heard Aunt Sarah screaming in the parlor. Emma rushed out of the room, white as a ghost, and the two of us ran downstairs. Papa was slumped on the sofa, bent to the side. He…"

Emma finished. "His head was back. All the blood on his neck, his shirt. Mama was bent in front of him, quiet, you know, stunned by her bloody fingers."

Ella went on, "Aunt Sarah screamed and screamed. We didn't know what to do."

Jacob added, "I had just fallen into bed, ready for a nap, half asleep, and the screaming jarred me. When I ran downstairs, it was—like pandemonium."

"You'd just come home?" I asked.

He squirmed as he tried to remember. "Yeah, maybe a little while before."

"Did you walk through the parlor?"

He was uncomfortable. "In the hallway, yes. Not *into* the parlor but in the doorway."

"Your father was there?"

"I saw him on the sofa. I thought he was sleeping."

"Slumped over?"

He flinched, nervous. "I glanced in, I think. I can't remember. Sometimes he napped there. I knew he was home sick from the butcher shop. I didn't say anything. I went upstairs, washed my face, lay on my bed."

I waited a beat. "Jacob, you didn't tell the police that you saw your father on the sofa."

He sputtered. "Well, of course, I did. I *saw* him…"

"No," I said firmly, "I've read the newspaper accounts"—that surprised the three of them—"and I remember the police were quoted as saying you hadn't seen your father since breakfast—and you said you had been napping for an hour—that you'd been in your room since lunch."

"I don't think…"

But I knew what I'd read in the news clippings. Jacob specifically said he'd heard his parents quarreling earlier and he'd hidden in his room, emerging only after hearing Sarah's wailing.

Now he sputtered, "Maybe I'm remembering wrong." He snickered, "It was fifteen years ago, for God's sake. You know, a person can forget things. It was a bad time—I wanted to block out some things. I don't remember *what* I told the police." Now there was an edge to his voice. "C'mon, Edna, you expect me to remember stuff like that. Maybe I'm thinking of another day. You know, Papa slept on the sofa a lot. A lot of times I walked by, and he was there."

"But not during the day. He was usually working at the store."

"Sick that day, yes. I don't know…" His voice broke at the end.

Emma spoke up in a clipped voice. "Jacob never had a memory for things."

Ella shot her a cautionary look, nodding furiously. "He can't remember what he did *yesterday*."

Emma agreed, echoing, "Yesterday."

"Jacob is always a little boy."

"A boy," Emma echoed. She was smiling at her sister.

Jacob's eyes dipped into his lap, his lips quivering. "It's all a jumble in my head. So long ago…"

Ella spoke loudly. "You know he's a poet, Edna."

"I've heard that," I answered. "But what does that have to do with his memory?"

"Nothing, but you can't expect a man like him…to…he's a wonderful writer, Edna."

"Brilliant," Emma said.

"You know *Poetry*, the magazine here in Chicago? Real prestigious."

I admitted I did. In fact, I knew Harriet Monroe, though faintly. A friend of Lillian Adler, my friend who ran the Maxwell Street Settlement House. I'd watched her teach dancing to awkward Polish and Russian and Jewish girls.

"They published his poem."

Jacob interrupted, "Emma, that was five years ago. One poem." He smiled sadly. "About our grandmother who'd died when we were all very small. My Bubbe."

And then, as though auditioning to be the best student in elocution class, Emma stood, prompted by Ella. "Now, Emma, now. Yes, now." Still holding her teacup, Emma recited in an oddly stentorian voice that doubtless carried out into the street and gave Mrs. Goldberg an immediate heart palpitation:

My grandmother
Was supposed to live till ninety
Though she had no legs
(We'd wheel her around
Until the flowers were dust)
She died at eighty-one
Not quite making it.
When I was small
She made old-country challah
Covered herself with eggs flour salt
Until the bread rose in the oven
Like evening in her eyes
And the smell took us both back
To a land I never saw
She'd never see again.

When she finished, Ella applauded, and I followed suit, though self-consciously. Jacob was pleased, though he pooh-poohed the whole performance.

Emma bowed and sat down.

Jacob stood up. "Edna, it's time we left."

Both twins immediately began clearing the dishes. Neither one looked at me.

Chapter Seven

The next morning, lying in bed but wide awake, I delayed going downstairs for breakfast. Though my door was closed, I could hear muffled voices—Esther's high soprano laugh and my mother's deep rumble —bits and pieces of their discussion of a theater performance they'd seen five years ago at Glickman's Yiddish Theater. An absurd rendering of King Lear. *Der Yiddisher Kainag Lear.* My mother kept saying it was too melodramatic and far-fetched; Esther insisted it was so sad she cried just thinking about it.

"Esther," my mother laughed, "you cry when the first flower blooms in spring."

Cracking my door slightly, I heard my mother telling Esther that lamentably, we'd not stay the full two weeks—another cousin insisted we visit in Evanston for two or three days. Blather and nonsense, of course, simply an excuse to secret her wayward daughter from the explosive household.

Yet another reason kept me in my room, tucked into a chair by the window and staring out at the leaves of the sugar maple tree wilting under the unrelieved heat. An awful reason: the visit with Jacob to Emma and Ella's rooming house. Jacob's careless dissembling, that slip about what he saw on the day his father was murdered. Perhaps meaningless, perhaps not—but curious. And Ella and Emma's spirited defense of his memory—and that curious sleight-of-hand maneuver of having Emma recite his poem, a preamble to my being shooed out the door. It bothered me, his failed memory. You'd remember every step you took on such an awful day, no? Stunned at that moment, of course, dazed, but later, recollecting in the painful days to follow, you'd order your thoughts, check off the moments in your head. But maybe not the helter-skelter Jacob—and his two bizarre sisters, his hip-hip-hurrah cheering team, panicky in their defense of a much-loved brother.

What to make of it all?

I waited until I heard Molly, Esther, and my mother leave the house, headed to the markets, then went downstairs into the kitchen for coffee and Esther's butter-slathered rye rolls. But the house was not empty after all. Ad was munching on toast, his face buried in the morning newspaper. He yawned and smiled. He was wearing a crisp white cotton shirt, unbuttoned at the neck to reveal a sunburned neck.

"Good morning, Ad."

"You hiding, Edna?"

"I thought everyone was gone."

"They've gone shopping." He chuckled. "I guess you were not invited. Papa's at the cigar store, of course. Only Lazy Ad stays home to masquerade as the leisure class. Lawn tennis at noon with Mrs. Potter Palmer, then a spin around the Loop in her ritzy fliv." He smiled. "Actually I'm leaving now. I've been helping Old Man Feinstein in his hardware store—he pays me practically nothing, but it keeps the folks from exiling me from the castle." He started to fold the newspaper. "Jacob told me you visited Ella and Emma yesterday at Mrs. Goldberg's. That woman scares me. The twins scare me. Ah, Edna, you and your acts of courage."

"Why? I found them delightful."

He narrowed his eyes as he smirked. "Yeah, sure, Edna. Convince me of that, can you? The silly Siamese twins. Ella giving marching oom-pa-pah orders to her sobbing sister. You probably didn't witness Ella screaming for hours at poor Emma, 'You don't have the brains you were born with.' It ain't pretty, let me tell you. Even though they put on a great act for the world to see, they don't *like* each other. That's clear. And yet they share a small, cramped room. Talk about your prison sentences. They hide from the world—they squeal if I say hello to them. They're so…scattered, those two. Yet, I suppose, harmless."

Ad's face got tight. Standing, he placed his cup in the sink and tucked his folded newspaper under his arm. "Jacob was *bothered* by what you said, Edna."

"What did I say?" I poured myself coffee, sat down, watching as he faced the outside window.

He hesitated, as though debating what to say to me. "I don't know exactly. Jacob only tells me just this much." He held up a thumb and index finger and punctuated the *this*. "He *avoids* sensitive talk, you know. Stuff about his mother. He thinks you've been asking a lot of questions about what folks remember." His hand flew to the air, a dismissive gesture. "He says you badgered Ella and Emma."

"I badgered *him*."

That startled. "Why?"

"He contradicts his own story."

A quizzical look. "So what? Why now? What does it matter?"

I munched on a bit of the delicious bread, moist, warm, scented with chewy caraway seeds, crispy outside, creamy inside. "Because now he suspects his mother is *innocent* of murder."

Ad started to cough, doubled over. When he leaned back, rubbing his cheek, he wore a quizzical smile. "He didn't tell me that you said *that*. That news must have stopped him cold in his tracks. Good God, Edna. You are something else. I can see why Jacob got depressed."

"Depressed?"

"He got moody. Maybe not real depressed. Sometimes he gets down in the dumps. There's no being with him those times. I back away. It's like this wave of melancholy drowns him."

"Maybe it's time someone in that family paid some attention."

Ad pulled a chair out, swiveled it around, straddled it. The newspaper slipped to the linoleum floor. Nervously, he lit a cigarette. "You don't think Jacob did it, do you?" Breathless, staring into my face.

"I don't know."

Ad didn't expect that answer and thumped the table with his fist. "Lord, Edna, do you hear yourself? This is Jacob. Sweet Jacob. He *loves* his mother. He never wanted his mother to be the one accused. But that's the way it happened. Problems with his father, everybody did, but he wouldn't *kill* him."

"He wouldn't be the first son to kill a father." I stared into his troubled face. "Sometimes those who love find themselves killing. That's the way it is. Because of the *love*, Ad. In a rage. A momentary fit. Passion. I read the articles in the Chicago *Tribune* about the murder, Ad. All of them…"

"What? Why?"

"I'm a reporter. It's in my blood."

"But it's so…long ago."

I bit my lip. "Yes, I know. Old news. Your grandmother so aptly dismissed it that way. That's the sentiment of the whole neighborhood. The only problem is that Leah has come back home. That's a wrinkle no one counted on."

He wagged a finger at me as though I'd said something amusing. He thought me one more nosy neighbor.

"You know, Edna, I just realized—you want a different ending. Leah Brenner fooled you, too. God, even now she can seduce, you know, entice. How many men fell under her spell and now…"

I cut him off. "You're missing the point, Ad. She didn't kill Ivan."

Ad's face got hard, his eyes dark and hooded. "Let me tell you something about Jacob." He counted a beat and then went on. "You gotta know this. When his father was murdered, Jacob got…miserable—crying jags, blubbering, sad, hiding in his room all day and night. Everything shut down inside him. It was horrible to watch. He fell apart, my best friend. Everyone but his sisters left him alone because they didn't know what to do. No mother, no father, and an aunt who didn't like him. His brother, Herman, kept saying that he should shape up and be a man, and 'What the hell is wrong with you?' His sisters baked him too many pies, like they piled up on the kitchen counter, insane. They gave him books of poetry by…by Ella Wheeler Wilcox, you know. 'Laugh and the world laughs with you, weep and you weep alone.' That kind of stuff. They'd read it *at* him. His Uncle Ezra mocked him. Ezra, his father's brother, a nasty man who was never around. Jacob cried all the time—I didn't know what to do with him. I thought he'd kill himself, so bad it was. He was a lost boy, really. I got scared of him. For him." Ad brought his face close to mine. "He ain't a strong guy, Edna."

I stood up. "Don't worry, Ad."

"I *am* worried. Don't make this into a game."

"I would never…"

With a sharp wave of his hand he left the kitchen. I sipped my coffee. It was cold.

• • ● • •

Upstairs in my bedroom, restless, I dabbled with my notes, reviewing some typed sheets, drawing a line here or there, striking out a paragraph, bored. Again, determined, I planned on a midnight run to the Haymarket, the South Water Street marketplace. I wanted to witness those dedicated Dutch truck farmers from outside Chicago bringing in their produce in the deep of night—the pivotal scene in my novel *Selina* or *So Big*—I couldn't decide which title I liked— Selina in her ramshackle wagon with her sleepy little boy Dirk nestled in blankets. But, again, that dirt farm grubbing world was far removed from the gritty pushcart world of Maxwell Street. The rich soil of New Holland had nothing to do with the tar and asphalt of Jewtown and Yiddish gab. Herring snacks on black pumpernickel. No—it wouldn't work for me. Not yet. I'd have to get away from Monroe Street.

Leah's story nagged at me like an old dog at my heel.

Downstairs, standing in the kitchen doorway, peering out the screen door, I could hear tinny music wafting across the yards. Someone in Leah's home was playing the radio loudly—fragmented words of that ridiculous popular song, "No No Nora" by Eddie Cantor. I find most popular ditties tedious. Eddie Cantor with that *wazza wazza* crooning drove me to distraction.

That adenoidal screeching. A house of noise—Sarah's booming music and Jacob's banging his way through the rooms. And Leah sat quietly by herself. But I lingered there, listening—and wondered: What had anyone in the Newmann household heard that morning years ago? Yes, they'd heard screaming. I knew that. Leah and Ivan's battle royal. But what else? What was said? The wailing of Ivan when he was knifed? The screams and weeping of Sarah and the children? Who heard what?

Had the police even talked to the Newmanns about it? I doubted that. After all, they scarcely talked to Leah.

Within minutes, standing on the sidewalk in front of Leah's home, I could hear the radio playing, but muted now. Impulsively, I climbed the stairs and knocked on the front door. Someone pulled back a curtain in a side window and then, finally, the door opened. Leah smiled at me. "I couldn't imagine who was here. Family always comes to the kitchen door." She pointed behind her. "Or through the back screen porch."

"I heard the music."

Leah raised her eyebrows and shook her head. The razzle-dazzle music was coming from an upstairs room, but at that moment the volume swelled so loudly that Leah and I had to raise our voices. Someone was fiddling with the knobs, searching for a station perhaps. A needle under the skin, that dissonant, staticky noise. *I wish I could shimmy like my sister Kate.* Claptrap music, utter novelty for a world of dancing fools in a speakeasy tavern.

"Sarah is telling me something," she yelled. "Ever since I got back home, she has discovered the volume control. Paul Whiteman thrills her—and he enters my nightmares. I tell her, beg her, but she goes against my wishes. Jacob pleads with her, but then he runs off. What can I do?" A weary shrug.

A sudden break in the music, a run of static as Sarah shifted the dial. But another crash of noise—stomping, a foot drummed on the floorboards, a fist slamming a wall. *Bam bam bam.*

"What?" I caught Leah's face.

She raised her eyes to the ceiling. "My Jacob."

"I don't understand…"

"A battlefield, Edna. Jacob staggers home and, like a restless boy, he thrashes around his room."

"A protest against Sarah's musical taste?" I joked.

She frowned. "The stomping around—a caged animal—even when Sarah is at the market."

"How can you bear the noise?"

She shrugged. "I have no choice." Again, the glance upward. "Jacob watches me too closely the last few days." She bit her lip. "His eyes accuse Sarah as she puts supper on the table."

Someone upstairs yelled, the music soared, the crash of a boot against the floorboards.

I motioned toward the Newmann house. "Join me for coffee."

She started. "Oh no. I—not there—Molly—"

Stepping close to the staircase, I raised my voice over the din. "No one is home, Leah. Molly and the others are out shopping. They're lost on Maxwell till afternoon. They'll linger at Nathan's Ice Cream Parlor. Trust me. I've been shopping with them. A sale at Louis Gabel's Clothing, and the hours go by. Come. There's coffee on the stove. Please. This noise is…impossible." I touched her elbow, though she backed away. "Please."

Numbly, almost mechanically, she stepped out onto the porch, shutting the door behind her. But her slow walk alongside me was a prisoner's plodding death march: short shuffling steps, a baby's tentative exploration. Once she sat opposite me in the Newmann kitchen, she sighed, relaxed in the chair, and folded her arms across her chest. "I haven't been in Esther's kitchen for—years."

"Did you come here often?"

She thought about her response, as if impossible to answer. "We were *friendly*. I *liked* her. She liked me, I knew. But she was always nervous *here*."

I smiled. "The shadow of Molly."

A slight wistful smile. "Molly didn't like me. Never liked me. Didn't trust me." A pause. "A *makhasheyfe*, she called me." A witch.

"I know."

Suddenly she stood, and I thought she'd flee. Instead, her hands fluttering, she walked to the sink and stared out the window toward her own house. Her back to me, she spoke quietly. "We moved here exactly one year after the Newmanns bought their place. May Day. May first. I mean, Sol and Esther, with Molly in tow, had already settled in, knew people, the rabbi." She turned her head, and I stared at her profile. "More than forty years back, a real neighborhood of greenhorns and off-the-boat boarders…and on windy days the sickening smells from the stockyards, sometimes from the I. C. trains. Our first home. Sol and Esther, new married. Me and Ivan, new married. Our home a wedding gift from his parents."

Now she faced me. Her eyes swept the kitchen as she ran her fingers across the counter, letting them rest on a cutting board. Her eyes took in the white-painted cabinets. "Nothing has changed here. Nothing. I used to sit in Esther's kitchen, here, friendly, you know. And then Ivan and Sol sat with cigars in the basement, arguing about something in *Forwards*, maybe. Molly made believe friendly, you know. But somehow—one day, maybe—Molly caught her Sol, a young man then, smiling at me a little too long. I was talking of something, and he laughed a little too long. Maybe."

Her face tightened. "It ain't my fault, Edna. Well—that day it wasn't. I was always blessed—or cursed—with the looks, you know. My mother warned me. Trouble, my little Leah. Trouble for you. My Papa said if we was Catholic I would be hidden away in a nunnery for good."

She shook her head back and forth slowly and dreamily. "A curse I didn't see coming, Edna. So Molly spotted Sol that day, real innocent it was…you know Sol, a nice guy always—you know him, such an innocent man—but Molly yells at him, and then at me as I sat there with a red face, and the rumors start."

For a moment she turned her face away, her lips trembling.

I stood up, touched the coffee pot on the stove to see if it was still warm, took the milk pitcher from the icebox, then lifted cups from the cabinet. She took one from my hands. Her fingers cradled it, turning it, and she whispered, "Nothing has changed."

Quietly, she poured coffee for herself, then took my cup from my hand. "I used to pour Esther's coffee while she chatted. Like sisters. It was…" A sigh. "Then she'd listen for Molly's step." We sat back down, but she jumped up to put the milk pitcher back into the icebox.

I waited until she sat back at the table. "Rumors."

A nod. "The fingers wagging. Coldness to me. At shul the whispers. People don't nod at me in the street. The families were very religious then, the first years in the neighborhood, always to temple, morning prayers, food. Esther didn't know how to handle it—she's just so…sweet and *good*. But Molly—I guess she was in her forties then—was cranky, sarcastic always, a gossipmonger. She had the rabbi knock on my door. The poor man, embarrassed, babbling, Molly's reluctant messenger. But it made my Ivan angry and he stayed away from shul."

I sipped my coffee but watched her eyes. "She wouldn't talk to you?"

Solemn, eyes locked with mine. "No. Forty years now, maybe."

I clicked my tongue. "She hasn't changed much, though the unforgiving part has become set in stone. Even with the stroke she has…a tongue on her."

Leah shook her head. She ran her fingertip around the rim of the coffee cup. "She got a tough life, Molly does—so Esther told me. The old village in Germany near the Polish border, Jews beaten, stones thrown, her home destroyed at Passover when the *goyim* accused a cousin of blood libel, killing a Christian child for blood to bake matzoh, horrible, horrible." She breathed in. "Then the long days in steerage, poor, a husband dying young and her alone with little Sol. A seamstress for years. In a sweatshop on Canal Street in New York. A grubby life till Sol grows and works in a cigar-making factory." Leah grinned. "Her biography is told over and over like a legend in that family. Struggle."

"As well it should be."

She stared into her cup. "So you can sort of see how the hardness takes over a person—gets in the blood. America saved her. Made her *safe*—allowed her dreams. So she thought I was a home-wrecker, maybe. So much to lose. I had no eye for Sol, of course. Believe me. A quiet, mind-your-own-business guy. Slap-on-the-back kind of guy. 'Come in, come in. My Esther gives you hot tea.' I had my own Ivan, a good man before he got mean. Molly badmouthed me and told the women to watch their husbands. That started my loneliness."

That last word jarred her. Standing, she walked to the doorway, peeked around the corner, then moved back to the sink. Again, she stared across the yards to her home as though somehow, in the minutes passed, it had vanished. Her eyes caught a framed piece of Esther's embroidery on the wall—a bucolic landscape of English cottage and trellised roses. Her fingertips traced the roses as she mumbled, "Esther's romantic world." A loving touch, lingering.

I raised my voice. "Well, you're still a beautiful woman, and you don't have to apologize for what God saw fit to give you. A gift."

She ignored that. "I confess something to you, though. I let the attention of the men go to my head. You know, Ivan and Morrie got the butcher shop together, but the real life of the shop was the friends who met there to socialize. Morrie didn't care for selling, really. He wanted the friends around him. That's all. Lord, you could walk into the back room there and you got six or seven men lounging around, a glass of beer or wine and a stack of cheese sandwiches—you know, like a second breakfast, *Zweite Früstück* they calls it—cigar smoke like a cloud you can't get through. Storytelling, laughing, bragging, arguing politics all day long. A club, you know. And when I went there for something, their…eyes, you know."

"I don't know."

She sat back down, facing me, her hand pushing her coffee cup away. "See, Edna, I married Ivan. I *loved* Ivan, sloppy fool that he was. That maybe *I* was. No one understood *us*—the quiet laughter, the—" She stopped. "The early days was good—always laughing. We joked about the looks given to me. Ivan was dumpy, always with mismatched buttons on the vest, his hair shaggy. I think it made him *proud* to have a pretty wife, but a *good* wife. One who kept a kosher kitchen back then. The proper Shabbas. Always. A good mother to his children. But sometimes I felt like a doll he showed off. That kind of…loving wears off."

"He changed?"

"He got suspicious, and for no reason. The silence in the house like a blanket thrown over your head. Stupidly, I let that fool Morrie touch me. A moment, and then it stopped, praise God. But Morrie brags about it to the boys in the back room—and to Ivan. By then, they fight all the time in the shop—hate each other."

I drank the rest of my coffee, and Leah, noticing, moved to the stove. As I started to stand, she held up her hand. "Let me." She opened the icebox and took out the milk pitcher, placed it on the table. But she didn't sit back down—as though she desired other tasks to perform. The rhythm of a mother in her kitchen, comfortable, sure, efficient.

I counted a beat. "Tell me about the fight you had that morning."

Her words low, hesitant. "We never fought like that. Yes, the little spats, yes. It started over Jacob and the way his papa treated him. He *hated* the *softness* of my boy. But the screaming, cursing that morning. And him being sick on top of it. He couldn't stop the yelling. Jacob, yes, but then Morrie, the rumors. All the ugliness of the—the indiscretion with Morrie. It was like someone broke…his doll. I cried and cried."

"Still, one moment shouldn't condemn you to a life of…"

She held up her hand. "Edna, I started *liking* the attentions of the men. I'm—what was I?—I was forty-four then, getting a little chubby, lines in my face, but the men still joked—whistled. Downtown even the *goyim*, the wolf whistles. How the old bearded men walking from shul yelled at me, accusing, watching, praying at me. I used to think I encouraged it—helpless to stop it, not *wanting* it to stop. One time Jacob and Ad were there in the back room, young men then, boys really, and someone made a remark. Not bad but…*wrong*. You don't mention another man's wife—or mother. Like *that*. You don't. I'd just walked in and overheard it. About me. I didn't know where to look. Everyone laughed but not Jacob. Of course, not Jacob, my son. But Ad laughed too long, trying to be one of the men. He ribbed Jacob, and Jacob struck out and hit Ad in the face. They didn't talk for a month. Ad was doing what all the men did, but Jacob wanted something better from his friend. Ad later apologized, I remember. He apologized to *me*—that was hard for a young boy to do, no? When Ad was a shy little boy, I teased him. How I could make him blush! This was before he got—religious." She threw back her head and laughed. "That was when he gave Jacob long lectures about such things. Quoting the Talmud. Jacob ran away from him."

"But Ivan knew you were loyal."

"Men have doubts. God knows what was said in that awful back room. And then Ivan's brother, Ezra, moved back from Philadelphia. The college brother, the swanky lawyer, the older brother, widowed now, childless, with gold in his pockets."

"So what?"

"I courted *him* first, Edna, when they were young men. The families chose *him* for me. Back then families told their children who to marry. And he wanted to marry me. He was a slick man, phony, too smooth. *Nu*. You know, a *gantser kener*." A know-it-all. "Ivan was down-to-earth, sweet then. I liked Ivan. Ezra didn't talk to Ivan for years after I chose Ivan. I fought my parents. Let me marry Ivan. Please. They had no choice, my family. Ezra, furious, missed the wedding. A huge slight back then in the close-knit Jewish family. Brother stopped talking to brother. Then Ezra came back, scooting around in a newfangled automobile, tossing coins at everyone, and Ivan got nervous. No reason to. I don't like Ezra. He makes my skin crawl. But he comes around then and befriends my Jacob. He sits in my parlor and waits for me to walk through."

"Lord," I commented, "the curse of beauty, magnified."

Leah squinted. "What?" She rustled in her seat. "I have to go." She half-rose, and her hand hit the coffee cup. It slid to the edge of the table. We both reached for it, and our hands collided. For a second I held her fingers—cold, clammy in the hot kitchen.

I wasn't through. Hurried, "Your Jacob looks just like you."

She laughed. "I know, though a skinnier version these days. His own curse—the playboy of Maxwell Street. A matinee boy from the magazines in his soft slough cap worn at an angle, just so—the brogans, the pressed London coat, the ear-to-ear grin. He hops off the El and the girls bump into one another."

"I confess, Leah. I had a crush on him way back when."

"Sooner or later everyone does."

"A charmer."

She rolled her tongue into the corner of a cheek. "And look where it got him, Edna. Nowhere. A poet who stopped writing poetry years ago. A drifter. Pennies here, there. For one week sweeping the floor of the barber shop in the Palmer House, then he can't get out of bed."

"Ella—or was it Emma?—recited by heart his poem from *Poetry*."

She chuckled. "I know about that. They *love* him to death." Her face got somber. "Edna, I heard all about your visit there. The twins were thrilled. You, the author of *The Girls*. I even told Ella to go to the public library to read that short story that meant so much to me, but she can't understand *why* it means so much to me. 'The Homely Heroine.' Of course, she never did. But Edna, Jacob wasn't happy with the visit. Your conversation made him a little crazy." She glanced toward the window and her hand pointed in the direction of her home. "So he comes home and the banging on the walls starts. The nervous pacing on the floor. Slammed doors. He sighs out loud. We don't *discuss* that day, Edna." Now a sliver of a smile, sad. "You've become drawn to it, he told me. The reporter. The moth to the flame."

"Well, I think you've been wronged."

"Jacob and the twins don't want to think about that day again. It's too horrible. I'm home. They want to believe that life is normal again. You're giving Jacob the idea that everybody got everything *wrong* back then. Everything they were told by the police to believe is false…"

"It *is* false."

"Edna, Edna."

Impatient, I stood up. I moved to the window. The Brenner home was quiet, the shades on the windows pulled down. I swung back to face her. "Leah, don't you want the truth to come out?"

She refused to look at me. A long silence, then she spoke in a soft, frightened voice. "No."

"This whole business smells."

She joined me at the window and grasped my wrist. "Edna, you come out of a different world. Yes, your feet are planted in the same Chicago neighborhoods—we all were—but you were built different from other folks. Your brain buzzing, your feet running up the street. Words humming in your head. What's out *there? Let me see.* That's who you are. You didn't want *this.*" Her hand swept around the tidy kitchen. On the counter a red-and-white enamel bowl of rising bread, covered with dishtowels. A jar of ginger snap cookies, never empty. Flowered curtains laundered twice a week, faithfully. A black-and-white tiled floor, scrubbed daily. A pot on the gas stove, diced potatoes in cold water. A similar kitchen up and down Monroe Street. Look in the backyards or on back porches of the apartment houses and you'd spot clotheslines of flapping laundry. A garden bed of mint and chives and parsley surrounded by Sweet William and mignonette. The same. Always the same.

A decent life, but not one I wanted.

"That's true."

"Of course, it is. Your picture in the *Chicago Tribune.* In the *Bookman,* clipped out by Ella and tacked to a wall."

"But I'm still the same little Jewish girl, almost forty, traipsing after a termagant mother who tells me how to behave."

Leah nodded, her face close to mine. "Some things will never change. Your widowed mother will never set you free, the unmarried daughter." She glanced over her shoulder. "It's a

Jewish commandment that only women understand. The cord cannot be cut. Don't even try."

"I'll see about that."

We started to laugh, a little crazily, enjoying the moment. Leah's eyes got moist and her nose ran. Idly, she removed the dishtowels covering the enamel bowl, peered in at the rising dough. She clicked her tongue. "Esther put the bowl where too much sun hits it." She ran her fingers under the cold-water faucet, then sprinkled drops onto the rising bread. Her fingers rubbed the surface. Satisfied, smiling to herself, she replaced the stack of dishtowels, but slid the bowl out of the shaft of sunlight. "There," she said to herself. "All right."

When we sat back down, she held my eye, dead on. "I don't want my children hurt, Edna."

I gasped. "I have no intention…"

"My son, Herman, called from across town. Jacob spoke to him about your visit to Ella and Emma's. He's a…fussy man, a little pompous, my Herman, he likes the gold coins in his pocket, jingling them. Lord, he should have been Uncle Ezra's son." That thought made her smile. "Which probably explains why they hate each other. Anyway, he wanted to know what was going on. What you're up to. 'I couldn't make much sense of Jacob's rambling talk,' he says to me. 'What is this reporter up to? Why doesn't she stay at the Newmanns' where she belongs?'" Leah chuckled. "Finally, the last solution we all run to. 'Do we have to have the rabbi talk to her?'"

"What?" I stormed, indignant, my shoulders hunched.

"I know, I know. I told him, 'I don't think that would work, Herman. Rabbi Kurtz ain't no match for Edna Ferber. Edna is her own woman.' He grumbled and hung up the phone, but not before he mumbled something about a call to you from him."

I rolled my eyes. "Ah, something to look forward to."

Leah's eyes clouded. "But I don't want my children hurt, Edna. They've been through enough."

"I promise you."

"I can't believe you, Edna. I like you—very much—but I don't know if I can trust you."

"You can trust me to do the right thing."

"That's what I'm afraid of." She watched me out of the corner of her eye. "The right thing ain't always the right thing."

The kitchen door swung open and my mother walked in, her arms filled with packages. She was glancing behind her at Esther and Molly as she complained about the need to haggle with a boorish peddler over some wilted cabbages. "You'd think he was offering gold leaf to…to Michelangelo, such treasures…"

She stopped short, and Esther, also loaded down with packages, collided into her back. Molly, still standing on the top step, grunted, "Am I expected to stand here with the sun beating down on me?"

Then, standing in a straight line, shoulders touching, backs against the kitchen counter, the three women stared from me to Leah, who'd jumped up so quickly she'd knocked her coffee cup to the floor. It smashed into little pieces and, confused, she bent to pick up the shards, then changed her mind.

"We're having coffee," I announced calmly.

Esther stepped forward, dropping her purchases on the table. "No matter, Leah. It's…it's an old cup." She smiled thinly. "It's nothing at all. I mean, really." She glanced nervously at Molly, frozen against the counter, with her cane suspended in the air, pointing. Bravely Esther extended her hand. Hesitantly, shyly, Leah took it, and Esther gripped the other woman's fingers. "Leah, welcome."

It was, I thought, as exquisite and touching a gesture as I'd ever seen—so quiet and…so right.

But that moment was shattered by my mother's consumptive rasp and her storming out of the room, bumping into a chair and toppling it over. Molly, bent and dependent on her cane, maneuvered her treacherous way around the broken cup and toppled chair. *Tap tap tap.* She paused in the doorway and eyed Esther.

"Esther, you need to clean up this mess. You never were the best housekeeper." With that, she turned and disappeared into the hallway. Angry whispers drifted back into the kitchen, punctuated by that infernal *tap tap tap*. Then silence.

Leah's face drained of color, sagging, drawn. She kept nodding at me and then at Esther, like a mechanical toy, though I noticed her look lingered on Esther, who was trembling. The two women stared at each other, and I marveled at the sudden and awesome transformation. Because, in that lightning-brief exchange, in that immaculate kitchen, Esther was the distraught woman, the shunned woman—and Leah, starting to move toward the door, was calm and sure, her hand gently touching Esther's quivering cheek. Her voice sweet and sure. "All right. It's all right."

Chapter Eight

Herman Brenner was inordinately proud of his new automobile. A *knaker*, he was, a big shot, happy to be one. Parked in front of the Newmann home, a deliberate act of defiance, he stood by the passenger door, his hand resting on the gleaming latch, waiting as I stepped from the porch. He spat into a handkerchief, and with the attention of a mother powdering a newborn, painstakingly rubbed off a spot on the ice-blue glossy surface.

When I approached, he stopped, half-bowed, very Prussian, greeting me. "Two days old, this masterpiece. A top-notch Roamer Auto made by Barley Motor Cars, built right here in Illinois, over to Streator. An exquisite auto, I must say." He bowed to it. It was glittery, long and spiffy, with sparking aquamarine paint, spitfire black tires, and monstrous headlights, its top down, grandly. A chariot of the gods—for one who saw himself as deserving of God's bounty.

"So pleased to meet you, Herman," I said in my friendliest voice.

He pursed his brow. "Have we met before? Jacob said you were here…." He was puzzled.

"Oh, no, I'd remember. I don't think we ever spoke. But I do recall seeing you walk by on the sidewalk."

"We didn't talk?"

"No reason to." I stepped toward the car.

That baffled him, but he opened the door and I slid onto the coffee-colored leather seat. So many gadgets on the dashboard—this was some Jules Verne futuristic vehicle, inherently dangerous. Ralph Waldo Emerson's better mousetrap.

Herman Brenner had called last night after supper. Esther handed me the telephone, her face a mixture of question and horror. He'd been speaking to Jacob, he told me. And Jacob had a lot to say about me. That lad did talk quite a bit, I concluded—Jacob as some kind of Semite town crier, indeed. Herman also understood his mother was fashioning a friendship with me. "Although," he went on, "I understand you'll be leaving shortly." I could detect relief in that last remark.

"A short visit, yes, as Jacob probably told you. My mother is an old friend of Esther and…"

He'd cut me off. "Suddenly you have taken on *our* family business."

"Meaning?"

A curt tone: "Edna, perhaps dinner tomorrow night with me and my wife. You'll like her. You'll meet the children."

I'd waited for an invitation for my mother, which was proper, but none was forthcoming. I'd nudged him. "My mother and I have obligations here." I'd repeated, "My mother…she…"

He would have none of it. "We need to discuss my mother's situation—and what you're up to."

"Up to?" I'd echoed.

"I'm not a fool, Edna."

"I never thought you were."

"I'll pick you up at six-thirty. In front of the Newmanns'." Click. The sound of a dial tone. I'd hung on the line, stupidly, until the operator came on and peevishly told me to end the call.

Which was why, at precisely six-thirty, I was gliding through the city streets, heading to the west side of town, to Lawndale, where Herman and his family lived. We drove past the railroad tracks, past the soot-blackened factories, until we came upon the smart-looking two-flat brick-and-stone homes surrounded by leafy parks. "Chicago Jerusalem," Herman told me, pointing proudly. Across Roosevelt, down Douglas. The automobile knew the way.

Instinctively, I'd dressed for a formal summer supper: a navy blue linen dress with a spray of red paper roses on the bodice, a pale rose-colored wrap over my shoulders. A tiny box hat, trimmed with lace. Annoyingly, I now realized that I'd inadvertently dressed in a way that seemed to accent the automobile—I was a Florodora girl in a back-page glossy advertisement in *Collier's.* "An automobile for the girl in your life."

Herman drove like a man expecting a bearded Russian anarchist, lit bomb at the ready, to step suddenly into his path. His gloved hands gripped the steering wheel, his face was grim, his body hunched forward, spine rigid. An automobile pulled in front of us, and he slammed on the brakes, hurling me to the dashboard. "*A brokh tsu dir!*" he screamed, A curse on you! Then, in English, "Damnation!" Again the slammed brakes as my body banged against the door. There was no apology.

This burly man was portly, pot-bellied, pompous, with a wide pancake face, iron-gray smallish eyes too far apart so that he seemed vacant, a little dumb, with large black spectacles shielding those pebble eyes, making the face almost clown-like. Yet despite that vacuous look I saw a flinty hardness in the eyes, and a stare that would not break. The round fleshy face, a simpleton's glance, was forgotten when his mouth moved—one moment a wide grin, all teeth, almost feral; the next moment a razor-thin line of disapproval. Despite the oppressive summer heat, even at that hour, he was dressed in a severe black broadcloth vested suit, with gold watch fob, a Rotary Club pin on a lapel, and a sensible black derby atop his slicked-back hair. A formidable man, this Herman Brenner, who, unlike his brother, had inherited none of his mother's delicate and wonderful beauty. No, it was as though, born with a physiognomy so distancing, he chose power and fierceness as traits to be cultivated. Frankly, he scared me, this man who oozed authority that I sensed he'd won by utter determination—paying a price for such victory.

"The purpose of this visit is what?" I began.

I knew I'd have to wait for the answer. This was a man who planned his strategies. A day calculated in half-hour blocks, regimented. Intrusive, smart-aleck young women had best cool their heels. He measured out his information in small doses.

So I waited.

We barely talked, but what feeble conversation we had dealt with my visit ("Such wonderful family, the Newmanns") or my burgeoning fame for *The Girls* ("Your picture in the photogravure some time ago was much talked of"). Finally, as though we'd sloughed through a barren desert, we drifted into uncomfortable silence.

When we arrived at his home in Lawndale, he purposely slowed down the automobile, inching its way on the long driveway, nodding toward the house. I was expected to *ooh* and *aah*, but those exclamations were difficult for me. So I sat there in stony silence, which annoyed him. He kept glancing at me, his brow wrinkly.

The house was a sprawling Tudor with sufficient windowed turrets to provide haven for damsels in distress or to warn of approaching infidels with spears and mace. Set back on a parched yellow lawn, with wilting nasturtiums and petunias in long green window boxes, the house appeared unoccupied—shades drawn, lead-glass windows shut tight despite the dreadful heat—and one of the two lamps left and right of the front door flickered madly.

He frowned at that. "What the hell!" Imperfections on the medieval canvas.

Parked under a manicured sycamore tree, we sat in the hot car for a minute, and he said in a gravelly voice, "The only argument my father and I consistently had was about moving to Lawndale. You know, the night before he died, we had a knockdown drag-out battle. My Papa was a stubborn man, difficult."

"About what?" Now I was curious.

"Come now, you've seen the old neighborhood. The old crowd is moving away, the old German Jewish folks, the Reform—the young ones, ambitious, they move here, or out to the suburbs. Lake View. Morton Park. For twenty or thirty years now, that migration. Things changed. Russian Jews streamed in to Maxwell Street with their burlap sacks and cardboard suitcases.

Up and down Halsted. They look at us and say—*goy*. A dislike
for us, the old-timers." He waved his hand at the landscape.
"Deutschland, they call this place. They're our people, of course,
but you've seen them."

"We're all Jewish."

"They're not rushing to become Americans like our families."

This was not the conversation I wanted. "You wanted your
parents to move here?"

He nodded. "Of course. A good life here. But Papa wanted
to stay on Monroe Street. He had that failed butcher shop. He
and Morrie always fighting. Morrie'd lost interest. The back room
was a den of…iniquity. A place to play poker and argue about
politics. Everything grimy and messy. I couldn't budge Papa."

"What did your mother want?"

"She said it didn't matter. She'd be happy there—whatever
Papa wanted. But the old customers started to go somewhere
else. Morrie indifferent, Papa tired of it all. Nathan's not *kashrut*
enough, they worry, the old ladies. Strictly kosher." Suddenly he
shut up. "I don't know why I'm telling you this."

"I suppose because you just came from there. Your boyhood
neighborhood. Those streets."

"Maybe. I don't *like* it there. You can't breathe there."

But the short conversation—this surprising revelation, so
out of character with his stuffy demeanor—abruptly ended. He
sucked in his cheeks, reached for a cigarette, and lit it. "Papa was
a poor businessman. Morrie, too. Talkers, they were. Oh, they
made money, sure, in the early days. Morrie lives in a big house
now, away from there. He collects rents for the old buildings he
owns on Monroe. A landlord who doesn't fix the broken pipes.
But Papa had no head for business." He preened. "I do."

"I understand you own a factory?"

He swelled up. "Brenner's Suits." He tugged at the lapel of
the suit jacket he wore. "The best." He opened the door, rushed
around to open mine, but then walked on ahead, leaving me
to follow. I lacked a requisite basket of rose petals to strew in
his path.

A man easy to dislike. All it took was a breezy ride in a hotsy-totsy convertible across town. From the peasant's hovel to the lord's castle.

"This is my wife, Naomi."

We approached a woman waiting in the doorway. She glanced at her husband and then shook my hand, immediately turning away, disappearing into a hallway. Herman acted flustered before motioning me into a parlor where two children stood at attention.

"Henry." A fifteen-year-old boy nodded, a freckled, gawky lad in knickers he'd outgrown, all stringy arms and close-cropped hair, a disarming smile, sweet. "Martha." A young girl, ten or eleven, dressed in a checkered gingham dress, an enormous bow atop her cascading ringlets, quietly turned away, shy. They both bowed, and I noticed that the boy sneaked a glance at his sister, the slightest trace of an impish smile on his face. I said hello, and we stood there, statues, the children helpless in this mandated audience. Children were difficult because they had their own language and customs, unfathomable. A kinship of sticky fingers and warm-milk breath. Of secret codes and schoolyard loyalties. Finally, Herman dismissed them, and, gleeful, they scooted up the stairwell, the boy fairly whooping at the top of the landing, as if to say he'd narrowly escaped the wicked spinster.

We sat at an oak dining table, Herman, Naomi, and the tremulous dinner guest in a room with glass cabinets of porcelain knickknacks and gaudy bric-a-brac and silver-plated bowls, served a dinner of apple chestnut salad, followed by a prairie chicken glazed with honey and mint, currant jelly, with pureed carrots and creamed onions the color of stagnant water. All passable, even the salad, but dismissible. The servant girl, a slip of a thing in a uniform, spoke in a thick Russian accent, but successfully ignored Naomi's clipped, abrupt orders.

"You have delightful children," I lied, which they expected.

Neither said thank you because both didn't believe what I was saying.

We talked of Chicago childhoods, of bitter winters with brutal wind off Lake Michigan (recalled fondly), of the recent heat wave (record-setting and unbearable), of their love of music (a Mel-O-Dee player piano occupied a wall in the parlor—if I wanted, they could play me Paul Whiteman, a favorite), until Herman, clearing his throat and watching the servant girl disappear with an empty platter, whispered to me, "Neither of my children knows *anything* about what my mother did."

A horrendous line, hurled into the quiet small talk. I stammered, "I won't say a word."

"We've *lied* to them," Herman frowned. "It's best. We are always afraid Jacob will slip up. He's not good with...lying."

I thought of an old Yiddish line. *A ligmer darf hoben a guten zikoren.* A liar needs to have a good memory.

"Someday they'll hear of it."

Herman rushed his words. "Not if I have anything to say about it."

"But people talk..."

"You talk, Edna. *You!*"

"I..." I stopped talking.

The servant girl reappeared. Silence.

Naomi had said perhaps ten words to me, none memorable. A cold woman in that hot room, a woman who never laughed. A white rose pinned to her white dress, a blue ribbon cinched at the narrow waist. Decorous, to a fault. She kept eyeing Herman, who did the evening's rehearsed narration, following his cues, supplying nods and at times a quiet "Yes" or "No," as needed.

The servant girl buzzed around us, deferential, seamlessly moving plates away, and our conversation was purposely circumspect in her earshot. I waited. Afterwards, the girl dismissed, the three of us sat in the parlor with coffee and a poppy-seed apple roll, and I waited. Herman offered me a cigarette, which I took. That seemed to surprise and annoy him. He seemed unhappy striking a match to light my Lucky Strike.

Obviously, not so lucky a strike.

"Ah, you're a modern woman, Edna," he said. "The New Woman I read about in *Everybody's.*"

"What can I say?" I ran my tongue over my upper lip. "Give a girl a reporter's pad and the dusty streets of Milwaukee, and hell and damnation come knocking on my door."

"What?" From Naomi, puzzled.

Herman waved his hand. "I've been talking to Jacob about your visits to my mother. You've been—become—prominent in our family, Edna."

"I like your mother."

"And Jacob?"

"Jacob is sweet…"

His hand flew up into my face. "Jacob is a ne'er-do-well, Edna. Let's be frank. A man who plays at his life. He's a Loop hound, nights traveling the El. He and that Ad at Dreamland, dancing with the Italian girls. He thinks every day is a…farce."

"You're very different people, you two brothers."

"Most definitely." Herman snubbed out his cigarette in an ashtray. He was tempted to reach for another, actually tapping the pack in his breast pocket, but decided against it.

Naomi spoke up. "My husband is the only success story in that family. He's held his family *together*."

I was tempted to remark on the very obvious unraveling of the Brenners but bit my tongue. Something was being told to me here, and I wanted to hear it.

"I'm glad you support your mother," I said into the silence.

That surprised him. "I've never stopped talking to her. I visited her at that…place, though the first years were hard. She stared at the walls and muttered back at me. Nonsensical syllables. Gibberish. But I would talk to her…telling her about Jacob and Ella and Emma. I didn't know what else to talk about." He squinted. "Then, one day, they told me she was talking."

Naomi faced me. "Herman came back a changed man."

Herman sighed, settling back into his seat, comfortable as a satisfied cat. Had he come to believe that he'd wrought that transformation in Leah with his chitchat? Yet I had to admire his loyalty to his mother—all those visits. That did say something positive about the man.

Herman watched me closely. "Her voice came back." A smile that was hard to read. "But there was too much silence. She often refused to see me."

Naomi made a *tsk*ing sound.

"What could I do? I still had to visit, no? She's my mother." A sigh. "No matter what."

I stared at him, perplexed. Had my initial dismissal of him as a self-important fool been premature? Usually my first impressions were on target, especially with smug and cocky men, certainly with moneybags rich men who took themselves too seriously. Yet Herman may have had a soul beneath that suit he conceived, manufactured, and sold to himself. Or not. He was a hard man to read.

"She startled me when she asked about Ella and Emma."

"Why?"

"Because I expected her to ask about Jacob, always her favorite. The boy who had to be taken care of, coddled. The darling boy, the little prince who wrote poems for her birthday and stuck them on her mirror." He smirked. "I was the doorstop that held the door open. It was, 'Tell me about Emma and Ella.' Very strange. Ella and Emma, bookcases without books in them."

An odd image, needlessly derogatory, but I left it alone.

Naomi spoke quietly to her husband. "Before I forget, Herman—while you were gone, Ella telephoned me. I meant to tell you. She said Emma insists on taking a job at Hull House on Halsted with that Jane Addams woman. Some sort of settlement work with poor Russian girls. Ella said you needed to do something about it—she wants you to stop it. She isn't happy. Emma hadn't told her she'd gone there."

Herman harrumphed. "Good for her. Ella should do the same." A sickly smile. "This doesn't sound like Emma, though. I never thought Emma'd have the courage to disobey Ella." Then a pronouncement: "Unmarried women find value in settlement work."

I drew in my cheeks and arched my neck. "We old maids are good for something."

There was no apology in his response. "I meant no...offense."

"That's not how it sounded, Herman."

He eyed me. "You don't know how to read a man like me, Edna."

"I'll leave that chore to your wife."

Naomi, who'd been following the exchange with her head swinging back and forth, made a clucking sound, very barnyard, and Herman frowned her into silence.

He withdrew a cigarette, tapped it on the arm of the chair, and lit it. A puff of smoke, followed by a clearing of his throat. He punched the air. "Jacob tells me you don't believe Mama killed our father." Flat, out there, blunt. He waited, his eyes narrowed, his head lost in wispy smoke.

"No, I don't."

"Based on what, my dear?"

"Instinct, for one." He scoffed at that, and sucked on the cigarette. "And," I added, "the fact that there was no knife found—and so little blood on her. A neck stabbing, a vein punctured, blood all over his shirt, and just a smattering on her fingertips? Really. Given her mental state when discovered, it seems to me she'd not have had the presence of mind to tidy up, hide bloodied clothing, scrub the knife…"

"Folderol!" he blurted out, and I jumped. Naomi bit a fingernail. "You are, indeed, the writer of fiction, Edna."

"I am that. But I was first a reporter."

"And you feel the need to solve a crime already solved?"

I hadn't thought of it that way, but—"As a matter of fact, yes."

"I believe Mama has told you she's content now—made her peace with it all—wants only to live a quiet life."

"In which, I gather, she cannot see her grandchildren."

"So…"

"And she lives with the knowledge that her own children believe her guilty."

"The police…"

"Did a shoddy, perfunctory investigation. No investigation, really. I'm tired of hearing what the police *told* you and the others. A cop observed a paralyzed, frightened woman, he notes blood on her hands—she probably reached out to her husband, disbelieving what she saw, a loving wife's panic—and he thought it was a simple case of husband-wife murder. After all, they'd had that nasty row in the morning."

"Still and all, Edna." He shot a look at his wife. "Please. Your voice." He pointed at the ceiling. "The children."

Frankly, had I been his fifteen-year-old son, I'd have spent the evening tying sheets together to lower myself out the upper-story window. A freight train to California, my belongings tied in a bundle on a stick.

I spoke with quiet fury. "No, listen to me. Let me be frank here. Your mother was—is—a beautiful woman. Men usually forgive such women *anything*. But those same men also happily and romantically condemn beautiful women when they kill in a fit of—passion or a heated fight or some frenzy. They know too many melodramas. They saw your mother as a woman who asked for trouble because, as neighbors happily told the police, your mother flirted, though innocently—and liked the attention she got. A lonely woman, hungry. She was found guilty not of murder but of being a loose woman—a violation of motherhood. Or womanhood. The obedient Jewish mother. Think about it. Men wink at such women but are ready to throw the first stones."

Herman was fuming, restless in his seat. "That's a lovely speech, Edna. Such talk comes of giving women the right to vote. Three years ago. Preposterous. This country sliding to perdition."

I laughed out loud. "I'll never win any arguments with you, Herman."

"I didn't think we were arguing. I've listened to you give me a long-winded essay on human misunderstanding."

"Edna, Herman, please." From Naomi, wide-eyed.

"So you believe your mother is a murderer. All those years you visited her when she was away."

"In my soul I believe she's guilty."

"And you still visit her, this woman who murdered your father. Jacob believes it, too, and he lives there."

"She's my mother."

"So like others—you both threw stones."

He shuddered. "A little extreme, no?"

"No other suspects?" I waited.

He exchanged looks with his wife. "Of course, back then—we *hoped* the police would find someone else—you know—but who? Some thought—Morrie? Jacob? Sarah? Aunt Sarah resented everything and everybody. Still does. The twins? For heaven's sake, Edna. They're afraid of their own shadows. The police even questioned me."

"Why?"

"I stopped by that morning to see Papa. I knew he was home sick. I drove there." He shook his head vigorously. "A brief visit, running in and out. People saw me talking to him on the front porch as I left. We'd raised our voices. Ridiculous." He drummed his fingers on the table. "I did *not* kill my father."

"No, you believe your mother did."

"I can't help what I believe."

He peeked at the clock on the mantel, and I suspected my visit was ending.

Naomi had become agitated when her husband mentioned his being questioned by the police. For the first time the cold, expressionless face cracked, and she hissed, "*Ezra.*"

"For God's sake, Naomi," he yelled.

"I'm sorry. We *did* talk about it then, you know."

"Ezra?" I asked. "Your father's brother. The lawyer…"

"Who'd moved back to Chicago from Philly around then."

"Naomi, tell me why you mention him."

She spoke through clenched teeth, a flat speech that sounded rehearsed. "He hated the butcher. He'd thought he was going to marry Leah, but she chose Ivan, the nebbish butcher with the bloody apron and the loud snoring, the dull man who fell asleep at the supper table. Not Ezra, the dapper lawyer with the Stutz Bearcat and the Chesterfield coat and the French cigarettes. A greedy, sneaky man, moving back after his wife died, stopping in all the time, grinning and teasing Leah."

Herman was fussing with the cuff of his shirt. "Now, Naomi, I know you like to believe…" He didn't finish.

She went on, louder now. "And he always hated you, Herman. And you hated him. He mocked all the children. Jacob, the wastrel. Ella and Emma, the wallpaper in the nursery, he called them. Now he befriends poor Jacob. Ever since Leah is back home, he's a...*presence* again. Edna," she held my eye, "Jacob and Ezra spend a lot of time together. Jacob relies on him, the shifty, treacherous...fop."

Herman added, "Jacob is so lost he can't tell a good sort from a bad one."

"And you're a good sort?" I asked.

"Yes, I am." He stood now, pointed to his watch. "It's getting late."

I remained seated a moment longer. "Why do you bother, Herman?"

"Let me tell you, Edna. All sorts of shenanigans were happening then—because of Ezra. Even because of Morrie, who wanted to end the partnership. Morrie had that cheap moment with my mother. I didn't trust anyone. I still don't trust Ezra. That house is in my name, as well as my mother's. *I'm* in control. Before Papa died, we talked about it. He was afraid if anything happened—well, Jacob and the twins would be clay in Ezra's hands. Even Sarah, flattered by Ezra into imbecility, though she once spat in his face. So we agreed that I would take over. My name on the deed. I'm a businessman. After his death, I sold the family share of the butcher shop to Morrie—for a pittance, true. To get *rid* of it—and him. I pay all the bills now while Jacob and Sarah rock on the porch and drink lemonade. Through Ezra, Jacob started going to the gambling houses on Clark Street. To drink at Magnum's, off the Loop. Can you imagine what would have happened if *he* had a share in anything?"

I turned to Naomi. "And you believe Ezra killed his brother?"

She wore a blank look. "Back then—maybe. I don't know now. No—I don't know."

"Why back then?"

She waved at her husband, helpless. "He still loved his

brother's wife. He refused to accept her decision. Read the Bible. The blueprint is there, I believe. Coveting—and all that."

Herman headed to the door, still talking. "My father knew I'd protect the family. And I will."

He opened the front door and stood too close to me. His breath on my neck: a hit of cinnamon from the apple cake. A hint of garlic, noxious, hot and dry. "Remember that, my dear. I will fight for my family. Even against you, Edna Ferber."

Chapter Nine

Ezra Brenner. The name stayed with me. In the past two days his name had popped into the conversations, first with Jacob and Leah, and then with Herman. The uncle who was the first suitor of the lovely Leah.

One afternoon, staring out the kitchen window, I'd spotted a sleek ebony Ford roadster convertible idling in front of the Brenner home, a man sitting at the wheel, arm half-slung out of the window, a cigarette ash flicked to the sidewalk. Called by my mother into the parlor, I'd not waited to see who was visiting the home. But on Tuesday morning, after my unsettling supper with Herman and Naomi, I sat on the front porch with coffee and a newspaper, instead of staying with my mother and Esther in the kitchen debating the merits of the smoked goose breast Molly had bought at Lyon's Delicatessen on Jefferson during her morning walk. So maddening their trivial preoccupation—"You figure the smoked chub is good, so why not? You'd think so, yes?"—that I escaped the hot room to the hot porch, though I sheltered myself in the shade of the overhanging roof.

Again, that sleek, expensive motorcar, a compact two-seater runabout, with a purposely noisy exhaust system and, occasionally, the driver's rude leaning on a horn that seemed a circus chime. *Wooza wooza wooza*. A boy with a new toy.

Finally, after the flourish of one more annoying horn blast, the driver stepped out and peered up at the house. The door opened and a disheveled Jacob, buttoning a cuff as he ran, yelled, "Hold on, Uncle Ezra."

I paid attention.

Uncle Ezra reminded me of one of those Broadway johnnies I spotted at stage doors in Manhattan: tall, rail thin, long angular face, bronzed, dressed in a white summer cotton suit with over-sized gold buttons, a silver-blue silk cravat, a diamond tie pin that caught the morning sunlight, and a flash of lilac handkerchief in a breast pocket. On his feet black-and-white country-club shoes, his long legs encased in expensive on-the-town spats. A dapper Dan dropped incongruously onto proletarian Monroe Street, the smooth operator who took the wrong turn in town.

Ezra shook his head at the errant Jacob, who rushed by him and jumped into the passenger seat. Uncle Ezra, unhappy, didn't move—he simply stood there, finished the cigarette he was smoking and then ground the stub out under his feet. A trace of a smile as he whistled loudly, a dissonant shrill sound that carried up to me on the porch. Within seconds, he slid into the automobile and sped quickly from the curb, the tires spitting up pebbles and dust. In the open convertible Ezra threw back his head, laughing. But Jacob, I noted, hugged the door, sink-ing into the seat. He appeared to me—although some distance away—unhappy to be there.

So this was the older brother who escaped smoke-blackened Chicago, went to Columbia University in New York, became a lawyer in Philadelphia, married, buried a wife, and came back a few months before his brother died. A man who never relin-quished his love for Leah.

I stood at the balustrade facing the Brenner household, as Esther and Ad walked out from behind me.

"Edna, what are you doing?" Esther asked.

I flicked my head to the street. "Uncle Ezra."

Ad bristled. "Did Jacob go off with him?"

I nodded. "In a jazzy roadster."

Ad grumbled, "Not good."

"Why not?"

"I don't like him. Never did. Never will." He caught his mother's eye. "He had no business coming back years ago and—and stopping in there, bothering Jacob and his mother. Especially his mother. He comes back, Ivan dies, and Ezra sits on the front porch. And now, suddenly, he's around even more these days."

"Because Leah is back home?"

He didn't answer, but his mother did. "He sort of disappeared again after they sent Leah away. But three years ago she's home and…"

"He's back," Ad finished.

"It's unseemly. It's—it's like he thinks he can start all over, like before Ivan, before the murder. Back to school days when they were all young." Esther's voice was hollow.

That surprised me. "So he's bothering Leah? How does she deal with him?"

Ad spoke up. "She ignores him, so Jacob tells me. She won't be alone in the same room with him. He stops in, she leaves—hides away. So it's—'C'mon, Jacob. You and me, let's go get a sandwich and coffee at the one-arm lunch room on Clinton.' Jacob nods. He always agrees because he doesn't know how to say no. Ezra is real…slimy."

"A snake," I said.

Ad grinned. "In the grass, Edna. In the grass."

Esther said she and Ad were going to lunch, though my mother and Molly were staying home. "Come with us," Esther pleaded. "A walk. You haven't been around much the last couple of days."

So the three of us walked down the block toward Maxwell in a comfortable silence. The heat of the day was rising, and Ad said, almost mournfully, "The paper says this'll be Chicago's hottest summer. Brutal."

Esther smiled at him. "You sound like your Papa, Adolph. That's his favorite topic—the heat. Every day he begins with the weather."

"I spend each summer in Chicago," I told them. "New York in the winter—for Broadway, my publisher, walks in Central Park.

But I need Chicago in the summer—Jackson Park, Hyde Park near the water, picnics in the woods south of the city. The Point. Lake Michigan. The Marshall Field's on State Street. The…"

"The heat from a blast furnace," Ad finished for me. "The red glow from the steel mills. The stink of slaughtered pigs." Ad wrapped his arm around his mother's shoulder. "It'll kill us, Mama."

"What will kill me is your father telling me the same story every day."

I changed the subject. "Ad, Jacob didn't look too happy getting into Ezra's automobile. He pushed himself against the door, huddled there like a reprimanded child."

He shook his head vigorously. "Yes and no, I suppose. He does like his Uncle Ezra, who dotes on him, flatters, spends time and money. Stuffs dollar bills into his pocket. Ezra is nearly seventy now, the fashionable gentleman with the fancy clothes. Jacob probably looks at his uncle and understands how *he'll* look as an old man. The same good looks. Not like his father Ivan— Herman is that—but like a romantic lead in a burlesque review."

"Really, Adolph," his mother chided. "You're exaggerating."

"No, I'm not," Ad protested. "Jacob is my best friend, but he's—he's a weak man. You can lead him anywhere. And Ezra does. A foolish man. I mean—Jacob. All Ezra talks about is Jacob's mother. 'Leah this, Leah that.' Jacob gets…uncomfortable. That's what he tells me over and over. Ezra calls and Jacob rushes out. Driving around the city—Jackson Park to the Midway, to Washington Park, to Garfield. Driving, driving, driving. Quail dinners with apple pie at the Palmer House. Tickets to the White Sox games at Comiskey Park. Every day is a holiday. It's intoxicating. He won't listen to me."

"You don't go with them?"

A pause. "I ain't invited."

"Thank the Lord," Esther said.

"But," Ad went on, sneaking a glance at me, "to answer your question, no, Jacob being miserable's got nothing to do with Uncle Ezra." He lowered his voice. "And I think you know why?"

"Why?" From Esther, doe-eyed.

"The comments I made?" I asked.

Ad's head bobbed up and down. "Jacob doesn't like it when things get confused for him. He doesn't like it when he has to…" Ad stopped short. "You rattled him, Edna." A quick glance at his mother, but he spoke to me. "You made him *doubt* the police."

I took a step ahead. "Good."

"Hey, I don't know if it's a good thing." He rushed to catch up with me.

"Of course, it's good."

At the corner at Maxwell, I noticed the front door of Nathan's Meat Market was propped open. Standing inside the doorway, facing out, was the old man I'd spotted there before, bent over, intent on adjusting an armload of wrinkled old clothing. A pair of tiny eyeglasses rested on the bridge of his nose. A black yarmulke on his head.

Ad saw me staring. "Levi Pinsky."

"And just who is he?"

"A junk man. A ragpicker. An old friend of Morrie. Maybe ninety years old now, maybe more, Orthodox you know, from a shtetl in Poland, and he'll tell you all about it. Once a *shochet*, a ritual meat-slaughterer. That's how he got to know Morrie way back when. A hanger-on from the old days, he lives in the Hebrew Home for the Aged off of Maxwell. Morrie lets him sort out the used clothing he scrounges up on the unused tables now, store his stuff, wander in and out at will, nap in back, then on Sunday he hauls it out to Maxwell. Pennies and nickels and dimes."

Ad waved to the old man who squinted, pushed back his eyeglasses. "Yes?"

"It's me, Adolph Newmann."

"I thought so," Levi said in a creaky voice. He stepped back into the room and dropped a pile of clothing onto the counter that once held butchered and trussed chickens.

Ad and Esther continued walking, but deliberately I turned into the doorway.

"Edna?" Esther called.

"I'd like to see the inside of the old butcher shop."

Esther frowned. "Why?"

Ad tugged at my elbow, but I resisted.

Levi backed up and leaned again the counter.

"I'm Edna Ferber. I'm visiting the Newmanns. I'm…"

He turned his back on me, pushing his arms into a pile of clothing, but then faced me.

A small wizened man, stooped, his nearly bald head covered with a yarmulke, *tzitzit* from his waist. Dull black pants, a tear at the back of one knee. A scraggly white beard, spotty. Splotchy, old-man skin, pale with dull red patches, bony arthritic fingers, and broken yellowed fingernails.

"So?" A word said without interest.

I surveyed the abandoned butcher shop, heavy trails of sawdust covering the floor. The rancid scent of dried blood and old wood, the whiff of decay and sweat, although the heaps of used clothing accounted for much of that. Used shoes stacked in a corner, laces hanging out like tangled eyes from old potatoes. Abandoned, this store—mouse droppings on the counters, the stink of old pulp newspapers piled in an uneven stack, yellowed now and sickly sweet with flakiness.

Old Levi watched Ad and scratched his head. "I remember you, lad. You're Adolph. The rabbinical student."

Ad grinned. "One of my many failures. Yes."

The old man narrowed his eyes. "No, one of *my* many failures." He shook his head back and forth, a look of disgust on his face. "The old days. Before Morrie lost interest. You and Ivan's boys. Herman and—Jacob." A deep sigh. "That Jacob."

"What about him?" I asked.

"Those were bad days here, you know." He arched his back, stretched out his withered limbs. "We sit in the back room"—he pointed behind him—"and I'd smoke my cigar while the fools carried on."

"The fools?"

"They were *all* fools." He leaned into Ad. "You remember, Adolph. You were a fool, but a boy. So maybe you I can forgive. You and silly Jacob and even Herman with his nose up in the air, sitting with the old fools who waited till Ivan left the room and then smirked and giggled about that beautiful woman. A mother, she was. Godless, them all."

Ad spoke up, "That was a long time ago, Levi. A lot of nonsense. Yeah, it was wrong, all that."

Levi spat out of the side of his mouth. "Respect for the womens, yes?" He wagged a bony finger. "I cursed at that Jacob— 'This is the way you let the mens talk of your mama? Shame, boy, shame on you. You, Adolph, you was being a rabbi, yes?—you alone shut up, turned away. I seen your red face."

Ad was flustered, unhappy with the horrible conversation. "I told Jacob to say something. I didn't *like* that—it was about his mama."

"Yet you smiled. You was nervous."

"What could I do?" Helpless, his hand waving in the air.

He yelled out in a shaky voice. "You curse them. What I did. That's what you do. I yelled at Morrie, the others. This is a married womans, the wife of your partner."

Ad, helpless, glanced at his mother. "Ivan seemed to find it...funny."

Levi exploded. "You simple boy. A man hears his wife talked of that way, and he likes it? A boy, you are. Listen to me. Such a rabbi you would have been, a fool."

A shrug. "That was a long time ago."

Levi narrowed his eyes. "It was yesterday, Adolph. Yesterday because the wife walks in and you can see she likes the way the mens looking. Eve in garden, temptress. And what happened? The worm in the soul. The spider in the web. A man dies. A knife. A good man." Angry, spitting out of the side of his mouth.

Ad was fidgeting, anxious to flee, stepping from one foot to the other. "Yeah, I told Jacob to ignore the talk."

A cackle, ragged and phlegmatic. "What? You the knight in shining armor? I sat with you, helping with the studies, read the holy words, talking, talking to you. How to behave." He touched his temple. "But behave is not *idea*—but action."

Esther spoke up. "Levi, what could Adolph do? A young man, involved with his Talmudic studies then, loyal to a friend."

"Jacob has a dark spot on his soul," Levi said. "He smirked with the rest."

Ad had moved to the front of the store. Sarcastically, he muttered, "A pleasure seeing you, Levi. You haven't changed. You're still the angel of no mercy."

Levi's eyes became slits. "I am the voice crying in the wilderness, and you and Jacob were little girls picking daisies in the field. Bah on you, boy."

At that moment footsteps sounded on the stairwell in a back corner and a small, squirrely man, hurrying down, stopped in his tracks. He sucked in his breath, a nasally whistle, and turned, ready to flee back upstairs.

"Morrie," Adolph yelled. "You here today?" He smiled. *"Vi geyt bay dir?"* How's by you?

"I heard noise. Levi, yelling."

Levi frowned. "No yell. I'm talking. You remember Adolph the almost rabbi, his mama, and..."

No matter the introduction here because Morrie disappeared up the stairs and out of sight.

Esther turned to me. "Ivan's partner, Edna. He keeps the upstairs apartment, which his wife won't come to. I guess he likes the old neighborhood..."

"But not the people in it," Ad added. "A couple nights a week he's upstairs heating soup by himself."

"Yet he lets the store stay empty—unrented?"

Ad shrugged. "He hasn't been happy since that horrible day."

So that was Morrie Wolfsy, the man who'd had that pathetic indiscretion with Leah, immediately regretted, who saw himself as a catalyst of the awful death. Or maybe not. Yet a man frightened out of living the life he had built for himself, stumbling, hiding out, yet still on the street. He interested me, this Morrie Wolfsy—what part did he have in that calamitous afternoon?

On the sidewalk Esther tucked her hand into Ad's elbow, protectively. "I never liked that Levi, Adolph."

He glanced back over his shoulder. "Nobody likes that man." Then he added, "He made Jacob nervous. The talk about his mother, wagging his finger at him."

We met Minna Pittman for a bowl of soup at Katz Dairy Restaurant off Halsted, Ad's intended grabbing a lunch break from her job. A grade-school teacher during the fall and winter, she worked a summer job as a seamstress. She had an hour break for lunch and was waiting when we arrived.

Ad was out of sorts, rattled by Levi's accusations. So scattered were his monosyllabic responses that Minna, a twitchy woman to begin with, became all jerky angles and jutting head. She kept asking, "You all right, Ad?" Over and over, a tinny question said too often, and never answered by Ad.

A curious couple, these two, with their epoch engagement, Minna's abiding trust that she'd be Mrs. Adolph Newmann someday. Esther had told me she'd bought her white lace gown after the engagement announcement a decade back, taking it in periodically as she lost weight. But Ad was in no hurry to commit to anything. He liked his unstructured, desultory life, the jack-of-all-trades, master of none.

They struck me as a couple who'd been married for decades, comfortably so, happily so, an old man and an old woman who knew the little things about the other: no strawberry jam on the rye toast, never bring roses or carnations, don't mention the crying jag five years ago in that restaurant on Des Plaines. That sort of picayune trivia—the stuff of a long but durable marriage. What was lacking was romance. No touching of hands, no fluttering eyes—no talk of moonlit nights. No picnicking in the park. No whispers as they watched the salmon-pink sunset over Lake Michigan. They were dependable, stalwart, loyal, dedicated. They simply *were*.

I asked Ad about Levi's comments, though I could tell the topic rankled him. "Why *did* Jacob sit by when the men said those things about his mother?"

Ad squirmed. "You know how it is, Edna. Or maybe you don't. It was easier to smile than to say something. Thinking back on it now, it seems like speaking out would have been easy to do. But we were young men sitting with older men. We wanted to be a part of things. That back room was the place to be. Our—hideout. Everybody talking at once—politics, baseball." He smirked. "Even religion, when old Levi had the floor and deemed us all sinners. These older men let us stay—that meant something then. Me and Jacob. Not Herman so much. Three or four times and he stayed away."

"Levi says you were quiet."

He cast a sidelong glance at Minna. "I was the holy of holies then. A make-believe rabbinical student kneeling before a wisdom-spouting Levi Pinsky. I was a moral prig, I admit. I didn't like the teasing. I *liked* Jacob's mama. She made me welcome at her home. Ivan didn't. At suppertime I had to leave their house. His rule—only family sitting at the table—and silence."

"He had his rules," Esther said. "The children could not talk during the meal. Imagine that."

Ad nodded at Minna. "Yeah, I thought his mama was beautiful. Everyone did. She was like…like Lillian Russell on the vaudeville stage. I was giddy when she smiled at me. One time I even said so to Jacob in earshot of his papa, Ivan the Terrible. 'Jacob, your mama looks like Lillian Gish,' I said. Or some star like that. I can't remember now. But Ivan told me I was an ass. And I was. But Jacob said nothing—it tickled him in some way to have a beautiful mother. Well, *he* was beautiful—like her. Mirror images. He liked that. When you talked about her, you were also saying something about *him*. But I was the one they all made fun of—too serious that year, too much the one who didn't fit in. The prude. I was Levi's special project, the old religious Jew mentoring me, giving me direction, choosing me. Jacob was the only one who liked me."

"Why?"

"Because I was the one who told him what he wanted to hear."

"You never discussed the nasty stuff about his mother? The two of you when you were alone? You must have."

"Yeah." He sighed. "But after a while I never mentioned it. I could tell Jacob got uncomfortable. It wasn't my business."

"But then Ivan was murdered."

Ad shivered. "Then everyone got serious—not only me. Everyone blamed everyone else."

Minna sipped her soup. "All we do lately is talk of Leah Brenner and the murder." She pouted.

I narrowed my eyes. "It seems to me that the event still colors Monroe Street."

She grunted and stirred her soup with a spoon. "I know. It's such a...sad street."

The line seemed a mournful benediction, so we rose, Ad heading off for his afternoon job of stocking shelves at the hardware store, Minna returning to alter the hem of a dress. Esther and I walked to the markets.

Esther whispered, "I felt Levi was attacking my Adolph for being *good*."

"He was."

"I never liked that man. Religion made him—horrible. He's sour."

"He's old and poor."

"Being old and poor shouldn't make you bitter."

"Sometimes you don't have a choice, Esther dear."

• • ● • •

Late afternoon, idling on the front porch with a book on Dutch immigration to Chicago, scribbling notes into a pad, I spotted Ezra's roadster speeding up the street, slamming to a stop in front of the Brenner home. Jacob jumped out but seemed reluctant to say goodbye to his uncle, standing on the sidewalk, his body leaning against the door.

I realized why: Aunt Sarah, arms folded, was perched on the top step, her body rigid, her steely eyes locked on Ezra, who'd switched off the ignition. Finally the man got out of the automobile. His intention, it struck me then, had been to visit Leah, who was nowhere in sight. But the sight of the indomitable Sarah, the hound of hell, stayed his movement. He stood sheepishly, ignored by Jacob, who didn't know what to do.

I tottered off the porch and called to Jacob. "Jacob, a minute?"

Alarmed, he was ready to flee, eyes darting in a continuous sweep from me to Ezra, even up to Sarah.

"Edna." A rasp, unhappy.

"So this is Edna Ferber." Ezra bowed, too grand a gesture, overly dramatic, mocking. "Jacob has done nothing but talk about you." Nothing friendly in his tone.

Shielding his eyes from the sun, Jacob hunched his shoulders, his head tilted away. A beaten child.

"Jacob, hello." I smiled at him.

With that, he fled into the house, bumbling up the steps, brushing past Sarah who never turned to watch him. No, she kept that unforgiving look at Uncle Ezra. Her dislike of her sister's brother-in-law was obvious. A dangerous man, her look conveyed. And probably rightly so.

"Uncle Ezra," I said to him.

"Charmed." Again the Prussian bowing from the hip.

The sun glinted off the diamond in his stickpin, making it seem a blinding sunburst.

"Jacob seems troubled."

His eyes searched the porch. Sarah had disappeared into the house and Jacob was nowhere in sight.

"We should talk, Edna Ferber." Ezra's voice dipped an octave, some of his words muffled. His voice had a natural high ring to it, fake laughter undercutting the spaced-out words. A glib man, practiced and imperfect, much as I remembered the gigolos from my post-war sojourn in Paris, those men *voulez-vou*-ing me in the night cafés.

"About Jacob?"

"About a lot of things."

He opened the passenger door and I slipped in. As we pulled away from the curb, I shifted in my seat and spotted Sarah peering out the front window, half-hidden by a curtain. And then, glancing up, I saw Jacob in a second-story window, his face pressed against the panes. I'd become, as my mother had warned, the neighborhood scourge. An indiscreet one, as well.

At Clark's Confectionary I drank a small chocolate egg cream with Ezra downing cup after cup of black coffee, which he declared vile. Each sip elicited a grimace from him, as though he were ingesting foul medicine.

"Don't drink it," I told him.

He ignored that and took another sip. "Jacob told me about your...nosiness about the death of my brother."

I smiled disingenuously. "I've come to like Leah. A melancholy woman, and—a wronged woman."

The soft features hardened. "So I hear. Do you really think your probing is prudent?"

I wiped a smear of chocolate from my lips. "When I was a reporter in Milwaukee, I covered the Schmattie murder trial there—a rich family, brewery people, scandalous, man's utter ugliness toward his fellow man. I learned that there is often a hefty price you pay for justice."

"And you're that instrument?"

A slight smile. "Possibly."

"Edna, the case was closed years ago. Fifteen years—a lifetime. Life has moved on. You are only stirring up old resentments, opening old wounds."

"Old news?" I tossed out Molly's glib summation.

His eyes got wide. "Exactly. Well said."

"Nonsense, Ezra. Nonsense. False accusations cannot remain...old."

"But Leah is home at last—and content."

"Content? Do you hear yourself?"

"Yes, I do." His voice dipped, harsh. "Would you have the street talk of this all over again? The busybodies of Monroe Street? The smirks, the pointing, the cruelty. Leave Leah to be...content."

"I don't think she's content."

"I know her better than you do." He stared into my eyes, unblinking.

"You're bothered about Jacob." My tone was blunt.

He sat back, breathed in. "Well, yes, I am. A gentle lad, breezy, carefree—at least he was. But now he's withdrawn, moody, quick to flare up. He *snaps* at me. That's your doing, Edna."

"He was convinced his mother was a murderer. Everyone told him that, the police…"

He interrupted me. "And now he isn't sure. You put doubt in him. You know what he said to me? 'Edna asked me where was the knife? Wouldn't it have been there? Wouldn't my mother be holding it in her hand?' He expects me to have an answer. I don't."

"Doubt, maybe some guilt."

He was seething now, though he tried to hide it. When he went to light a cigarette, he dropped the match. "How dare you, young lady? Tell me—guilt about what?"

"Hold on. I don't mean he's a murderer. I would never accuse him. I have no proof of that—"

"Yet?" he broke in, snidely. "Is that what you mean?"

"He's guilty of keeping his eyes closed. He allowed injustice to prevail."

"Are you aware of how his behavior has changed?"

"Yes. And the question is—why? Why so sudden this… moodiness? What does he know?"

He blew smoke across the table into my face. "He knows what the rest of us know—poor Leah, perhaps in a panic, killed my brother."

"And you believe that?"

A long pause. "Yes."

"And yet I understand your visits have increased to the house these past three years. You…squiring Jacob here and there. You knock on their door. You once loved Leah. You wanted to marry her—it was expected by the families. Before she chose your brother."

He actually grinned. "I'll never understand that misguided decision by Leah. Ivan the plodding, the overweight dullard."

"And you? The sleek expensive animal."

He laughed out loud, enjoying the description. "Good God, Edna, how you do go on. I'm not a beast. Yes, I love beautiful women. And Leah, to this day, still has about her that… exotic aura, that dark-skinned Rebecca out of a romantic novel."

I winced, recalling my own description of Leah as that memorable heroine out of a Walter Scott novel. "Anyway…"

"She's almost sixty and…you've seen her. I thought we'd marry someday, but Ivan stole her from me. I never knew how."

"Perhaps Leah was hoping for something beside a glossy finish."

He pulled in his cheeks. "Ah, a cruel and easy barb, my dear. The slings and arrows of the outrageous Jewess. And unworthy of you. Ivan had a secret weapon, which I discovered too late."

"And what was that?"

"He didn't talk about himself."

"And you did?"

He chortled, choked on the cigarette smoke. "All the time. I was trying to impress."

"It never works that way."

A light laugh. "So I ran away. I refused to go to the wedding— to the horror of my devout family. I buried myself at school, then in a marriage I paid no attention to. A wife who died too young in childbirth, though it was a convenient way for her to leave an unhappy husband. I practiced law in Philadelphia, and then drifted back here—just in time for the horrors that happened in that house. Bad timing, wouldn't you say?"

"Yes, especially for Ivan."

"I didn't mean *that*."

"You weren't close to Ivan?"

"Well, we spoke. We argued. He thought I'd come back to steal Leah away."

"Had you?"

He bit his lip and leaned in. "You want to know something? She was foolishly, annoyingly in love with my brother. He'd become a harsh man, terrible to Jacob, even worse to Leah who fought him over Jacob, but she still was loyal to him. But Ivan didn't want me around, he said. I supposed I oogled his wife too much." He tapped the table with a fingertip. "To this day, a whole part of me refuses to believe she killed him. It seems impossible.

You've met her. Impossible. But sometimes I think—why not? A nasty man with a cruel tongue. There were times I wanted to kill him." He waited a heartbeat. "But I didn't. Don't pursue me, Edna Ferber, with your pack of sniffing bloodhounds. There are times I blame her—too seductive, too *unconsciously* the siren, you know—though that added to my ardor. The *naturalness* of her attractiveness. Do you understand that? Yeah, she knew she drew me in, but she never understood how…how compelling was her power." Still the tapping on the table, rhythmic. "We were school sweethearts. Once you love Leah, you don't ever stop." A faraway look in his eyes. "Even now when she is an old lady."

"But she didn't kill Ivan."

"You keep saying that—without proof. You actually stunned poor Jacob, knocked him for a loop. Do you plan on spreading that venomous rumor far and wide?"

"Yes. Until someone tells me something."

"A dangerous pursuit, Edna Ferber."

"How so?"

He didn't answer.

He took a dollar from his wallet and placed it under a cup. "Even if Leah killed Ivan, I'd still marry her today." He winked. "This afternoon—if she'd have me."

I waited. "Is that your plan?"

"I don't have a plan." He went to put his wallet back into his vest pocket, but deliberated. He withdrew a small photograph mounted on hard cardboard, like a nineteenth-century *carte de visite*. He slid it across the table. I saw Ezra and Leah, youngsters, laughing into the camera. Perhaps they were seventeen or eighteen. Younger. He was dashing and handsome, dressed in some sports outfit—billowing pants tucked into black boots, a cotton jersey that said, quaintly, Maxwell Street Bengals, a cap on his head. Football? I had no idea. Leah stood there in a flowing wraparound sports skirt, a velvet bow in her hair, her dark hair resting on her shoulders. The ivory cast of her skin and those jet black brows. She was exotic, fire in her eyes, head tilted up, and, above all, a stunning face that held you, mesmerized. Circe and her awful powers. The whispering siren who wrecked ships that dared approach.

"A beautiful woman," I commented.

"She's still beautiful."

"You still love her?"

He sighed. "Yes, even though she now has a past."

"So do you," I said glibly. "But yours is harder to understand."

Chapter Ten

Sarah opened the front door but said nothing. She watched me closely, and for a second I thought she'd slam the door in my face. But she stepped back, frowned, and said in a low growling voice, "Leah is napping. I don't suppose you've come to visit me."

"I could."

She scoffed. "I saw that miscreant Ezra dropping you off. How could you get in that rattletrap machine with such a man?"

"You don't like Ezra?"

"He's not an easy man to like, Edna."

"True," I conceded, "but he's become a presence again in this house these past few years."

She clicked her tongue. "He's up to no good, of course. Whatever he's whispering in Jacob's ear is making him irritable and plain difficult. He's not a delight in the best of worlds with his breezy, bumbling manner. A fool staggering home from a speakeasy—such a nice Jewish boy. Add morbidity to that mix and these rooms are an undertaker's front room." She laughed at her own humor, though I didn't.

She motioned me into the room.

"I wanted to see Leah."

She drew in her cheeks. "My, my, my." She made a face.

What was there about her that intrigued me? Was it the calculated, blasé attitude she created? Her whole demeanor suggested indifference, a quick shrug of her shoulders and a cavalier rolling of her eyes. I could respect that in a woman—a curious defense against a world that routinely ignored her, this unmarried woman dependent on others for shelter and companionship. She did not strike me as a chronic whiner nor a gummidging soul. In a world she couldn't forgive, she'd found a way to survive.

"She's napping," she repeated.

"Then I'll…"

"Follow me."

She led me into a back sunroom filled with potted ivies lining a window ledge, yellow bamboo blinds shielding the room from the afternoon sun. A door led to a screened sleeping porch built to catch the wind from the prairies and breezes from the lake. Wicker chairs with sloppy red cushions and glass-topped wicker tables, magazines everywhere. *Good Housekeeping. Collier's. The Saturday Evening Post. Everybody's.* Piled high, well-read, the corners dog-eared. A novel on a table, its pages spread open.

"This is my room, really," she commented. "I hide out here. I even sleep on this porch these last scorching nights. Jacob avoids it because I'm usually found here. He's afraid of me—my acid tongue. And Leah is afraid of sunshine. She got used to shadows and clouds."

"That's sad, no?" I sat down in an old chair, sank deep into the cushions.

"Not really. At least she knows where she can be…I was going to say 'be happy' but that's not a word I use with Leah."

"Are you happy she's back?"

She poured me iced tea from a pitcher.

She debated her response. "I don't care one way or the other. My life goes on, boring and uneventful. It's just that someone else is in my line of view these days. And we do talk, although I never can remember what we've talked about the minute she leaves the room."

"But you lived here so long without her. You and the twins and Jacob…"

"What can I say? Ella and Emma nodded at me, like they were surprised I was still alive. Jacob, as I say, hides."

"But why?"

"I'm not the mother he missed." She sipped tea. "Edna, you have to realize—I don't *care.*"

I locked eyes with hers. "I don't know if I believe you."

A phony laugh. "Well, that's your problem. When Ivan was alive, I was the drone who swept the hallways. The charity case in the closet. The dressmaker's dummy, stuck with pins. Leah was his life. He barely paid attention to the twins, and only liked Emma because she was quiet, thought Ella was pushy, didn't trust Herman, and found Jacob intolerable and weak. The happy-go-lucky swell who staggered home drunk on Shabbas. No kaddish for Papa. So much for the next generation of Americans."

She laughed at her own words, searching for something cynical to hurl at me, but finally, shaking her head, sat back, summing up. "I am the calendar on the kitchen wall, always one month behind."

I compared Sarah with her sister, the differences startling. Yes, both similar, attractive women, though Leah had inherited looks that necessitated words like *stunning* and *ravishing.* Radiant. Dreadful words: the carnival language of besotted or smitten stockyard boys or fawning drummers. Both were dark complected, with deep-set eyes, oval faces with Roman noses over cupid's-bow mouths, a Mary Pickford-cum-Theda Bara marriage. Yet there the comparison stopped. Sarah had none of Leah's sensuality, so elusive it was hard to define—that wave of an arm, that lifting of a finger, that tilt of a head that suggested rarity that made Antony stumble blindly off Cleopatra's drifting barge. No, Sarah was brittle, angular, refusing soft edges, a woman hell-bent on scaring you away. With her hair skewed into a utilitarian knob secured with a long tortoise-shell hairpin, she struck me as the dreaded schoolmarm. The stepmother with the broom, the maiden with the midnight cackle.

"You're so different from Leah."

"Thank God. Men always trailed her like alley cats in heat. Me, they handed their school tablets so I could write their essays for them."

I laughed. "I don't believe you're so…blasé."

"Believe what you want." She drew in her cheeks. "Who is Sarah, who is she, that all the men deplore her?" Then, abruptly, she sobered. "You *are* determined to find the real murderer, assuming Leah didn't kill Ivan."

"Sarah—what?"

She watched me carefully. "Edna, you're hardly questioning and probing in a vacuum, my dear. We're not simpletons. You, a novelist, a journalist, your picture in the paper, here asking questions, displaying more chutzpah than a good Jewish girl is allowed to, trailing Jacob like he's the twenty-year-old handsome lad you followed a hundred years ago."

I started to protest, but didn't. Here I'd thought my schoolgirl crush a secret back then. "What have you heard?"

"Sitting on my porch, I heard your own mother sitting on the Newmann porch and loudly labeling you the town snoop. 'We always had a problem with her, back to Appleton days. How the townsfolk *talked*. She never changes.'" Sarah burst out laughing, but, again, a quick locking of eyes with mine. "You're a dangerous young woman."

I breathed in. "What?"

Rapid-fire words now. "Somebody already died, Edna. Long ago. In this house. And life went on. Now it's like it happened *yesterday*. That makes everything scary all over again. Don't you see?" She leaned forward in her chair, grasping her knees with her interlaced fingers. "You *have* to see the trouble you're stirring up."

"I don't think your sister killed Ivan."

She rolled her eyes, her voice assuming the world-weary laziness. "I know, I know. We all know your thinking."

"Do you think Leah did it?"

She counted a beat. "Do you think *I* did it?"

"I don't know."

"I could have, you know. Ivan was a hard man, truly, but kind to me. We never said a cross word to each other. But I was in his way, the starved pullet sister-in-law, not aging as beautifully as his centerpiece wife, who reminded him that I would always be here, stuck like a piece of linoleum to the kitchen floor."

I held her eye. "A good reason to kill him, no?"

"If you say so." Sarah now was tired of the conversation, glancing over my shoulder, stifling a yawn. She'd had her fun with me, an afternoon's light entertainment over a glass of tepid iced tea. Now, spent, she'd rather I'd be gone.

"You could have moved out," I offered.

Unwittingly, she betrayed a flash of anger, her dark eyes blinking. "Do you remember that brief, glorious war we orchestrated for the world's amusement—the Spanish-American War, back in 1893? America stretching its raw-boned limbs like a spoiled child—Hey there, old tired Europe, look at me. I'm grown up. Anyway, there was a boy who loved me, drifting after me down the streets, handing me wilted roses. My father spotted him, and that was the end of *that*." A melancholic smile, genuine. "His name was Tim Mahoney. Timmy Mahoney. Freckled and red-haired and speaking with an accent that sounded alarmingly vaudevillian. But not a boy you'd invite to Friday night Seder, if you know what I mean. Thank God he got killed in the Philippines. It saved everyone a lot of trouble. Especially me."

"I'm so sorry."

She stood. "Well, I need to start supper. I need to choose the appropriate knife to chop the string beans…"

"Just a moment," I insisted. She sat back down. "Since we're talking candidly—I assume we are, right?—I'm curious. Tell me what you remember of *that* day."

"Oh, no. Please. I'm not going through that again."

"Only what you told the police."

She laughed too long. "They scarcely talked to me. A few words. I was the hysterical sister screaming out of control, the maddened woman by the fireplace woodpile. Other than—if I recall—one remark on the spot. The policeman said, 'You came downstairs to find your sister leaning over the body, right?' To which I nodded, sobbing into a handkerchief, 'Yes, sir, indeed, I did.' And that was it."

"Unforgivable."

"Edna dear, we barbaric Jews are known for our murderous rages."

I tilted my chin. "Well, my desire to slaughter a few folks is certainly there, and well known, I'm afraid, but I resist the temptation. Prison bars do not appeal to me."

She sat back into the cushions. "What happened that day…" She drummed her fingertips against her chin. "A Homeric epic. It was a quiet day, a typical day in the neighborhood. I'd had hot tea and a slice of poppy-seed roll for breakfast…"

"Don't be frivolous with me, please."

She was quiet for a long time, regarding me with narrowed eyes. Then, resolutely, "You are a grim young woman, Edna Ferber. Probably not very likable, although I sense we could become good friends, the two of us sheltered from the storm out there."

Impatient: "Tell me."

"My, my. Another woman destined for spinsterhood."

"Which, frankly, I welcome."

"We all say that."

"I don't say anything I don't mean."

She deliberated a moment. "You know, I actually *believe* that. Most of what I say I don't believe as it's escaping from my tongue."

"Then we could never be friends."

"Just as well." She interlaced her fingers and hid the lower part of her face. I noticed her nails were jagged, with a line of dried blood on one or two. Here was a woman who gnawed at her nails and I wondered why. "Let me see." Now she rubbed an eyeball.

"About fifteen years to the day, Edna. I'm not gonna fool you. No, I know exactly what happened. You have to remember such things clearly. The last day when there was peace in this household. Since then we live suspended in space here. We all held out breaths for years and years…until we disappeared. And since Leah's back home, there is even less air to breathe."

"Tell me."

Her voice got soft, yet matter-of-fact, a mechanical recitation. "In the morning Leah and I went to the market, as we always did. Ivan was home sick—upset stomach, chest pain, and a little bit of a fever. So unlike him, you know. He'd traipse to his shop through blustery winter snow and whooping cough. He didn't trust Morrie. All the men ogled Leah. All the boys, too. Herman and Jacob's school buddies wanting the mother in a room when they visited. Can you imagine? All schoolboys *run* from mothers. Anyway, Ivan lay on the sofa, grumpy and complaining. Here you have a big, growling man, a butcher notorious with a kosher cleaver, reduced to a little boy begging for soup."

"Did anyone visit him?"

That stopped her. "I heard Herman was here briefly early on. Ivan went onto the porch to say goodbye, or so the neighbors told the police. They were loud, but they always yelled at each other. I know Morrie called from the shop. I could hear him yelling on his end of the telephone. He'd had it with Ivan and didn't believe he was sick. That marriage of butchers was coming to an end."

"So Ivan knew that?"

"Ivan was not much fun to be around. In fact, the day before, after supper, he overheard Jacob and Ad on the porch, talking about the…scandal. I know Jacob was bothered by what folks said about his mama, even though he laughed about it, claimed it was funny. Part of the problem was that Ad, his best friend, was then a little too religious for everyday life. Under the sway of old Levi Pinsky, that hand of a malevolent God. Ad defended Leah, though he accused her. I suppose he didn't know what to say. It was…awkward, to say the least. He was intoxicated by her beauty, too. He always got giddy around Leah, which tickled her. All men and boys did. 'It's not *her* fault,' Ad told Jacob. 'Hey, it's not my papa's,' Jacob countered. Back and forth, really stupid. Jacob even shoved Ad. But Ivan, inside, heard the whole thing, and, flying onto the porch, slapped Jacob in the face. Ad skedaddled across the yards, but Jacob was crying, that grown man. You could hear him up and down the street, wailing. So Ivan hit him again."

"What did Leah do?"

She thought a bit. "I don't think she was at home. Otherwise, she'd have rescued Jacob, her darling boy, the one who shared her beauty. She'd have fought Ivan who never understood Jacob. He really was Herman's advocate, and the porcelain-doll twin girls, Emma more than Ella, of course—but Jacob, the poet, the drifter—no, that boy was a mystery to him. So, no, Leah couldn't have been home."

"But Leah and Ivan fought the very next morning, no?"

"And brutally, I gotta tell you. They *never* fought like that. But Ivan was sick and irritated and fed up, and Leah was feeling guilty about brushing her lips against Morrie's, but Leah can only take so much yelling at her. That—and Jacob complaining that his papa had slapped him—twice. She gave it back, and royally so."

"You heard the whole thing?"

"Most. At first it was stupendous entertainment, I admit, like an over-the-top scene from the Yiddish Theater." For a moment Sarah turned away. She wrapped her arms around her chest and shuddered. Then with a deep sigh she looked into my face. "But it went on too long, you know, a fight that got…dangerous. I don't mean physical—I mean dangerous in a way where people say things they can't take back. Ivan had always been perversely flattered by the ogling of Leah, some badge of victory for the *schlemiel*. Frankly. But Morrie had crossed the line—and Leah foolishly let him. I think Morrie did it on purpose—a slap in Ivan's face. Maybe she was lonely. I don't know. I don't care. Ivan, the older he got, was not *there*."

"But the fight had ended."

She nodded. "It ended. I'd closed my bedroom door upstairs, tired of it, but at one point when I opened my door, I heard her rattling around in the kitchen. Quiet downstairs. Ivan still on the sofa, but breathing hard. Then nothing. I closed my door." She bit her lip. "I know at one point I walked by the window that faces the backyard, and Leah was there, picking tomatoes, putting them in a basket. She had a small garden and liked to putter there. I started reading, and thought the day would drift by as usual."

"Where was Jacob?"

She clicked her tongue. "I was waiting for you to ask that. He's been going crazy since you caught him on that...that contradiction. Edna, Jacob can't remember anything—least of all sequence. Even on *that* day. So now you've made him doubt his memory—and himself. Worse, you've taken a man hopelessly devoted to his mother and planted doubt here. But it's all cockeyed. He was told his mama killed his papa. End of story. Now he wonders. Confused. It's like he wanted to keep believing she killed his papa. Cockeyed, as I say." She pointed finger at me. "Shame on you."

"That wasn't my intention."

"Of course it was. You like to shake the bushes to see what form of life emerges. When you pick up a rock, Edna, I bet you smile at that white worm slithering there."

"I'm not a cruel woman, Sarah."

A heartbeat. "No, I suppose not. Just a pesky one."

"True."

Her eyes danced. "Anyway, the twins were in their lair, but Jacob—in my memory—was not home earlier. I heard him leaving *before* the argument. So he must have missed the battle. But he came back at one point."

"You saw him?"

She paused to organize her thoughts. "I *heard* him. I think I heard his bedroom door shut. I know he said he came downstairs afterwards. He also told you he walked by his papa on the sofa, but—I don't know."

"Leah was still in the backyard?"

"I don't know." She waited. "I heard voices at one point. She was talking to a neighbor over the fence. From the street in back of us. I had stopped paying attention. So I don't know when she came back into the house. I remember she'd told me she'd be running to Maxwell for some groceries. But I heard what I thought was mumbling from the parlor. Ivan, I thought, hacking away. Then a grunt—maybe a shout. Loud. That startled me. Then nothing."

"Then you went downstairs."

"Only later. For a drink. And saw Ivan on the sofa, slumped over, and Leah bending over him, her fingers tinged with blood, this blank look on her face. I started screaming and couldn't stop. I went on and on." A smirk on her face. "I'm not good with murder, Edna. I remember staring at the twins who came flying downstairs. But as I did so, I spotted Jacob. He was already standing in the back corner by the Victrola, leaning on it. I don't know how he got into the room."

"Had he been upstairs?"

"He says he was."

"Maybe he followed Ella and Emma down."

"Maybe."

"Your words indict him, Sarah."

"You asked me what I saw."

"True."

"Don't shoot the messenger." She drummed the table with her fingers. "Everything happened so fast, really. I still can see Leah's face—stark, empty, white."

"It sounds as if you don't believe your sister killed Ivan."

"I don't really know. She could have, I suppose. I could have. The man who delivers eggs on Tuesday. I don't know…"

"I don't understand Jacob's place in all this. I think…"

"Edna." A voice broke in. I jumped, nearly knocking over my glass. Turning, I saw Leah in the doorway. Dressed in a robe tied at the waist, her hair a jumble and her eyes heavy with sleep, she leaned against the doorjamb, her arms wrapped around her chest. She was facing Sarah, and I wondered suddenly if Sarah had seen her standing there, even as she continued talking to me.

"Edna was telling me what really happened the day you didn't kill Ivan." Sarah's voice was chilling.

I gasped, furious.

Leah's face was transfixed on me. Frightened now, those luminous eyes held me, demanding.

"I don't want my children hurt, Edna," she said in a raspy voice. "I told you that."

"Leah, I would never…"

Ferocity in her words, chilling and desperate. "Nothing else matters, Edna. I don't want my Jacob hurt. Do you hear me?"

Chapter Eleven

I worried about Jacob. From the kitchen window as I chatted with Esther or Molly, I'd spot him moping on the sidewalk, or walking in and out of his home as though he'd forgotten something, or, worse, sitting on the front steps with his head dipped into his lap. Once, hearing banging, I hurried to the kitchen window in time to see him slamming a tree limb against a porch railing, over and over, until he flung the branch across the yard. Helping my mother as she made her cherry cobbler one afternoon, I heard Ezra's hearty greeting, followed by Jacob's meek hello, and then the slamming of a car door. The blare of a horn as they sped away.

I worried. Had I fostered this emotional wreck? And Leah's words as I sat with Sarah—those heartfelt, if bitter, words stayed with me. A shattered family had finally assumed some semblance of quiet, and I blazed into their lives, the cocky reporter on a mission. Was I wrong? And yet—

And yet I believed the story hadn't been told. Or, rather, the story had been given the wrong ending, trumped up, convenient. Strings tied around a bloody package. That bothered me.

At breakfast Ad listened absently as I pummeled him with questions about Jacob's state of mind. He didn't want to talk about it, fumbling with the coffee pot, flipping over the pages of the newspaper he held, even eying the doorway into the hallway. Idly, he emptied the drip pan from underneath the icebox, carelessly splashing water on the hard-swept floor.

"Jacob looks so unhappy," I summed up. "I'm bothered, Ad. Aren't you?"

He grunted and turned away.

At that moment my mother was walking in, settling into a chair opposite me. "Is it any wonder?" Her good-morning greeting. "Edna, stay out of it. For Lord's sake. Must we be the guests who arrive with pestilence and doom?"

I ignored her. "Can you talk to him, Ad?"

He shrugged. "You know, Jacob keeps things to himself. Private."

"But Jacob will listen to you."

Esther and Molly walked in, Molly rubbing her lower back. *Tap tap tap.* The cane banged into a cupboard. She'd been muttering to Esther about her lumpy feather mattress but, hearing the end of my words with Ad, she straightened up. "Do you begin every morning at full gallop, Edna?" No kindness in her words, and my mother nodded furiously.

"It's conversation," I said emphatically. "I'm just talking. Ad and I."

Ad eyed his frowning grandmother and grinned. "Jacob's not gonna listen to me."

"I don't want to hurt him."

"A little late for that," my mother grumbled. Ad poured coffee for everyone. My mother slathered a roll with butter, licked her fingers, and watched me over the top of the cup. Her look said, brutally: *Stop this! Stop this insanity now!* I refused to look at her.

"*You* should talk to him, Edna," Ad said finally. "But he's afraid of you."

"Impossible." I was smiling. Then I added, "People *like* me." A pause. "Jacob likes me." Another pause, purposeful. "Everybody likes me."

Said, my words brightened the mood in the kitchen, a ripple of laughter growing.

My mother whooped, spilling her coffee, and Esther giggled. "Your daughter is a hellion, Julia."

"I've heard other words used, I'm afraid."

"I will talk to him," I said to Ad. "He has nothing to fear from me."

Everyone at the table chortled, except for Ad, who shook his head. When I caught his gaze, he saluted me with a wave of his hand. Esther had tears in her eyes but reached over and touched my wrist affectionately. She was still giggling.

Molly wasn't happy and wanted the last word. "Sooner or later everyone you meet will be afraid of you."

• • ● • •

Of course, Jacob didn't cower in fear when I met him on the sidewalk. In fact, he seemed eager to walk to Maxwell Street with me. The handsome face was drawn, true, but he gave me a wispy smile.

"Everyone says you're afraid of me."

That startled him. A long drawn out "Nooo," though there was question in his eyes. "I admit I've been a little...morose. Is that the word I want? You *rattled* me, Edna. Let me just say *that*. I still don't know what to think. I don't like to *think* about things, really, and you..." He went on babbling, a little incoherent. What was really going on? Finally, the sputtered nonsense stopped. "I'm afraid of what you *said*."

"About your mother being innocent?"

"Yes, of course." His lips trembled. "I hate to think of what they did to her." A heartbeat. "What *we* did to her. Me!"

"Because you love your mother."

"Yes."

As we walked, he became jittery. He darted ahead of me as though in a rush, only to stop, lag behind, shuffling from one foot to the other. Peck's Bad Boy, sent home from school.

For a moment he stopped and faced me. "I have to tell you—you got me thinking, Edna, and not good thoughts." His face tightened. "I can't sleep at night. But I'm not *mad* at you. This has to do with me. Maybe I *have* to do this. You opened wounds. In me."

A troubled face, a welter of confused emotions. How handsome, I thought—still, after all the years—but bags under his eyes, ragged lines at the corners of his mouth, wrinkles in his forehead. Puffiness around the jawline. The face of a late-night rouser, some café patron. The man who never slept.

His voice got lazy and confidential. "Your words reminded me of how much I hated my father."

"What are you telling me?"

"These past few days I keep asking myself—why? Why did it happen that way? To my mother. Why? But I mean—how was I a part of it?"

"Were you?"

He winced. "That's just it. I don't *know*. Did I do something? You know, that—that thing with Papa the day before when he overheard me and Ad talking nonsense. The way he slapped me in the face. I saw his face, all bloated and red and…and you know what I saw there? Disgust. He didn't like me. My own father. I always knew it, though he never said anything outright. The way he ignored me. The way he slapped Herman on the back, praised him—'What a mind for finance, my boy! You're a chip off the old block, son'—and I was the Romeo fool writing stupid limericks for the girls who followed me home. I was the one who resembled Mama." A wry smile. "That was my biggest sin. He thought there should be no one else like her."

"He didn't understand…"

He snapped. "I hated him."

"But why *hate* the man, Jacob?"

A perplexed look on his face. "I couldn't help it. I started hating him when he came home from the shop, a bloody apron in a bag for Mama to wash. Blood everywhere. Then the way he slobbered his food. His dirty fingernails. The way he got drowsy and slumped at the table late at night, a bottle of Manischewitz tipped over. The sweet sickly smell on the tablecloth. You know how little things start to drive you crazy? The way he held a glass of water. The way he kicked his shoes under the sofa. Stupid, stupid things like that. And then that day he slapped me. Twice. Me, a grown man. Ad running home like a scared little boy, shocked. His papa never touched him—ever. I used to envy the Newmann family because Sol was the father I could only dream of. Lucky Ad. And I felt a little dirty because the slap had to do with Mama and the way men talked about her. Ad and me talking about it. It made me feel unclean."

"And the next day he died."

"And the next day he was murdered."

"But not by your mother."

A helpless look, pleading. "But that's what they *told* me—us." A sob escaped his throat. "I was in a daze, crying, crying. Edna, I said nothing to defend my mother. I accepted…"

"But now your mother is back home."

"And I still don't know."

"Jacob, you have no idea what happened?"

He stopped walking, planting his body in front of me. His cheeks were streaked with tears. "You know why I can't tell you *exactly* where I was—what I did? Every story I tell is different?"

He waited as I shook my head.

"Because I blacked out. A whole chunk of time is dead to me. How did I get downstairs? They tell me I was upstairs, as I told everyone. Or just coming home. I don't know."

"What are you saying, Jacob?"

"I'm saying that maybe I killed Papa."

I drew in my breath. "Jacob…"

He held up his hand. "I don't know." He started up the sidewalk, hurrying, aimless, brushing the shoulder of another stroller. Over his shoulder he said, "I can't answer any of your questions." He stopped, ten or so feet ahead of me, waiting.

But at that moment, staring at him, mesmerized by his rocking stance, his arms wrapped around his chest, I felt that he *knew* something. I didn't know why I felt that, only that he was hiding something—possibly something he'd not understood himself, something buried in that roiling, frenzied brain. A secret he would not—maybe could not—face.

It was an awful moment, a close one, but I believed that Jacob's despair stemmed from some kernel of knowledge of who the murderer was. Something had clicked inside him… something bit into his soul…

Part of him believed he'd been the killer. Another part said...
no...it was—

But he didn't have the answer yet.

As I came alongside him, he strutted ahead. "Wait, Jacob,"
I called out. "You can't tell me this stuff and then run away."

He scrunched up his face. "I told Sarah about it back then,
fifteen years ago, about my...blackout...and she told me to
keep still—that no one would believe me. I should just accept
the way things happened."

That bothered me. "Tell me about Sarah."

"What's to say—a woman you can't get at. Like...she put up
this shell years ago, and speaks *at* you and never says anything."

I broke in. "I don't know that I believe that blasé front she's
created."

He shrugged. "Who cares? When Mama came home, which
none of us expected, she put on this act. All lovey dovey. *My
sister, my sister! Welcome home!* It didn't even *sound* like her, to
tell you the truth. But I'd catch her at odd moments—her lips
drawn into a thin line, her eyes just slits. You could tell she was
angry." He spat out the words. "She plays the radio so loud—like
she wants to make the walls crumble."

"She was used to a household without your mother. You and
Ella and Emma."

He gave out a false laugh. "She barely spoke to us those years.
Herman was paying the bills, grudgingly. When she *had* to, she
talked to us."

"But why? Help me to understand."

"An unhappy woman. She lived her life in the shadow of my
mother. 'Oh, you're Leah's sister? Really?' That's gotta wear after
a while. You get sick of being the *other* one in any family. The
drab sister, though I gotta say a smart one. Trust me, I know."

"Do you ever fight with her?"

"No, we dodge around each other."

"What about the...lover who died in the Spanish War?"

Again, the phony laughter, exaggerated now. "Yes, we heard
all about him. She claimed he took her for a ride in a Victoria

with two chestnut horses, and the two drank chocolate at a carnival—unchaperoned, no less. Grandfather lost his mind. She made it up. She made it *all* up. He was more a story than a flesh-and-blood man. I never met him. *Nobody* did. The story surfaced years after the war was over. One day she mentions how my grandfather put the kibosh on her romance. I remember Mama saying, 'What are you talking about, Sarah?' Then the story comes out. We stared at her like she was crazy. She *was* crazy. *Abie's Irish Rose. Sarah's Irish Moze.*" He laughed at his own joke. "It was a convenient tool for my aunt to take the light off my beautiful mother."

"You're hard on the woman."

"She hasn't made life in that house easy these years."

I waited a second. "You could have moved out."

"And go where?"

"A life, an apartment, a wife, children. A bungalow on the North Side."

Now he was serious. "I *wanted* all that. A Lake Shore home, eventually. But I didn't know how to make it happen." He scratched his head. "There was always another pretty girl who stared at me when I went to Dreamland or to a basement club. I got"—he closed his eyes a moment—"lost." Then his eyes got wide, brilliant. "I left that life to Herman. Money, a cold fish of a wife, a boy and girl we never see. Ever. We are diseased, we folks on Monroe Street. Herman, I think, believes too much socializing with me, or Sarah, or even the evil twins, will sully the chosen children. We're kept at a distance."

"Unfair."

"Well, you've met Herman." A grin. "By the way, he's on the warpath. Against *you*. Rumor is afoot in the Jewish oral tradition we cultivate here in the quarter. You, Edna Ferber, sort of a female dybbuk with a pad and haystack hair. He sits in temple and prays: *May the Lord protect me from Edna. Her evil eye.*" He laughed out loud. "They sell incense on Maxwell to remove jinxes, you know."

"Yeah, and Dragon's Blood herbs down in the Black Belt."

"Ah, superstitions. Not Herman's cup of tea."

I frowned at that. "I'll deal with Herman."

"A greedy man who treats Ella and Emma like invisible waifs who disappear when you blink your eyes. He watches Ella browbeat Emma, and says nothing. And me, the vagabond non-poet who hasn't written a line in years, the son who still worships his mother."

"What do Ella and Emma think of Herman?"

"They're scared of him, mainly."

"They moved out when your mother returned."

"Herman thought it best. Better for everyone. It would make the household less tense. Emma believes Mama murdered my father because they told her that. She's afraid to change her mind. Ella—well, she's hard to read. Yes no, yes no. Each sees the other as another limb on the same body. So many years now that they can't separate. Herman feeds them money. He feeds everybody money, enough to reinforce his hold. It's a curious form of slavery, wouldn't you say? Buying people. Money takes away the desire for freedom."

"Did it work with you?"

That gave him pause, though he smiled. "Of course. He paid for this summer suit I'm sporting." A boyish smile. "Actually, he manufactured it. His label on the collar. He put a tag on me in case I get lost along the way."

"You don't have to bear it, Jacob."

"Oh, but I do. It's my own medieval hair shirt, Edna. Jacob Brenner howling in the wilderness. I spit three times to protect myself in this unclean place."

I pointed to the entrance of Katz's. "Coffee?"

He checked his watch. As he did so, he grumbled, tapped it emphatically. "Another gift from Herman. Order, precision, time, cleanliness, discipline, morality. Lord, my parents gave birth to a Semite Ben Franklin."

"I believe in hard work, too."

"I don't." He bristled. "But I need to get back. Uncle Ezra is picking me up."

"Ezra. The uncle who lingers on the edge of all your lives."

His face tightened. "What does that mean?" He headed home, and I scurried to walk alongside him. He slowed his pace.

"I gather he's around more these past few years now that your mother is back."

He eyed me suspiciously. "That's being mean, Edna. He *is* my uncle. A blood relative, a…"

"How much was he around those years when your mother was away? Tell me that."

He spat out his response. "Mean, Edna. You're mean."

"I'm only asking."

"Ezra was always around." But I could tell he didn't believe his own words.

"Did he get along with your father?"

He walked for a while, dragging steps. "No, of course not. You've seen him—dapper Dan. Razzle-dazzle man. He sparkles in the sunlight with all those diamonds. Papa was a butcher—down to earth, blunt, happy in his easy chair."

"But Ezra came around after he moved back from Philadelphia?"

"For a while we thought he was interested in Aunt Sarah. A marriage that would be made in hell, frankly."

I touched his sleeve and he stopped moving. I could feel a tense muscle in his forearm. "Uncle Ezra still loved your mother, Jacob."

"Good God, Edna." He stomped his foot on the sidewalk.

"He did. But let me ask you one thing, Jacob. Was he aware of the fight you had with your father? When your father slapped you. Or the fight your mother and father had that morning?"

"Why do you ask?" He started walking faster.

"Humor me."

He stood still then, hands interlaced behind his back, swaying back and forth. A puzzled look on his brow. "There was no reason for him to know all about the fights—mine or Mama's. Yes, he stopped in that morning. But real early. *Before* the fight. I remember seeing his car in front, parked there. I remember thinking—so early he comes to visit? I remember hearing laughter. My mother was in the back garden. Before anybody was awake. God, she'd be out there weeding before the hot sun forced her inside. Laughter. Uncle Ezra's roar. But then, later, as I left, I noticed the car was gone."

"Where was your mother?"

"I could hear her in the kitchen. Singing."

"Did she say anything?"

"I didn't talk to her. I left." He paused. "There was a package on the hall table. Uncle Ezra sometimes dropped off books for me." He was nodding his head, happy. "That had to be it—he dropped off books, said hello to Mama, and left." He reflected, "I know Herman stopped in because I heard him talking to Papa on the porch. Loud—they always boomed at each other, like they were talking at each other from twenty feet away. Ezra was long gone by then."

"So he wasn't around during or after your parents had that fight?" I drew in my cheeks. "Where was he?"

He didn't answer at first. Then, "I don't like what you're saying, Edna."

"I'm not saying anything."

He sneered. "Oh, yes, you are."

As we neared his home, a few houses away, I spotted Uncle Ezra's roadster at the curb, with Ezra in the driver's seat. Seeing us, he gunned the automobile, spinning away from the curb, cruising alongside us and braking so abruptly I smelled burnt rubber. Jacob started, jumped back.

"Uncle Ezra, I was almost home."

But Ezra was focused on me, none too kindly. Staring back, I tried to look winsome, Lillian Gish venturing out onto an ice floe with girlish trepidation. My palms on my cheeks, the helpless ingénue. Menaced virtue, the maiden scanning the horizon for a hero.

"I've been waiting," he snarled.

Jacob faltered, turning from me to him, his face sagging. "We were taking a walk, Edna and me."

"I'm not blind, Jacob. I can see the two of you *walking*." He stressed the word, stretching it out, fierce. He wasn't happy.

His shoulders sinking, Jacob leaned on the fender of the automobile, as though stabilizing himself. The automobile rumbled, idling in place.

"Ezra," I said softly, and waited. "Ezra, we were talking about you."

He ignored me. "Get in, Jacob," he said in a harsh, guttural voice laced with fury. "Now, dammit."

When Jacob didn't move, paralyzed there, his hip against the fender, one hand holding the back of his neck, Ezra leaped out of his seat, slammed the door behind him and glowered. I marveled at the transformation: the sleek, polished man who sat opposite me as I sipped a chocolate egg cream, so purposely charming, the *schmoozer*, was gone now. Instead the distinguished face was flushed and dark, the old man seeming much older now, threatening. The lines around his mouth and under his eyes deepened, got blood red, but what most alarmed me was the look in his eyes: gleaming, frozen agates. I caught my breath.

"What did you tell her?" he yelled at Jacob as he pointed at me.

Jacob stammered, "Nothing. We were just talking…"

His voice broke. He wagged a finger at Jacob. "She wants to pin the murder on *you!*"

"I do not." I threw back my head, indignant.

"She's got you all confused. This was not an innocent walk." Fire in his eyes now, a catch in his voice. "She is not an innocent girl."

Jacob rocked back and forth, his body slipping from the automobile. Ready to sink to the pavement, to curl up, he sputtered like a frightened child.

I touched Jacob on the shoulder. His look scared me—starved, pleading.

"Get your hands off him," Ezra seethed.

Jacob swung around and actually smiled at me, a madman's smile, empty and dangerous.

"What are you afraid of, Ezra?" I was blunt.

"Leave him alone."

I turned to Jacob. "Your uncle is scared. He believes you might be the murderer."

Said, the words punched the air like an exploded firecracker.

Jacob found his voice. "Uncle Ezra is afraid that you think *he* is the killer."

Ezra stalked around the automobile and grabbed at Jacob's sleeve. Jacob fought him, pulling away, but Ezra pushed him against the automobile. "Just shut the hell up, Jacob."

Jacob struggled to break free, but Ezra, though an old man, kept a tight grip on Jacob's shoulder. Jacob shook like a caged animal as Ezra kept barking. "Shut up, just shut up. You always say too much."

"Or not enough."

Ezra glared at me. "You've ruined everything, Edna Ferber. Everything."

At that moment, in a blind frenzy, he smashed his fist into Jacob's shoulder, so sudden an assault that Jacob, groaning, toppled away, bounced off the fender of the automobile. Freed, he let out a squeaky wail, a mouse trapped, and he broke into a run. He moved sloppily, as if he hadn't run in years, this middle-aged man who ran by twisting his ankles and bending his knees, a parody of flight. He headed not to his home behind him but toward Maxwell Street. Wailing, sobbing, distraught. Heads turned, people stepped out of the way.

Ezra stared at me, icy. "Do you see what you've done?"

"You hit him, Ezra, not me."

Chapter Twelve

The heat wave stayed with us. Waking up in the morning, the streets still dark, the windows wide open with night creatures brushing against the screens, I could feel the day's heat. The temperature never seemed to drop with nightfall. Everyone moved with beads of sweat running down their skin, clothing sodden and sticky, irritation swelling in their bellies. Another blistering, appalling day.

Last night Sol grumbled, "The hottest Chicago summer on record. And I've been here sixty years. Too hot to live."

Lying in my bed, I rolled over: too hot to live. Like being in the open flames of the steel mills, the red glow that washed the sky.

Esther was in the kitchen, setting the table for breakfast. As I walked in, she was humming softly to herself, preoccupied, and I startled her. She tittered, "Good Lord, Edna dear, you walk as softly as a kitten."

I gave her a quick hug, "Yet I growl like an old lion."

She chuckled. "Edna, some folks are born to rile the world. You may be one of them." She winked at me. "But that might not be a blessing."

"You're being kind, Esther."

"I *do* love your visit, dear. Remember that." She kissed me on the cheek, then stepped back, eyes twinkling. "It's gonna be another hot day, Edna. Again. Sol will talk of nothing but the weather. He'll quote the newspaper. Only on Shabbas does he stop about the weather. For a few minutes, at least." Laughing, she handed me a cup of coffee. "Fresh and hot. You like it black."

The *tap tap tap* of a cane as Molly, grumpy and sleepy, walked into the room. "I'm gonna die of the heat."

"Some coffee?" Esther handed her a cup. "Fresh rolls from the oven."

"Least downstairs there's a little breeze from the backyard. Though not much." Molly frowned at me. "You're in my old room, Edna. Upstairs. Hottest room in the house, sorry to tell you. The only good thing I got from the stroke I had last year was moving downstairs to the back." She grinned at Esther. "Of course, I had to take over Esther's sewing room." She glanced back at me. "Your room is hell, Edna." Molly was happy with that shared news—the proper place for the errant guest.

"I don't mind. We can't have you falling down the stairs."

"Don't get old, Edna," she told me. "A curse, it is."

Behind her, Esther rolled her eyes.

"It's something I'm looking forward to," I said. "Then I can speak my mind."

Molly smiled but never blinked. "I think you got a head start on that, dear."

Molly sat down while Esther waited on her. She kept the cane at her side, gripped in her right hand, every so often tapping it on the linoleum. Then she'd rub her lower back and groan. I caught Esther's eye, her swift glance telling me Molly would have one of her crotchety days. She'd find fault with her daughter-in-law, the quivering *hausfrau* that Esther was, though Esther had learned something I refused in myself: patience with whiners and malcontents. Molly, at eighty-eight—she insisted she was eighty-six, as though that shifted the axis of the earth dramatically—thought it her privilege to kvetch, to make everyone around her stand at attention. My mother attended the same school.

She turned to me, her chin trembling. "You're up early, Edna. I heard you in the kitchen late last night. Rattling around."

"I couldn't sleep. A glass of water. I was trying to be quiet, Molly. I swear. How'd you know it was me?"

"I heard you clear your throat. Twice, in fact. An old lady is a light sleeper. After all these years, I know the souls of my own home."

Grinning, I teased her. "Molly, you're our Sherlock Holmes."

Cranky: "No, just an old lady who likes a quiet house at night and would prefer for folks not to wander around in the dark."

Lord, I'd tiptoed downstairs, aware of Molly's bedroom behind the kitchen, her door open to catch a breeze, moonlit shadows in the hallway. I'd lingered by the front kitchen window, idly watching the house next door shrouded in blackness except for a light switched on at the back of the house, probably Leah's bedroom. Two in the morning, someone sitting up, a lamp casting a glow out into the backyard. Leah, unable to sleep? Leah, hungry for light? A woman afraid of darkness.

Molly was watching me. "Edna, you enjoying your visit?" Slyness in her tone, an unfriendly sidelong glance at me.

It was an untoward question, and Esther gasped. Hurriedly, Esther began chatting about the warm bread on top of the stove, the black pumpernickel, the failure of the yeast in the dead air. The cold mutton and apple sauce she'd be serving that night. The cherry cobbler, lumpy, dry. Babble, all of it, a little crazy, though I appreciated her attempt to salvage civility.

Molly was oblivious, prattling on. "You prefer the occupants next door." A grimace that showed ivory-blue false teeth, stained.

Esther chatted on. "Well, that Jacob is a handsome…"

Molly interrupted her. "It's bad enough our Adolph insists on keeping that… friendship with that lad. Such a bad influence on Adolph. The mistake we made years back of moving into this house. He could have—I suppose he will"—she deliberated—"flower." She sipped coffee and peered at me over the rim of her cup. "Had Jacob not been next door, Adolph would be a rabbi."

Esther frowned. "Adolph played at that, Molly. The way he plays at being a puller, or a handyman, or a…"

Molly drew her lips into a straight line. "He looks like my father, you know. In the old village. The spitting image, really. So wonderful. I look at him, feel a tug at my heart. His great-grandfather's nose, the jawline, the eyes, even the way he walks—that shuffle, as though he is afraid the earth beneath his feet will cave in. Like my father, he'll marry late and find happiness in old age."

Like you did, I thought horribly, though I was pleased at my own observation.

Sipping coffee, she'd become almost rhapsodic, a beatific smile on her lips, though I noticed Esther, doubtless often the recipient of this blissful song to her shiftless son, fiddled with the loaves of bread and paid no attention. In the middle of this paean to one man's uncharted future, Ad trooped in, his father and my mother close behind him.

My mother was rubbing her eyes.

"Mother, you all right?" I asked.

She put on her aggrieved face, one I'd seen since I stumbled around in pigtails in a Kalamazoo kitchen. "A sleepless night."

"I'm sorry."

"This is an upside down household," Molly said.

Sol grunted at his mother. "The heat is driving everyone crazy. People crack from the heat—go nuts. The papers said…"

His mother, cane tapping the floor, hissed, "We can't change the weather, Sol darling."

"All I'm saying is that…"

"All right, Sol." Esther affectionately drummed her fingers on his shoulder as she moved to the stove.

Molly smiled at her grandson, slumped over the table, head to the side, heavy-lidded eyes, not even trying to stifle a yawn. One leg of his gray cotton trousers was tucked into a high-laced shoe, the other hanging loose. He tugged at it with his fingertips but finally sat back, reaching for a buttered roll Esther slid across the table at him.

"Hmmm." The picture of contentment, the family pet finally fed.

Then, gulping coffee and sitting up, Ad spoke to me, a tickle in his voice. "What happened yesterday, Edna?"

"A lot of things happened yesterday, Ad. Could you be more specific?"

He made a crooked smile, one lip turned up. "With Jacob."

"We went for a walk."

"I was coming home from the hardware store, and I cut through the park on Halsted and Elm. Jacob was there, bent over on a bench, sobbing."

A catch in my throat. "Sobbing?"

"Yeah, and he wasn't happy to see me approaching. 'Go away, Ad,' he yelled. 'Can't a man sit by himself?' But he mumbled your name—or at least I think he did. You…and Uncle Ezra. What in God's name happened?"

Every face on me, waiting, unhappy.

"He had a spat with Uncle Ezra."

"Edna," Molly asked, "what did you tell Jacob?"

I shrugged. "We were talking."

Ad smiled, the rabble rouser. "She made him cry."

My mother sighed. "Sooner or later Edna makes everybody cry."

I ignored her, compelled to say, "Sooner or later everyone tells me that."

Molly grumbled. "That is an unstable family. Look at the lot of them. Jacob—I know you persist in that dead-end friendship, Adolph—is a bomb ticking away, getting worse. I see him from the porch. A *farblondzheter*, that boy. Lost." A lost soul, baffled, confused. "He ambles, he talks to himself, he stumbles, he laughs out loud at a joke only he hears in his head. He slams the front door."

"I don't care," Ad insisted. "A boyhood friend."

Molly rolled on. "The twins are squeamish little mice, though that Ella can be a bully. I've heard her. Lord! Ezra, well, I've known him for decades. He's always one step away from a shady deal. You can't trust a man who wears a diamond stickpin."

"Molly, please…" pleaded Esther.

"That family teeters on the edge of a cliff. Sister Sarah won't give you the time of day. Over the years I tried to be friendly." A deep breath. "And need I mention the unpardonable sinner,

Leah, with the knife in the poor slob Ivan's neck?" She stopped, triumphant.

Esther gasped, hid her face over a pot on the stove. Ad stared at his grandmother, dumbfounded, unhappy. Sol *tsk*ed and reached for his pipe.

My mother spoke up. "Really, Molly, your words stun the breakfast table."

Molly harrumphed with a good measure of Victorian bile and venom. "I don't care. A subject long buried when Leah… left us. Over with. Finished. Thank God. Justice in an unjust world. And now, unwanted, back at us. We talk and talk—and our eyes shift over to that horrible house." She aimed her cane at the kitchen window. "And you, Edna, the reporter on holiday, no less. Needling a weak Jacob, having coffee with that murdering woman, throwing our world into chaos. It's unforgivable."

I said nothing because I wanted this conversation to end.

Esther cleared her throat. "You know, that horrible day, that hot, hot day, we sat in this kitchen and listened to Ivan and Leah fighting."

"You could hear it here?" I asked.

Esther nodded. "It was *that* loud. Summer. The windows open. A hot summer. I knew to my soul that life would never be the same. A strange feeling in my gut. It had nothing to do with us—with me—but a chill sweeps through me. Such yelling I never heard. Nasty and cruel and bitter, with crying and… and awful silences in between. Never in my life, I tell you now. Like something ripped open a part of the street, this neighborhood, this quiet block of good Jewish people, law-abiding, God-fearing, and said, Look, look inside, all this simmering evil is here, underneath, waiting, waiting, everywhere…I swear I never thought of people the same after that." She closed her eyes. When she opened them, they were wet.

A long speech, especially for Esther, and so deadened and low that many of the words were lost or slurred, though we all listened closely.

"It was that bad?" I asked. "The fight."

Ad nodded. "Edna, it *scared* us. You can hear noise from over there, people on the porch, the radio, the gramophone." He smirked. "Leah cranking away her Caruso records. Listening to opera on KYW. But that was...ferocious. Mama is right—it went up your spine."

"Adolph wanted to go over there," Molly told us. "We were going to leave, the two of us, shopping downtown, meeting a friend of his, but we just listened. We couldn't move. I told Adolph, no, please no. Stay here. They have to deal with it."

"What was said?"

Molly frowned at Esther, who glanced at Ad. "It started about Ivan hitting Jacob the day before. Leah had just learned of it—from what she was screaming. Then the—you know—little kiss with Morrie, Leah's apology, her pleading."

"I got real afraid," Ad said. "Ivan was scary."

For the first time Sol spoke. "Such a bitter man, that Ivan. Once so good to everyone. A friend. We smoked cigars together."

"He wouldn't hit Leah?" I asked.

Ad shrugged. "I was afraid of that. We all were. After all, he did hit Jacob twice. A mean man, but he never was...violent. And I knew Jacob wasn't home—I saw him walking up Monroe earlier." He exchanged looks with his grandmother. "You should have let me stop it, Bubbe. Look what happened afterwards."

Molly wasn't happy with the conversation. "You could not have stopped *that*. In the middle of such craziness. Family business." She paused. "Then, suddenly, it stopped. Just like that. Adolph and I left and I saw Leah carrying a water pail from the front porch to her garden out back. Like a normal day. Daily chores. She didn't look up as we walked by. Silence in the house, Ivan somewhere inside. Silence."

"You didn't hear anything later on?"

"We were gone a long time, came back later, tired, Adolph and I upstairs in our rooms. I woke from my nap to hear screaming. At first I thought something happened to Esther because it sounded so close. But then I thought it was Leah's howling and thought, oh no, here they go again. But Adolph comes flying out of his room and yells to me, no, it's Sarah. Sarah is hurt. Something was wrong. You could hear her—like someone was killing her. Adolph ran over, Esther behind him. The neighbors. You know the rest." She frowned. "I've told the story too many times." She bit her lip. "Too many times—and now again."

"The day was hot like today," Sol commented.

"And now," Ad added, "Jacob sits in the park and cries."

"Because," I said quietly, "he has his mother back but he doesn't believe she killed his father."

A collective groan, my mother's falsetto cackle breaking above Molly's squealing protest and Esther's quiet whisper. Ad's look conveyed the notion that I was a pesky disturber of the peace.

Only Sol, portly and fleshy, sitting with his hands resting in his lap, wore an enigmatic smile that alarmed me more than their expected responses.

"What?" I asked him.

At that moment we heard a heavy footfall on the front steps, followed by an insistent *rap-rap-rap* on the front door. Everyone jumped, though no one headed to the door. Finally Sol shuffled to the front door, then followed an irate Herman Brenner into the kitchen. Once there, planted in the doorway, Herman repented his brash invasion, grunting and fussing, half turning toward the front door.

He stammered, "I'm sorry." He addressed Sol, then Esther. "I've come from my mother's. Ezra telephoned her about Edna, telling a horrible tale. Little of it makes sense. Jacob is slobbering and is accusing *me* of God-knows-what. That I *betrayed* our mother. I lay all this at the feet of this questionable young woman who plays with my family's…tragedy for…for sport."

Sol placed his hand on Herman's shoulder. "Sit down, my boy. We haven't seen you in such a long time." He nodded at his wife. "Esther, a cup for Herman. Some rolls with butter. Please."

Rattled, Herman dropped into a seat, his mouth open, suddenly aware of where he was, where we all were. His eyes swept the kitchen and rested on Esther.

A sheepish smile. "Lord, I haven't been in this kitchen for years and years." So simplistic an observation, so naïve that Esther, watching him, teared up. Herman struggled to stand. "I'm intruding. Unforgivable, my temper. I didn't mean…I'm sorry."

Esther placed a cup of coffee before him, smiling at him, and Sol nodded at him. "Drink some, Herman. Please."

As if by habit, he sipped the coffee, though his hand trembled. He nibbled on the crust of a roll. A smile lit up his face. "Esther, your rolls. Heavenly. As a boy we made sure we wandered in here in the morning. The aroma from the sidewalk…" He stopped.

"Is Jacob all right?" I asked.

Herman's words were bitter. "The happy-go-lucky fool we all got used to now moans and blames and starts at any noise. My mother doesn't know what to do. She walks the hallways, waiting for him to come out of his room. She's crying. He's crying. The only one who isn't crying is Sarah. I stop in and find a topsy-turvy home. Jacob says to me, 'We did a horrible thing to Mama.' What can I say to that? 'We put Mama in hell. Who is the murderer, Herman? I'm afraid it might be me.' Then he looks at me and says, 'Or you.' Can you imagine such words from his mouth?"

Sol nodded toward Herman's coffee cup. "Drink, my boy."

Herman stood up. "No more. I'm sorry. A mistake, my rushing in here. I came here in poor taste—to confront Edna." He nodded at me, not angry now but with a hint of melancholy. "My mother's house is filled with ghosts today. That's what drove me here. I'm sorry. I'll leave you all in peace." He half-bowed to Molly and Esther, even to my mother, but not to me. He was gone.

A minute of stunned silence.

Sol spoke up. "Herman, after all these years—and so crazy a visit."

My mother fumed. "Look what you've done, Edna."

I faced all their stares, but didn't care. "I don't understand why everyone is content to let a wronged woman wear a stigma. What about justice?"

Tap tap tap. Molly exploded. "And you know more than the police, dear Edna?"

"The police never investigated this the way they should have. No investigation at all. Leah was an easy target."

In a small, unexpected voice, timid, Esther began, "I never believed Leah did that horrible thing."

Startled, we all turned to her.

"What?" said Sol, befuddled.

She shrugged. "It just seemed…impossible then. Like the big pieces of a puzzle were missing somehow." She faltered. "A thought, that's all." Then, staring into my face, "It seems to me that someone knows something—if Edna is right."

"But she isn't," Molly screamed.

Ad stood and his glance took us all in. "Nonsense, all of this. Do you hear yourselves? When everyone turned away from that family, left Jacob to flounder, helpless, I was the one who stayed at his side. I got him through it all. I made him laugh again. When people pointed at him on the sidewalk, I …I sheltered him. Me—me. And now, he's slipping back into that black pit. I never thought Leah would be *allowed* back home, but what do I know? All I do know is that it's…it's like somebody took a family photograph way back when, everybody standing in their Shabbas best, but now, years later, someone is shredding the picture, piece by piece, ripping it all apart."

He paused. "And now *we're* in the picture."

Molly sputtered, "Leave us out of it. Your love for Jacob is a curse, Adolph. *A tropn libe brengt amol a yam trern.*" A drop of love may bring an ocean of weeping.

"Stop, Edna," Ad said. "Stop! Can't you see what you're doing to them?" And his outstretched arm pointed at his own family.

• ● ● ● •

I sat on the front porch, alone, crying softly. What had started as a glance from an old woman on her porch had led me to a conviction that something was wrong. I stumbled through my questions, driven not by meanness but by a heartfelt belief that there was, indeed, rightness to life. If Leah was innocent—as my gut told me, and the smattering of evidence suggested—then there was a murderer among us. One of the folks I'd met, socialized with, talked to, followed, probed, debated. Everyone saw me as hard and insensitive and maybe cruel. But a murderer lurked in the shadows of Monroe Street. When was the world going to be fair to Leah, with her lost life, her dark corners, her fears? "I don't want my children to be hurt," she'd said to me over and over. A prayer. But she also didn't want her children to have a murderer for a mother. What mother did? I believed that. A mission, a—

"Edna!"

I jumped. Sol had slid into a chair next to me.

"Sol, you startled me so."

"You're crying, Edna."

I turned my head away. "I'm all right."

Sol shuffled his seat, edging it closer to mine. He reached out and grabbed my hand, squeezing it tightly. "Dear Edna," he said with affection, "a problem for you, this whole story." He waited. "Look at me."

I faced him. Strangely, he was smiling. "Sol…"

"No, no." He put his hand in front of my face. "You're young, a modern woman. Maybe one of those girls I don't understand. It's a different world nowadays. I'm old. But you want to do the right thing, always. You want to make the world *better*. Most people don't. Yes, they *say* they do. Everybody is on the side of right. Everybody jumps back from evil. From doing the wrong thing." He waved back toward the kitchen. "Everybody believes they are good people. And they are. But you're—what?—a different girl. You *do* things, Edna."

"And everyone hates me." Self-pity, a trait I disliked in others, especially myself.

"No one hates you." He chuckled. "Maybe a little irritated with you, I tells you, yes. They don't understand what's inside you. You push and push." He laughed. "They should make you a puller up on Maxwell. Imagine the sales!" Then his voice deepened, serious. "Edna, don't worry. Follow your heart. You gotta be…Edna. Yourself. Like the Talmud says, 'A man's name is his soul.' You understand? That's you…inside. They"—again he pointed inside—"can never understand a girl like you. The passion."

"I believe in Leah."

A long pause. "So do I."

Startled. "What?"

"I'll tell you a secret. Like my Esther, I never believed she killed poor Ivan. She *loved* that man, and he was a hard man to love sometimes. Not good with his children. Mean to Jacob, so bad. I used to ache for what he did to that boy. One time I says to him, 'Leave the boy be. Jacob is a good boy.' And he says for me to mind my business. Okay, so they fought. But we all fight. I seen her that day when the police come here—frozen, dead eyes. The face of a grieving woman, not a murderer."

"Then who?"

He shrugged. "I don't know."

"That's why I…"

"I know, I know. And let me tell you something, Edna. I'm proud of you. You need to do this. You are a girl with a heart so big it makes others tremble. You know the saying, yes? *Dos hart iz a halber novi.*" I shook my head: no. He watched me carefully. "'The heart is half of a prophet.' You walk on a road that looks into the future. The others…you can't help the way they thinks. You will always be a mystery to your own mother. In the end they will still love you." He winked. "As much as they can."

"But this isn't going to have a happy ending."

"It don't matter. It will finally have a…ending. That is enough."

Chapter Thirteen

Minna Pittman telephoned me to check if we were still on for the theater on Sunday. "I hope you don't cancel," she said nervously.

Of course not, I told her, annoyed. I'd been wishing to see Sigmund Romberg's *Blossom Time* at the Auditorium on Michigan Avenue.

"But," Minna went on, as though I'd vacillated, "I am really excited about it. We are, Ad and I. But this whole thing with Jacob and…" Her voice trailed off, a squeak at the end. She waited. Then quietly, "I hate when people don't talk."

"Minna." I raised my voice, confused. "What are you saying?"

"Ad told me about Herman barging in and how Ad told you to…he told you to leave things alone. To *stop* it. Hurting his family."

"Minna, is that why you're calling? I am *not* mad at Ad. Is that why he's been sulking around?"

She didn't know what to say. Finally she blathered, "He thought he hurt your feelings."

I shook my head "Good Lord, Minna. Tell him—oh, never mind, I will tell him."

She hung up.

So that explained the silence in the hallway, Ad's sheepish avoidance, the hesitant hellos and goodbyes. Our minor kerfuffle over breakfast was forgotten, though my mother had reminded me, once again, that I was a guest in the house. Good Lord—how thin-skinned did Ad think I was? Though, considering it, I smiled to myself: ah, the unnecessary gentleman that he was.

So on Sunday as I walked with Ad and Minna up Monroe to Maxwell Street to catch a streetcar, Minna did most of the talking, Ad silent beside her, grim-faced.

"Ad," I told him, "I'm a big girl."

He made a face. "The women in my family—and the woman in *your* family—told me I wasn't...polite to you."

I laughed out loud. "Ad, didn't you ever learn to fight back?"

"I only win battles with Minna." He flicked his head toward her. "She lets me."

The remark seemed dismissive. The girlfriend with lukewarm water in her veins, the faint-hearted child who lacked the iron blood the women in his household possessed. Minna—destined to be the *alte moyd*. The spinster much pitied yet coddled. At that moment, listening to him, Minna heard that condescension, and I watched her squirm, bite her lips.

Curious, that scene, because Ad immediately sensed his error, stammering, "Minna never finds fault with me." But that cavalier line was dreadful, a deeper cut, utter disregard. Finally, groping for an apology, he simply walked ahead and muttered over his shoulder, "I should keep quiet."

"Advice most men fail to learn," I commented.

Ad showed me his crooked smile, which failed to charm.

Minna was blinking her eyes rapidly, an idiosyncratic behavior I'd noted once before in her—a girl who would never be comfortable in the matriarchal world of Molly Newmann, Monroe Street martinet.

"Jacob won't answer the door." Ad spoke suddenly, a line not directed at Minna or me.

"I told you, Ad—he's sad. Leave him alone." Minna touched his elbow, reassuringly.

Ad banged one fist into the other. "I knock on his door. Yesterday. Today. He won't answer. I'm getting worried. It's always been him and me. Blood brothers. He *knows* that. Through the bad times. I held him up when he fell apart." His eyes got wide, round. "Now, I'm afraid."

"He'll come around," Minna said softly.

Ad's eyes rested on me. "His mother told me *she's* worried. Edna, you should've seen her face—like…like a ghost."

I glanced back down the block. "I need to stop in to see Leah. She hides away, too."

"Everybody hides in that house." Ad breathed in. "It's a locked-up fortress. Sarah, the guard dog at the gate. Jacob's mad at the world. His knuckles bruised—a fist against his bedroom wall." Then, a helpless look. "But he cannot be mad at me, can he?" He shook his head back and forth. "It's crazy."

Minna touched his elbow again. "Call him later."

He scowled at her, impatient. "Why would he be mad at me? He always *comes* to me."

"C'mon, Ad. Please."

He had no interest in the play, though I did. The American version of the Viennese musical, *Das Dreimäderhaus*, Sigmund Romberg's adaptation of Franz Schubert's melodic tunes, was a jolt of old-fashioned melodrama, depicting the sad (and final) days of the celebrated composer. Lovely, I thought, a soothing balm after the open wounds on Monroe Street. "Serenade," an enticing ballad, made Minna cry. It made me miss my father.

Ad fidgeted throughout the musical, though the spirited song of "Three Little Maids" did elicit a snicker from him. Minna was overly solicitous, tugging at him, the mother hen with her awkward runt offspring, though Ad shrugged her off. At intermission when he was away in the lobby, Minna whispered to me that Jacob's new disaffection was Ad's only story.

"Ad doesn't like people being mad at him." She leaned in. "You know that Jacob had a real bad breakdown after his mama was taken away. Ad cried for days."

When Ad returned, Minna's jerky laughter confused him, and he shot a penetrating look—not a kind one—at me. Edna, the spreader of gloom and doom throughout the Western hemisphere. The wicked stepsister rubbing her foul hands together with glee over the cauldron of steaming poisons.

Ad offered to treat us to coffee and dessert at Henrici's Fancy Bakery and Café on Randolph Street, though I said no—since he'd provided the tickets, that snack would be my pleasure. Minna squealed as if I'd paid for catastrophic surgery. But we were all in a genial mood now, the afterglow of splendid theater, always so bolstering for me, covering us, making us giddy and foolish. Ad played the clown as we strolled along—he warbled "Bei Mir Bist du Schein" too loudly, and purposely off-key, but Minna frowned him into silence.

Over walnut rolls and robust cherry phosphates, I faced the two of them in a booth. Ad had whispered something in Minna's ear, and she'd blushed to her ringlet roots. Watching Ad's curiously distant yet still solicitous gestures, I understood, yet again, the calculus of their love. Ad would be the perennial bachelor under his aged grandmother's doting care, Peter Pan in a Friday night yarmulke. The boy who never wanted to leave his bar mitzvah party.

I wasn't paying attention to their bantering, engrossed as I was in my own splendid summation of the overgrown yeshiva boy before me. I was startled back into the conversation by Minna's uncharacteristically brusque, clipped tone. The surprising mention of Herman Brenner. Minna had been talking of Herman's abrupt visit to the Newmann kitchen, followed by his tepid and embarrassed apology, but her mention of Herman's name seemed particularly bitter. Amazing, I thought, how someone can say a name—in the case, *Herman*—and the word dripped with bile. What was Sol's quotation from the Talmud? *A man's name is his soul.*

I sat up, alert. "Herman?"

Minna narrowed her eyes. "I mean it."

I had no idea what that meant. Unfortunately, now as a habit, I never listened to Minna.

Ad was shaking his head. "Edna, Minna has a history with Herman."

I turned to her, this pencil-thin, frail woman, as brittle-boned as a skeletal bird, forgettable. Or not. "Tell me."

"Nothing to tell," she stated, her eyes dipped down at her plate. Now those words always infuriated me. They were any inquiring reporter's least desired response, an indication of so much left unsaid, the rich ore under the sandstone earth. *Nothing to tell.*

"Tell me." I spoke so sharply Ad spit soda pop onto his sleeve.

"My first beau." Said quietly, an epitaph etched in the soul.

"Herman?"

She giggled. "Impossible, no? That...that stiff collar, that over-starched man."

"When was this?"

"We were young, well, eighteen, nineteen. For a real short time. A foolish time, let me tell you. Our parents arranged it, of course, as they did back then. They planned for us to *love* each other, very Old Country, no? And we were determined to be real Americans, red, white, and blue to the core. We enjoyed being together, me and Herman, though always under the eye of one parent or someone. Ice skating at the Midway Plaisance, box suppers in Humboldt Park, volunteering at the Davis Square Settlement House because they had an ice cream parlor downstairs. As proper as can be, our relationship. And Herman used to laugh a lot back then, before he was told he wasn't supposed to."

"What happened?"

Minna wrinkled up her face, which made her look like a disgruntled ferret. "His father took a dislike to me."

"Can you imagine that?" said Ad, tapping her wrist.

"Ivan? But why?" So innocuous a girl, so invisible in a room.

"He never gave a reason...I always felt he wanted someone else. Like he was *thinking* already of someone else. But Leah *liked* me. We spent a lot of time in the kitchen. She once told me that maybe Ivan favored a rabbi's daughter from North Chicago, Rabbi Goldman's distant relative. Some money there. Living up on Calumet Avenue. But my parents and Leah arranged..."

The more Minna talked, the more shrill her voice got, edged with a fury I'd not thought her capable of showing. She, this diffident woman, twittering around the Newmann family for years, had mettle. And spirit, though that spirit was tinged with smoldering resentment. A spitfire woman here, and I marveled at this delicious new revelation. Ad, the un-handyman of the neighborhood, would be no match for the redoubtable Minna Pittman, once aroused and passionate.

"Ivan the Terrible," I said.

She rapped her knuckles on the table. "Herman was a coward, despite his bluster and yelling. 'I don't care what my father says'—that's what he told me. But he kowtowed to his father, though Leah fought him—quietly. Ivan always talked to me like I was a dumb farm animal. I'll never forget it."

I widened my eyes. "So Herman left *you*?"

Ad was nodding furiously. "But lucky for me."

I didn't know about that, frankly, a dull buffoon like Herman giving way to a layabout gadfly like Ad, two members of the male species who'd fallen out of the monkey tree.

"He left me," Minna thundered. Her eyes blazed. "He said he still loved me. He would always love me—the love of his life, said with the passion of a scared boy. Imagine that?" Her eyes got moist. "We *did* love each other. Then. I mean—then."

"Yeah, sure," Ad said. "Herman was always a bump on a log." He winked at Minna. "I remember when you and Herman courted."

Minna pursed her lips, unhappy with the depiction. "My parents were nervous about Ad marrying me." She grinned. "I told them that he'd once thought of being a rabbi."

Ad laughed, too. "No one believes that. Jacob could never understand that dream of mine."

"I don't see you as a Talmudic scholar, Ad," I grinned.

"I had a moment—way back then." His eyes got sad, dark. "Long, long ago. Before Ivan's murder. Jacob *fought* me. A baseball player, a hot dog vender, a ditch digger. But not a rabbi. 'Don't get crazy on me,' he said. That was my holier-than-thou year, preaching and spouting Scripture like some Jewish Cotton Mather, thunder and lightning. God, you should have heard me at Nathan's Meat Market."

"Why there?"

"Because of old Levi Pinsky," Ad told me. "You know, the ragpicker that still squats in the empty shop. A religious Jew, that one, fanatical, he wouldn't even sneak a pretzel on fast days." He chuckled. "He watched everyone, quiet mostly, except when he came in with some Biblical truth. He started talking to me about old Judaic lore, myth, superstitions, and I guess that's what got my attention—for a while. But I couldn't stay with it. He's not happy with me to this day."

"What kind of teaching?"

"Stories of how in Rome Jewish girls lined the Appian Way and sold dream charms and notions to those walking by. How demons carry on in the shade of trees—in the shadows cast by the moon. How demons are all around us, invisible, because, if seen, we'd go crazy. Demons everywhere, waiting, waiting. The night before a boy's circumcision is the most dangerous one in his life." Ad stopped, embarrassed by his enthusiasm. He dropped his eyes. "Stuff like that, designed to make a young man curious. I got…caught up. Most don't know stuff like that. So I talked to our rabbi, but he wasn't happy. He said Levi had some confused view of our religion—true stuff, but not what I should be focusing on.

"The rabbi set me studying seriously, on the path that petered out. Once I got past the late-night spookiness of medieval Judaism—hocus pocus and razzmatazz—once I stopped boring my friends with bits and pieces of history, I lost interest. Hebrew floored me, made me black out. Not the memorized routines of the bar mitzvah but the sheer power of the language, the sheer weight of its history. Suddenly my religion was so…important. Magnificent. It was all so…beautiful, that history, so awesome. I couldn't…" He shrugged his shoulders. "I couldn't do it. I walked away."

"Hmm," I said. "I suppose Levi thought he was doing the right thing. Levi the Teacher."

Ad's voice a low rumble. "Yeah, the ragpicker prophet, sorting clothes on the butcher block tables where carcasses once lay. No one cares anymore. Morrie Wolfsy, a couple nights a month he's there, alone, collecting rents, away from his wife and her French Provincial furniture and the gold-gilt bathroom fixtures, behind the locked doors of the upstairs apartment. Or he's downstairs, sitting with old Levi, the two lost in the past over cigars and knishes bought from a cart on Maxwell." He laughed. "Go in sometimes. The front door's unlocked. A big bare room now."

"Obviously Levi's still disappointed you abandoned your studies."

He thought about that. "He didn't seem to notice at the time. After Ivan's death, Morrie discouraged the men from haunting that back room, a place we loved. I loved—a place to hide away. Morrie lost interest. Even old Levi disappeared for a while. He was unhappy with the whole nightmare. 'Jews killing Jews,' he screamed one afternoon. 'Is that what we do now? Ain't it bad enough the Russians got a head start?' Then, one day, I heard he was back. But Morrie told everyone to stay away. He wanted to close up shop. So I never returned there. Jacob, of course, stayed away. How could he go back there? Ivan was gone. Morrie liked the back room—the talk, talk, talk. Then he didn't." A dark smile. "Another thing Levi taught me. When bad luck touches you, you and your family can't shake it off. It stays, grows."

"No one ever suspected Morrie of the murder?" I wondered out loud.

"Yeah, of course. The partner? The man who wooed Ivan's wife? We thought the cops would question him—but they didn't. Nothing came of it."

I grumbled, "The police already named the murderer."

He nodded. "Yeah, on the spot."

"Tell me about the back room."

He raised his eyebrows, suspicious. "A place where we could smoke cigars and talk about things."

"Talk about women."

Ad squirmed. "Sometimes." He sighed. "A refuge that wasn't shul. I felt at home there. So did Jacob."

"The women never came in?" I asked.

"Leah would step into the doorway, but Selma never did. Morrie's wife. But the men would, you know, watch Leah…"

"Barnyard antics," Minna piped in.

"She'd smile at us." Ad reminisced.

"I'll never understand Leah's…indiscretion—if that's what it was—with Morrie, Ad."

Minna spoke up. "Edna, Morrie never *liked* Leah either. He thought her foolish, a distraction. He didn't like it when she walked in. Everything in the shop went off kilter."

Ad went on. "He used to push the boys—me, others—to joke with her—to make her uncomfortable."

That news flabbergasted me. "Why then the…indiscretion?"

Ad sat back, smug and confident. "You wanna know why? Simple. Because he *could*. Because he could take something away from Ivan. Ivan was talking of breaking up the shop, going out on his own. Morrie found a way to hurt him."

"My God!" I exclaimed.

Minna concluded, "Little boys playing rough in the schoolyard. Nasty." A wide grin on her face. "The land of the cavemen."

"C'mon, Minna," Ad admonished her. "It wasn't like that."

"Well, Ad, when you bar women from your door, you risk chaos in the land. You men won't be content until you make yourselves extinct."

"That makes no sense, Minna."

Minna's expression was blissful. "Edna understands what I'm saying."

• ● ● ● •

The land of the cavemen. The infernal back room. The dark recesses of the male species.

Ad and Minna decided to look at the shop windows up and down Michigan Avenue, but the afternoon sun exhausted me. I headed home. Turning onto Monroe, I stopped at the corner by the entrance to the old meat market, caught by the dusty plate-glass window, the faded signs over the door, the yellowing cardboard notices in the window advertising chicken and beef for so much a pound. On sale this week. Today. A kosher market, unintelligible Hebrew (to me, at least) in black lettering, chipped now.

On the hot afternoon the front door was wide open, a block of wood under the bottom of the door, securing it. Staring in, I expected to see old Levi sifting through piles of old, smelly clothing, hunched over, a Uriah Heep with the bony scalp and hawk nose.

"Hello." My voice echoed against the back wall—all those empty cabinets, those glass-topped display cases, the racks, the shelves, everything empty of the deadly paraphernalia of butchery. A shell of a store. No one answered.

Too seductive, of course, an invitation to probe. That sacrosanct back room, the lair of the clubby men. "Hello," though now I expected no response, and happily so. I stepped through the doorway and moved quickly into the back room, a cluttered hovel: mismatched chairs with torn fabric, a Franklin cast-iron stove with a broken hinge, tables with overflowing ashtrays, not emptied in years, stacks of newspapers and magazines, even a scurrilous *Police Gazette* propping up the uneven leg of a table. Empty bottles, dirty glasses, a turned-over box of hoar-frosted peanuts. The stench of unventilated mayhem. Along all the walls were the counters and cabinets where, doubtless, poultry and beef carcasses made their inglorious entrance from a back door, preamble to dissection and trussing with cleaver and twine. Three of the walls held cubbyholes and ramshackle drawers, some half-open with papers and receipts and yellowing pulp spilling out. One wall once held knifes, the slots empty now but menacing, a knife-thrower's vaudeville act or, rather, the basement of the Spanish Inquisition. Torquemada's private pleasure. Chills ran up my spine seeing that vacant wall of deadly weapons, stripped now, but haunting. Had the knife that pierced Ivan's neck come from here?

Standing there, overwhelmed by the packed and worthless accumulation, I thought: There are secrets here, a story unexplained, a room that no one wanted to touch. I doubted the police, in their hurry-up investigation, considered pulling out even one of the drawers—or peeking into one of those jam-packed cubbyholes.

What notorious talk in this back room led to the murder? What questionable comment? Or did it?

I sensed an answer buried among the mountains of decay and dread.

My fingers gingerly touched the pull of an oak drawer, slightly ajar.

A voice bellowed from behind me. A gargled grunt.

I swirled around, my hand sweeping up thick gray dust, to face Morrie Wolfsy and Levi Pinsky, both furious.

"What means this?" Levi bellowed, quaking. "*Vos iz das?*" The veins in his temples bulged dangerously, blue-black, purple. Nostrils flared. Shoulders shook. A bony finger accused. "Trespasser."

Morrie, arms folded over his chest, simply said, "Edna Ferber." As though he were a jury foreman rehearsing a death sentence.

"The door was open and I..."

"Trespasser!" Levi screamed again. He sputtered, "You... you...*noodsh.*" A pest.

Morrie approached me. "The stories come back to me, Miss Ferber. You befriend the murdering woman and they tell me you get ready to point the finger at me, the surviving partner. They tell me you suspect me." He pointed to the rack that once held all those knives. "Morrie Wolfsy, he took a knife." Almost a child's chant, the words rhythmic. He said it again. "Morrie Wolfsy, he took a knife." Singsong, Lizzie Borden—that awful refrain.

And took from Ivan his precious life...
Morrie Wolsy took a knife...

"But I never..."

"Word on the street, Miss Ferber."

"I give you my word."

"*Ikh zed azoy lang lebn.*" I should live so long.

Levi rocked back and forth, this ninety-year-old hunched man, a bell-ringer of doom. "The good Jewish girl belongs in the home. Her mama's kitchen. Not here." His arthritic arm took in the cave. He shuddered. Disgust covered his features.

In a flash, I realized that Levi, the old crusty celibate, despised women. An unhappy man. I thought: Ad studied at his feet and learned the persistent alienation of affection. Another thought: poor Minna found the back room amusing but didn't realize it was most likely the wellspring of her perpetual engagement. She'd never walk down any aisle that was not stocked with gefilte fish and macaroons.

I was through defending myself. I marched between the two men, striding boldly, Scylla and Charybdis parting seamlessly.

"Goodbye."

Behind my back I could hear Levi cursing Leah. "Such beauty in so horrible a woman. Lilith, that demon woman with the long, long hair. Lilith who fled the Garden of Eden. A curse on all of us."

Chapter Fourteen

Detective Tom O'Reilly's name had been mentioned in the newspaper accounts of the murder, but fifteen years later, he was reluctant to talk to me. Ready to retire, he told me—"The old ticker needs Florida, Miss"—he sat behind a desk with two pieces of paper on it, one of which, doubtless, was his retirement application. The other paper a brochure of a clapboard beach home in Porto Gordo, Florida. He was a pot-bellied officer of the law with out-of-focus eyes surely in need of spectacles, and a few strands of vagrant white hair teased and encouraged over a bald head—a hopeless journey from one grotesque floppy ear to the other. A button red nose, speckled with polka-dot red blood vessels, and a tobacco's chewer's gamey breath. Detective O'Reilly eyed me with a look that suggested I'd interrupted a day of calculated idleness.

"Miss Ferber," he chortled, "they tell me you're famous."

"Hardly. A novel of mine…"

"I don't read."

"I could have guessed that."

His eyes narrowed. "Captain Mooney ushered you in, all buzzing and waving his arms. He claims he knew you when."

"Yes, when my family first moved here after my father died in Appleton, Wisconsin, we lived with my mother's family for a few years over to Calumet. Jimmy Mooney was a young patrolman on the block then, someone the neighborhood liked and respected."

"Yeah, yeah," he broke in. "A real sweetheart, that Mooney. Blarneyed his way up to captain."

"He remembers the Brenner murder."

He sucked in his breath. "Not much to remember about it."

"You were the chief investigative lawman."

"Open-and-shut case, my dear."

"Are you sure of that?"

That gave him pause, and considerable digestive surprise, given the rumbling and rasping and clucking that erupted from his throat and bursting belly. "Sort of dim in my memory—after all, this is Chicago where folks kill for sport. You have heard of our beloved mobsters, no?—a husband catches a wife *in flagrante delicto*, a spat breaks out, real messy, and the good wife kills cuckolded husband."

"In twenty words or less."

"You're the reporter, lady."

"I am that. But if you'll indulge me, sir, I'd like to review the evidence."

His eyes got wide. They flickered a moment as if I'd shined a light into them. "A young woman like you playing detective? My, my, my." He chuckled. "How times change!"

I didn't chuckle. "As I say, sir, indulge me."

He'd been leaning back in his swivel chair, his tremendous girth suggesting imminent catastrophe, but now, quick as a slap to the brow, he shot up, spine rigid, and banged a fleshy fist on the desk. "I sent the killer away, Miss Ferber."

I smiled winsomely. "And now, would you believe, Detective O'Reilly, Leah Brenner is back home, cooking in her kitchen. Grinding poppy seed in a mortar and pestle."

"What?" He tapped the desk impatiently. "They let her out?" He stared over his shoulder as if he expected Leah Brenner, white-haired now and demonic, to smash through the wall, cleaver at the ready.

"The asylum, I suppose, deemed her suitable for the safe streets of Chicago."

"Very funny."

"Thank you. Most of my humor is met with derision—or bafflement."

His face tightened. "Look, Miss Ferber, I heard all about you because of that novel you wrote about Chicago. So I suppose now this…this conversation we're having is the stuff of a new book, though why you want to dredge up some domestic squabble is beyond me. You can read all about it in the papers"—I nodded—"but police business is police business."

"The news accounts in the *Chicago Tribune* suggest a rush to judgment."

"She was caught red-handed."

"Without a knife," I broke in. "Without *evidence*. How is that *red-handed*?"

He struggled to stand. "I don't think I can help you, my dear."

"Sir…"

He scratched his neck. "Oh, I don't think so."

Unceremoniously, I was pointed out without any goodbye and certainly with no thanks from me, only to find myself downstairs facing a grinning Captain Mooney. Still with that red, boyish face and round blue eyes that I remembered from years ago, Captain Mooney was scratching his head. He watched my face, admittedly set in a stony grimace, and held out his arm. In it a green-backed folder, thin, bound with cords.

"He's a bastard," Captain Mooney whispered. "And lazy." He pushed the folder at me. "Here is what you want."

On my way in I'd told him my mission, though he'd not spoken a word. Clever boy, this old beat cop, and kind.

"Sit in there"—he pointed to a small alcove, windowless but with a door—"and leave it on the table when you leave."

"You'll be in trouble?"

"This will be the least criminal act committed in this building today." Laughing, he motioned me toward the open door. As I went to thank him, he simply bowed, threw out his arms like a stage performer at the end of a revue, and disappeared.

A quick hour, but an intense one, focused, my pencil scribbling furiously in the notebook I'd carried in my purse. A skinny file, granted, but its chaotic notes—was that Detective O'Reilly's illiterate penmanship?—intrigued me. Notations later ignored or forgotten—and ones that never made it to court or to the skimpy Fourth Estate accounts. What particularly intrigued me were the desultory—and largely trivial—interviews with relatives and neighbors. O'Reilly misspelled names, and in one case began a paragraph describing Sarah, quoting her, and then at the end of the same paragraph decided the quotation was by Ella (which was crossed out and "Emma" inserted). Folderol, most of it, a man in a hurry to head to Bath-House John's Groggery or to his browbeaten mistress in a fourth-floor walk-up.

But what I gleaned made the visit worthwhile. After all, I was at the point of asking the central question: Who was where that fateful day? How did the hapless players in this sordid drama move, interact, or absent themselves from the fatal scene? Yes, I knew what I'd been told by the players, some reinforced by the skimpy reportage in the *Chicago Tribune*, but here, in the detective's rambling and bumbling narrative, was a beggar's opera of tidbit and anecdote.

First, Jacob, the wandering Jew, the sensitive artist whose perfected art was avoidance—and now absence. The report said he was upstairs the whole time, all morning, emerging only with Sarah's screaming. So his current story of walking in and seeing his father on the sofa was perhaps fanciful, failed memory. Or perhaps he'd lied to the detective. I'd lie too, confronting that supercilious buffoon who'd convict out of convenience.

But there was an appended follow-up to Jacob's scattered behavior that day. Leah, dazed and silent, had been taken to Cook County Hospital, which surprised and pleased me, though, according to Detective O'Reilly, her moaning essentially admitted guilt. I gathered he somehow deciphered the words "fight" and "Ivan" and "sorry" from the sounds she spilled out. All of which the perfunctory detective interpreted as an outright confession. That same night, released from the hospital, she'd been summarily arrested for murder. Jacob, sitting in the hospital hallway with Uncle Ezra, wailed and smashed his fist into the wall. His intended target was supposedly some cop who was holding onto Leah, but Jacob, maddened with a welter of confused emotions, missed, bloodying his knuckles on a door-jamb, an inept assault on a police officer that luckily spared him handcuffs and arrest.

That same night Jacob disappeared. Sarah called the police the next morning, saying her nephew hadn't returned home, nor had he taken a suitcase or a change of clothing. The notation on the typed sheet stated, crassly, "Out on a drunk? Drowning his sorrow? Or at Hattie Beeber's brothel?" I imagined the smirk that accompanied such scribbling.

When Jacob was gone for a week, even the cops sat up and paid attention. Another murder perhaps? All in that misguided and hot-tempered family? A call from an old cousin in Bloomington Hills, Michigan, however, let the family know that Jacob had arrived there, distraught and exhausted, the night before. He wouldn't say where he'd been the day before, though his grubby clothing and unshaven, haggard face suggested tenderloin flophouses and waiting rooms in train stations.

He refused to return. "Dead. Everything's dead there." Jacob's words on the telephone, as recorded.

Uncle Ezra asked Adolph to ride with him to Detroit because Jacob said he'd only speak to Ad. Nothing followed the summary, save a remark that Jacob was finally coaxed to get into the automobile. He returned home.

There was nothing written about the nervous collapse Jacob shortly would experience.

Sarah's comments were routine, cursory, though she seemed to contradict her own statements on her second (and apparently final) interview, the first that afternoon, the second the next morning after being informed of the arrest. I recalled that she'd told me emphatically that she'd *not* been interviewed at all. She'd lied to me. At first she told the police she'd spotted a knife on the hardwood floor, feet from the dead Ivan. But, questioned further, she'd balked—she was so hysterical she *looked* for a knife. After all, Ivan had been stabbed. You could tell from the blood on his neck. On his chest. She swung around. The afternoon light through the curtains, the tilt of sunlight, the shadows. But she was wrong. Of course, she was wrong. As she was quoted, "There was no knife. We all know that now." She'd also said she'd rushed down the stairs to find her sister standing back from Ivan, just by the kitchen entrance, immobile, facing *her*. That detail was transmogrified within the same interview to Leah's bending over the body, inches away, as though she'd topple onto him. But one fact was consistent both days: Leah said nothing. She stared blankly at a questioning and screaming Sarah—and couldn't speak. Now and then a low moan. The awful silence, the stillness that underscored the horror of the tableau.

Sarah did provide information not in the news accounts nor, obviously, in her brief talk with me. And I wondered how true—or forgotten—that information. She told Detective O'Reilly that she'd been reading upstairs and vaguely heard the front door open. She was asked why not the back door—the door that led to the garden where Leah had been earlier. Or the side kitchen door. Had Leah left for errands? No, Sarah insisted, it was definitely the front door, massive and oak and a little warped, so that it made a dragging sound, a creaking wail. No other door did that, but only on opening it. When you closed it, there was only a quick *pop*. So, she said, she thought maybe someone had entered through the front door. But in her second interview Sarah said she wasn't sure now—it might not have been that afternoon. After all, folks walked in and out all the time. She thought it was that afternoon—but—

I scratched a note on my pad. What was that all about? If true, something very different was evident: someone walked in from outside when Ivan was in the parlor. Through the front door. No knocking or bell ringing. Jacob, returning? Which door had he used earlier? If, indeed, he'd been out earlier. Ivan on the sofa, watching. If true, that person was free to approach Ivan. But who? Leah returning from errands? Wouldn't she have used the kitchen door? Unless she was sitting on the front porch. That was possible. But would the door be shut behind her? Herman? Ella and Emma? Morrie, sneaking away from the butcher shop.

The butcher the baker the candlestick maker…

Sarah, upstairs, waited for the *pop* as the door closed. It never did. The door left open?

The police had found Morrie at his store, surprised at the visit, greeting them in a bloodied apron and gripping the cleaver he'd been using moments before they arrived. No, he told them, he never left the shop. A cup of coffee upstairs, running up, few minutes maybe with his wife there, his counter helper, Manny, still downstairs with customers. Even upstairs he could hear the front door jingle. No, no, Ivan was home sick, yes, no, no, such a busy morning it was, yes. Such a story you tell me now! Oh my God! Let me sit down, collect myself, let me.

Morrie's story, recorded by a transcriber, complete with vaudeville dialect.

Buried deep in the paragraph was a brief mention of Levi Pinsky, described as "Morrie Wolfsy's helper," a man who came out of the back room having eavesdropped on the conversation, and said one thing to the cops, which totally baffled them: "Evil everywhere, you men. Demons. Everywhere the night falls during the daytime." With that, he turned and retreated into the back room.

That made no sense to me.

Morrie had confided to the detective, "Everything that happens can be found in some line from the Torah."

Which made no sense to Detective O'Reilly who noted, "Crazy kike."

Nice touch, I thought, his sorry attempt at alliteration.

I skimmed through the comments by random neighbors who'd gathered on the sidewalk. A half dozen names that meant nothing to me—and offered nothing concrete. But what did startle me were the words offered by Esther and Molly Newmann—not Ad, I noticed—who stepped onto the Brenner lawn that afternoon. Molly, I gleaned from the notes, had considerable nonsense to offer, none of it of value, so labeled by

O'Reilly—"An old biddy next door thinks I'm there for coffee and a cruller"—while Esther, described as "the old lady's niece or daughter," kept tugging on Molly's arm, directing her back home. As Leah was led away, Molly muttered, "You reap what you sow," to which Esther, suddenly sobbing, reached out to Leah, trying to lay a comforting hand on her, though she never did. A bad scene, Molly playing Greek chorus to that awful tragedy. And decent Esther, always forgiving, an ineffective antidote to her mother-in-law's nasty and unnecessary homily.

• • ● • •

Back on Monroe Street, fevered, my notepad bursting with jottings, I knocked on Leah's front door. She seemed surprised to see me, wariness in her eyes. Dressed in a shapeless Mother Hubbard, coarse gray, with a white lace shawl thrown casually over her shoulders, she held a book in her hand, clutching it to her chest. Despite the broiling heat of the afternoon, she appeared chilled, her skin pasty, clammy. She'd pulled back her white hair into a careless bun, bound with a red ribbon, but vagrant strands broke free, giving her the look of a wagon-train gypsy.

"Edna," she whimpered, but offered only a cool, distant smile.

"Are you all right?"

She winced, her voice thick. "Has something happened?"

"No, no," I said hurriedly. "Ad told me Jacob is troubled—won't talk to him. Hiding away…"

She motioned me inside, watching the street as I moved by her. A woman expecting to be shadowed, watched, questioned.

"I don't know what to do."

"Is this my fault?" I asked quietly.

She sighed. "I suppose it's all my fault, if you think about it. I did come back home."

"It *is* your home."

Resignedly, "I suppose so. But what that means I no longer know—a roof over our heads, sure, but too many ghosts in the woodwork."

"I'm sorry, Leah, if I hurt you or your family."

"I know you are, Edna." A sigh. "Nothing to be done about it now."

She pointed to a chair, but I didn't sit. "I'm not staying. I'm expected home. I wanted to see about Jacob."

Her eyes brightened. "Thank you."

She was turning away, glancing toward the stairwell. Jacob, upstairs perhaps, listening. Or Sarah, eavesdropping. Ghosts in the woodwork. I longed to question Sarah about her remark to the police about the front door opening, but this wasn't the time. The atmosphere had shifted in the home since my first visit. Then, there'd been warmth, a soft glow to the light, bodies eased into overstuffed armchairs, the tinkle of ice in glasses, conviviality. That was my visit with Leah, of course. My scattered talk with Sarah on the sun porch was a different matter. Now, however, late afternoon shadows swept the parlor, darkening corners, exaggerating the stark light from a solitary lamp switched on in the hallway. A mausoleum, that room—that house. Sarah's gaudy figurines an eerie circus panorama. A crypt in a Gothic romance. Leah sat at the edge of the shadows, most of her face in darkness.

I seemed an intruder now, a violator of a hard-won serenity that was dangerously close to being lost. My fault. Mea culpa. My blame. Edna, who never allowed herself the luxury of guilt—now consumed by it.

My voice choked, I turned to go. "I only wanted to help."

Suddenly Leah grasped my shoulder, made me face her. The move seemed to surprise her as much as it did me, but she spoke tenderly, a catch in the back of her throat. "You've done nothing wrong, Edna."

My head turned toward the stairwell. Jacob and Sarah, up there, listening. The hum of a radio. "But…"

She was rocking me gently, a mother's soothing grip. "Nothing. You don't think I wondered all those years? You don't think I felt blessed when you stepped onto my porch that day?"

Tears escaped the corners of my eyes. "This can't have an happy ending."

"Nothing in my life will ever have a happy ending, Edna. It can't be, not now. Not after all these years." She let go of me. "All I ask is that it have…an ending."

• • ● • •

The Newmann kitchen was alive with preparations for supper as I walked in. My mother was peering into a huge pot of boiling water, preparing to drop in handmade rolled egg noodles. Esther sat at the table, dicing burgundy-red beets into thick fleshy slices, her fingertips tinged red. Molly, leaning against a counter, her cane resting at her hip, was breading chicken legs, dipping the pieces into egg and then rolling them in the flour. A deep-dish apple pie, heavy with the smell of grated cinnamon and nutmeg, sat on a wire pie rack, cooling, tantalizing. They'd been chatting amiably, but they stopped, almost on stage cue, as I banged through the back screen door.

"Edna," my mother said, "we expected you hours ago."

"Research downtown." I told the truth.

"Truck farms in High Prairie? The Dutch farmers?"

I nodded, dumbly, but I said to Molly who held up flour-coated hands, "I didn't know you and Esther spoke to the police the day Ivan died."

My mother groaned, ready to explode, but Molly squinted at Esther, puzzled. "So? All the neighbors did. We stood on the front lawn, watching." A pause. "And how did you know that?"

"You were quoted in the police report. Lots of people were."

Molly stared, unfriendly. "And what did I say?"

"In Leah's yard. 'Reap what you sow.'"

Suddenly the three women exchanged looks, a gurgle rising from Esther's throat, and then they burst out laughing. Though I had no idea why, I joined in, that infectious community of women sharing some laughter in the steamy kitchen. "*What?*" I manage to say. "What?"

Esther had tears in her eyes. "Molly *always* says that. To Sol, even now. To Adolph and Harriet when they were little babies. To me." The corners of her mouth twitched. "Especially to me."

"Wisdom for the ages," Molly added, nodding. "Perhaps you should heed it, Edna." She glanced at my mother, nodding back at her.

I got serious. "But why hurl it at Leah that afternoon? She was a stricken woman."

Molly was perplexed. "If I remember correct, I was saying it to Sarah. Leah was already gone. Not to Leah."

Now that made no sense. Leah, the rumored adulteress. Leah, the murderer. Leah, the neighborhood leper. Sarah, the skittish spinster sister.

"But why Sarah?"

Molly waited a heartbeat. "Well, I suppose it *was* for Leah, a shameless harlot. But they were already carrying her off. Sarah was standing there, a snippy look on her face that said to me: Get off my lawn. This is not your affair. I don't *like* you."

Esther faced me. "Molly and Sarah have had long clashes over the backyard fence."

Molly pouted. "She once accused me of being a yenta. A busybody. That Sarah was always a brat. Leah was the pretty flower, vacant as an abandoned house, so far as I was concerned. But Sarah, she was like sandpaper against my skin. 'Mind your own business,' she says to me. She complained about me to Herman who talked to me. Said he'd send the rabbi to talk to me. Imagine that! Him and his wife, Naomi, that dreadful cold fish. Both of them are like Sarah, a form of life best left under rocks." She smiled maliciously. "So *there!*"

"I didn't know this," I said. "The feud between the Newmanns and the Brenners. The Hatfields and the McCoys."

"No feud," Esther insisted. "Leah had coffee with me at this table. She was my friend—one of the few I had."

"Against my wishes," Molly said. She banged the cane against the cupboard door. *Tap tap tap.*

"Sarah also suffered that day—what she had to see, no?" asked Esther.

Molly would have none of it. "She put her two cents in. That's why I tried to catch her eye on the porch."

"What are you talking about?"

Molly covered the platter of floured chicken and then rinsed her hands in the sink. The cane rattled to the floor as Esther rushed to pick it up.

"Edna, that bruising fight that morning. Above Ivan's yelling and Leah's wailing there'd be Sarah's voice yelling, 'Stop!' or "Just stop!' It was almost comical—like a child trying to stop a speeding train."

"You never mentioned Sarah as part of that fight."

Molly shrugged. "I told the police."

"It isn't in the report."

Molly's voice cracked. "That ain't my fault." She paused. "I must have told them."

Now Esther spoke up, befuddled. "Molly dear, you *never* heard Sarah then. This is the first time I'm hearing about it."

The old woman teetered a second, squinted. Now she deliberated. "Or was it another time?" She tossed her head back. "What does it matter now?"

"It does confuse the story," I said.

"Edna, you're being ridiculous. I can't remember *everything*."

Ad opened the screen door and walked into the kitchen, Molly wagged a finger at him. "You're late."

"I didn't know I was expected." He kissed Molly on the cheek.

His mother poured him a glass of lemonade, which he gulped down. "Adolph," she asked him, "tell Edna about the fight Leah and Ivan had that morning."

He rolled his eyeballs. "Didn't we have this talk before? A thousand times? Is this the only story left in the world?"

"Your grandmother now says Sarah kept telling them to stop." She waited.

"What are you talking about?"

Molly jumped in. "It's no big deal, dear. I recall Sarah stepping in and trying to end it. We all heard her, no? She yelled 'Stop!'"

Ad started to walk across the room. "I didn't." He smiled at Molly. "Are you sure? We talked about it, you and me, as we went shopping. That was *all* we talked about. That I remember.

I know their house was quiet when we walked by—the fight over with, but...no, Sarah was not part of it. This is the first I'm hearing about it." A heartbeat. "What is this all about?"

"I must be losing my memory." She lifted a dishcloth off the platter of chicken to inspect her work. "It was a brutal fight, those *two*."

"Do we gotta relive it all over again?" Ad complained. "Didn't it color too much of our life? Days afterwards, horrible. The world turned upside down. Maybe if I'd gone over there, that day...wouldn't have happened."

Molly cried out, "Oh, Lord no. I didn't want you anywhere near that craziness. Ivan would have turned on you. Leah waving that knife...You could have been..." She stopped, her voice shaky. "You could have been *hurt*." Her voice shook. "Exhausting it was, listening. Then, later on, Sarah crying out like that. To wake the dead, that woman's screams. I can still hear it. I woke from my nap and thought the screaming was here—in this house. I thought somebody—my Esther—fell, maybe—hurt. I rushed across the hall and pounded on Adolph's door."

"And scared me half to death. You yelled, 'Something happened to your mama.'" He shook his head. "But I knew it was Sarah, I could hear her myself."

Molly's lips quivered. "Everything changed then. Everything. Leah, that harlot..."

Esther *tsk*ed, glanced at Adolph as though he were five and not forty. "Now, now."

"That woman." Molly smiled. "I was right what I said then. You do reap what you sow. So many times I was convinced that Ivan would kill Leah. He had such a temper, that man. A husband made a fool of. Sooner or later he'd kill her. She drove him to it. That woman was too...alluring. You gotta know—that beautiful woman was a curse on both our houses."

Chapter Fifteen

Another Saturday afternoon on Monroe Street, the pavement breathing its silence. Shops closed, doors shut, no distant sounds of two-wheel pushcart vendors drifting over from Maxwell Street. A family in black moved down the center of the street, headed to shul. Mostly the street was silent, deserted under a white hot July sun, heat waves rippling above the pavement. A toddler squealed in its mother's arms. A street that watched and sighed under a day meant for God.

By myself, I strolled the empty streets after lunch, listening to the bark of a chained dog or the sudden blare of an unreligious horn or the profane violation of a husband and wife spat or the hint of the passing Illinois Central.

Back home at mid-afternoon, I found Sol Newmann sitting on the front porch with Ezra Brenner. That gave me pause. But of course they knew each other, friends from years back. But not exactly the friendliness of two old men leisurely smoking cigars on a hot afternoon—Ezra sat upright, one hand holding the arm of the chair as though ready to flee. Although his posture might have been the result of spotting me strolling up the sidewalk.

I cringed. How I disliked the man, especially after that unnerving altercation the other day as he tried to drag an unwilling Jacob into his automobile.

Sol waved to me, cheerful. "Edna, you disappeared after lunch."

"A walk through the quiet streets."

Sol continued, "My favorite day on Monroe. You can almost hear the prayers in folks' houses."

Ezra frowned at him. "Sol, you're not a religious man."

"No, Ezra," Sol answered, a smile on his face. "And you're not a religious man. No decent Jew wears such a tie on Shabbas."

For, indeed, Ezra, dressed in a sharp-pressed gray linen suit, sported the most ostentatious turquoise tie and accompanying handkerchief. With his black-and-white shoes and snappy spats, his white hair under a summer straw sailor hat, he resembled a barker from a rag-tag Punch-and-Judy revue.

Ezra laughed. "Jealousy is an awful thing."

"Are you visiting next door?" I asked him. I waited a second. "And found no one at home?"

"Edna, with such a tart tongue you'll not find a husband."

"Then I need to employ my tongue even more than I do now."

Ezra leaned into Sol. "Ah, the modern woman, Sol. Bicycles and lawn tennis and Camel cigarettes and dance slippers and… and miscast votes."

But Ezra was through with the banter, bored, his eye watching the street. "I wondered if Ad has had any luck?" A question to Sol. Again, the sweep of the sleepy street.

Sol followed his eyes. "Poor Jacob."

I moved closer, panicked. "What happened?"

Sol made a dismissive wave of his hand. "The lad wanders. You know that."

Ezra fretted, tapping his cigar against the rail of the chair. "As you know, poor Jacob, distressed over the latest turn of events"—with this, he narrowed his baleful eye at me, registering blame where he supposed it to be—"has pretty much hidden in his room, even cold-shouldering Ad. I thought I'd drive over to take him for a spin." He sucked in his breath. "I seem to be the only one he'll talk to. Even poor Leah finds herself excluded. But he'd—fled."

"Ad went searching for him?"

Sol spoke softly. "I sent him. We think maybe Jacob went to visit with an old school friend, Sy Bloom, over to Roosevelt

Boulevard. Ad, too, old friends from school, but years ago. Sy calls now and then. A wild goose chance, we figures, but why not?"

"We got to do something," Ezra said.

"I never knew what was wrong with that boy." Sol shook his head.

Ezra was nodding. "A lad who never had roots, that one. An adventurer."

Yes, I thought: an adventurer who never stepped away from his father's home, the middle-aged man who wrote one poem in a magazine and then drifted through five or six streets, this adventurer who now hid in his mother's house. Hardly the circumnavigating hero headed around the world. A man committed to nothing, though he wrestled with demons inside that no one took seriously or, at worst, ever even noticed. Poor Jacob, indeed.

"So you're worried?" I asked Ezra who was doing his best to act friendly toward me, a plastered-on smile covering his features, though his eyes were wary, distrustful,

"Of course. It's as though the murder of Ivan happened yesterday. It's an open wound with him, that emotional, that..." He hesitated.

"That unanswered," I finished for him.

A flash of anger in his eyes. "So you say. Poor Jacob talks like a crazy man, colorful nonsense. He acts like a..." His voice trailed off.

A shock to the system, that sputtered sentence, because at that moment, like a wallop, I experienced an epiphany: Ezra feared that Jacob in his confused, rambling state would *say* something. But what? A confession? Or something else? Maybe something about Ezra? Or someone else? Staring at Ezra, the polished mannequin so shallow and decadent and *fin de siècle*, I realized that he might believe Jacob was, in fact, the murderer. He wanted to shield him—or shut him up—or...or what? To silence him.

All along I'd felt Jacob had something to say but perhaps didn't realize what it was. Now, more than ever, I was convinced of it. Something crucial, deadly.

"...a murderer?" I finished for him.

"No," he stumbled. "God, no!" His voice broke as he hurriedly went on. "Edna, no one seriously considered Morrie Wolfsy, the disgruntled partner, the smarmy…seducer. Did you know that the day before—the day *before*, let me repeat—Morrie waved a cleaver at Ivan? They were at each other's throats, and Ivan got so scared he hid in the small bathroom in the back room. He locked himself in. All the time he's yelling, 'Help! Help! Call the police!' While in front Morrie is waiting on customers lined up, weighing out a pound of lean beef, some rib-eye steaks. A customer told me this later, of course. Customers were lined up, and Ivan in back hollering 'Help! Help!' It was almost comical, really, some zany skit out of a Yiddisher nickel show."

"What happened?" asked Sol, fascinated.

"Nothing, it turns out. They always fought, even before the…the thing with Leah. A half hour later, calmed down, Ivan opened the locked door, stumbled out, and got behind the poultry counter. 'May I help you, Mrs. Rabinowitz?' he says to the next in line. 'A good-looking bird, plump, this one, the best, look at this wonder.'"

"Then why do you say they should consider Morrie as a murderer? If, in fact, they entertained each other with these little spats."

Ezra drew in his cheeks. "Because Morrie never took them seriously, but Ivan *started* to. He *did*. Near the end. A game to Morrie, the customers even laughing, but after Leah and the nonsense there was a look in Ivan's eyes—and at the end Morrie saw it. The violence under the chitchat. Hair-trigger moments. Sooner or later…"

I wasn't happy. "Based on what? All the police information puts Morrie solidly in the shop that morning."

Ezra scoffed. "Yeah, that reliable witness, Levi Pinsky."

"Do you know anything?"

Ezra stood. "I told you everything I know."

And with that, positioning his hat on his head, adjusting it carefully, and putting out the cigar in an ashtray, he nodded at Sol but not at me, and stepped off the porch.

• • ● • •

That night, long after sundown, the heat of the day making the air sticky and close, I left by the kitchen door, skirted by the Brenner yard—there was only one light switched on, at the back of the house—and strolled up the block toward Maxwell. People sat on front stoops, fanning themselves. A few children ran after balls in the street, though such activity was listless. The whole street seemed to sweat, to wilt. Ad had never returned home, so I didn't know if he'd located Jacob. An automobile squealed by, Ezra with the top down, elbow resting on the open window ledge, a cigarette drooping from the corner of his mouth. Coming from Leah's? Searching for Jacob? I doubted that—the preening peacock. I disliked the fact that such a dissembling, devious weasel could so infuriate me.

A light flickered in the front room of Nathan's Meat Market, the door propped open, and I expected to see a doddering Levi Pinsky issuing a proclamation rescinding woman suffrage, scribing his diatribe on a piece of ragged linen cut from a five-cent tattered trouser leg.

Sitting quietly in the center of the room, leafing through a stack of papers under an overhead naked light bulb, was an old woman, eyeglasses slipping off her snub nose. I was staring, true, surprised, but she stared back, then raised a welcoming hand in the air.

"Edna Ferber," Harsh, bold, her voice dropping.

I started. "Why, yes."

"My husband described you perfectly."

"I can imagine…"

"Late thirties, sallow skin, short, reedy, a nose from one of the lost tribes, and a hayfield bonnet of wiry hair."

"How attractive."

She grinned. "Morrie is not a nice man. And never to women, unless they're beautiful and in need of money."

"You're his wife, I take it."

"A badge of dishonor I refuse to relinquish, don't ask me why."

"Why?" I asked, stupefied.

Her eyes got wide, not amused.

She was a smallish woman with a little girl's bony frame, four-feet-five if she exaggerated, thin papery arms and neck, so scant they resembled twigs, breakable; a face lined with deep wrinkles that nearly eclipsed the small nickel-sized round eyes, as metallic as dull silver. A homely woman, one who'd never been pretty, but a woman who, with advancing age and teeth-clenching grit, had become doggedly handsome, like a piece of ancient statuary rusted and weathered in a forgotten park. The patina of forgotten silverware. As I watched, she simply dropped the stack of papers to the floor where they scattered, some sliding under the chair she sat on. She shrugged and ignored them.

"I'm Selma Wolfsy. You gathered that already. You're smart. At least you're smart enough to realize that Leah Brenner never killed Ivan."

That shocked me.

"You know that, too?"

"Of course." She smiled at me.

"But you never told the police."

She roared in a thick, whiskey voice, ending by coughing into the back of her wrist. "What do I know? Do you think I have evidence? I'm talking common sense here."

"Then who...?"

She groaned. "Oh, please don't ask me that. You've probably bored everyone on Monroe Street with that tired, unanswerable question. Do you really expect an answer from one of the crowd around these parts? Everyone naming Leah but secretly pointing to their least favorite person. A wink—look at *him*. Look, look. It's bad enough my husband thinks you're planning to pin the murder on him—the fool—an idea whispered by our own resident misanthrope, Levi Pinsky, who fears he might actually touch my hand by accident someday—so Morrie spends his waking hours hiding upstairs and running from you."

"Does he have anything to hide?"

She laughed and wagged a finger at me. "Dear, we all have things to hide. By the time you're my age—I'm seventy next month—you'll probably be annoyingly famous and hated by most folks you've skewered in your writing, and living alone, hiding your loneliness with wisecracks."

A beat. "I do that now."

"So you found your destiny early, young lady. Good for you."

"Why are you sitting here alone?"

She waved a hand around the room. "I want to sell this fire-trap. I've been begging Morrie for years since he closed up shop. I rarely come here. But I had to sort through some delinquent leases. Apartments we own. The Russians we rent to make believe they can't read English. They're all hiding in shul today, of course. Morrie is visiting someone over on Canal. He'll be back in a bit." She grinned. "You better not be here, Edna Ferber. You'd hate to see an old sickly man topple over in fear, right?"

"Will Morrie sell?"

"Morrie is a sentimental fool. He remembers with affection the old days, the rough-and-tumble off-the-boat days, the romance of being poor in squalid houses. He holds onto the old ball of string that tied his first rump roast together. Lord! I'm a practical woman. I like my new kitchen with the electric refrigerator and the electric stove and…and my green lawn and sycamore trees. Even if Morrie comes with the package."

"A loving marriage."

She watched me closely. "Sarcasm is unattractive in a young woman. In an old woman it's sometimes all we have left."

I leaned against the doorjamb. "You don't care for him?"

"Of course I do. I love him. It's just that I've never *forgiven* him."

"For Leah Brenner?"

She grunted. "You don't know the half of it."

"Tell me."

A harsh, unfriendly grin. "You *are* a public nuisance, my dear. The rumors about you don't do your peskiness justice. In other centuries they'd have burned you at the stake. To thunderous applause, I'd say." She laughed at her own joke. "Leah Brenner.

Ah, where do I begin? A woman born to woo ships into the rocky harbors. Not her fault, you'll say. Let me ask and answer all the questions here. Well, that's true, but it's no great consolation for a plain Jane like me. Or, sad to say, you, my dear. We're the scraggly ragweed growing on the side of the road, wild-blown, dusty, as the speeding roadsters sail past with Lorelei with her red lipstick cooing in the driver's ear."

"You can't just blame a woman. A man—your man—is part of the equation."

She shook her head back and forth. "And don't I know it, but I can still condemn Leah. Look, dear Edna Ferber, Leah was only one, maybe the last, of a series of women over the years. Some I closed my eyes to, others I confronted. Leah was one frivolous afternoon, a second in time. Nothing happened. There were so many others—a week, a month, so long as Morrie had nickels and dimes for the nickelodeon—or an evening at Haverley's Minstrels followed by supper at Gold's. Cheap girls, all spangled up and shiny under a streetlight. He destroyed our marriage years ago, but Leah was off-limits. She was the partner's wife. Ivan's wife. Lord, there have to be some boundaries, no? You can't be friends with a woman who looks—*looked*—I mean, she's an old woman now—like *that*."

"She suffered a horrible fate—for a murder I don't believe she did. But to accuse her because she was beautiful…"

Sharp, angry. "Who cares? C'mon. Who cares?" A sliver of a smile. "I actually met her a few days after Ivan unearthed—is that the word?—the tawdry moment, the kiss heard round the shul? She was shopping with sour Sarah of the salt mines. That unhappy woman. Leah approached me, brazen, and apologized. Can you believe that? Her arms filled with packages, the dutiful *hausfrau*, shopping for Shabbas supper, and she gets teary-eyed and begs forgiveness. I turned away."

I swallowed. "But it must have pained her. It took courage to do that."

"Sarah stood there with a smirk on her face. A big joke to her. Laughing at me."

"But Leah wasn't laughing."

For a second she closed her eyes. "Everyone in the neighborhood was. A disgraced woman—*me*. Not her. I kept away from shul for a month. 'Here's the prune-faced wife. How sad! How horrible! Married to a squat, spindly Lothario with loose coins jangling in his pockets.'"

"You stayed married to Morrie to make him pay?"

A slow, lazy grin made the old wrinkled face contort. "Now, at last, you understand the whole story."

I shuddered. "I wouldn't be you for a million dollars."

"I agree. I wouldn't be me for a million dollars."

I glanced toward the back room, jerked my head in that direction. "All the fantasies and foolishness that came to life in that room. Men with their games. What happened in there, I believe, was the hotbed that ended with the murder of Ivan. Something those men never expected."

She followed my gaze. "A no man's land. A dump. But you're right. The men schmoozed and planned lives they never got 'round to leading…fantasies that couldn't be realized or—or…"

"Or had dreams that had no hope. Women breathe hope into men's souls. We temper men's folly."

She chortled. "Ah, a feminist. I should have suspected it. The New Woman. Susan B. Anthony casting off her ritual wig."

"You sound bitter."

"Actually, I'm not. I'm enjoying this conversation. You're tremendously innocent of things."

I bristled. "You make innocence sound childish."

"And it isn't?"

She stood, tired of the talk, and glanced at the wall clock. "Morrie is late." She was peering into the back room, dark now, the door half-shut. "What a pigsty. If we sell the place—if I twist his arm enough—it'll take a month to clear out those shelves and cubbyholes. Can you imagine if it caught fire? A fire you could see from the rim of hell."

I stood beside her. "Lucky you."

She faced me. "It always surprises me that someone *wanted* to break in there."

I started. "In the back room? What?"

She laughed pleasantly. "For a nosy detective, you sure miss a lot, Edna Ferber. No one told you? On the same day Ivan was stabbed to death, maybe around eight that night, dark out, someone pried open the back door. Morrie and I were away, maybe at the police station, I don't know. But when we got back the door was smashed. The latch…"

"What was taken?" I broke in, eagerly.

"A small tin box with some change was emptied. The box was knocked onto the floor. Maybe five dollars in quarters, nickels, dimes. Nothing. Pocket change."

"Nothing else? Was anything moved around?"

"Hard to tell. Back then, especially, it was the same disgusting pile."

"Did the police investigate?"

She narrowed her eyes. "Well, somebody came out. But keep in mind Ivan's murder got more attention than some petty burglary. There were other break-ins in the neighborhood that summer. The police thought it was just one more. Some youngsters, bored, daring."

I rushed my words. "But didn't the police make any connection with Ivan's murder? The same day, a break-in at his store? It seems to me…"

Her hand in my face. "For Lord's sake, Edna, you do take wonderful leaps of imagination. By that time they'd already condemned Leah to perdition. Based on what—I'll never understand." She smiled. "A body and someone standing over it. Case closed."

"But…" I stammered. I wanted to yell: madness, this investigation. Something happened that night, yet no one decided to add one and one to get two.

"Pittance, Edna. Change. I don't see how you are connecting those dots. It would be one thing if we stepped on a bloody knife, conspiratorially dropped onto the floor. Or lifted a bloody shirt. Follow a line of bloody footprints out the front door. Or upstairs. Evidence pointing to Morrie. It was nickels and dimes. Hardly a pirate's booty."

"Somebody wanted to get inside that back room, and it had to do with the murder."

"Preposterous." She stepped away. "Enough. Really." She headed to the front door but shot a glance back at me. "So, my dear, what have we concluded?" The gravelly, irreverent laugh. "Have I given you the answer you need?"

"I'm thinking about that break-in."

Her eyes flickered. "You think it had to do with the murder?"

I didn't answer her.

"Now you're trying to scare me." Her voice was hollow.

I shook my head back and forth. "I don't think that's possible."

Chapter Sixteen

Late the following morning Esther walked in from watering the flowers on the front porch, a puzzled look on her face. She held up a long white envelope, sealed. "*Vos iz dos*? For you, Edna dear. And no stamp on it. Dropped onto the porch. How odd." The envelope simply said "Edna Ferber" in thick black ink that had smudged at the edges. "A mash note?" A twinkle in her eye.

I took it from her. "More likely a death threat."

But those were poorly chosen words because Esther drew in her breath and scrunched up her face.

"I'm joking, Esther."

"I hope you are, Edna. I don't understand today's humor. You young folks."

Sitting across the table, spreading boysenberry jam on some toast, my mother quipped, "This new generation of young women refuses to be humorous."

"No, Mother," I answered back, "we just refuse to be humored."

Perversely, I declined to open the envelope, though both women insisted I do so. Molly, hobbling in, wondered what the fuss was about. Told of the note, she gave me an in-my-day-no-respectable-girl look that left nothing unsaid about decorum and civility and suspect missives dropped casually onto a fair maiden's doorstep.

Back in my room, hurriedly, I ripped opened the envelope. What I found intrigued me: a yellowing piece of paper, typescript on one side, and neat penmanship on the back. It was, bizarrely, from Jacob, though I was baffled why he chose to drop it onto the front porch.

"Edna," it began. "It came to me—at last—about years ago. I finally remember you. I was cruel." Below that:

Edna, Edna, sugar and spice,
An orchid locked in frozen ice.
Edna, Edna,

Not nice—
Dramatically he'd drawn a huge "X" through that bit of old childish doggerel, and below it wrote:

Edna, Edna
Let's hope I'm wrong.
When I sing you a comrade song
That goes on too long.
Edna Edna
Here's some advice
An orchid in ice
Please be nice.

And below it, separate from the silly verse, were two words in bold block letters:

TO ME!
Please be nice to me!

At the bottom he also scrawled: "This is the first poem I've written in seven years."

Hardly poetry, I thought. Not exactly a love-smitten Robert Browning writing to (and wooing?) the frail and welcoming Elizabeth Barrett. The scribbling was, frankly, unsettling.

None of this made sense, except as indications of Jacob's disturbed state of mind. Jacob, playing a game. Jacob, groping along in some darkness he'd fallen into.

Jacob's mind taking him back to the past—and remembering me. Finally. But also, I wondered, what other bits and pieces of the past were at last surfacing in his mind these days.

The paper crackled in my hand like opening an old letter, long stowed away in a drawer, brittle. On the back I found what was obviously an old poem from the days when he listened to some poetic muse. Poorly typed, under the title "Poem," with cross-outs, hatched lines, a fading typescript read:

The movement of my mother
Suddenly turning in her beautiful flesh
Makes us watch
Stars move through untouched heavens
And the boys gather from the street:
She lifts pots from the stove
And licorice from the cabinets.
In summer she sees them to their end.
I shouldn't be here, this moment—
Lapping tongues that mock.
Not my fault.
Even the dead know more than I do.

I reread the old words—a rough draft? Rambling, confused, and, for some reason, I thought of Stephen Crane's stark, enigmatic verse, which always intrigued me, though I never liked it. Was it an accident, Jacob's choosing this old sheet of paper with that particular poem in order to pen the doggerel intended for me? Who knew?

What was he telling me?

Jacob worried me. I watched for him to leave his house. I drifted to the side windows overlooking the Brenner yard, or read on the front porch, or glanced out my bedroom window late at night, unable to sleep. I waited, holding my breath.

Which, surprisingly, was how I finally spotted him: at midnight, the houses and street silent as dust.

Just after midnight, as I sat reading by a small table lamp, unable to sleep, I noticed a light switched on at the back of the

Brenner house—on for a minute or so and then extinguished. I switched off my own light and peered outside, where I noticed a faint shadow moving out from the back steps, someone leisurely walking around the side of the house toward the street. A man, I could tell from the build. Jacob Brenner, obviously. The erstwhile poet wandering under a hazy moonlit sky.

Hurriedly, foolishly, I threw on my robe over my dressing gown, tied a sash at the waist, and quietly, cat-like, opened my bedroom door, closed it carefully, and moved down the stairs. The old house creaked and moaned with night noises, the labored breathing of old boards, so my careful footfall on the oak stairs produced a few groans and sighs as I walked. I wasn't certain of my behavior. Certainly I could never follow the nomadic man through Chicago streets at this unseemly hour, especially dressed for bed and unchaperoned by my dowager mother. Yet curiosity overwhelmed me. The front door squeaked as I opened it, so I paused, waiting. No one in the house stirred. Molly probably popped awake—but so be it. The rest of the household sound sleepers, I trusted—as I usually was.

Though the night remained unrelentingly hot, a slight chill made me shiver. Nights in Chicago usually shuddered under the wind that came off Lake Michigan. Even in the dog days of summer, boiling, no one could forget the awful power of any Chicago winter. So now I shivered, drew in my robe tighter, and huddled in a corner of the porch. Silence: no one visible. Jacob Brenner, disappeared.

Gingerly, in violation of all I considered proper, I walked down the steps, surreptitiously secreting myself behind an over-grown bank of hedges, and peered up the block. Not an auto-mobile, not a soul in sight. The darkness was relieved at regular intervals by fuzzy streetlamps. Dim lights in some apartments, here and there. A tomcat disappeared under a car fender. But mostly blackness on this quiet, respectable street of hard-working lives. The streetlamp in front of the Brenner house cast blocks of yellow onto the pavement.

Moving in the middle of the street, slowly, dully, was Jacob's shadow. From my hidden spot, I could discern his lanky figure moving, moving, moving, and steady, with purpose. At the corner where Monroe met Maxwell, he stopped, conveniently under a streetlamp. A tiny figure now, almost difficult to see, except for the movement of arms that waved at nothing in particular. He stopped directly in front of Nathan's Meat Market—that lodestar at the heart of his papa's murder. He stood there for a long time, though perhaps it was but minutes, and soon I saw the ghostly silhouette headed back.

Quietly, I slipped into the house, tiptoed into the parlor where I stood by the front window, concealed in darkness, my hand pulling back the curtains. Within seconds, Jacob reappeared, still in the middle of the street, as though savoring the exquisite freedom of a city street with no automobiles, no bustling strollers, no noontime yelling and rattling.

Yet he danced around, loose-limbed, a marionette freed from the confining strings, because he swirled, stepped left, stepped right, a tap dance on the pavement. I heard—or imagined I heard—a humming, or was it a plaintive keening coming from his throat?

He stopped, stooped down, hunched over, and rocked on his heels. He stared at his dark home. Silent now, arms folded on his chest. He was waiting for something. But what?

Then he moved quickly. I jerked back in the parlor, gasped as I bumped a table, a box falling to the floor with an loud thud. Energized, he walked toward the Newmann home. Had he spotted me on the porch earlier? Had he caught my reflection in the window, a shadow caught by moonlight and flickering street lamp?

He stopped in front of the house—directly in front of the window where I stood, paralyzed now, helpless to move. As I held my breath, he crouched down again, the same frog-like stance he'd assumed before his own home. Now, rocking like a children's play toy, he stared at the Newmann home and I feared he'd be there all night, with me—the nosy investigator—afraid to shift my body lest he catch sight of me. Dawn would find Jacob still on watch, and my mother would discover her wayward daughter wrapped in a parlor curtain like a pesky servant spying on the household.

I waited.

But of course Jacob finally moved, standing, nodding as though waking from a dream, and walking home. No jerky movement now, no flailing of arms, no *danse macabre*. Simply a man strolling home without a care in the world.

I slipped into an armchair and realized I was breathing heavily, my heart pounding. Good Lord, I thought, what was that midnight romp all about? What demons drew poor Jacob from his hot bed and compelled that midnight trek?

My mind sailed to the scrap of doggerel he'd sent me—a message? Trivial, a lingering vestige of the old, flirtatious Jacob? The ladies' man, Romeo, the foolish gigolo. But then I thought of the poem on the back, that dark poem to his mother, the neighborhood cynosure of the hungry boys, and that haunting last line: *Even the dead know more than I do.*

The dead? His father? For, indeed, his father knew his assailant. Yes, I thought: Ivan let the killer come near. No stranger, of course, that killer. Someone free to approach him, to bend over and stab the man to death. A knife to the neck. A curious place to strike—as if by chance, anger, confusion. Unpremeditated?

Ivan knew his killer. And well.

At that moment, I guessed that Jacob knew the name of the killer.

• • **●** • •

A police car pulled in front of the Brenner household, and the street held its breath. Late afternoon, a lazy and sweltering day, I sat on the front porch with my mother, Esther, and Molly, scarcely moving, nursing tart lemon phosphates and saying little. Too hot for conversation. Earlier Molly had asked me what I was doing roaming around the house late last night. "I recognized your steps in the parlor. Something dropped on the floor—knocked me wide awake."

"Sleepless," I'd told her. "The heat."

Still eying me suspiciously, she dozed off, a whisper of a snore coming from the back of her throat. Every so often a passing car—a horn tooting or an explosive backfire—would startle her and she'd open her eyes, surprised to see the rest of us staring at her. Esther was talking in a weary drawl about the wilting of her petunias alongside the front steps.

My mother pointed. "Look."

The policemen stepped from the squad car, adjusted their trousers, and one shifted his body and nodded to the other.

Roused, excited, Molly wanted to walk to the Brenner home, but Esther, alarmed, held up her hand: No, please, no. Not our business. No.

Within minutes the front door opened and the two lawmen escorted Leah and Sarah out.

Molly made a rasping sound and shook her head. "What new black spot is that woman bringing to our street?"

Esther stared her down. "Really, now, Molly."

I walked to the edge of the porch, quietly watching. What I saw told me that this was no arrest. The police walked alongside the two women, one of them leaning into Leah's neck, saying something. But the way he held his body—the tilt of his neck, the way he held onto Leah's elbow—suggested comfort, solace.

And Leah looked shattered, drawn, stooped over, an old dragging woman. None of the vibrancy or spunk I'd seen in her before. Even Sarah, stone-faced with her head thrown back, her fingers gripping a handkerchief, seemed unusually solicitous, her hand touching Leah's lower back. That rare display of intimacy scared me more than the policeman's reassuring touch. Sarah, the woman with sass and vinegar, her sister's harsh critic, now lending comfort.

It had to do with Jacob. I felt it to my core. Standing there, I trembled.

Then, like that, they were gone.

Molly's craggy, lined face was ghostly, white. The life of the street had shifted again, and she knew it to her marrow. The new twist on old news. When I turned to Esther, she was sobbing.

• • ● • •

We knew nothing until later that evening when Ad, ashen and shaky, walked into the house. Sol, home from the cigar store, was the first to approach him, his hand grazing his son's shoulder.

"My boy," Sol said, his voice a rumble. We stood, all of us, to greet him, panicked.

Ad pulled out a kitchen chair and toppled into it.

"Ad..." his mother said anxiously.

He was shaking.

"Jacob?" More my statement than a question.

He nodded, his eyes moist.

"He's dead?" From Esther.

"Thank God, no." Ad smiled thinly at his mother. "But he's hospitalized. He's unconscious. In a coma."

"Tell us," I demanded.

Across from me my mother sat with her eyes closed.

Ad sighed. He didn't know where to begin, a run of incoherent speech, a voice so soft that his mother nudged him quietly. "Please, Adolph. I don't understand."

His voice cracked. "I heard it on the street so I stopped back at their house. Leah was at the hospital but Sarah had come home." He sucked in his breath, his words broken. "Sarah told me the horrible news."

"Is he going to be all right?" Real concern in Molly's voice. "That poor boy."

Ad deliberated. "I don't know."

"But what happened?" I begged. "Jacob doesn't leave the house. He hides away." Except nights, midnight ghosts in the deserted street. The dancing shadow silhouetted against a white-hot sky.

"Uncle Ezra got real worried. He stopped in but Jacob refused to see him." A sad smile. "The same with me, his oldest friend. Shutting us out. Going a little crazy, maybe. But Ezra kept at him, even banging on Jacob's bedroom door. He talked to Jacob, whispering through the door, demanding, according to what Leah told Sarah. Leah told Ezra to leave him alone. But he convinced Jacob to go with him. Leah, rushing in from the kitchen, saw them speeding off in Ezra's car."

"How did Jacob look?" I asked.

He shrugged. "She only saw them leaving. She was surprised—and bothered. She doesn't trust Uncle Ezra."

"No one does," I commented. "Too oily a confection."

"Edna, for Lord's sake." My mother cast a baleful eye on me.

I wasn't happy and drummed my fingers on the table. Ad's eyes watched my nervous hand, mesmerized. "Jacob had something to say," I told him. "I'm convinced of it. Ezra wanted him to keep still."

"How do you know that?" Ad asked.

"I don't."

My mother *tsk*ed. "Edna, please stay out of this."

Impatient, I cut in. "Tell us what happened."

"Well, Ezra's version."

"He was there?"

Ad bit his lip. "Right there. He was trying to shake Jacob out of his blue spell, afraid there'd be another period of…of depression, so he breezed around the streets with Jacob, out to the lake, stopping at a chop suey place on Thirty-first Street, stopping for ice cream at Nathan's Ice Cream Parlor, even going to a movie at the Vista up on Forty-third Street. Weird, he said, the way Jacob acted there. They saw *Within the Law*, you know, the Norma Talmadge movie. I saw it last week with Minna. Halfway through the movie, Jacob got agitated, jumping up. He left the theater and Ezra followed him. Outside Jacob said the movie put salt in the wound he'd already opened."

"I don't know that movie," I said. "Tell me."

Ad volunteered. "It's about this girl, Mary Turner, a shop girl at this emporium, falsely charged with stealing, a trumped-up charge. She's sent to jail for three years—even though she's innocent. She didn't *do* it. Maybe the scene where she gets out of prison got Jacob all riled up. She wants revenge, but within the law, the people that did her dirt paying for it—but make them pay in a way she couldn't be touched. Anyway, Jacob ran away from Ezra, up the street, pushing through the crowd, bumping into folks, rude, staggering, loud. Ezra says he caught up with him, grabbed hold of Jacob's shoulder, trying to hold him back, maybe calm him down, but Jacob shrugged him off. 'Stay away from me. All of you.' That's what Ezra said he kept yelling. Embarrassed, folks staring at them, Ezra stepped back." Ad paused, hesitant to go on. His mother reached across the table and touched his wrist.

"And?" I prompted.

"And Jacob was standing on the corner as the streetcar approached. Ezra said Jacob was quiet, even turning toward him with a slight smile on his face. So Ezra relaxed, as they stood shoulder-to-shoulder with crowds of folks ready to cross the street. But someone jostled the crowd, some woman slipped, someone reached out to grab her, to pull her back to the curb. Everything shifted suddenly and Jacob stumbled, just feet from him, toppling in front of the streetcar. He was knocked to the ground and smashed his head."

"Oh, my Lord." Molly was trembling.

My mother's face tightened. A mixture of sadness and accusation. Lightning flashes in my head, a roar in my eardrums, panic. I turned away from her look.

"Or a suicide," I said into the silence.

Esther gasped, covered her mouth with her hand. "Oh no, it had to be an accident. Streetcars hit people all the time. I've seen…people stumble…"

Molly was staring at Ad, her jaw set, rigid. "What do you think, Adolph?"

"I don't know. I wasn't there."

"What do you think happened?" I asked Ad.

A long, unhappy silence, Ad fidgeting with the buttons on his shirt until he snapped one off. It rolled onto the floor, and Esther stooped for it. Ad's mouth went slack, his eyes half-closed.

Finally, breathing in and out, almost melodramatically, he faced me. Me—not his mother. His eyes were dull pieces of stone.

"You wanna know what I think? I think Uncle Ezra pushed Jacob in front of the streetcar."

"Adolph, no!" From his mother.

Molly gasped, clutched at her throat.

But Adolph gathered steam now, his voice booming across the kitchen. "C'mon. Face it. Uncle Ezra murdered Jacob."

"But why?" his mother pleaded.

"Because Jacob had learned that Ezra was the one who killed Ivan."

Chapter Seventeen

Jacob Brenner lay in a coma.

Two days passed, suspended time, all of us holding our breaths, frantic yet calm. Waiting. A deathwatch. Conversation muted, if at all.

Renovation completed, the five-room apartment we'd booked at the Windermere Hotel in Hyde Park was ready for us, lovely spacious rooms, morning walks to Lake Michigan one block away, to Jackson Park. My routine for summers: writing nine to four, a walk, back home for a bath. Quiet rooms, except for the rumble and toot of the Illinois Central suburban trains as they passed.

But now I was hesitant to leave the Newmann home. Not yet, a few days more, graciously invited by Esther and Sol, and the reason was Jacob Brenner. Though my mother said nothing, I sensed she also wanted to be nearby. A harsh woman, my mother, but one easily made sad by the agony of others.

Esther busied herself in the kitchen, baking a Black Forest cake that we'd all ceremoniously carry to Leah's home that afternoon. I'd called, asked whether such a visit might be acceptable, and Leah hadn't spoken for a moment. An awkward moment, but she finally said yes, though I could hear the hesitation in her voice.

Hearing of our planned visit, Molly balked. She was snide. "Have a good time."

"Please," Esther begged her.

"You bring cake after a funeral," Molly insisted. "Not before."

"We've known Jacob all our lives."

Molly said nothing. The old woman was sitting on a kitchen chair, her lethal cane resting on her lap. At Esther's "Please" she gripped her cane, tapping firmly on the floor, her fiery punctuation.

Molly turned to my mother. "You going, Julia?"

Tap tap tap.

My mother was startled, unhappy being singled out. She glanced at Molly, and in a croaking voice said quietly, "This visit is for Jacob, Molly."

Molly snorted, struggled to stand, waved the cane menacingly in the air, barely clipping Esther, who ducked, and slowly tottered out of the room, exaggerating her movement, her slight limp.

Esther whispered, "I'll pay a price for this long after you two leave."

I spoke up. "Leah will wonder where she is, no?"

Esther shook her head. "She'll *know*. Molly harbors a lifetime of resentment. You don't give up such dislike easily." A thin, mischievous smile. "Her first words about Leah, I recall: 'A beautiful woman ain't no gift from God.' Then she said, 'No good will come of this. You mark my words.' So, I suppose, Ivan's murder and Leah's arrest proved her…her dire prophecy. Molly has never been one to forgive—or forget. Ask her about the time Sol was fifteen and forgot to come home from a park for her birthday." She shuddered. "Still talked of."

"She has one weakness, though," I noted.

"What?" Esther stared into my face.

"Ad. She indulges your son as though he's the golden child,"

Esther bit her lip. "I know. Poor Adolph, the heir to the throne. But what throne? My Harriet, two years younger than Adolph, a quiet and pretty girl, smart as a whip, was ignored."

"How sad!"

"That's why she married young and moved to Cleveland. She got tired of sitting in darkness, though Sol and I fawned and flattered. Adolph got all the smiles. So…so Old Country, no? The man is the…chosen of God."

My mother, surprisingly, muttered the old ritualistic prayer. "'Thank God I was not born a woman.'"

"How sad!" I repeated.

Of course, I'd spent a lifetime in the shadow of my sister, Fannie, now married and happily away from my life. True, my mother grudgingly accepted the generous alms I offered from my increasingly large bounty. A short story sold to *Cosmopolitan* garnered her that new fur coat she coveted or some glittery bauble, shrilly demanded but then denigrated. So I understood Harriet's flight from family…but I was bound, the indentured servant in the Ferber household…

Esther was talking softly. "Molly has spent all of my married life waiting for me to blunder. After over forty years of a good marriage, Sol and I, I still got to prove myself." She sighed as she glanced toward the doorway. "It gets a little…exhausting."

As she said that last word—an "exhausting" that was world-weary but strangely comical, elongated and in a purposely Old Country inflection—my mother and I burst out laughing. Then Esther, surprised at herself, joined us, and we sat there, giggling like small girls in a schoolyard.

Leah's house was an oven. The windows were shut against the afternoon heat, the quiet rooms deadly. As Sarah let us in, deftly taking the cake from Esther's hands and disappearing into the kitchen with it, we noticed Leah standing back against the fireplace mantel. She was staring over our shoulders, probably for Molly, but I was watching my mother, whose exclamation of "The nerve!" had begun my treacherous journey into the facts of the murder. A flicker of disapproval in her face, though she was long practiced in the art of deception, the actress who'd learned to deal with the annoying patrons of the family notions store she once ran back in Appleton. So her smiled "Hello" was acceptable, though I noticed she didn't extend her hand. Leah pointed to chairs in the dining room, and we sat down around the table.

Sarah served iced tea and the cake, but she said nothing, watching us warily. Once, accidentally, I caught her eye, but her stare was difficult to read—peculiarly, a trace of anger that baffled me, though in seconds her eyes assumed the blank look she always wore. That also troubled me.

Surprisingly, Leah was dressed in a current style, not the dowdy, matronly dress she'd worn before, but, rather, a modish lavender blouse with filigreed lace around the neck, and a straight-lined black skirt, snug at the hips, knee-length, modern. She looked younger than her sixty or so years, nervously jumpy—someone wide-awake because something unexpected might happen. Her snow-white hair, luminous, was pulled into a schoolmarm bun, secured with a black velvet bow.

"Any news on Jacob?" Esther asked.

Leah shook her head and suddenly, gulping, began to sob. She turned her head away, closed her eyes, and breathed in. "No, he's dying."

Said, the awful words stung the room, sucked the air out of us.

"Oh, my Lord," Esther whispered. "We're sorry."

"He never woke up."

"A horrible accident," Esther said.

Sarah made a growling sound, deep and loud, that made us start.

"Yes?" I asked.

"There are all kinds of accidents," she told us.

"But Ezra said…"

Sarah broke in. "Ah, yes, beloved Uncle Ezra, tour guide through the dangerous Chicago streets, the guardian angel."

Leah snapped at her. "Stop this, Sarah. For heaven's sake."

"I'm only saying what you are thinking."

The two sisters eyed each other, a penetrating look I couldn't read.

"You've never been able to read my mind, Sarah," Leah countered.

Sarah smirked. "Just as well. Dark, unchartered territory there."

Leah made a clicking sound, her dark eyes flashing.

Esther was following the nasty exchange, confused, ready to cry. Exasperated, my mother bridled, shifted in her seat, half-rising. She adjusted the sleeve of her dress, pulling at it, a nervous gesture I recognized—a signal to me that she was ready to leave. "*Nu,*" she said, "we must go."

No one had touched the iced tea or the cake.

But I wasn't ready to leave. "Sarah, certainly you don't think someone pushed Jacob in front of that streetcar? On purpose?"

My mother screamed. "Edna, have you no decency?" She glanced at Leah, who was watching me carefully. At that moment our eyes locked, and I realized she'd also wondered. She was nodding her head.

I didn't apologize but addressed Sarah. "Now what are you saying, Sarah?"

"You've met Uncle Ezra."

Leah reached out and touched her arm. "Maybe not now, Sarah."

Sarah jerked back her arm. "Then when?"

"Not now."

Sarah flicked her head to the side and rolled her tongue over her lips. Flushed, jittery, she was readying some remark when the doorbell chimed. Leah turned to her sister. "Who?"

Reluctantly, Sarah ushered Ella and Emma into the dining room. They stood behind the chairs, not happy to discover the neighbors sitting at the table. Speaking in a low, trembling voice, one of them said to Sarah, "We've come from Mount Sinai."

Leah tensed up, her hand raised against her cheek. "And?"

"Nothing. No change." She stared blankly at her mother.

"Sit down, Ella. Please." Then she spoke to the other sister. "Emma, I'm happy you've come."

Emma glanced at Ella, as if to say: Are you satisfied? I came, after all. Emma, the twin who believed in her mother's guilt. The prodigal daughter, grudgingly visiting the home she'd left three years ago. She sat down and avoided the staring faces, the stranger at the wrong party.

Ella had an edge to her voice, "Emma wanted to come."

Emma scowled as her head bowed into her folded hands in her lap. But when she caught her mother's watchful eye, her face softened. "I'm sorry," she said simply. Then, a catch in her throat, she echoed her own words, but louder now. "I'm sorry."

So she'd moved past the belief in her mother's guilt, at least for now, perhaps because of Jacob. Or, more likely, Ella's emphatic order. No matter, because her words "I'm sorry"—heartfelt, spontaneous—cracked something within her, and her body slumped in the chair. She'd wanted to come home, I realized. She'd wanted this overdue reconciliation. Silent now, but content as an old cat by the hearth, she half-closed her eyes as though ready for sleep. A curious transformation—the reluctant daughter back at home. Strangely, though, Ella, the sister who visited her mother, the one who professed her mother's innocence, now was on edge, anxious, her eyes blinking rapidly, as if she'd been accused of some transgression and didn't know how to respond. She was the one ready to flee the room.

Leah asked Emma about Hull House. "I understand you're working for Jane Addams with the young Russian immigrant girls."

Emma seemed surprised that her mother had heard that news. "Volunteering. Three afternoons a week. I'm teaching sewing to young girls. And English at the same time."

Ella grumbled. "There's no money coming in." She shot a look at Emma. "This won't last."

"I like it." Emma's voice rose. She smiled at me. "I was working two days a week as a seamstress. For a cruel woman. We both did, me and Ella."

Ella's tone got bitter. "But we need money for the rent, Emma."

Emma frowned. "No, we don't. Herman pays…"

"For everything," Sarah finished. "The rich brother."

"I don't like it," Ella said. "Emma is making a mistake."

Leah put her hand to her head as though squelching a headache. "You can move back here, Ella."

Ella jumped. "Oh, I don't think so."

"We may have to," Emma said, surprisingly. Then she whispered, "Although I think I'd like to live on my own."

Emma, the dormouse under Ella's severe control, had found some spunk. Feisty, I thought, this girl who'd had a taste of independence, and now, so late in her life, was daring to counter her sister.

"A single woman can't live…" Ella began, but stopped.

Sarah snickered, "Just like when you were little girls. If one said left, the other said right."

Ella bristled. "I always knew what was best for Emma. Because…"

Emma glared at her.

Leah finished for Ella with a nervous laugh, "But they both ended up headed in the same direction."

"Because of Ella." Emma's voice had no kindness in it.

Ella glowered at Emma, the muscles prominent in her neck. "Not anymore."

Silence in the room, my mother again mumbling about leaving. This time, nudging me, she stood, adjusted the seams of her dress.

The doorbell chimed again, but before Sarah or Leah could move, the front door opened. Uncle Ezra walked in. Nothing sheepish about his entry, unannounced, because he planted himself in the entryway, his face flushed. Leah started to speak but Ezra spoke over her words. "No one answers the telephone in this house. Why pay for that infernal contraption if it's not used? It seems to me…"

"Because we knew it was you," Sarah said snidely.

He narrowed his eyes. "I told you I'd call at nine, Sarah."

"I know," Sarah said again, cheerfully. "As I said, we knew it was you."

"I was at the hospital," Leah said, placating. "I didn't…"

Ezra addressed Sarah, "At times like this, a family must come together, support…" He paused. "You know…*mish pokhe…* the family."

Sarah rolled her eyes. "Oh, please, Ezra, don't you get tired of being an ass?"

"Enough," said Leah. "Ezra, please sit down. Join us. We have guests."

But he didn't. He surveyed us all, his steely gaze condemning. Finally he rested his stern glance on me, and waited.

"What?" I asked.

"I'm surprised you are here, Edna."

"I'm concerned about Jacob—and Leah."

He grunted but said nothing at first. Rather, he tapped his foot on the floor, the pouting child. Then, purposely, he spat out the words: "I suppose you came to apologize."

My mother spoke up. "My Edna doesn't need to apologize for anything."

I held up my hand. "I can fight my own battles, Mother."

Ezra, eyes bright, mimicked a look of innocence. "This is a battle?"

I glowered at him. "A skirmish, really. My opponent woefully at a disadvantage."

"And why is that?"

"You don't understand that you've already lost."

That confused him, but he stopped talking. Sarah was grinning, actually pointing a derisive finger at him.

"Outnumbered, dear Ezra," she told him flatly. "Look around you. Women in the kitchen, in the dining room...they *overwhelm*." She counted. "Seven against one. Lucky seven. You make us unlucky, Ezra—eight is doom."

Leah was tired of the squabble. "What's wrong with you two? Do you hear yourselves? We should be thinking of one thing now." Once she started, she went on and on, a sad ramble, until all of us—not me, really—tried to look penitent and sorrowful. Ezra, too—he never altered his look of disgust and condescension.

The doorbell chimed. "Good God," Sarah said, "is this a hub of the Illinois Central?"

A sheepish Ad walked in, trailed by a jittery Minna. Ad said nothing and seemed surprised and bothered by the number of folks gathered there, but Minna entered talking, thrusting out a white box tied with twine. "Cookies from Bremmer Cookies." She was holding out the box toward Sarah but recognized her error, swung around and bumped into Ad's side as she searched for Leah. Ad watched her, annoyed, but Leah approached her, accepted the box and embraced the woman. Minna stepped back, colliding with the edge of a table, and kept muttering, "Sorry, sorry, sorry." She viewed the room in a panic and said, "I haven't been here in ages."

Leah followed Minna's gaze. Perhaps some in the room flashed back to a time when Minna had been the sweetheart of Herman until Ivan, finding fault with the bumbling girl, had nixed that union. Minna once sat at that very table…dinners, plans, dreams. Leah, of course, had given them her blessing, so she'd liked Minna—something apparent now as she held her, Minna's face buried in her shoulder.

"Ad told me. I didn't know. How is…?"

Leah shook her head slowly, comforting. "It's all right, Minna. Sit, sit. Please."

Ad sat at her side, though all the attention centered on Minna, frail and trembling. I watched Ad. Drawn, weary, shattered. He'd shaved but missed a spot near his left ear, a faint patch of beard stubble that seemed endearing to me. The Arrow collar he'd clipped to the pale blue shirt was coming undone, poorly fastened. Despite his sharp-pressed pants and the polished button shoes, he looked disheveled. A man who hadn't cared that morning as he bathed and dressed for the day.

"Were you at the hospital?" I asked him.

He nodded. "Yeah, I stopped in before I got to Minna's. Nothing doing. They wouldn't let me into his room."

Ezra spoke up. "Family only, young man."

Ad's face got hot. "Jacob is my best friend. Always has been."

"It's all right, Ad," Leah reassured him. "He *knows* you're his best friend. No matter what. Some things don't got to be said."

Ad's expression got dreamy. "I keep thinking about my last talk with him. A few days ago. Just before he started to avoid me—to avoid everyone. He shuffled along like an old man, shoulders down, droopy eyes. You couldn't shake him out of it, and I kept asking what was wrong. 'Tell me, tell me. C'mon, Jacob. Tell me.' But he'd get this funny look in his eyes, that lazy sleepwalker's look he sometimes had, and stare at me. Like he was already far away from the world. Lord, it scared me. It was so—crazy…deep. But at the same time I felt he wanted me to *help* him. So close to me, the way he stood."

"What happened?" I asked.

Ad stopped a second, catching his breath. "What he said chilled me." Another pause, his eyes half shut.

"What?" I prompted.

Ad peered into my eyes, but he glanced for a second at Leah. "He said he'd failed his mother."

Leah tensed up. She wrapped her arms around her chest, and swayed. "But he never failed me. He knew that. He had nothing to do with…"

Ad couldn't look at her now. "He believed he *did*. Then, like that, his eyes got hard as glass, real scary like, and he said to me, a finger jabbing in my chest, 'Don't you know it's time?' 'What?' I asked. 'Time, time, time. It's time.'" Ad swallowed. "It was like some chant."

Sarah spoke too loudly. "What does that mean? Are you saying he planned to kill himself?"

Ad gasped. "God, no." Then, fiery, "No, dammit." He shot a look at Ezra, then at me. Ad had announced Ezra as Jacob's attempted murderer last night. Now, as Ad's eyes focused on him, Ezra squirmed. He'd been lighting a cigarette and dropped the wooden match. He swore under his breath.

"Ad," I said, "Jacob was sinking into his troubles. It's hard to know what he meant by that."

"I dunno." Helpless, a whimper. But he went on. "Then he said, 'Should I let the past stay dead?' He mentioned those days when we all sat around the back room at Nathan's. 'Disgusting, all of it,' he said. Then, like that, he closed up."

Sarah said, "If Jacob comes out of his coma, maybe he'll tell us what really happened."

Ezra glared. "Be realistic, Sarah. He's not going to make it."

Ad shot him a look. "How convenient."

"What does that mean?"

Ad didn't answer.

By chance, I'd been watching the twins as Ad told the story of his last conversation with Jacob. Ad had a drifting, rolling voice. His narrative was intoxicating. I watched his handsome face, the deep lines under the eyes and at the corners of his mouth that, in a man like Ad, added to his charm. Though not to everyone, especially Ezra, ready to pounce. But to Ella and Emma, rapt and attentive, mouths slightly open, heads tilted back, Ad's tale was powerful, the stuff of heroes. It struck me then that both women, bound by sisterhood and spinsterhood and the awful poverty of women on their own, shared an abiding infatuation with Ad, one that probably dated back to childhood years. The plain, forgettable sisters watching the handsome, debonair play-boys, Ad and Jacob, cavorting on the porch, in the yard, squiring the popular girls to basement clubs and sandlot baseball games. Quietly, they held onto their hunger, unspoken maybe even to each other, but clearly still alive. Ad must have known—how could he not? Such unabashed devotion in their eyes. Because even now, sensing their riveted looks, he faltered, smiling, and then, embarrassed, he reached for Minna's hand.

"We have to leave." He nodded toward Leah.

Ezra made a dismissive sound, then seemed to regret it.

With a mystical power I'd not anticipated, Leah slowly began to shoo us toward the door, the loving mother hen, tending, pecking, a flicker of an eyelid, the curve of her chin. It was magnificent to watch, so effective, so seamless. There she was, the woman sprung from isolation in the leper colony, the disgraced woman, the alleged murderer of the man who once lived in that house with her—there she was, benignly leading everyone to the door, the schoolteacher herding stubborn or dim-witted children. *Thank you, thank you, so kind...*

As Emma and Ella moved, they whispered to each other, saying something we couldn't hear but nevertheless communicating some bitterness. Bickering that would probably end with a sisterly feud that would last for years—the deadly silence, the nasty gossip, the noxious bile. I knew that cruel story because my sister Fannie and I didn't speak for years at a time. So, too, Ella and Emma, Siamese twins joined at their loneliness, had now found a way to leave each other. Ezra seemed loathe to leave, smiling at Leah who ignored him—that sleek, expensive man, gussied up with pomade and moustache wax and a flashy garnet pinky ring—a man no one ever trusted, could never trust again. And Sarah, watching her exiled sister take control of a house she'd ruled for years, the prison matron with the cruel jibe—she herself stood back, watching, her jaw set in disapproval, her eyes wary.

And, of course, Jacob's spirit hovered over us, the lost lamb, shattered, now dying...or already dead...

I was the last one to leave, trailing after my mother and Esther. Ad and Minna were the first, in a hurry. Ella and Emma and Ezra moved, then stopped, debated, then left together.

Leah shook her head as she leaned into my neck.

"Edna."

I turned back. "You all right, Leah?"

"Of course, I am." A pause. "I have no choice now." Then her voice trembled. "You know, Edna, I didn't kill Ivan, but somehow I destroyed my family."

She walked away.

Chapter Eighteen

The trouble began as daylight waned. All afternoon the heat built, miserable, the air clammy, and we waited for the thunderstorm that would do nothing to end the long hot spell. The sky darkened and we waited. A few drops fell, a sprinkle, teasing us, wisps of steam rising from the hot asphalt. Then the light began to fade, the heat getting worse, a furnace. Everyone wilted. I sat on the porch and waited for the storm to come.

Herman Brenner and his wife, Naomi, pulled up in his town car, idling in front of Leah's home. They debated stepping out—I could see Naomi's head swiveling back and forth as though she were arguing with her husband—but finally Herman stepped out and slammed the door. He wasn't happy.

A shadow moved in the rear seat, leaned forward to say something to Naomi, and in seconds Emma opened the door and walked out. Naomi stayed in the car.

Emma yelled to her brother, "She won't get out."

"Then leave her, for Christ's sake."

Emma without her sister? Sitting in the backseat of brother Herman's automobile? So here was the recalibrated twin, long convinced of her mother's guilt and hammered into obedience by Ella, now visiting—without her sister.

She spotted me on the porch, said something to her brother, who waved indifferently. He walked to the passenger door, leaned in to say something to Naomi, and she finally got out, though not without grunting her unhappiness. The three stood on the sidewalk, waiting, watching one another. Naomi glanced up into the twilight sky, and pointed. Again, Herman waved, but this time the gesture seemed a salute, very Prussian military. I waved back. Then, in a body, they moved toward me.

"Edna," Herman yelled, "no one answers my telephone calls to the house." He jerked his head toward his mother's home. "Have you seen signs of life there?"

"I have no idea, Herman. I don't keep track of the neighbors."

He scoffed. "Edna, Edna. You expect me to believe that?"

"Believe what you will, Herman." I turned to Emma. "Emma, a return visit? Where is Ella?"

Emma waited for her brother to answer for her. When he didn't, she said, "My sister is not happy with me."

"And why is that?"

Naomi bent into her, her fingers brushing Emma's sleeve. As she whispered something I couldn't hear, Emma shrugged her off. "She resents my…I was the bad sister, the unforgiving one. She trumpeted my mother—I refused. Now I want to return home and she…she's unhappy."

"I don't understand."

Herman was glaring at Emma, but he spoke to me. "You don't have to, Edna. This has nothing to do with you."

Naomi was tugging at her sleeve. "Could we go and get your mother?"

Herman explained to me, "The doctor called earlier. We need to be there now."

"Jacob."

"We're losing him today."

My heart raced. I stepped off the porch. "I'm so sorry to hear that."

Herman stepped closer to me, ready to say something, but simply stared at me.

The door behind me opened, and Minna strolled out onto the porch, though she was speaking to someone behind her. When she spotted us, she stopped, alarm in her face, took a step backward, and then forced a smile. "Herman." Again, her voice lower, "Herman."

Probably Herman was a man who rarely got flustered, had long practiced his stoicism, but staring up at the woman he'd once planned on marrying, the woman he swore undying love to and then abandoned, he stiffened, his mouth twitching, and insanely one of his hands gripped a thigh. His shoulders hunched up. He stole a look at his frowning wife, someone doubtless aware of her husband's first love affair, but Naomi wore a cruel smile, nervously pleased with her husband's unexpected discomfort.

"It's been a long time, Minna," Herman got out.

"Yes, it has." Cold, distant, so unlike the bubbly, scattered Minna who giggled into Ad's ear.

"How've you been?"

"Fine." Minna managed to make the throwaway remark biting. She was wearing a pink bow in her hair, a Mary Pickford affectation, and she checked to see whether her little-girl look was intact, running her fingers through her ringlets. A failed move, however, because she made it lopsided so that she seemed the madcap ingénue in a vaudeville farce.

"It's been a long time." Herman repeated the words, then regretted them, flicking his head away.

Emma tried to maneuver him away, but he was rooted to the sidewalk.

It dawned on me then that Herman still loved Minna. Settled now, middle-aged, moneyed, the father of two children, ages fifteen and thirteen, and a loyal if plodding husband, pragmatic Herman still held a lingering romanticism about the girl he had loved when he was a young man. A carefree bachelor then, his father's awful edict—exiling unacceptable Minna—had driven him into a marriage that probably satisfied his father but no one else, least of all Herman. Minna represented a moment of freedom he'd walked away from. And a real love had blossomed in the mechanical man. Now, on the hot sidewalk as we waited for the thunderstorm, Herman froze. This was what his dead father Ivan had wrought. This...this awful paralysis.

"Fine." Minna repeated the same word. A curse now, wrought with steel.

Herman shrugged. "You visiting Esther?"

Perhaps he didn't know about Minna's long courtship with Ad, though that surprised me. Yet it was possible. Since Ivan's murder fifteen years back, Herman was an infrequent visitor to the neighborhood, and the Newmanns kept their distance from the cursed house next door.

"I'm marrying Ad."

Herman seemed puzzled. "Adolph?"

"Of course."

He squinted. "But I'd heard you were seeing him *years* ago."

She faltered. "Yes, we were—I mean, are. Have been…" The troublesome conjugations threw her off, and she finished with: "We'll be…still."

"Minna." My voice was sharp. "Minna, go back into the house."

She didn't move. There they were, the two of them, back twenty years ago, ignoring the intervening years of other marriages and other engagements and other disappointments. And the horrific murder next door—something not to be imagined.

Minna dropped into a chair, her face crumpled. Oh my God, I thought: Don't let her cry. Not now. Not on the porch.

At that moment Molly came outside and, smart woman, understood what was happening. "Minna," she said firmly, "Ad is waiting for you." Then, cane tapping, she addressed Herman. "Herman, if you are intending a visit to your mother, you'd best be on." She lifted the cane and pointed dramatically to Leah's home.

But Herman still didn't move.

A sudden *wooza wooza wooza* jolted us, as Ezra pulled up in his roadster. He leaned on the insulting horn again, pulling alongside the three people standing on the sidewalk. Emma let out a mouse-like squeal, was embarrassed by it, and then giggled. Naomi, eying the interloper with steely eyes, took a step toward the idling car and cleared her throat. Herman, however, produced the most bizarre response—he cursed Ezra roundly, a string of *goddamn yous* while raising his fist into the air. I could never imagine Herman so out of control, so maddened, nor could he, because almost at once he froze in place, blinking furiously, affronted by the behavior of a street lout.

Meanwhile, Ezra put the automobile in gear and slid to a halt in front of Leah's home. He threw back his head as though he'd just heard the most hilarious story. By the time he stepped out of the car, Herman was right there, face crimson and hands flapping at his side.

"My heart went into my mouth," Herman roared. "That infernal horn. Do you have a brain in that head of yours?"

Ezra ignored that. "Is Leah home?"

"She's not answering the telephone," Naomi told him.

"Maybe she's not home."

The two men stood there, facing each other, their dislike palpable. Ezra was spiffy in a charcoal gray summer seersucker suit, a creamy white shirt open at the neck, and a rose-colored silk handkerchief peeking out of his breast pocket. On his head he wore a bleached straw bowler. Next to him, Herman, the younger man, came off as the drab poor cousin in his wrinkled black suit, buttoned up to the neck, an old-fashioned business-man's black cravat, and a brimmed cap with attached goggles that he always donned for motoring. A tad ridiculous, his look, especially the ludicrous goggles, and made more so next to the dapper uncle. Herman's blurted out curses made no secret of his dislike of Ezra, and Ezra—long used to being the despised blood relative who visited—couldn't have cared less.

"I thought I'd take her to the hospital," Ezra said. "To see Jacob."

Herman glanced back at me—and his eyes lingered on Minna, watching from a seat on the porch. He sneered, "I *still* don't know what happened that day with Jacob."

That surprised Ezra, who fumbled. "He slipped…"

"And you couldn't stop him?" Tense, snide.

Ezra squirmed. "I couldn't reach him."

Herman persisted. "I can't get a picture of it, Jacob falling, toppling." A sneer. "With you at his side."

Ezra spoke through clenched teeth. "You have more of an

interest in your brother *now* than in all the years he walked these streets." He glanced up and down Monroe Street.

"What does that mean?"

"C'mon, Herman. You never *liked* Jacob."

"He's my brother."

"You saw him as a lazy, foolish poet, some silly boy who looked like your mother and flirted with the girls."

"He's my brother!" Yelling now.

Ezra insisted, "I'm the one who was his friend. Me, Herman, my boy. And Ad next door. His own family laughed at him."

Herman stepped closer. "For three years now you slink around here since our mother is back home. You don't think I hear about that? Uncle Ezra, knocking on the door. Uncle Ezra, bringing baskets of food. Uncle Ezra, taking little Jacob for a ride in his tin lizzie. Uncle Ezra taking Jacob for a boat ride on the river. Ezra, Ezra, Ezra."

Ezra snarled, "So what?"

"The truth is that I don't think you ever cared for Jacob. It's my mother you were visiting."

Uncle Ezra glanced at the Newmann porch. Minna had stood up, moving closer to the front steps, though Molly reached out to touch her elbow. "Meaning?"

"You know damn well what it means. You've crawled around here for years now, even when Papa was alive. *He* knew it. He warned you. I *heard* him tell you to get lost. Mama tossed you over for Papa but that didn't stop you. Flattering, smiling, laughing, a silly little boy. My father warned you to stay away." He faltered. "A…a *shedim*…you demon."

Ezra said nothing, checking out the quiet street. He glanced up into the sky, watching for the thundershowers. The sky was darkening. Finally, he grumbled, "A street brawl, Herman? Is that what you're reduced to?"

Red-faced, Herman poked him in the chest. "The way you ogled my mother."

Ezra stepped back, unsure of his footing. "*Everyone* watched your mother, dear Herman. A beautiful woman. Ivan *liked* that.

He had his precious little doll. He got meaner and meaner as he got older and older, jealous, cruel."

Herman's voice was a low rumble. Another poke in the chest. Ezra flinched. "You want to jump back into her life now. You want to go back to when you were young and…and you thought *you'd* be marrying her." Unwittingly, he spun around and stared at Minna on the porch. It was a knee-jerk reaction, its meaning not lost on himself, or me, or doubtless the listening Minna. She tensed up, a trickle of tears streaming down her cheeks.

"C'mon," Herman's wife pleaded, tugging his sleeve. "Do you realize how foolish the two of you look in the street? Street urchins, pushcart boys."

Herman ignored her.

Ezra put his face close to Herman's—and suddenly, bending his neck, spat onto the pavement. Herman sucked in his breath.

The door behind me swung open and Ad, hearing the brouhaha in the street, stormed out, slamming the screen door behind him. "Jesus Christ," he yelled, "what's going on out here? I'm in the kitchen…" He hesitated. "Minna?" She stood there, crumpled up, tears on her cheeks. "What the hell happened?"

"Ad," I began, "it's nothing. Don't…"

"Minna, what's the matter?" He glanced toward the skirmish in the street. At that moment, regrettably, Herman heard Ad's bluster and turned, though his eyes rested on Minna. Ad fumed. "What did he say to you?"

"Nothing," she muttered.

"Ad," I went on. "Nothing."

Molly said to him, "Go back into the house, Adolph."

Ignoring her, Ad touched Minna's shoulder, a quick, comforting gesture that made her sob harder, which in turn enflamed him. Always the neighborhood knight, the tilter of imaginary windmills, Ad repeated, "Minna, did he say something to hurt you?"

She shook her head vigorously and tried to smile. "I don't know why I'm crying, Ad. It's all this…yelling…Herman and Ezra…in the street. Jacob is dying and…"

Her words ignited Ad's temper, and he pounded one fist into

the other. Madness—the next act in this silly street revue, men acting like loutish boys.

"Herman," Ad yelled.

But Herman ignored Ad's fury. Instead, he'd turned back to Ezra who was sneering something about the roly-poly burgher in the rumpled suit. Herman said something unintelligible and stepped back. He nodded at Naomi, though she regarded him coolly, then sought Emma who'd stepped off the sidewalk and was standing in a clump of bushes.

He took a step away.

But Ezra, still raging, lunged forward and, thrusting out his arm, slapped his nephew full in the face.

So resounding and unexpected a blow, so marrow-deep ugly, so...so *wrong*. I breathed in, and Minna, behind me, cried out, "No!" She started to hiccough.

Stunned, Herman blubbered, rubbed his face with his palm, and sputtered, "You..."

Emboldened. Ezra pushed his palm against Herman's chest, and Herman stepped to the side. His foot turned and he nearly toppled, but he grabbed onto Ezra's sleeve. His uncle shrugged him off, but slapped his face again. Herman bellowed but then, grunting, hunched over and plowed his head into Ezra's chest. Ezra let out an *oomph* sound, the air out of a balloon, and staggered back against the fender of his car.

Out of breath, heaving, the two men stared at each other, eyes hooded. An ugly space between then, wrestlers ready to grapple.

Suddenly Herman's eyes found Minna, locked eyes with her.

Ad, incensed, flew off the porch, nearly falling over, and stood between both men. He spun around, furious, pointing first at Herman, then at Ezra.

From the bushes, bent over as though in pain, Emma whimpered, "Jacob. Think of Jacob."

Ezra stormed at her. "Yeah, you love your brother, little sister."

She cried out, hurt.

Ad yelled at Ezra, though his frantic glance took in Herman.

"Yeah—Jacob. How he hated the way you…you followed his mother. He stopped. "Evil Ezra."

Brutal, frightening words, belligerent. Ezra scrunched up his face. "You—you hypocrite. Ivan warned all the boys…even you." Ad made a fist, but it was Herman, rubbing his cheek and breathing hard, who gripped Ad's arm. "No, no. He's not worth it."

But Ad would have none of it. Hotheaded, spinning around like a wobbly top, he wasn't sure what to do. Back on the porch, Minna was rocking, mewing loudly, her tiny hands fluttering around her face like jittery birds. "Ad, no, no. Please." Her voice hollow, words so mumbled that only I could hear her.

"Damn you, Ezra." Ad was panting. "Jacob dying—my buddy." His voice a ragged blend of yelling and sobbing now, sailing over the street. "He wanted you away from the house—because of his mother. He went with you to keep you from coming *into* the house."

"Nonsense," Ezra hissed. "Funny, though. These last days the *only* person he'd see was…me. Not you, Ad—he kicked everybody away from him. Only me. *Me.*"

A long, dead space. Ad spat out, "You thought that he killed his father…" He stopped. "He told me *you* kept *asking* him—'What do you remember? That day. Tell me. Tell me.' Why did you ask?"

"Because he *knew* something."

The words made Ad see red. Blindly, he thrust out his arm at Ezra, an ineffective jab that grazed his cheek. Surprised, Ezra punched the air, grunting, but immediately grabbed onto Ad's sleeve, tearing it.

"Goddamn you," Ad swore, and spinning around, yanked Ezra's necktie, bunching it in his fingers.

Ezra made a gurgling sound, stumbled, but, sidestepping around Ad, lunged at Herman who'd taken a step toward him. Ezra barreled into him and Herman staggered back. Getting his footing, Herman assumed a cartoonish pugilist's stance, one foot in front of the other, fists thrust out in front of him, elbows bent.

A dark laugh escaped Ezra's throat as he pointed at Herman, mocking his ridiculous stance. Dancing around Herman, Ezra didn't expect his nephew's sudden punch to the mouth. Ad laughed out loud.

Ezra, mumbling that Ad should get out of the way—"Mind your own goddamn business"— ran the back of his hand across his mouth. A smear of blood from a cut lip. He whimpered, blubbered "Blood, blood," as Herman, still in that outlandish pose of a gentleman boxer, rocked on his heels.

Ad shot a look back at the porch. Minna was sobbing. He hesitated—waiting. But I realized—and he realized—that Minna was staring at Herman, her body trembling.

Huffing, head bobbing like a circus clown, Ad crashed into Herman, who toppled back and bounced off a car fender. He slapped at Herman's face, but Herman kept striking out, loose-limbed swings that missed his target. Circling the other two men, Ezra poked and jabbed, the pesky gnat. Herman kicked Ezra's shin, and he howled. The three men slammed against one another. A tangle of awkward bodies—tripping, bumping, arms and legs that aimed but mostly missed. Roustabout vaudeville slapstick. Helter-skelter sad sack comics executing exaggerated kicks that knocked them off balance.

Then, out of the tangle of flailing arms, a vagrant kick—Ad's foot into Ezra's groin. The old man bellowed, fell to his knees, and cried out.

Exhausted, the men fell apart, bodies sprawled on the hot pavement, Ezra moaning, Ad wheezing, Herman's breath a scratchy rasp.

Over—the slapdash scuffle of men who never thought they'd ever raise a fist at another. A trickle of blood across Ezra's cheek. Herman picked street gravel from a bruise on his forehead. Ad's head buried in his shoulder, a patch of bare flesh exposed where his shirt had ripped.

It was over—we waited. A stunned Greek chorus, we held our breath. Emma whimpered in the bushes. Minna had fallen into a chair, her face buried in her lands. Naomi had disappeared—I spotted her inside the car, the door open.

An eerie silence—only the labored breathing of the men.

Herman rolled onto his knees. Ad struggled to sit up. He grasped Ezra's forearm, pulled him into a sitting position.

A crackle of thunder, the sky suddenly dark and awful, the air heavy, the setting sun masked. In the distant sky a flash of lightning, brilliant. Big droplets began to fall, *splat splat splat* on the hot pavement. Hobbling, bent at the waist, Ezra hurried to put up the top of his convertible, clumsily falling into the automobile. He rested his head on the steering wheel. Herman groaned as he lumbered to his car to crank up his windows, then sat still inside, his head inclined against the seat rest. Only Ad didn't move. Standing now, he wrapped his arms around his chest, swaying. Raindrops covered him. He was sobbing.

Dark now, the storm gathering steam.

One drop, another, *plop plop. Splat.* A hot breeze blew rain onto the porch. The thick-leafed maples rustled. No one moved now, Ezra and Herman still in their cars. Naomi in the passenger seat, facing out, the door still open.

The front door of the Brenner home opened, and Leah walked out onto the porch. She'd been home all along, though she was dressed in a nightgown and robe, as though she'd spent the afternoon napping under the covers. She walked to the edge of the porch, looked up at the looming heavens, and then at her family. Her confused glance swept from Emma to the Newmann porch. Her eyes rested on Ad, still standing in the street, shoulders heaving, sobbing. Seeing her, Herman stepped out of the car.

The rains broke, ferocious, hard.

She spoke to Herman, her voice flat. "They just called me, the doctors. My Jacob is dead."

Dripping wet, Herman sucked in his breath, but then pointed at Emma who was running toward the porch. "No one cries. Do you hear me? No one cries. I don't want tears."

A strange line that made little sense.

But Leah, watching him, began to cry.

Chapter Nineteen

After the funeral, Sarah invited everyone back to the house where Leah sat quietly on a low chair, stunned, lovely in her dark sadness. No one spoke to her, though a few approached, began words of consolation, but then, startled by the stark upturned face, retreated, apologetic. Hers was, I told myself, the frozen face she wore fifteen years ago—the haunted look that greeted the police when they first arrived at her doorstep. That unfathomable mask that led them, in their glib dismissal, to assume her guilt. Now, tucked into a chair in a corner of the room, her arms wrapped around her body, her feet planted solidly on the floor as though she feared she'd lose her balance, Leah occasionally surveyed the small group of mourners gathered in her home. Surprise there, and wonder. What was wrong with this day?

She was dressed in a dull black silk dress with a frilly lace collar, ankle-length and a little worn at the seams. A small black ribbon pinned to her chest. A dress from an earlier century, found in an unused closet, with a musty mothball scent, though she looked seductive, the alluring grief-stricken woman, the alabaster skin and the snow-white hair and the black-shadowed, inky eyes. A Renaissance portrait, this woman, painted by Raphael. She reminded me of another Jewish mother, grieving over a crucified son.

An exaggeration, of course, my words, on the impact of her sitting there. Such beauty that was paradoxically so unapproachable.

Sarah buzzed around, officious, greeting the scattered few who came into the home. The presence of Leah, returned from her confinement, must have kept many away, though others visited out of perverse curiosity. A gaggle of loose-limbed middle-aged men in a pack came out of love for the hapless Jacob, a man who'd made so many women smile or wilt or fantasize. Most of the women stayed away.

Sarah urged the few of us to try the whitefish. She kept whispering, "It's from Lyon's Delicatessen," as if that imprimatur would create appetite in us. "Eat, eat," she hummed. "B'rith Abraham delivered it. An offering."

My mother nibbled on a bit of fish on a piece of bread. Earlier that morning, before we'd dressed for Jacob's funeral at Congregation Sinai, with Rabbi Glickman officiating, she'd packed her hidebound travel trunk and pushed it into the hallway outside her bedroom door. Her brocade valise was open on a stand in the room, pieces of clothing placed inside. When she saw me watching her, she nodded toward my room.

"Best be ready, Edna."

For, in fact, early the next morning we'd be leaving the Newmann household, headed for Hyde Park and the Windermere Hotel, where my luxurious rooms were ready. Quiet days, long walks, outdoor concerts at Ravinia. During the rest of the long hot summer, away from the Newmann home, I planned on finishing my novel. Serial publication as "Selina" in *Women's Home Companion* that fall, a book from Doubleday next spring, probably as *So Big*, then painful oblivion for me as a writer—my feeble tale of a battered farm wife and her contemporary, shallow son. A book in which nothing happened, the climax a wagon ride to market in the deep of night. I feared a scolding letter from Nelson Doubleday himself.

"No, Mother, that can wait," I'd told her. "A little unseemly to pack now. We have a funeral…"

She'd interrupted. "Unseemly? Edna, I'd suggest you rethink your vocabulary. After all, your horrible behavior set into motion this…this catastrophe."

"That's cruel."

"But true."

"All I wanted was justice for an innocent woman."

She'd smacked her head, dramatically. "After all *this*"—she pointed through walks toward the Brenner household—"you still persist…"

"I know now who killed Ivan."

She'd gasped and peered down the staircase from the landing. "Quiet, Edna. For God's sake. You know *nothing* of the sort."

I'd whispered to her. "Things have happened and it seems to me…"

She'd interrupted, pulling her face close to mine. "It seems to *me* that you're going to accuse an innocent person—and the nightmare you've created will continue, worse than ever. Leah Brenner killed her husband, Edna. Can't you get that through your thick skull?"

I'd held her eye. "Oh, I don't think so. I *know* so. Because the pieces fit together, maybe sketchily, though I regret them." A long, deep sigh. "But I don't know how to prove it—after fifteen years."

"Then leave it alone. We have a funeral to go to, Edna."

"For Jacob's sake, and for his mother's, the murderer must be named. There has to be a rightness to things."

For a second she'd closed her eyes. "It's going to be a long day."

"I'm afraid you're right, Mother." I'd whispered to myself, "For once."

• • ● • •

Someone was saying something to me, so I focused. Emma Brenner was talking about her mother. "Jacob was always her favorite. I suppose because when you saw his face, you saw her. The rest of us—Ella, Herman, me—took after our father—the unlovely children. There were too many mirrors in this house to look into. Jacob was the only one who liked them."

Mirrors on the walls, though thankfully covered today.

"You're hard on yourself, Emma."

She tossed her head back. "I'm a realist, Edna." Then, a crooked grin, she added, "How the world loved poor Jacob. The girls giggled and fussed. Once, in shul, sitting quietly on Yom Kippur no less, humble, the rabbi found a note on the floor, Jacob's name on it, dropped by an anonymous girl. Girls followed him off the streetcars, boys wanted to be his friend. Everyone wanted to walk with him. He had it all." A melancholy tone entered her voice. "Except ambition. A dreamer, my brother. But sad all these years since…that day…"

"Yes, he took his father's death hard. The breakdown." I watched her face closely.

She shook her head back and forth. "Not because of Papa, Edna. Because of what happened to Mama. Too sensitive, Jacob always was. Even as a boy he'd hide away, lips trembling, acting out parts from the dime novels we all read. The murder"—she glanced across the room at her mother—"the murder leveled him. You know, I think he was waiting to die from that day on, spiraling downward, waiting, waiting. You could see it in his eyes. He was never happy again. Something…drained out of him. I believe some people wait for death—they *decide* that. It's like the book is done with. I'd catch him crying, alone, slumped over in the bushes outside. We thought we'd lose him that first time, that awful breakdown." She clicked her tongue. "And now we have."

"He was never close to your father? Even as a little boy?"

She spoke too loudly for the quiet room. "Lord, no. He *hated* Papa. Well, Papa never understood Jacob—mocked him, spanked him. Worse—looked *through* him. Too mean to him. Jacob was a little boy who kept bringing him gifts that were ignored. Worse—ridiculed. 'Papa, Papa, look at me.' Papa was a hard man to love, Edna. Very Old Country. When he got old, the worst stuff inside of him surfaced. He wouldn't even go to shul. 'Obey me, do you hear?' We couldn't talk at the supper table. Silence. No warmth, no weakness."

"Jacob had Ad, thank God."

Emma nodded. "Thank God. The defender of the fortress."

"What?"

She laughed. "That makes no sense, I know. But one time, a couple years back, we all went to see the movie *The Golem* at the Apollo Theater. You know, the Jewish hero created from mud, the defender of Prague in the middle ages. A stupid melodrama but Jacob and Ad joked that they were *our* heroes—me, Ella, even Minna. One made from clay, the other from mud. But Jacob, for days, walked around saying, 'I wish I was a real hero.' There was something so sad about it."

"Everything about Jacob turned out sad," I said.

Emma's lips trembled. "Poor Jacob."

I changed the subject. "Are you reconciled with Ella?"

She started, resented the question. "I'm moving back here, I decided. We both are. But I want my own room now. We're not little girls anymore. I have a job at Hull House, which I love, something vital, important, and maybe it'll lead to something else, maybe a salary—but Ella fights me. She still works as a seamstress. I quit that. What she's afraid of…she wanted to remain little girls, scared, the two of us together, feeding into each other's loneliness. I won't have it any longer. It used to be easier not to fight her."

"That can only last so long."

"Edna, she always told me I wasn't too bright and I believed her." She threw back her head. "That proves she was a little bit right, then. No? If I learned anything from what happened to Mama, it's that silence covers a multitude of sinning. Strangely, what happened to Jacob lately…it sort of liberated me. I watched him sinking…lost, and I woke up and thought about my world. I may be an inconvenience to Ella—to others, though Herman grudgingly accepts me—but I don't care. An inconvenient woman is just what a family sometimes needs to straighten itself out. Do you understand me, Edna?"

I tapped her on the back of her wrist. "Of course, I do. Inconvenience may not be the word I would choose, but it'll work. I like to put myself in the way of folks' expectations. Women need to do that more. Sometimes they'll notice you. Sometimes they'll listen."

She giggled like a little girl. "Tell that to my sister. Look at her." Ella was sitting across the room, watching us talking, unhappy. Uncle Ezra was chatting into her neck, but she was focused on us, not him. Absorbed, he didn't seem to notice.

Herman and Uncle Ezra kept their distance, except for exchanged hard and angry stares, the two weary soldiers separated after carnival fisticuffs no one won. At the services Ezra sat at the back, refusing to join the family. When the twins sobbed, he bowed his head, and from where I sat I could see his pale face. Surprisingly, he was dressed in a conservative suit, sans flashy and colorful handkerchief, though the *kippah* he withdrew from a pocket and placed on his head was a brilliant sky blue, inappropriate. He spoke to no one, though I noticed him nodding at Leah. I was surprised he'd come back to the house, but he remained at Ella's side, protectively, assuming his new role as her confidante. At moments, she did her best to slide away from him, not even subtly, once rudely turning her back on him. He didn't seem to care. No one else in the family acknowledged him.

When I'd first arrived, he was one step ahead of me. He'd turned on the top step and watched me. My mother, at my side, squinted at him, disapproving, but he held his unyielding stare. A mixture, I'd concluded, of disdain, wonder, and, fantastically, humor.

"What?" I'd said, perturbed.

"Oh, nothing at all, Edna dear. It's just that you are always one step behind someone, the barnacle on the underbelly of a hurting family."

"A refreshing image," I'd quipped.

He'd hurried inside, disappearing into the kitchen.

Lagging behind me had been a resistant Molly. The old woman mourned Jacob—that dismissive epithet "poor Jacob" would be the way he'd be remembered forever, sadly—and said yes, indeed, she'd go to the services. She'd even give condolences to Leah, the woman she believed began the decline of the Brenner dynasty. It was only fitting and right, she lectured, the dictates of a loving God.

"I'm an old lady," she announced to us at supper. "I don't need someone telling me how to behave."

Leah watched Molly and her family walk toward her. If she was surprised by Molly's extended hand and murmured sorrow, she didn't react. A simple wispy smile, a quiet thank you, and Leah added, "Jacob always loved living next door to your family. He was always at your home as a boy. You were his family, too."

The words touched Esther, already weak with grief, and she burst into sloppy sobbing. Immediately Sol draped one arm around her shoulder and used the other to touch her face. She smiled at him, a soft and loving look, and it was, I thought, a beautiful tableau of a long, cherished marriage. The man who spoke so little but always so aptly, Sol bent over Leah and took her hand, squeezed it. Again, the perfect gesture because Leah's face relaxed, softened.

Minna dragged Ad to Leah, though he resisted. He'd sobbed loudly through the service, the loudest keener, his shoulders shaking as he swayed back and forth, a mournful metronome. Disconsolate, he'd walked out, stood on the sidewalk smoking cigarette after cigarette. Minna tried to talk to him, but eventually gave up, herself crying softly. Nearby, his father watched him but didn't approach. Sol kept nodding at Minna: Help him. Help him. Help the lad. Molly kept an eye on him as well, though she seemed embarrassed by his public histrionics.

Jacob and Ad, a boyhood spent together. Grown men, the friendship now ended.

Inside Leah's home Herman sidled up to Ad and tapped him on the shoulder, muttered a soft "I'm sorry for...outside." He flicked his head toward the street. Ad didn't answer. Herman said something I missed, but Ad slowly nodded, his handkerchief dabbing his eyes. Finally he slumped into a chair, staring at the carpet, with Minna hovering over him, a twittering humming-bird, solicitous, anxious. "Ad," she kept whispering at him. "Ad."

A dreamlike world, that gathering, a lazy stream of Jacob's friends coming in, awkward, not knowing whom to talk to, and then, relieved, turning to leave. A heartfelt *mitzvah*. The rest of us sat or stood, mutely watching them, until finally the few of us lingered there. Molly kept nodding to Esther and Sol, an obvious nod accompanied by her redundant cane tapping, signaling a need to leave. But Esther and Sol were reluctant to leave Ad who was nestled into an armchair, his body heavy and immovable, as though he'd lost the will to stand.

"Esther," Sol said to his wife finally, "we gotta leave the family now. They gotta grieve by themselves."

Sitting shiva for a dead son. A hard-backed chair, low to the floor.

Mirrors covered.

Seven days.

Seven nights.

The door opened and Sarah cried out. Morrie Wolfsy and his wife, Selma, walked in, accompanied by a bent-over Levi Pinsky. No one expected Ivan's old partner to visit the home, though all three had been at the services that morning. As expected. Morrie paused in the entrance, doubtful of his welcome, this old partner who'd battled the dead Ivan—and whose illicit moment with Leah had begun the sweep of trouble that ended in Ivan's murder. Herman bristled at seeing him. The twins actually glanced at each other. Uncle Ezra, though, was smiling thinly, reveling in the happenstance juxtaposition of old acquaintances who never should be in the same room together.

No one moved.

"Hello." Old Levi yelled out in the silence.

It was an unintentionally comical moment, the old man's crackling voice breaking at the end. Uncle Ezra smirked.

My mother nudged me. "Edna. Leave."

I had no intention of doing so.

Levi waited for Leah to address him first, so he watched her closely.

Leah struggled to her feet, disoriented, but she stepped forward, extending her hand to Morrie's wife. The poor woman, obviously uncomfortable, was relieved and muttered condolences. And like that, as if Leah had sprinkled some midsummer night's magic elixir on the room, everyone settled, eased into chairs, sipped cold water, gabbed, and smiled. Leah herself fell back into her seat, assumed her silence, though her eyes watched the room. It was a marvelous transformation, her magic trick, however she achieved it, and even Molly gave the grieving mother a look that had equal parts wonder and admiration in it.

For some reason Levi began to share stories, recalling a young Jacob hanging out in the back room of the old meat market late at night, sitting by a small green-glass secretary's lamp, fashioning his poetry. "Alone. By hissef. Everybody gone home. He said he liked the quiet, the feel of the old room."

"That back room." Herman spoke up. "I never understood its attraction." He nodded at Ad. "You, too. You and Jacob sitting there with the older men."

"A home for us," Ad said.

Levi glowered at him. "You was gonna be a rabbi."

Ad raised his eyebrows. "Ancient history." But for the first time that day he smiled. "We felt so grownup there. Well, Papa and...Morrie." He pointed a finger at Morrie, then stared at Levi.

"I never liked it," Herman said, "A couple times there and I stopped going."

"I never felt welcome there," Ezra added. "But it didn't stop me from going."

Ad watched both of them. "It was like a private club."

"No Jews allowed," Ezra said, snidely.

Ad faced him. "Maybe you weren't Jewish enough."

"Being Jewish is not a...gradation," Ezra said.

"No," Ad said, "but it can be a special beat of your heart. The bond that..."

Ezra scoffed. "Yeah, that special haven. A filthy room packed with junk." He purposely eyed Levi. "A ragpicker's paradise."

"And yet someone broke in to steal," I added, loudly.

Old Levi furrowed his brow, squinted at me. "Yes, so strange, that. The long darkness of that day. On the very night that poor Ivan died. Like God telling us something."

Silence in the room: images of Ivan with a knife slicing into his neck. In this very house. On that sofa. A knife. Blood. All over. The paralyzed widow. The screaming Sarah...the murder...murder...

Emma started weeping loudly, her face buried in her sleeve.

"I'm sorry," Levi blathered. "I talk too much."

"Or enough," I said.

"Edna, please." My mother nudged me in the side.

Everyone turned to look at me. "I always thought it strange—the coincidence—both events on the same day."

"No connection," Morrie said hurriedly. "A few coins stolen. Those days a few robberies in the street, I remember."

"But the police never investigated."

"What's to investigate?" Morrie shrugged. "They come out for a minute. A petty burglary. It's nothing. A broken door. Pennies."

I stood up, raised my voice, the moment I'd wanted.

"Edna." My mother, warning.

"What are you saying?" From Herman.

A hissing sound from deep in Uncle Ezra.

I heard gurgling from Leah, behind me. I ignored it.

"I've wondered about that break-in. I'm sorry, but I want to say something here. Tasteless but necessary. Now."

"Edna." My mother, thunderstruck.

Esther tittered, reached for Sol's arm. Molly gripped her cane. *Tap tap tap* on the floor.

"This is not the time for..." Sarah's voice broke.

"Am I the only one to wonder about that? A knife never recovered. Perhaps bloodied clothing. After all, a stab to the neck. All evidence disappeared. When I saw that cluttered back room, walls of...of *stuff,* and then learned about the break-in, I thought, what a wonderful place to *hide* evidence."

"Stop!" Ella, furious.

"The knife."

Two words, explosive in the room.

Ad spoke up. "That makes no sense. Why there?"

"The police would naturally search Ivan's workplace. The back room. Such evidence would then cast suspicion on Morrie. A logical suspect. If the cops found it *there*—well…" I glanced at Morrie. "Or a place to hide it permanently…or to be removed later, at a safer time."

"Oh my God," Ella cried out. "Have you no boundaries?"

My voice trembled. "Why not there? Not in *this* house. Away from here. Maybe a place that lots of folks always gravitated to, comfortable, reassuring…"

Ezra scoffed. "You're saying one of us hid the evidence there? In the…rubble?"

"Maybe."

"Maybe not."

"Could be still there."

"Preposterous."

"Crazy," said Sarah.

Then the room exploded. Some yelled out, others cried, others damned me. Molly, bewildered at the cacophony of noise, banged her cane on the floor but no one listened to her. Ad was shaking his head, a quizzical grin on his face.

In the din I said, loudly and purposely, though I didn't believe a word I was saying, "If it's still there—and I believe there's a chance it is, all these years later, a knife and maybe incriminating clothing. Hidden in a convenient cubbyhole. If so, then there could be a way of identifying the true killer."

I didn't believe a word of it.

More pandemonium. My mother banged on a table, maddened, grabbing at her errant and improper daughter, whose disgrace had no limits. Thank God her bags were packed. After my inappropriate and unforgivable outburst in front of a grieving mother and her family, we'd have to make a hasty retreat out of Dodge.

"The police need to be called," I went on, gathering steam.

Leah had folded her body into a ball, curled into the chair like a scared child, but her eyes locked with mine. Slowly, trembling, her lips formed a curious smile. A nod of her head. One hand lifted from her curled body, and it was, triumphantly, a benediction. We nodded at each other. Her blessing to me. Mine—to her. A *mitzvah*.

Suddenly Ella was at my side, too close. Her hot breath covered me.

"What?" I said into her wide-eyed face.

"Edna Ferber, you're a dangerous woman. You should not be in this house."

Chapter Twenty

My mother had pushed her travel trunk into the middle of the hallway, purposely in my path, a bulky monument to the failure of her daughter to behave. It sat there as a reminder that we'd be moving to our apartment in Hyde Park early the following morning after a robust breakfast Esther insisted on making for us. I stared at the trunk with its plastered-on shipping and city labels my mother generously applied: Berlin, Budapest, Vienna, Paris, Rome, Florence—the grand tour of cities we'd visited just before the Great War, returning on a German boat as the 1914 war erupted. Now, after more than two weeks at Esther and Sol's there'd be no labels stuck on, of course, unless there was one mimicking Hester Prynne's inglorious "A"—in this case, perhaps a "D." For Disgrace, Dismay, or Disdain. Disaster? Or, simply, Dunce.

Because, emphatically, as we left Leah's house earlier, no one spoke to me, except the occasional *tut tut* or *tsk tsk* that slipped from Molly's cranky mouth. Tight-lipped and stony-faced, my mother said she'd skip supper, though I didn't. Esther had a savory roast in the oven, paprika-speckled potatoes, and a beef-barley soup simmering on the stove. Esther picked at the meal, Molly ate one potato and fussed about it, but Sol had an appetite and devoured two helpings. A man after my own heart. He who does not value good food, especially in moments of abject shame and humiliation, is a weak-kneed sap. As far as I was concerned.

Finally, the women gone from the table, I sat alone with Sol as he drained the last of a frothy glass of root beer, homemade and kept in an oak barrel in the basement. A twinkle in his eye: "You done a good thing, Edna dear."

"You think so?"

He shook his head vigorously. "You beat the bushes with a big stick, my dear, hoping a jack rabbit will scurry out."

I smiled at that. "A dangerous game."

"It had to be done."

"So you believe me, Sol?"

"I always have."

"I figured that…" I stopped because, in fact, I knew exactly what I'd been doing.

He was still shaking his head. "But the old back room. You think somebody stuffed a knife and bloody clothing in there? Broke into that place? Fifteen years ago? And still there?"

"Not at all."

"But clever, what you said." He raised his eyes to the ceiling and pointed upstairs. "You drive people crazy, Edna."

"So I've heard. I don't do it on purpose."

"Yes, you do."

A sigh. "I guess I do."

"So everybody goes into hiding." He chuckled, but sadly. "Maybe nobody believes you about the back room, but maybe somebody wonders…what? What's there? Maybe this Edna knows something. Maybe not the back room but somewhere else. Something hidden—in plain sight? Maybe…Who knows? Someone running around now. Nervous like a chicken with its head cut off. Give themselves away, stupid. I bet Morrie Wolfsy is pulling out the drawers in that room, piling up the papers and junk dating back to the last century." He chuckled softly.

"I doubt it. Not now. Did you hear Selma after my…performance? She grabbed him and said, 'I need to get home. Now. Away from here. These people.'"

"The air was filled with poison."

"Yes, from Edna, the anarchist's bomb, hurled into a grieving room. A good way to begin shiva."

Sol shook his head. "Ad took Minna off to the movies tonight. Up at Central Park Theater. A comedy, he tells me. A night like this—a comedy? Can you figure that? Chinese food at Joy Yen Lew's, to top it off. He tells me as they're leaving, 'What in the world was that Edna thinking?' Minna whispered, 'A trouble-maker, Edna is.' And I tell both of them, 'Maybe we need to have more such trouble in our lives.' So Ad punches me on the shoulder like I'm an old school chum and they go off to laugh at some antics on the screen. Movies—I never seen one, you know. Don't want to. Young folks, not caring. A movie today. A box of popcorn. A quarter for nothing. A walk home after dark. Young folks. *You* young folks. Such a generation." He waved a hand at me.

Though I said nothing, I thought Sol's definition of "young folks" somewhat skewered. Ad, at forty. Minna, fortyish. Me, careening unhappily toward forty. I was young when McKinley was president. I was young when it was hardly a golden age. Now *these* were days I reveled in—me, the short story writer in the pages of *Ladies' Home Journal* or *Everybody's*. Six months in New York, six in Chicago. A novelist. A move from short story land to novel country. Furnished apartments with oriental carpets, Victrolas, and supercilious doormen.

…with my mother…

…whose trunk was a punctuation mark on a failed day.

I stood up. "I'm going to hide in my room."

Sol winked, grandfatherly. "Under the covers where the goblins can't get you."

• • ● • •

I turned the doorknob slowly. At first the old door refused to give. No one locked that door, I knew, probably hadn't for years. After all, Levi walked in and out all day, left the door wide open. There was nothing left to steal except his piles of used clothing, unsorted, smelly, worn, sifted through. A vacant room now, though the stink of raw meat and gamey bird lingered, odors that warred with the stink of mouse droppings and old paper pulp. After he shut down his butcher shop, Morrie never locked up. No need to. Everybody knew that. And, maybe, others. At least one other soul who might surprise me.

...with any luck...

Eight o'clock at night, dark now. At the Newmann household all was quiet. My mother was in her room, probably writing letters before she turned in. Esther and Sol in their room. Molly, when I walked into the kitchen for water earlier, was in her bedroom at the back, the hum of a radio on low, some staticky song. I heard her coughing, some phlegmatic jag that alarmed. But then silence. The radio suddenly switched to another station, and then switched off. A house that went to bed early, and happily. That middle-aged youngster, Ad, was at the movies with Minna. Or treating her to chop suey on Clark Street. The house creaked under the summer heat, the steamy attic, and the groaning eaves. Another hot night.

I'd slipped out by the back door, pushing open the screen door, edging my way up the sidewalk until, away from any possible sighting, I hurried toward Maxwell. At the corner I paused to check out Morrie Wolfsy's second-story apartment over the meat market, but saw only darkness. Home with his wife, probably reviewing my shameful performance. "I told you she was a crazy person, that daughter of Julia's. Imagine the nonsense that comes out of her mouth." No one around now. A streetlamp cast flickering shadows on the façade, black-sooted like so many Chicago buildings, the awful dirt and grime of distant I. C. trains carried by wind and rain until so much of Chicago resembled a darkswept Hogarth print.

The door gave, though it squealed and yawned, loud enough to make me hesitate. But not for long. Inside, sweating but calm, determined, I switched on the light, and the miserable room lit up: counters of unsorted clothing, empty butcher-block surfaces, sagging shelves, and on the floor a nasty crumble of old, dried sawdust. Quietly, I moved across the room, reached the back room, found the light switch, and turned it on. I rushed back to the front entrance, switched off that light. The same procedure in the back room, as I located the small bathroom at the back, turned on that light, went back to switch off the back room light. On off, on off, a frantic rhythm. I pulled a hard-backed chair into the bathroom, shut the door but not completely, an inch opening perhaps, and then plunged the small space into darkness.

A little foolish, I sat in complete blackness, hands folded in my lap. And waited. Waited. Waited—though I thought—not only is this most likely a waste of time—but *foolhardy*. Proving what? A suspicion I'd had the day before—a mishmash of bits and pieces that led me to suspect someone of murder? Impossible to prove—except…maybe *this* plot…this…this sitting in the dark. Would someone show up? So there I sat, waiting.

A knife had been thrust into a man's neck, probably a sudden, unplanned moment, quick, quick, the spurt of sudden blood. The horror of it all. Not pretty, any of it. Ivan's murder had been impulse, chance. I believed that. Someone not used to murder. Someone surprised at the act itself. One of *us*.

A murderer who now felt safe, untouchable.

Except for something—maybe *someone*—unable to be controlled.

But…what possibility fifteen years later? So much to lose.

Getting away with murder. The perfect crime, the murderer untouchable. Maybe forever.

I waited.

An hour passed, uneventful. Bored, hot, I nearly dozed off in the tight, close room, windowless, when I heard the creak of the front door. I shot awake, spine stiff, eyes wide. My heart raced. I sucked in my breath.

Now.

My God. Now.

The answer.

At first nothing. Then a tentative step, almost inaudible, the front door closed, a dragging sound as though something were being shuffled across the floor. Through a crack in the bathroom door, I saw the light come on in the back room, though I sat back, in darkness, hidden, scared now, heart pounding. For a moment I closed my eyes: lightning flashes of red yellow blue, blending, colliding, sparks flying. I nearly gasped out loud.

Then I heard it: a wall cubbyhole opened, a drawer pulled out. One drawer, followed by a crash of papers and something metal. Something clanging onto the floor. A pause, deafening. Then a second drawer, opened, rifled through. A rhythm, though sloppy and rushed. I waited.

A tapping. Something moved. *Tap tap tap.*

I had no choice. I snapped on the bathroom light, swung open the door, and heard a woman's piercing shriek, breaking at the end.

Molly Newmann faced me, her face ivory with fright, one hand grasping a sheaf of bound papers, the other gripping her cane. *Tap tap tap.*

I stared, frozen, my mind blank, my throat parched.

A low hissing sound from the back of her throat. "Edna, what...?"

"Molly." I barely got the name out.

She dropped the papers, spun around, banging into a table with that cane and hobbled toward the door. She hesitated a moment, faced me with sad and stark eyes, ready to blather some excuse—*I lost my way, I wandered—I—I don't know how I got here—*

Shoulders dropping, resigned, she ignored me, leaving the back room but, nervously, switching off the light behind her. Plunged into darkness, I reached for the bathroom door, got my bearings, but my body refused to move. When I touched my cheeks, I felt hot flesh, my skin tingling. I burned with shame. It was like opening a door to find someone naked sitting in front of you. You, the intruder, stammer, apologetic, babbling. The naked soul, aware of her own nakedness, simply watches you. In the case of Molly, she simply walked out the door, though slowly, an old woman's fragile step. My whole body shook.

• • ● • •

Molly sat in her kitchen and ignored me when I walked in. I'd stayed in the back room, righting the drawers, obsessed with returning the room to its original look. But it was more than that, really. I couldn't bear the sight of the aged Molly, crippled now, moving down the sidewalk. *Tap tap tap. Tap tap* tap. She was headed to the house where I was a guest. So I lingered, sad and dizzy, until I had no choice but to follow her dead man's path.

She was preparing a cup of hot tea. As I watched, she carefully removed the tea leaves, added a bit of cream, two teaspoons of sugar, and took a sip. She watched me over the rim of the teacup. A civilized woman, but the cup rattled when she replaced it on the saucer.

"I need to understand." I sat opposite her.

She watched me for a while, her face horrible, wrinkled, old, old. "It wasn't supposed to come to this."

"Tell me."

"I knew you'd come to suspect"—she faltered, the word catching—"him."

Her clipped words, so blunt and hurting, were like a jolt to the system. Of course, she'd sensed that I knew. The little slip-ups. The little nagging suspicion and inconsistencies that suddenly came together, flashed before me, emblazoned.

"Ad." One word, awful in its fearsome weight.

She closed her eyes.

She mouthed one word: Adolph.

Her hand knocked the tea cup, the tea sloshing out.

For I had realized, earlier, that I'd known it on a gut level for a day or so now. Maybe more. The little things, I reflected. I found my voice. "Little things you said. When you heard Sarah screaming, you stepped out of your room to find Ad standing in the hallway. Another time you said you knocked on his door, and he was waking up from a nap. A small inconsistency, true, but it made me wonder. And that nonsense about Sarah being part of the fight the morning that Ivan and Leah had. You were forgetting things, slipping up, and so you rambled, threw stories out, helpless, trying to push me away. You were forgetting what you'd told me. What you'd told the cops."

A thin smile. "There was never a reason for me to rehearse a story."

"Until I arrived. Until Leah came back home."

She shuddered. "A seductive hoyden, that one."

"Tell me."

"I never knew anything." She refused to look at me, her voice dipping.

I broke in, angry. "Of course, you did. Molly, you're lying to me."

A long pause, the rattling of the cup. "He's my grandson. My favorite boy. The one blessing to this family."

"I wondered about the boys in the back room. I grant you that. Something always bothered me. In all the stories Ad was different. Under Levi Pinsky's moralistic instruction, he frowned on the others teasing about Leah, though I gather he once did so and Ivan yelled at him. That deadly conversation he had with Jacob on the porch. The day before the murder. The failed rabbinical student, a lark for a moment, intrigued by Levi's stories, but he saw himself as chivalric, the one who had a rarefied view of women. Levi's insidious gift to him. It explained his long, unfulfilled engagement to Minna. So many times he saw himself as a hero. The clay hero, or mud, saving others. A little thing, but maybe not."

Molly shook her head. "Maybe. Maybe not. But even when he was a small boy, he had a boyish crush on Leah. His best friend's mother. A beautiful woman who teased him then. He became a little...protective..." A sigh. "The hero nobody needed."

"Or possessive."

Bitterness in her tone. "That fight Ivan had with Leah. That morning. Adolph hated Ivan—so many times, hearing them fight, he—seethed. Adolph with his hot temper. Back to when that man hurt poor Minna—shattered that poor girl. Adolph stepped in, sorry for her. Always the knight hungry for a—a battle to show off. Adolph didn't want to marry her—he wanted to *defend* her."

She stopped talking, her eyes watching the doorway.

"Go on, Molly."

She breathed in. "That morning he wanted to go there—to *fight* Ivan. He was afraid for Leah. 'I got to help her. That...that bastard!' The way Ivan smacked Jacob the day before—hated his own son, mocked him. Adolph, the protector. Adolph, the savior."

"But you left, went to Maxwell Street."

"I made him go shopping with me—to get him away. But I could see the fury in his face. His eyes—so...crazy. I lied and told everyone we were together the whole day, as if we'd never left each other's sides. And we were—most of that day. The truth. But later on, back home, I napped in my room. I heard screaming. Sarah screaming." For a second she closed her eyes. "You know, I'd heard Adolph running up the stairs a short time before, out of breath, sobbing, slamming into his room. It woke me up. No, Adolph wasn't in the hallway. When he came out after I called him, he was scared. Shaking. His hands shook. I *knew*. But what could I say? My boy. Adolph. Everyone calls him Ad. Everyone loves him—a good boy. Edna, he never found his way. He's an unfinished boy."

"A scared man." I waited a second. "You never asked him?"

"How could I, Edna? How?"

"And he let Leah take the blame."

She didn't answer except to say, "He changed after that day. I could see it. He'd stare, he'd get white in the face, he'd get that faraway look in his eyes. He lost...ambition. Minna pursued him, got him—but what did she get? A shell, a vacant-eyed wanderer, lost in this house, on the streets. A thousand jobs."

"But Leah..."

She raised her voice. "Leah was sent to a home. Not a prison. I could see how he thought that saved everyone, like Leah was visiting out-of-state relatives. He stopped thinking about it. I doted on him, but he'd see me watching him because he knew I *knew*. The way he looked that day when I came out of my room. And now and then he'd spot me staring at him, something in my eyes that he saw there. I don't know. At those moments I saw fear, a look that said: Don't tell, help me, don't tell help me

I don't know what I did help help help me. Like words strung together without a breath between."

"But he watched Jacob have a breakdown. Jacob, filled with his own self-doubt. Jacob, blaming himself, Jacob willing himself to die."

A sob escaped her throat. "You saw how Jacob drew apart from Adolph lately, no? Adolph was baffled. Your doing, Edna. You put that doubt into Jacob's head, and he obsessed about it and somehow wondered about Adolph. A suspicion, maybe, the way Adolph acted. Back then."

I agreed. "That's what got me thinking about him, Molly. God knows how Jacob's mind worked, but something triggered such thoughts. He sent me a poem, asking me to be nice to him, but talking about a 'comrade song.' Something that made no sense. What 'comrade song' did he have? Only one. Written on the back of an old poem about the boys watching his mother. He must have known Ad's attitude toward Leah. I wondered about that. And his last conversation with Ad—something about it being time. 'Don't you know it's time?' His best friend, he realized—and it was time to come clean. Time!"

Molly's face was tear-streaked. "How Adolph hated Ivan." She shuddered. "And adored Leah."

"Ad on a moral crusade, starting in that back room."

"A good boy…"

"Somehow when it came together for Jacob, he couldn't be around Ad. It bothered him. It ate at him."

"You scared me at Leah's this afternoon, Edna. You made me wonder. What does Edna know? Did I miss something? It made no sense, but I couldn't take a chance. A whole part of me knew there was nothing in that back room—how could there be? why would there be?—but I couldn't sleep. I'm an old lady—confused. Fifteen years—of course nothing, though Morrie left it cluttered, untouched. I had to *be* there. I couldn't *ask* Adolph."

"And so you headed there."

"The evidence still there? Impossible. Fifteen years. But that news about the break-in that same night. I never heard that before. Never. A locked back door—broken into. It frightened me. I could see Adolph doing that. I thought—yes, I thought—yes, hide something. Hide a knife. Adolph broke in, hid the knife and bloody clothing so that the police would blame Morrie."

"I don't think the police even considered…"

A sharp look. "That's why I thought…maybe…"

"But there's no evidence. I never believed there was any."

A dusky chuckle. "Which is why Adolph went to the movies. He knows there's nothing there. And anybody else hearing you today. Everybody else but…but me." She eyed me. "You knew I would do something. That news about the break-in that same night. You probably saw my face." A sickly smile, those ivory-blue false teeth. "The only hope you had was—me."

I shook my head. "I didn't know. But there was no other way to prove my theory. Too many years have gone by. Who would believe me? What proof? The only way was to get the only other person I suspected who knew what happened that day to…to go there."

"Me." She could barely get the word out. "An addled old lady. Adolph believed he was safe."

"You didn't."

Her voice broke. "I *had* to go there."

"And so did I." I sighed. "Molly, I swear I didn't want to see you there, but there was no one else who would come. The only person who might come—you."

Her laugh broke at the end. "So in walks this little old lady, crippled, banging away with her cane." She saluted me with her teacup. "I was panicky. Yes, that's the way he thinks. Blame Morrie. Stupid Morrie—the philanderer." She locked eyes with mine. "The idea drove me—*crazy*. But, you see, I couldn't take a chance."

My voice trembled. "I'm sorry for you, Molly. Of course, I am. For your family. For Ad. You are people I care about. You have to believe that. But I'm not sorry for what I did. Leah had to have that black stain taken off her."

"Leah! Temptress. Look what she did to Adolph."

I stared back, stupefied. "Look what *he* did to her, Molly."

Footsteps in the hallway, a door slammed, an ebullient Ad bursting in, giving Molly a peck on the cheek. She held up her hand.

"What?" he demanded. "The two of you are so serious…"

Molly took his hand in hers, held it, squeezed it. "I've told Edna." She started to cry.

He knew then, he had to.

His jaw dropped. He spun around, maddened, glanced toward the back door. A coward, I thought—a callow man, a bounder. Worse…a killer.

"But…no." He yelled out the word. It sailed across the kitchen.

"It's over, my Adolph. I'm old and I'm tired."

"What?"

She reached for his hand, but he pulled it away. "Edna knows what you did."

"No."

"I told her."

"No."

"Sit down, Ad." I pointed to a chair. He debated what to do, but finally he did, hunched over. "Now tell me."

For a moment there was a flash of anger and resentment, of utter dislike, but it passed. What surfaced was the little boy, the town bully who hopes you'll pity him, console, forgive. *My excuse is weakness, frailty, I'm all too human. I didn't know…Forgive me. Love me. It wasn't my fault. It was an accident.*

Believe me. I—

So he blubbered, ugly, but I reached over and gripped his arm. Steely-eyed, I demanded, "Tell me."

"He made fun of me."

Molly patted the back of his wrist. "Adolph, my Adolph."

He refused to look at her. "That day, yes, but it wasn't the first time. He was a hard man—cruel. What he did to Jacob. To me. 'You look at my wife, you lousy creep.' He struck me once. I never told you that—I was so ashamed. And that morning, the fight. Horrible. Leah crying and crying—the sobs carrying across the yards. I was so afraid he'd hurt her. So when we got back from shopping, I snuck over."

Molly frowned, "You didn't have to, Adolph. I stopped you that morning, but that's all you talked about with me. You got so crazy." A sigh. "Always a *hitsiger*, my boy." A hothead.

"I had to. You were napping. I heard Leah crying on the back porch, and then I saw her go into the back garden. She was sobbing in her garden. Pitiful." His voice became a whine. "When I walked in the front door, he was there—on the sofa. He laughed at me. Again." He swallowed. "He's sick and irritated and… and…I snapped. He was doubled over, but suddenly he reached out and pushed me. I snapped. I had the dumb pocketknife I always carried. Lord, we all carried them, and I pulled it out, opened it. I waved it at him. He laughed and laughed, tears in his eyes. 'That little knife. You'll never be a butcher if you use a knife like that. Oh, you'll never be nothing.' I don't remember what happened. I don't. But all of a sudden that knife was in his neck, a vein, and all this blood was gushing out, and he was choking, gagging. One loud shout, I remember, and then this gurgling sound, desperate. His hands pulled at his neck—all the blood. It was awful. Awful. I folded the knife, covered with blood, and tucked it into my pocket. I rolled up my sleeves, soaked with his blood. I wrapped my handkerchief around my fingers. I got out of there."

"Adolph." Panic in Molly's voice. "Adolph."

Ad watched his grandmother. "Yeah, you heard me running up the stairs. I knew that. That ruined everything. You saw what a mess I was—I could see the question in your eyes. That *hurt* me."

"So Jacob suspected you? He avoided you."

He nodded. "I was stupid. Crazy, he said to me, 'A knife. There was no knife.' And I said that maybe the killer took it with him. 'Yeah, running out the door with a cleaver?' But I said—maybe a small knife, a pocket knife.' A blunder, really. We both carried pocketknives, and he gave me the strangest look. It chilled me."

"What did he say?"

"Nothing. He walked away. But I thought—Christ, trouble."

"Ad," I began, "why didn't you speak up when it happened? Years ago?"

He ignored that. He was still staring at his grandmother, his eyes moist. "I haven't been happy since that day."

"Happy?" I screamed. "Ad, no…sense of honor…or proportion. Ad, do you hear yourself?"

Surprised, mouth twitching, growl of barely suppressed anger. "You shouldn't have come here, Edna."

"No, Ad…"

Suddenly he stood, so abruptly I started. His fingertips rapped the table nervously. "I need air."

"Sit down, Ad," I told him.

He shook his head, his eyes white with panic. "This kitchen is too hot. It's too damn hot. No one ever opens the goddamn windows here. You can't breathe in here. No one can breathe in this house. What's the matter with you people? How do you expect a man to breathe in this house?"

"Sit down, Ad," I repeated. "We have to talk to the police in the morning…"

He started. "No."

"We have no choice."

Molly made a choking sound. "No, Edna, all the years."

"No." My voice firm. "It's over, Ad."

He looked down at his grandmother and mouthed the word—over.

"Over," he said out loud. Then, in a small, tinny voice he rambled, sputtered nonsense, but dark, frightening. At one point he mouthed the name Jacob—"Oh Jacob, Jacob"—and he sobbed. Then, his eyes weepy, he said, "I always knew my story would have a bad ending."

He bumped into the cabinet, banged his fist on the sink top. Blindly, furiously, he stared out the window at the black night.

He rushed to the door, though Molly screamed, "No, no. Don't go."

"Not this way," I pleaded. "No, Adolph."

But he was gone, the door slamming behind him.

Molly had her eyes closed. When she opened them—when she caught my eye—it was as if she'd seen a ghost. Her hands flew to her neck as she struggled for breath. Her fingers rubbed the right side of her face—the sagging jaw from her stoke—and she rocked in her chair.

The look we shared was horrible. In that moment we both understood that there would be a dreadful knock on the door the next morning.

Her face was ravaged now, ancient, the map of wrinkles deeply rutted, a dull purple. She tried to stand, reaching for the cane, but her elbow knocked it away, and it clattered to the linoleum floor. She stared absently at it but made no effort to bend for it. With one foot, jerking out, she kicked it across the room. It banged against the stove, a thud, the white enamel chipped. "Good."

"You did a horrible thing, Molly."

She spat out her words, an epitaph. "My own grandson, Edna." She sighed. "*A mane hot oygen fun gloz.*" A mother has glass eyes.

I shook my head. "No, Molly. You can't close your eyes to this."

"Edna..."

"You let an innocent woman suffer for fifteen years. You condemned her to ridicule and exile and shame and..."

She pounded a fist on the table. The teacup slid off, crashing to the floor. A ragged voice, icy. "And I didn't suffer all these years, Edna? You don't think I suffered? Every waking moment of these years has been my hell. Tell me I haven't suffered, Edna. You can't, can you?" She started to cry, thin, breathless gasps. "You can't. You can't."

Sing
a
Song
to
Jenny
Next

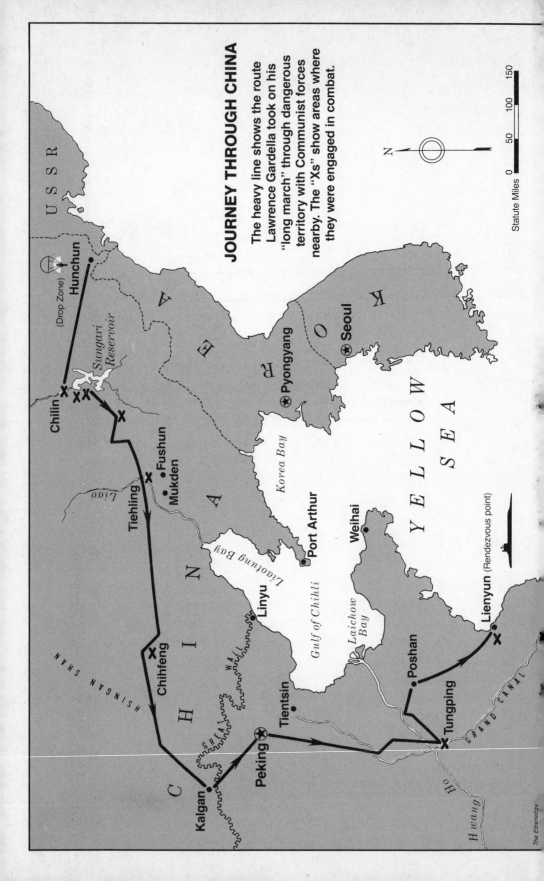

JOURNEY THROUGH CHINA

The heavy line shows the route Lawrence Gardella took on his "long march" through dangerous territory with Communist forces nearby. The "Xs" show areas where they were engaged in combat.

Sing a Song to Jenny Next

Lawrence Gardella

E. P. Dutton · New York

Published in the United States by
Elsevier-Dutton Publishing Co., Inc., 2 Park Avenue, New York, N.Y. 10016
Library of Congress Cataloging in Publication Data
Gardella, Lawrence, d. 1981.
Sing a song to Jenny next.

1. Korean War, 1950–1953—Personal narratives,
American. 2. Gardella, Lawrence, d. 1981. 3. Spies—
United States—Biography. 4. Spies—China—Biography.
5. Korean War, 1950–1953—Secret service—China—
Manchuria. I. Title.
DS921.6.G37   1981   951.9′042   81-7788
AACR2

ISBN: 0-525-20462-8

Published simultaneously in Canada by Clarke, Irwin & Company Limited,
Toronto and Vancouver

Designed by Nicola Mazzella

10 9 8 7 6 5 4 3 2 1

First Edition

Dedication

To my wife, Marie, for the love she has given me throughout our marriage and for the understanding and support she has granted me during the making of this book.

And to the rest of my family: my mother, Muriel; my two daughters, Susan and Janet; my twin sons, whom I have never seen; my grandson, Robbie; my brother, Michael; and my late father, Edmund.

I pray that none of you will be bitter over what you are about to read. I am not and never will be. What happened, I chose freely. May we enjoy the miracle. I love you all.

Acknowledgments

There are many people who put their lives on the line so that I might survive the events described in this book. Scotty, Audy, Charlie, Nancy and Sally, and my numerous Chinese and Mongolian friends; I will never forget you. Gunny, my Marine Corps father and steadfast friend; someday I know we will meet again. And how can anyone ever forget the Dragon Lady, who took so very much upon herself for her cause and for me. Or Kim, the Dragon Lady's sister, whom I can picture today as clearly as when she was a little girl. And those five Americans, friends, who endured with me so many years ago —the promise has finally been kept.

And those others who have given of themselves in recent years so that I might tell my story. Dr. Mortimer Greenberg, who has added years to my life. The staff of Mt. Auburn Hospital,

Cambridge, Massachusetts, whose compassionate care has sustained me. Maurice and Alma Woodman, friends who showed me how to begin. Asa Cole, a journalist who believed. Chuck Corn, my editor, who worked so hard in fashioning the final book; you have my lasting gratitude. And Jacques de Spoelberch, my literary agent, a person Marie and I can truly call friend; a man of his word, a man for all seasons.

1

On Friday the thirteenth of July 1979, I was working at a construction job in Cambridge, Massachusetts, right next to Harvard Stadium. I ate my lunch alone, sitting in my car, then went for a little walk in the empty stadium, as I'd been doing every day. It had gotten to be a routine. On this day, when I came out of the stadium, three men were standing directly in my way. They were well dressed, in business suits and shirts with ties, and they looked so young that I had to smile. It wasn't hard for me to guess that they were here to see me about something that had happened twenty-seven years earlier, when they would have been playing in the sandbox.

I walked right up to them, close enough that we could have reached out and touched.

"Forget about trying to have your story published," one of them said, "and we'll pay you twenty-five thousand dollars."

I don't know why I thought that was funny. Anyhow, I started to laugh. "You can take your money," I said, "and stick it . . ." I started walking, and when they didn't give ground, I put my arms up and brushed them out of the way. I kept on walking, and never once looked back.

The story they didn't want me to tell is the one I'm telling now.

I do not get frightened easily, especially now that I have leukemia, and don't know how long I can expect to live. That is the most important reason I decided to tell my story after waiting nearly thirty years. Until I made that decision I had told the story to one person, a priest. I hadn't told anyone else —not even my wife or my daughters or my parents.

For one thing, I was sworn to secrecy. For another, it's a very strange story. Suppose I told you that in the space of three weeks back in 1952, I traveled a thousand miles through China while our troops were fighting the Chinese in Korea? That I attacked a couple of Chinese Communist bases, one of them manned by Soviets? That I crossed the Great Wall, walked into Peking dressed like a Chinese—in 1952? That I met a cast of characters straight out of "Terry and the Pirates"—a Mongol chief six and a half feet tall, who could hit bull's eyes on a target over two hundred yards off with a bow and arrow—and a Chinese noblewoman who led a band of mountain fighters with no allegiance to either the Communists or the Nationalists?

Suppose I told you that I killed scores, maybe hundreds of people, some with a machine gun, some with grenades, some with a flamethrower, some by slitting their throats with a knife?

Suppose I told you that I made love to the noblewoman and now have twin sons, twenty-seven years old, living in China, that I've never seen?

Suppose I told you that I believe I may have contracted leukemia blowing up an experimental atomic laboratory built by the Chinese in caves deep under a reservoir in Manchuria?

Would you believe me?

Frankly, if I heard such a story I might not believe it either. All I can say is that as God is my witness, it happened, all of it, and it happened to me.

For twenty-five years, from May 1952, to May 1977, I had no reason to tell the story. But in May of 1977, everything started to change. I was working as a foreman on a construction job in Danbury, Connecticut, when I got sick. Three times in two weeks I went to the hospital emergency room, and they couldn't find anything. The third week, feeling worse than ever, I went back to the hospital, and they took some tests. This time they told me I had acute leukemia. They wanted to put me in the hospital right there, but I said no. I called my wife, Marie, and told her I was on my way home. I was so weak that a couple of times I almost drove off the road, but I made it. The Danbury hospital had called my doctor, and when I got home, Marie had us driven straight to Mt. Auburn Hospital in Cambridge. Dr. Mortimer Greenberg, who took over the case, came straight to the point: "If we don't start you on massive chemotherapy, I give you three, perhaps four months."

I asked him, "Will that stuff work?"

He laid out the risks and the side effects. What hit me was that I might have a heart attack or go into a coma. I didn't know what to do. Marie and I talked it over, and she persuaded me it was better to try something than just wait. I stayed in the hospital forty-five days, getting blood transfusions and chemotherapy. For three weeks of that time, I was in a semicoma. Marie tells me that one arm and one leg swelled up so that they were hideous. I don't remember any of that, and there's a lot besides that I don't remember from that time, but that Marie and other people told me about afterward.

They said that when I was in a delirium, I kept talking about tunnels, blood and monsoons—that I kept calling a Chinese woman doctor Dragon Lady.

Marie was mystified. She knew I had been in the Marine

Corps, but that's all she knew. In the nearly twenty-four years of our marriage, I had never told her about my experience in the service and now she was upset as well as curious. When I got out of the hospital on July 1, 1977, I was feeling better, but Marie was feeling worse—angry, confused, on the verge of a nervous breakdown.

We've been married since 1953. It's been a wonderful marriage. And here was Marie, who means everything to me, wondering and feeling hurt about a whole chapter in my life that she knew nothing about. I decided I owed it to her to tell what had happened. Once she had heard it, she felt I should put the whole story down on paper.

I still didn't know what to do. Telling Marie was one thing, but having others know was another. I decided to get help, and went to Father Chambers at St. Mary's Church in Franklin, Massachusetts, to ask his advice. He told me to have faith, to be strong—and to tell my story.

So I decided to try. I decided that the American people ought to know what we did there. For one thing, I now have a grandson, and I want him to know. For another, though I'm happy to say that I'm in a state of remission now, who knows how long that can last? The doctor doesn't. Whatever happens to me, I want it all on the record—for Marie's sake, for my daughters' sake and for my sons'—the sons I've never seen.

I had reason to believe that once word got out about this book, there were people who'd want to stop me, and that I'd hear from them. I did—and not only on that day in Harvard Stadium but a few other times that were a lot less pleasant. I'll come to those later on.

But I ought to explain right away that there are some questions I don't know the answers to and maybe never will, and some about which I can't even explain why I've got to remain silent. As a reader, your main question will be: Is this story true? Did it really happen? I can only repeat what I've said before: I believe in God, and as God is my witness, it happened, all of it, and it happened to me.

2

The adventure started on a day in April 1952. I'd been sent to
the Marine Barracks at Annapolis, Maryland, full of piss and
vinegar as any marine who's only seventeen years old and just
out of boot camp. While I waited for a permanent assignment,
I was doing routine guard duty and training exercises.

That day, I remember, I'd just come in from a two-day
field exercise. After I'd put away my gear, the next step would
have been a shower. Before I got that far, a captain and two
MPs came into the barracks and ordered me to go with them.

I asked if I should take my gear.

No, they said, no gear.

They led me to the orderly room and from there to a van
that was parked outside.

I asked myself what could be going on. I'd been in the
Corps only since February and hadn't done anything to screw

up that I could think of. Anyhow, I had no choice but to get into the van for what turned out to be an eight-hour ride—where, to this day I still don't know.

When the van finally stopped, I was led into a room in a one-story building. There stood a marine colonel, a major and two men in civilian clothes. Why I rated the attention of so much brass I had no idea, but in a minute I would find out.

It seemed, according to one of the officers, that I'd falsified my enlistment papers. When I asked what he meant, he said I had fraudulently concealed an item in my medical history, that as a kid I'd had asthma. Now that they had found out, I was going to be discharged.

I just sat there in angry silence, wondering how in hell they could have found out, and at the same time realizing that it didn't matter. All that mattered was that I wasn't going to be a marine anymore.

Then one of the civilians said, "Ricky, there's a way we might be able to keep you in."

I was startled to hear him use my nickname. Somebody had obviously done some checking up with people who knew me.

"You haven't shown any signs of asthma lately. We might be able to get around it—if you'll agree to something we have in mind."

"Sir," I told him, "I'll agree to anything."

It might be hard now for some people to believe I honestly said that. But at the time we were fighting in Korea. I was young and I believed in my country—I still do—and as far back as I could remember, I'd wanted to be a fighting man. So I didn't ask any questions. I just listened while the civilian talked about needing a small group of men for a mission they couldn't even discuss. "This mission is important to your country," the civilian said. "And if you go through with it, the chances are very good that you'll be allowed to make the corps your lifetime career."

Thinking about it later, I realized that what the civilian

actually meant was not "If you go through with it" but "If you get through it at all."

Well, I never saw things happen so fast. Within minutes after I'd agreed, I was taking off with the two civilians in a small plane. I had no idea then where we were headed and still haven't, other than that we landed in about an hour in a terrain that was barren and mountainous. All I could see was a low building, a kind of adobe hut. Inside it was another marine colonel, along with the same major we'd left an hour before—how he got there I don't know, but he wasn't on our plane—and seven other marines. I spotted one set of lieutenant's bars; the rest were all enlisted men. It soon became clear that they were "volunteers" like me.

One of the civilians told us to sit on the floor. This was where we would sleep that night. There was to be no liberty, no passes—in fact, we wouldn't even be able to walk out of the building until told to—and what went on here was all top secret. No one else spoke. We were given mats and blankets, and told to sack out.

Sleeping was one thing they couldn't order you to do, and I didn't do much of it that night. At one point I thought I'd get up for a breath of fresh air. When I tried the door, it didn't budge until suddenly somebody opened it from the outside. There stood three armed marine guards.

One of them spoke: "Nobody goes outside."

I said okay—what else was there to say?—went back to my mat, sat down and lit a cigarette.

One of the guards stuck his head in: "Put that butt out. No smoking."

"Suppose I have to go to the head?" I asked.

"You'll have to hold it till morning," was his answer.

Before long the door opened again, and in walked the major and the two civilians. It was still dark outside. One civilian switched on a bare light bulb. The civilian who'd given us the instructions the night before now told us to strip, to take everything off, including rings, watches, bracelets, even dog tags. We each got a bag to put our stuff in, and then we stood there naked, wondering what kind of mission this could possibly be. Then we each got a pile of clothes and were told to put them on. They looked just like the pajamas you saw Chinese and Korean peasants wearing in news stories about the Korean War.

The civilian who seemed to do all the talking asked if any of us had ever used a parachute. Two men said yes: the one I'd get to know as Lieutenant Damon, and a gunnery sergeant who would become one of the closest friends I ever had. His name was Robert Masters but he was known to us as "Gunny." For the rest of us, the answer was No.

The civilian said, smiling, "Well, you're all going to use one today." It began to look as though there would be no instructions, no chow and nothing to drink. My mouth was already parched—maybe because of the dryness, the heat, or maybe just the thought of my first parachute jump. We were soon fitted out with chutes and loaded into a transport plane. As it climbed, we were given three pieces of advice: first, as you were about to hit, keep your feet together, the knees slightly bent; second, don't let yourself start swinging (you might land on your back or stomach that way, and get hurt); and third, when you hit, roll to the side.

Half an hour after being told about jumping, we were ready to do it. At a thousand feet we were hooked up and literally kicked out the door. I felt the chute open with a jerk, then I seemed to be floating—until I hit the ground. Even though I tried to do everything the way they told me, I came down hard.

We were picked up and the civilian asked if everyone was all right. I didn't say a word and neither did anyone else. Then we were put back on the plane for another jump, this one at just six hundred feet. My chute barely opened before I was on the ground.

This time we were marched back to the hut and given some cold rations. Almost before we had time to finish those, we were told we were going up again, with a special harness because we were going to jump from between three hundred and three hundred fifty feet. After a little rest we were airborne again, and had hardly fallen free of the plane when the chutes opened. It was a much harder landing than the first two, but everybody made it.

Back we went to the hut for a little longer rest and, at last, some hot chow. While we were eating we were informed that we were going to participate in a night maneuver. We would be divided into two groups of four and dropped, in the dark, from about five hundred feet. Each group was to try to capture the other but there was to be no physical contact. Just how far apart we were to be dropped we had no way of knowing. After one group had captured the other, we were to make our way back to the hut. We weren't to know how far from it we were, or in which direction. A lot was never explained. But after all, we were marines.

I was in Group Two, headed by Gunnery Sergeant Masters. Lieutenant Damon was in charge of Group One. It was getting dark as we boarded and took off. After twenty minutes the order came: "Group One out!"—and down they went, one right after the other. The plane circled and my group was ordered out. Gunny ordered us to hide our chutes behind some bushes and then split us into two pairs. Corporal J. F. White was with him, and I was with PFC Jake Craig. The two of us headed up the mountain. After we'd gone about a hundred yards I said, "Let's hold it, sit down and see what's going on." Craig agreed there was no sense in just rushing around. So we stayed quiet, getting our eyes used to the dark—it wasn't really pitch-dark—for about half an hour. Then we heard some movement and I could see two figures silhouetted against the skyline to the west. Those were Gunny and White but we didn't know it yet. To the east we spotted two more figures coming over a ridge. "Shh," I said to Craig. "Don't move." We'd lost sight of the first pair, but I could see the second making their way toward us. I told Craig to stay where he was and keep a lookout while I moved forward cautiously, making my way down into a dry river bed. When I'd gone about thirty yards, there was a tremendous explosion on the mountain. I just lay there frozen, not moving. After an instant I saw two figures racing at me down the mountain. When they were almost on top of me I could see that they were Lieutenant Damon and his partner, a sergeant whose name was Mike Holden.

I shouted, "You're mine!"—and for them the game was over. Lieutenant Damon lit a flare, the signal for the entire party to regroup. Craig came up first, then Gunny and Corporal White. The six of us waited for the other two, but they didn't appear. I never saw them again.

Lieutenant Damon ordered Gunny to go with him and the rest of us to stay put. They were gone for an hour; then they came back, just the two of them, and Damon led us back to the hut. There was no way I could ever have found it, but he seemed to know which way to go. Altogether it must have taken us two hours to get there. When we did, the civilian who did the talking was waiting for us.

He asked coldly if we had any questions.

Of course we did. We wanted to know about the explosion, first of all, and then what had become of the other two men.

He ignored the first question, and to the second all he said was, "We're fighting a war. There's no cheap way out." I never learned anything more about the two men, not even their names. The names I've given for the others are their real ones.

Gunnery Sergeant Masters, whom I would always call Gunny, was the one I would get to know best. He had had nineteen years in the Corps after joining up at seventeen, which would have made him thirty-six at the time. He was everyone's idea of what a marine should look like—rugged, about six feet tall, weighing over two hundred pounds, with a jutting jaw and a dark look on his face. He'd grown up in the streets of New York City, where I'd lived the first eight years of my life. That was one thing that brought us close—a lowly "snuff" and a senior NCO.

Lieutenant Kenneth Francis Damon was slender, about five feet ten, the shortest man in the group, brown-haired, brown-eyed, and in his mid twenties. He never pulled any chickenshit about rank, but he always seemed to have something on his mind. I had the feeling, when I thought about it later, that he must have been an insider on this mission, not a last-minute "volunteer" like the rest of us.

Sergeant Mike Holden was also in his mid twenties, with brown hair and brown eyes, but he was more heavily built and a more outgoing sort than the lieutenant.

Finally there were the three of us who were still in our teens. We looked so much alike that we could have been brothers. J. F. White was a corporal, Jake "Slade" Craig and I were PFCs. We were all over six feet tall, weighing about two hundred pounds, and we were all blond and blue-eyed. The other two were less excitable than I was, and didn't ask as many questions.

One thing all six of us had in common was that we were in great physical shape. Otherwise we couldn't have taken the twelve grueling days that lay ahead.

I had another night without much sleep—and then the ordeal began. There was nothing orthodox about it, none of the usual calisthenics. And no rest. We were pushed continually, we never knew what was coming next, and we never walked.

Each morning Lieutenant Damon had a new set of maps showing the area we'd be jumping into, and the routes we'd have to cover in our allotted time. It might look easy on the map, but on the ground it was something else. We made three jumps every day: in the morning, again in the afternoon and once again at night. And then there was the running. You don't know what exhaustion is until you've run and run and run up and downhill, over rough, broken terrain. The amount of time it takes to cover a mile of that comes as a shock.

Our first day of this workout kept us at it for nearly twenty hours, with short breaks for rations. I had never in my life been as tired as I was then. I hardly had time to wonder where I was, but I did wonder a lot.

The next morning, we'd no sooner hit the ground than live rounds of ammunition were being fired over our heads. I knew they were live because I could hear them whistling and hitting. The firing did not stop—and neither did we. By this time we'd learned not to ask questions. We just took off, sprinting, while the firing over our heads continued—not too high over our heads either—until we were out of range.

From then on, after every jump the firing of live rounds was standard operating procedure. What was good about it was that it made us move even faster and keep our heads down. What was bad about it was that we were terrified. But none of us asked the civilians a single question. We knew they were trying to psych us, but it made no difference: they kept on shooting and we kept on running. Sometimes even at night, after we'd staggered back to the hut and collapsed onto our mats, one of the civilians would wake us and run us again for an hour.

After a few days, *I'm not sure just how many,* we were told we would now begin working with weapons. The three daily jumps and the running went on as before. We looked forward to the break in our routine, but it was a shock to be handed Soviet M43-PPS-43 machine guns. Of course we'd learned not to ask what they could mean.

The weapon had a folding metal stock and a circular magazine holding thirty-five rounds, and it didn't take us long to learn to handle it. From then on we carried it on all our jumps, and used it on the targets that we found along our routes— human shapes that popped up at us as we moved. We'd fire away at them and cut them to pieces. At least it was a great way of taking out our frustrations.

Besides targets—which didn't fight back—there was hand-to-hand combat training. This was with knives, and our instructors were Orientals—Koreans, I assumed, but never knew for sure. Though we were all a lot bigger and stronger than any of them, at the beginning we were pretty awkward, and they never made it easy for us. I got whacked on the head with the dull side of a knife a few times, the lieutenant had a dagger put to his throat, and even Gunny, who was saltier than the rest of us, had a hard time. But with our greater size and strength we learned almost to hold our own against them.

Days went by and we hadn't bathed once. We were filthy. The two civilians, who wore denims, were just as filthy as we were. One day they told us that from now on we would bathe every day in a lake that was near by. The route after our next jump took us right to it. When we got there, the two civilians were waiting in a rowboat. We all piled in, and when we'd been rowed to the middle of the lake, we were told to jump in and enjoy ourselves for a while. Then we were to swim to shore.

While we were splashing around, we saw that one of the men in the boat was aiming a machine gun at us. By this time nothing really surprised us. We swam around frantically, submerging and then coming up again. Sure enough, in a minute or so the son of a bitch began firing! I suppose he wasn't shooting to kill, but it's something of a miracle that no one was even hurt.

Now our "bath," complete with machine-gun fire, became a part of the daily routine, along with jumping, running and hand-to-hand combat training. The two civilians seemed to enjoy putting us through it all, especially firing the machine gun at us. As a group we began to feel a bond, and there was no doubt that the training was sharpening our reactions and fine-tuning all our senses.

As to why we were there, the mystery remained. The pilots stayed out of sight. The marine guards and the colonel and major had disappeared after the second day. We saw only the two civilians and the Orientals—no one else but each other. We were completely out of touch with the world—except for a curious thing that happened just before our training ended, when one of the civilians gave me some sheets of lined yellow paper and told me to write three routine, undated letters to my parents, saying that I was well and everything was going all right. I suppose the others did the same thing, but we never talked about it. There was very little talking of any kind among the six of us.

On what I guessed was about the thirteenth day, the civilian who generally did the talking told us that the next day our training would end and that the day after, our mission would take place. Now we learned for the first time what it was. We were to jump, using the quick-jump chute, from about three hundred feet, armed only with knives. When we landed we'd be supplied with Russian or Chinese weapons. We would be leaving the next day.

We were in fact to be a special force like the Marine Raiders in World War II. But then came the stunner. "If you are caught," the civilian told us, "there will be no acknowledgment by the United States government of your existence, where you were or what you were doing."

The Oriental clothing had told us something about where we were going. Scared as we all were, I figured that whatever was ahead of us couldn't be any tougher than our training. But then I still had a lot to learn.

After the civilians left, we sharpened our knives, checked and rechecked our chutes and got ourselves ready.

The next morning we were up before dawn, ate and climbed aboard the plane for a flight that never seemed to end. One reason it seemed endless was that the windows were blackened so that we couldn't see anything at all. When we finally set down, the six of us were still kept aboard until finally the hatch was opened and we stepped into a huge crate on a truck that had been backed up to the plane. In this way we were transported to another plane, again with blackened windows, for a flight of six or seven hours—something like that. None of us had watches. When that flight ended, we were once again loaded into a crate. This time, after riding for an hour or maybe a little longer, we were led out of our box into a building that looked like a Quonset hut. Before us stood a marine colonel with rows of ribbons on his chest. He launched into a pep talk about the job we had ahead of us and about what it means to be a marine. I must admit that talk got to me.

Then we had our first really good meal in days. The colonel said we'd be getting four hours' sleep. I showered and walked out into the warm sunlight. It felt good. As soon as I sat down, I began to feel groggy. The next thing I knew, I was being awakened. Possibly I'd been drugged to make sure I slept; anyway, those four hours left me feeling a hell of a lot better.

Then it was back into the crate for a ride to a landing strip and still another flight, this one maybe three or four hours long. Waiting for us at our destination were the two civilians from the adobe hut and a marine colonel we'd never seen before. We all boarded a truck, which we were told would be taking us to our mission plane.

The civilian who'd done the talking said, "Boys, may the good Lord take a liking to you, and may we see you back. Good luck."

The other civilian had never said much. He said only one thing now but that one thing came as a shock: "Your pilots are Chinese."

The plane we boarded was stripped bare inside and we sat on the floor. Holden broke the silence by asking, "Would you say we're going to China, fellas?"

"Nah," I said. "They fired MacArthur for wanting to go to China!"

Lieutenant Damon broke in, "Let's cut the chatter. We're only getting ourselves excited. We'll find out soon enough."

In less than half an hour, the order came to stand up. We stood, hooked up for the jump, and moved toward the hatch, which had been unbolted and slid back. Through the opening

I could see mountains—so close it was as though I could reach out and touch them. I don't know how the pilot kept from crashing. But then the word sounded: "Go!" And out we went, headed God knows where.

3

I was born in New York City on November 22, 1934. My father, Edmund Gardella, worked as a laborer and a hospital guard; my mother, Muriel, was a nurse's aide. They named me Lawrence Frederick Gardella, but my grandmother, who thought that was too long a name for a little baby, started calling me Rick and the nickname stuck.

About the first important thing—important to me and to a lot of other people—that I can remember is the start of World War II. At the time we lived at 170th Street and Amsterdam Avenue in Manhattan, and after the U.S. got into the war, there was a military camp—tents, soldiers, all—in a park right near us.

I couldn't stay away from that place; I spent so much time hanging around that the soldiers got to know me and treated me like a mascot. It got so that when my mother wanted me she always knew she could find me hanging around the camp. I remember one year bringing eight or ten soldiers home for Christmas dinner. In those days we didn't have all that much for dinner ourselves. But my mother and father, God bless them, managed to feed everybody.

That was my first encounter with the army, with men in uniform, and from then on I was hooked. I knew what I wanted to be: a soldier, a fighting man. That feeling never changed. It hasn't to this day. That I couldn't stay in the Marine Corps after 1952 is one of the few major regrets in my life.

During the war, we moved to Englewood, New Jersey. Our old neighborhood was getting bad, gangs were starting up, and my parents wanted to get out. But often on a Sunday my mother would bring my brother Michael and me into New York. Those were the days when big movie houses like the Paramount and the Strand had stage shows along with the movies, and we loved to go to those.

One Sunday, while we were walking in Times Square, I spotted a group of marines in dress uniform. I was so hypnotized that I kept following them, and got separated from my mother and brother. My poor mother finally went to the police; and three or four hours later they found me with the marines in a bar. I was maybe nine at the time. My mother was furious, but I wasn't really bothered. I knew then that being a soldier wasn't enough. I was going to be a marine.

In 1947, after the war, we moved to Allston, a suburb of Boston, where my grandparents lived. My grandfather had spent nineteen years in the army and was now the chief armorer at the Commonwealth Armory in Boston, which was the headquarters for the Massachusetts National Guard. He used to take me there all the time, and naturally I loved it. I got to know the men, I read all the manuals, I got to know weapons. Some guard officers who were close friends of my grandfather would let me field-strip the weapons at the firing range after the men were finished, and my grandfather would let me fire. Before I was sixteen I knew how to handle the M-1, the Springfield bolt action, the carbine, the four-point-one rocket launcher, the flamethrower. And I don't mean just take them apart and put them together. I mean fire them, hit targets with them—hit *bull's eyes* with them. I took to those weapons, my hands seemed made for them—even as a kid I had big hands. When I joined the Corps at seventeen, I was six feet and weighed 190. I am not boastful by nature and don't pretend to be anything I'm not. Ask me now how many books I've read in the past ten years, and I'll tell you: I've read two. Ask me how I handle an M-1 or a machine gun, I'll tell you. I'm the best.

In 1951, when I was sixteen, I decided I couldn't wait any longer, and I got my grandfather to talk my parents into letting me join the National Guard. Of course I was underage, so I did something I'm not exactly proud of. I fixed up my birth certificate so it would make me old enough. I was a big kid, and had no trouble joining the Guard. By this time, I had finished two years of high school. I was no student. Now I was at the armory every day. I never missed a practice at the firing range. Some days I'd be the only one there, but that just gave me more firing time.

In the summer of '51, our unit went to Camp Drum in upstate New York, where I got some field experience. I was a private, E-2, serial number 21261628, with Battery C, 180th Field Artillery Battalion of the Massachusetts National Guard. I loved it.

But I was still not a marine, and I became one by getting myself into trouble. In December, someone in the Guard asked me if I could drive a truck. I had no license, and I had never driven any vehicle, let alone a truck, but I didn't want to admit that I couldn't.

I drove that truck right through a garage wall—and was brought up on charges. The brass found out I'd falsified my birth certificate and was underage when I enlisted, even though by that time I was of age. My grandfather did what he could to help me. Finally I was told the charges against me would be dropped if I joined the regular army. "How about the Marine Corps?" I asked, and they said okay.

All of this may sound as though I had only one thing on my mind as a kid. But before then I had been a normal enough teenager. I played sandlot football—I was a tackle—and baseball, where I was a catcher. I got into my share of fights, won a lot but lost some, too. I did about everything the average kid does. But ever since that Sunday in Times Square, when I followed those marines, my one overwhelming ambition had been to be a marine.

When I filled out my medical form I did not mention that I had a history of asthma because I was afraid they might not take me, even though I'd been practically cured by treatments at Massachusetts General Hospital. I hadn't had an attack in a long time, and I wasn't allergic to grasses, trees, dust or pollen anymore—just animals. My father had to sign for me because I was under eighteen, and it may be that he hoped the Corps wouldn't accept me because of the asthma—not knowing that I wasn't telling them about it.

Anyhow, January 31, 1952, I was honorably discharged from the Massachusetts National Guard, and on February 1, 1952, I was inducted into the USMC. I remember asking the recruiting officer if I could get into a paratroop unit—I didn't even know whether the marines had one—and hearing him say he'd put it down on my papers. And I remember boarding a train at South Station along with a bunch of other guys for the long ride, twelve or fifteen hours, down to South Carolina. Then came the bus to Parris Island. As we got near the gate, and I saw the statue of Iron Mike, I felt like shouting, I was so proud and happy just to be there.

My feelings today are the same as they were then. I'm honored to have been a marine. The story of what happened to me I do not blame on the Marine Corps.

Saying it felt great to be there is not to say boot camp was easy. Its whole purpose was to get the civilian cockiness out of you. The DIs, the drill instructors, knew how to do that. You could get thumped for blinking an eye or for scratching a flea you thought had landed on your nose. You were kept from going to the head for hours at a time. And there were other punishments, too, such as having to stand with your arms straight out in front of you, supporting your M-1 on the backs of your hands. But the favorite of the DIs was a fist to the stomach, which knocked the wind right out of you and left no marks. I wasn't a troublemaker—never have been—but I got my share of all those punishments.

Also, there were pushups, chins, and other calisthenics, and there was the time on the firing ranges. There, for the reasons I've already mentioned, I had a head start on the others. I fired sharpshooter on the M-1, qualified with the carbine and the .45 caliber pistol. I was proud to be a marine, and proud of what I could do.

When boot camp was over, I requested combat duty overseas, which in the spring of 1952 meant Korea. I had been told then that I was too young. But now here I was, somewhere over Asia. . . .

4

We were in the air, and this time it wasn't a training exercise. We hit the ground hard—but no harder than we had been doing three times a day for nearly two weeks. We'd landed in what turned out to be a mountain meadow, not a moment too soon either. In the distance we saw the dinky little transport plane being attacked by a couple of fighters. It fell apart in front of our eyes, before the pilot had a chance to maneuver.

And someone already knew we were there. As we were getting our chutes together, a band of about twenty-five Orientals came toward us. I expected the worst. But they seemed cautious rather than menacing. One of them said what sounded like "Quick," and then I heard Lieutenant Damon answer, "Sand." The Oriental seemed satisfied. So *quicksand* was a password and countersign. Where the lieutenant had gotten it, I don't know and didn't ask, though I wondered again whether he knew more about this mission than the rest of us.

The Orientals led us quickly over several miles of this rough, hilly country. Once again I had to be grateful for the training we'd gone through. They brought us to what turned out to be a cave. We kept going deeper and deeper, for maybe three hundred yards, with no light but the flicker of torches, until we got to a blazing fire.

Here, finally, I got a good look at our hosts. They were not in uniform, but all wore pajamalike outfits of light brown or gray. Their pants and collarless shirts were like the ones we wore, but they had twine wrapped around their legs from ankle to mid thigh, so that the loose-fitting pants wouldn't catch on brush or rocks. Some wore black caps and others had cloth bands tied around their straight, silky, jet-black hair. They wore low-cut shoes, a sort of cross between a sneaker and a sandal, similar to the ones we'd been issued.

The big difference, of course, was in their looks and build. The biggest of them was no more than five feet six inches tall, and weighed no more than 125 or 130 pounds. Some were a lot smaller, and when I looked more carefully I realized that six were women—none of them much over five feet tall and weighing no more than a hundred pounds! But every one of them looked strong and lean and fit.

In a moment or so the one who seemed to be their leader spoke in English with a fluency that surprised me.

"My name is Yen. On behalf of the Nationalists, I welcome you to Manchuria. Please sit."

Manchuria! We were all stunned. The lieutenant had turned pale. He might have known more than the rest of us, but I could see now that he hadn't known everything. We were deep behind enemy lines!

Yen told us that we were in the mountains near the town of Hunchun. Our objective, he said, was the Sungari Reservoir north of Hautien, where the Chinese Communists were using several huge caves for experimental work on atomic weapons. The reservoir, he told us, was about 175 miles away.

"We're going to fly there?" I asked.

Lieutenant Damon answered. "No," he said. "We're going to walk."

"Walk?" I was almost shouting. "And what are we supposed to do when we get there? And how do we get away again?"

Before anyone could reply, a figure came striding out of the darkness and into the circle of the fire. Yen said, "It's all right. He is with us."

We were even more startled when the newcomer spoke. In his "Good morning, lads," we could hear the burr of a Scotsman, and when he got close to the fire I could see that though he was dressed like the others, he was indeed a Caucasian. He was perhaps five feet nine or ten and weighed 170 or maybe less. There was gray in his reddish-brown hair and I could see that he was in his mid forties, but lean, hard and fit like the others.

He told us to call him Scotty, and we were soon to find out that he was the leader of one of the pockets of resistance that were left after the Communists took the mainland from the Nationalists. He explained that he'd come to China in 1935, had worked for Chiang Kai-shek and gone through the Japanese occupation and then the Civil War.

Now he sat down with us and outlined his plan.

We'd be divided into three main groups, each made up of two Americans and three Nationalists who knew the terrain. I didn't like the idea of being split from the other marines, but I could see why we had to do it. These three groups would travel the valleys leading to the reservoir. Two units of Nationalists would be guarding our flanks on the ridges alongside us. The movement of our three groups would be in the form of a spearhead, with Gunny and me on the point, Lieutenant Damon and Sergeant Holden behind us to the left, and White and Craig behind us to the right. The remainder of the Nationalists would travel behind me and Gunny and between the other units. Our communications were to be with lights that could be seen at night only if you wore special glasses. There was a code. For example, one flash would mean "Danger, stop"; two meant "Come quickly, we need help"; and the meaning of three flashes was "Get the hell away as fast as you can."

Next the Nationalists had a little argument among themselves, through which I could hear Scotty speaking rapidly and easily in Chinese. When that was over, Scotty told us the six women would be divided two to a marine group, increasing the size of each group to seven. I was worried that the women might slow us down. I'd learn later how wrong I was about that.

We were each issued two grenades, two bandoliers of ammunition, and a Soviet machine gun, along with dry food and animal skins full of water. The gun was not the M43-PPS-43 we had trained with, but one with a clip instead of a circular magazine, and it fired a 7.62 mm round. But it did its job perfectly well.

Now that we had our weapons, Scotty made a point of warning us to avoid contact or confrontation with the Communists wherever possible. If we did make contact, we were to break it off as soon as we could, and there was to be no signaling for help except as a last resort. Which meant that we were pretty much on our own.

Scotty's usually genial face turned grim as he reached into his pocket for a bottle, out of which he gave each of us a little pill in a plastic case.

"This is in case you get captured," he said. "You just take it quickly and it's over with. For I tell you, lads, no one can bear up under what they'd put you through if you got caught."

I looked at the thing for a second before finding the pocket in my pants. This was no training exercise. And nobody who fired at us would be doing it just to scare us.

"All right," Scotty said, "we're ready to go. We'll give the groups who are going up to the ridges a start of an hour and a half."

The two groups of three men each got to their feet at once and were off. While the rest of us waited we began getting to know each other. Two of the three men who were going with Gunny and me couldn't speak English. They were brothers, both in their mid thirties, solidly built and missing several front teeth. They looked so much alike that the only way I could tell them apart was by a long scar that one had running from his left ear down the side of his face and neck. We called him Sam One and his brother Sam Two. The English-speaking Chinese in our party was called Charlie. He was smaller and a bit older than the two Sams—maybe in his late thirties. Right away I noticed a special warmth in his smile. Later the thing I'd remember about him most was his great courage.

The two girls with us—and girls is what they both were, teenagers—were called Nancy and Sally. They were cute and tiny, Nancy about five feet tall and weighing less than a hundred pounds, Sally perhaps two inches taller and a little heavier. I couldn't believe the way they kept the pace under the same gear the rest of us carried.

Of course Sam One and Sam Two, Charlie, Nancy and Sally, weren't their real names. What their real ones were we didn't know and didn't want to know: as Scotty had pointed out, if you were captured, the less you knew the less you had to reveal. Though I know their real names now, I still wouldn't want to take any chance of endangering those who are still alive or any of their families.

I tried talking to Nancy and Sally, who had gone to mission schools and could get by with the English they'd learned there, though it wasn't always easy to understand them. I think they said that for a year they'd been moving around with this group, and had had much more fighting than schooling.

We were making our way through the conversation when Scotty approached us. "It's your turn, lads. God bless you. Success to your mission."

Gunny and I and the five "friendlies" took off. Charlie, who knew the area, led the way. We were traveling in the dark, at a trot or faster, the whole time. These people didn't seem to know what walking was, and again I had to think back to the training we'd been given by the two civilians, whoever they were.

After a few miles I said to Gunny, "You're the sergeant here and I'm only the PFC, but don't you think we should separate? Let me stay here with Charlie on the point, you fall back with the girls and the two Sams, so no one can catch us both together."

He took it the right way. "You got something there. Sounds good." Gunny dropped back, leaving me and Charlie up front. Without seeming to make any special effort, Charlie speeded up the pace, and we kept it through the night. Just before sunup, we signaled the ridges that we were stopping, and pulled in behind some rocks. My legs were aching and I was so happy to stop that I didn't even mind the cold dried rice that was all we had to eat.

Soon Gunny, Sams One and Two, and Nancy and Sally were up with us. We couldn't move toward our objective during the day—there were supposed to be as many Communists as there were rocks in this area—and so we chatted again, always with one of us out on guard.

Though Sally wouldn't talk about her background, Nancy told us that her parents and two brothers had been killed by the Communists, and she thought of Scotty as her father. Pointing to Gunny, she asked, "Is he your father?"

I said, "He could be, he has more time in the Corps than I am years old." We laughed at that.

After a while I had a few minutes alone. I stretched out and put my head back to look at the beauty of this strange country, the distances all bluish-green in the morning sun. Before I could think about it, I was asleep, and the next thing I knew, Charlie was waking me for my turn at guard. As soon as I was relieved I went to sleep again, and when I woke up it was late afternoon. I checked my weapon and ate some more rice.

When it was dark we started out again. We had traveled for three hours when we spotted a signal—one flash from the ridge to our left. Danger. We stopped, moved off the trail and squeezed in behind some rocks, where we spent several tense minutes before we got an all-clear and could move on again. All through the night we kept going at the same fast pace. I found it hard to imagine how the people on the ridges could keep up with us in the terrain they were covering.

When it got light we stopped and rested again through the day, hidden away in those mountains that seemed to go on forever.

After it got dark, we hadn't been traveling long when from the left ridge we got two flashes, the signal to come quick. Charlie and I hooked up with Gunny and the rest of our seven, and Charlie led us to the left into a pass, where we were intercepted by someone from the left ridge. The man explained to Charlie that there was a fight going on at our left rear, which was the spot assigned to Lieutenant Damon and Sergeant Holden. We climbed rapidly onto a ridge where we could look down into the valley. Damon and Holden and four friendlies were firing, fighting their way toward us. We added our firing to theirs while the six of them came toward us, and suddenly everything was quiet.

But now we learned that one of the girls in the lieutenant's group had been caught.

We crept along the ridge until we could see the fires of a camp up ahead. When we got within four hundred yards, we could see the girl, strung out naked on a barricade. They were torturing her. What they had in mind to do, I guessed, was to bring us into the open. Her screams made my gut crawl, and I started to get to my feet; I saw Craig look at me and begin to get up too. None of the seasoned people, marines or friendlies, had moved a muscle—but when we started forward, the friendlies grabbed the two of us, knocked us both down, and literally sat on us. I lay there powerless, listening to that poor girl scream all through the night; I didn't see how I could take it, but at the same time I knew it wouldn't do anyone any good to try to go in and save her.

At daybreak we sent out scouts, who came back with a report that the girl was the only one left in the camp. Craig and I were the first ones to the barricade. What I saw was too terrible to describe, even if I'd been able to do it. Blood was everywhere, and pieces of skin. The worst thing was hearing a moan, and knowing she was still alive.

That was more than I could stand. I turned away and was sick. Charlie came up alongside me, touched me on the shoulder, and said he would take care of it. I was walking away as I heard the shot he fired. I didn't dare look back. This was certainly no training exercise, and I had stopped being able to imagine what might come next.

We resumed our journey, which by now took us into canyons so deep that it was safe to travel during the day. After we'd gone for a long time without saying anything, I asked Charlie, finally, who the torturers had been.

"Probably bandits," he said. "With no loyalty to anybody but themselves. If they had been Communist soldiers they would not have gone away."

For another night we just kept going, and with the first light of morning we signaled the people on the ridge that we were stopping for a rest. God knows I needed it by then. But after a while I got edgy. I turned to Gunny, who'd caught up when we stopped, and asked, "Why not let Charlie and me go out on recon, to see what's around?"

Gunny thought for a moment, then said okay, but that we'd be taking off in two hours. "So be back by then. We've got a lot of traveling to do."

Charlie agreed: "Tomorrow we shall be at the reservoir."

I shouted, "What? Have we gone that far?"

"We are getting close."

Why it should have given me a lift to be that close to our

objective I don't know, but that is the way I felt when I started out with Charlie.

"We'll be back in time," I told Gunny, "but just in case we're delayed, why don't you start forward and let Sam One lead you? We'll meet up with you one way or the other."

We headed northwest, and after more than an hour Charlie put his hand on my shoulder to stop me. While we ducked behind some rocks, he whispered that there were troops ahead. He'd heard the footsteps. Then I heard them too, and from behind a huge boulder we could see at least six soldiers. They stopped about two hundred yards from us and sent out two flankers.

"They are setting a camp for a stationary patrol. We're close to the reservoir, we shall see many of these," Charlie told me.

"How long will they stay?" I asked.

"Possibly for an hour, possibly for a week."

I asked, "Can we get around them?"

He replied, "With some of the men out patrolling in these mountains, it would take too long. We must go through them."

I realized now that we'd never get back in time and that Gunny and the others would be coming. "I'm heading back," I told Charlie, "to let the others know about these guys. You stay put and watch them. If they move, drop back and we'll meet you."

He agreed and I started back, keeping low. I'd traveled about two miles when I ran into Gunny and told him the situation: that it was either wipe out the patrol or make a long detour.

"Christ," he said. "That's lousy. We can't use guns, we're too close to the reservoir. The place is probably crawling with Commies."

"If you give me and Charlie two more people, and we can catch them asleep, we can take them without guns," I said. I may have sounded like a pro, but my palms were wet and my pulse was racing. I'd never killed anyone.

Gunny thought for a moment and then said, "Okay, you got the two girls."

"What?" I said. Girls? To kill soldiers? I thought he was kidding.

"They tell me they can do anything the men can do," Gunny said. "And Charlie told me the same thing yesterday."

I still didn't care for the idea, but he looked determined, and reluctantly I said Okay.

Nancy and Sally came up and the three of us headed back for Charlie. He didn't bat an eye at the idea of attacking the patrol with a force that was half female, and that reassured me a little. The four of us sat behind boulders waiting for dark, keeping an eye out for the two sentries, and listening to the noises from the camp—loud voices, laughter, a bottle breaking on the rocks. We had four hours until dark, and no water. I cursed myself for not bringing an extra skin of it from Gunny's position.

Waiting, we talked about a plan. We'd have two teams; Nancy and I would be one, Charlie and Sally the other. One on each team would be the throat man, the other the leg man. First we'd go for the two sentries. The idea was to get close and wait for the guard to change before we attacked. As for the others in the camp, we'd wait to catch them asleep or drunk.

When it got dark Nancy and I moved to within fifty yards of our sentry. We waited two hours for the change of the guard. I had plenty of time to think, more of it than I wanted. This was the real thing: I was about to kill somebody. I began to sweat, and soon my clothes were soaked. My heart was thudding and my stomach was jumping. I had to make myself calm down. Nancy must have noticed; anyhow, she came closer to me and put a hand on my shoulder. Then I really had to calm down; I couldn't let her feel me shaking. I began to feel a bit better, and actually smiled at her.

Finally we saw the new sentry arrive. We took advantage of the change to come within twenty yards, edging closer while the new sentry sat on a rock. The signal we'd agreed on was one, two, then go. When finally we were close enough, I put up one finger, then two, and we made our move.

While Nancy tackled his legs, I put my left hand over his mouth, and with the knife in my right I did what I had to do, slashing the blade from left to right, straight through his throat. He didn't make a sound.

We began moving toward the main camp, counting on Charlie and Sally to have gotten their sentry too. The soldiers had a small fire going; some of them were asleep, and the others were sitting on the rocks. One was drinking, and occasionally he would say something to the man next to him. Hoping no one would suddenly go out to trade places with a sentry now, we moved closer and closer until we were just outside the ring of firelight. We watched as the last two men lay down, not sure whether they were drunk or asleep. We didn't dare wait too long.

Wondering again about Charlie and Sally, I signaled to Nancy and we started forward, into the light of the fire, and as soon as we did that I saw movement on the far side of the camp. It was Charlie and Sally, there waiting for us.

I pointed to the nearest man. We went for him, and I'd cut his throat almost before Nancy could get his legs. He never moved. I was shocked by the amount of blood that poured from his neck, but I knew I couldn't stop to be sick. We went for the second soldier, then the third. Charlie and Sally had gotten to the fourth before we could. It was over. Four bodies lay there, besides the two sentries—each one with his throat cut.

Standing at the fire, I realized that I had blood all over me. I think if Charlie hadn't come over and started talking I would have thrown up right there.

"You did very well," he said. "Was this the first time?"

"Yeah. And I didn't think I'd make it past the first one. Is it always this hard?"

"Not this hard. Not easy either."

"We'd better get away from here," I said. "Because when they find the bodies . . ."

"We fix that," Charlie said. "We make it look like bandits." He and the girls went to work stripping the bodies and collecting weapons. I was glad they didn't ask me to help.

I went back to tell Gunny it was all clear, and we started moving again, faster than before, to make up for the time we'd lost. I was grateful when Charlie finally held up his hand to signal a rest. I was gasping as I fell back to tell Gunny so he could signal to the ridges. The ten-minute break had never seemed more welcome—or shorter. Before I knew it we were moving again, at the same agonizing pace.

We'd gone another couple of miles when Charlie signaled a stop. "I can smell water," he said.

I was amazed at how sharp his senses were, and delighted to be so close. This meant we'd be at the reservoir before sunup —which was crucial, now that we'd gotten back into territory where daytime travel was dangerous. We'd covered another four or five miles when Charlie motioned for me to stop, and pointed to two figures on a ridge, outlined against the sky. We crawled toward them, saw that they were soldiers and decided to take them ourselves. Later I thought this was probably stupid, because if there had been more we would have been in trouble. As it happened, we were lucky. This time my knife must have gone straight into an artery, judging from the blood that spurted onto my shoulder and ran down my arm. I stood there frozen until Charlie gave me a slap to get me moving again. An instant later we saw that the two men had been guarding an approach road to the reservoir.

"One mile to go," Charlie told me. "We must hurry."

He didn't have to say why. There was already a touch of light in the east. We broke into a dead run and from the last ridge we saw open land below us, sloping down to the reservoir.

Soon Gunny came up and signaled to the groups on the ridges. Damon's group came in first, followed by White's. Then, to my amazement, Scotty appeared.

"What the hell?" I said. "I thought you'd stayed behind at the caves."

"I was just a few miles behind you all the way, lads," he answered. "I wasn't going to miss this. It's too big a job. And we have to do it quickly, while we can still surprise them."

"I see a road and a reservoir," Damon said. "I don't see any caves."

"The road leads to a tunnel and the tunnel leads to the caves. They are under the reservoir," Scotty said. "The laboratories were built for the Japanese by Chinese prisoners, about ten years ago."

"Is there any other way in?" the lieutenant asked.

"No," Scotty said. "Just that one."

I couldn't help wondering if there would be any way out for us.

5

I stood there with the blood of half a dozen men hardly dry on my shirt, but ready to go on with the mission. Looking back, I don't know how I got over the shock of what I'd done. Part of it was that I was just seventeen, and when you're that young you can bounce back more easily. Part of it, too, was being in a kill-or-be-killed situation. Anyhow, it was lucky that I had no idea what was waiting for me in those caves.

"Twelve of us will go in," Scotty said. Although Charlie argued that Scotty was too important to be one of the twelve, he insisted. "This is too big for me not to go in," he said. "Besides I am the only one who knows the way at all."

The other eleven would be made up of eight friendlies along with Lieutenant Damon and two others of his choosing. He pointed to me and Holden. Of the Chinese, Charlie, Yen,

Sam One, Sam Two, Nancy and Sally would be going in, with two others whose names I was never sure of.

"We won't be able to just walk in," Scotty said. "We'll have to get hold of a truck that's on its way in, and take it over."

I pictured the twelve of us, all in one place—and all dead. But there was nothing I could say. And before I could even think any further, we had started moving. We had to back-track a couple of miles to a winding path that led down along the canyon walls. It must have been eight or nine in the morning when we started down.

When we'd gotten to the bottom, we stayed hidden but close to the road. Several vehicles passed, none of them big enough to hold us all. After half an hour we saw a covered truck. Sams One and Two had put on the uniforms of two of the guards we'd killed. Now they stepped out onto the road and signaled to the driver to stop. While they approached him, the two girls slipped up on the other side and leaped for the passenger. In a minute or two the bloody work was done, and the driver and passenger lay dead. The rest of us jumped onto the back of the truck, which turned out to be empty under the canvas except for a few crates.

As we drove toward the reservoir we began to see more and more soldiers, dressed in uniforms of brown or gray— loose, floppy trousers, long jackets with wide black or brown belts and fatigue caps. They paid no attention to us. I found a part of me wondering why we didn't just turn the truck around and get the hell out while we could.

After a few minutes we arrived at a gate and the Sams spoke to the guard. I don't know what they said—or whether it was because the guard was especially stupid or because the Sams were especially smart that they let us through. As we drove on, we passed barracks, several small buildings, and dozens, maybe even hundreds of soldiers. I could see a radio tower, and near the reservoir there were storage tanks— whether for fuel or water there was no telling.

Then we reached another gate. Peering from underneath the canvas cover, I guessed that we'd reached the entrance to the caves. We slowed and then stopped. We'd done so well up to now that I wondered how long our luck would hold out. I could see a soldier who looked like an officer staring at the side of the truck. He spoke to Sam One, and then waved us through. At least we seemed to have picked the right truck!

The road began to dip so sharply that we pitched forward. Then we entered the mouth of the cave, and the road was suddenly steeper than ever—something like a thirty-degree incline. There was plenty of artificial light. I could feel the sweat running down my neck and back, and my mouth had gotten very dry.

I saw that Scotty was fiddling around with the explosives he was carrying. They were light—they had to be—but he'd said they were powerful enough to do the job. I could only hope he was right.

Deeper inside the cave, the road turned left. I guessed that it must be taking us underneath the reservoir. Then it leveled off. Along the side walls we now saw concrete bunkers with steel doors.

The truck suddenly screeched to a halt in front of a gigantic steel door. As we sat there, it began rising. When it got up to about ten feet, four armed guards came out, two on either side of us. One of them started talking to Sam One, who said something back. Their voices grew harsh, and I could see Charlie getting his machine gun ready. I picked up mine too, while the arguing went on, and we peered through the canvas to watch. Suddenly Sam Two fired a burst at the two guards on his side. Charlie poked his weapon through the canvas and opened up on the other two. He almost blew their heads off. The truck lurched forward, then came to a stop directly underneath another huge door. On Scotty's orders we all jumped out and rushed forward. We heard shouts and then we could see men running, lots of them, many in white laboratory coats, the rest in military uniform. At first I saw no weapons and heard no shots. Then Scotty began firing, and I did the same. Masses of men were coming at me and falling as I blasted away. Still they kept coming and falling. Then there were shots from the other side. I could see the lieutenant moving off to the left; I took off to the right. Standing there in the open was Holden, with Nancy and Sally. I screamed to them to take cover, and they raced toward the wall. I could hear the bullets hitting the walls and feel the showers of rock fragments that followed.

Men were charging at us from the front and from a second corridor off to the right. I changed the clip in my gun and resumed firing; we must have knocked over fifty of them in those first few minutes, while we still had the advantage of surprise.

We moved forward, and since I could see that the weapons had been dropped, I slung my machine gun over my shoulder. Many of the dropped weapons were Soviet M43-PPS-43s, the very guns we'd trained with. I'd fire one until it was empty, then drop it and pick up another. There was no shortage of them, and none had been fired very many times.

But now the firing was heavier. Charlie and Yen came scurrying over to me, and the three of us made it to a large metal door with Chinese lettering on it. When I leaned my weight against it, the door opened. Inside was what appeared to be a laboratory with tables, test tubes and other apparatus —now deserted.

From the rear I could hear someone screaming at me. The voice sounded like Scotty's but I couldn't make out what he was saying. I grabbed one of my grenades and pulled the pin. Now I could hear Scotty yelling, "Close the door! Get the hell out of there!"

I tossed the grenade, and a blast of flame came at me as it exploded, knocking me off my feet and leaving me dazed. I felt pain in my legs. Looking down, I saw that my trousers were in tatters and that there was blood on them too, but I didn't think I could be badly hurt.

I got to my feet and started forward. The noise of gunfire was so loud that I felt deafened. About twenty yards ahead of me and to my left, I spotted Lieutenant Damon sprawled on the ground. I started running, then fell onto my belly and crawled toward him. I managed to drag him to an angle in the wall, which gave a little cover. He had been hit in the shoulder and was bleeding. As I lay there and wondered what I could do for him, Sally came over and pointed to herself, apparently meaning that she'd look after him. As I started to move off, I saw her looking at my legs, and waved my hand to tell her I was okay; I guess I looked worse than I felt.

I made my way to Holden, who also looked at my legs. "I just slid into the plate too hard," I told him, not sure whether I was reassuring him or myself.

With us now were Charlie and the two Sams. That made five in all. I assumed the others were along the opposite wall, though I couldn't see them. I must have been on my third enemy gun by then. Half the time I couldn't see anyone because of the gloom and smoke, but in that corridor, with those men coming at us, it would have been hard not to hit someone every time I fired. Still they kept coming. I wondered then, as I did afterward, whether they might have been drugged. Whatever it was that kept us alive, I thank God for it.

I came to another door, like the one I'd gone through, opened it, and tossed a grenade—only this time I got out of the way at once. Again there was a blast, and a fire that filled the place with such thick smoke that it was hard to see anyone. I was on top of Scotty and Nancy almost before I recognized them. Scotty was leaning over trying to fix an explosive onto a big boiler. Yen was at the far end of the boiler, firing like hell. To the right I saw another door, opened it, and went in. I reached for a grenade and was getting ready to pull the pin when something made me stop. It was a pile of crates. Going closer, I saw that my first quick glance hadn't been mistaken. Stenciled on them were the words MADE IN U.S.A.

I stared for a moment longer, then headed for the door. I

lobbed the grenade on my way out, then slammed the door and made my way back to Scotty. By this time he had fixed the charges with a timing device. He looked up at me and said, "The time has come for us to make our exit."

The piles of bodies in that murky tunnel would be almost impossible to describe. And still people kept coming at us. We backed our way to the lieutenant, who by this time was only semiconscious. For his sake and ours we had to get out of there. I said to Scotty, "Why don't you and the others take the lieutenant and start moving out? Yen and I will come right behind and cover you."

He started to say No; but he knew I was right, that we couldn't all stick together. So he got the others moving, half carrying, half dragging the lieutenant with them. While they retreated, Yen and I stood still and kept firing as fast as we could. The others had piled a few enemy guns near us to make things easier. We began to back off, still firing; and just as I was thinking there was some kind of miracle about our not being hit, Yen groaned, twisted sideways, and fell on his back. He lay there motionless, and I saw that he was dead, killed by a shot in the middle of the forehead. I went on backing off and firing, in a scene as near to hell as I hope I ever get—the bodies, the smoke, the flames from fires started by the explosions, the new blasts as the fires spread.

I would fall back, stop and fire, fall back again, until finally, turning around, I caught sight of the truck where we'd left it parked, directly underneath the doorway. Sam One had been clever; the Communists had tried to close that door to trap us, but the truck had kept it from dropping all the way. As I backed up under the door, the shooting seemed to have eased off—maybe because of the fires and explosions. I lobbed a grenade under the truck and took off up the ramp, hearing the truck blow, and looking behind me as the steel door dropped down the rest of the way. After about fifty yards, I caught up with Scotty and the others. "How come you haven't gotten any further?" I yelled. "Yen is dead. That place is an inferno. Let's go!"

I could see from Scotty's face that he thought I was getting hysterical. Maybe he was right. While he was telling me to calm down, a tremendous blast sent us all toppling. "There goes the boiler!" Scotty shouted. He seemed almost cheerful.

As we started up the ramp again, I noticed a locked wooden door. I fired at the lock, breaking it open, and went in. The place was an arsenal, with countless stacks of weapons. In one corner stood case after case of .30 caliber ammunition, each one stamped WATERTOWN ARSENAL, WATERTOWN, MASSA-CHUSETTS, U.S.A. For a couple of seconds we just stared. But we knew we weren't safe there.

When we stepped out of the bunker, streams of soldiers were coming at us. This time they were moving down the ramp. We dropped to the ground, set up our weapons and started firing. Again, I couldn't understand what must be going through the minds of those Chinese, pouring in and letting us knock them off as though they were ducks in a shooting gallery.

I yelled to Scotty, "Don't you think we should get back into the bunker?"

"We'd be trapped. We'd never get out!"

"Yeah, but they're going to run over us here!"

The stench from the smoke was worse than ever. Many of the lights had been knocked out, and visibility was down to almost nothing. The less they could see, the better; but still, if they fired enough, they'd hit something. All we could do, meanwhile, was fire up the ramp.

Next I heard small arms fire hitting near where we'd left Lieutenant Damon. I crawled over to him and saw that he'd been hit again, this time in the neck, and that his left ear had been shot off. Nancy and Sally were trying to stop the bleeding, but they didn't have any medical supplies. Damon was in bad shape, but since there was nothing I could do to help him,

I moved back and went on firing up the ramp. Thanks to the Watertown Arsenal, Watertown, Massachusetts, one thing we had plenty of was ammunition.

Suddenly the firing at us stopped. We stopped firing too. The quiet was terrifying. We all stared up the ramp, and then Holden said, "There's another bunker up there. Let's go and have a look at it."

Scotty opposed this. "Some of those bodies on the ramp might not be dead ones."

"Yeah," I said. "But all the same, there might be something in there that we could use. It's a chance. If we just stay here, we've got no chance at all."

Scotty thought for a moment. "Well, at any rate it's thirty yards closer to the top. Try it, but be careful."

Holden, Charlie and I started moving up in the semidarkness, around and over the bodies. The quiet made it even scarier. There was a lock on the bunker door. Holden shot it off, and the sound of his gun in that stillness was awful. Going in, we found another arsenal, but with heavier stuff—bazookas, grenade launchers, rockets—along with more ammunition, all of it made in the U.S.A.!

We emptied a crate, loaded it with an assortment of weapons, and pulled it out of the bunker. We'd intended to drag it down the ramp, but Scotty was already moving the group up to us. We got down quickly, and I looked at the lieutenant. He was unconscious, but the girls seemed to have stopped his bleeding. I asked how they'd done it.

"With earth, wrapped in cloth," Scotty said.

"But that'll infect the wounds, won't it?"

Scotty shook his head. "It works. I don't know why, but it does."

The stillness was broken by the rumble of something that sounded like heavy machinery. I asked what. "Sounds to me like tanks," Scotty said.

Holden picked up a couple of bazookas from the box we'd filled and handed one to me. He gave Charlie some rockets and motioned for us to go with him to the opposite wall of the tunnel. When we got there, Holden asked, "Did you ever fire one of these?"

"Oh sure," I said. And I had, actually—three times in training. Looking across the tunnel, we saw Scotty standing with another bazooka. Nancy was behind him, ready to supply him with rockets. He called out, "If we can get one or two as they come around the bend, they'll block the tunnel."

Holden waved back; the noise was getting closer. I wondered whether the tanks would be carrying napalm. If they did, they could fry us right where we were. All we could hope was to knock out the first couple and hold back the rest with them.

"Here they come," Charlie shouted, and as the first tank appeared, we all let go. That first round tore the turret off. We reloaded as fast as we could. The second tank got past the first before we could aim. I fired at the tread, Holden at the turret, Scotty at I'm not sure what. Anyhow, we stopped that one too, and set it afire. No more tanks could make it through now. But then men started coming down on foot. I fired one rocket at them with the bazooka. When I saw Holden drop his and reach for his machine gun, I did the same. We started firing, and some of the men fell, while the rest backed out of sight behind the shattered tanks.

Another lull—for how long we had no way of knowing. We used it to get back to the others near the bunker and resupply ourselves with ammunition—and it was a good thing we did, for almost at once we heard something bouncing down the ramp at us—something that might have been a rock, until it exploded. So they were just going to lob grenades down at us. We heard more of those come clattering down, and Scotty yelled, "Back into the bunker!"

We made it somehow, dragging the lieutenant with us, and slammed that heavy wooden door behind us. Then we just sat and listened to the grenades going off on the other side. I thought, Now we're trapped. They can come for us whenever they want. The barrage of grenades went on for what felt like ten or fifteen minutes, though it may have been a lot less than that. Then everything was quiet. I looked around, began counting, and realized that two of Scotty's Nationalists were missing. Dead or captured. Counting Yen and the lieutenant, that left four casualties and eight of us still able to fight. I wondered if the other side knew how few of us there were.

Breaking the lull Scotty said, "Let's go!" and threw open the door, firing as he stepped out, with three of us just behind him. We surprised a couple of dozen soldiers at point-blank range, wiping them out almost before they could fire.

More lights seemed to be going back on, as though there had been a switch to emergency power. The longer we stayed here, the smaller our chances of getting out would be.

"Let's head up to the tanks," Scotty said, and we started out, moving as many weapons and as much ammunition as we could, while the two girls dragged the lieutenant. All the way, we were having to step over the bodies of the men we'd killed. The idea that twelve of us had been able to do all this was stupefying. Even though there was more light now, the air was thick with smoke, which cut down the visibility. We could still hear an occasional explosion somewhere in the tunnel behind us. As I remembered, the bend in the tunnel was about half-way up. That would be a good point to defend. I kept fearing that sooner or later one of those explosions would bring the reservoir down on our heads, which may have been nonsense, but the higher we went the safer I felt.

We reached the burning tanks and looked around the bend at a sight I hadn't believed I'd ever see again—daylight. But we weren't out into it yet. Two more tanks were approaching, followed by men on foot. While Scotty prepared to aim a bazooka, I remembered something I'd seen back in that last weapons bunker—a flamethrower. I started back for it. When Scotty screamed, "Where are you going?" I yelled, "Be right back" and kept on going. Inside the bunker, it took me a while to locate the flamethrower. Just as I was thinking I must have been mistaken, I saw it—another item marked MADE IN U.S.A. I picked the weapon up and mounted it on my back.

When I got back to the others, the second group of tanks had already stopped. The Chinese soldiers were now ahead of them, firing and moving down at us. Our people lay on the ground, trying to use the two burning tanks near us for cover and firing back as hard as they could.

Wondering if the flamethrower would even work, I dropped to one knee, ignited the spark, and opened up. A stream of fire came shooting out that all but scared the hell out of me. What it must have looked like to those poor guys while I waved it back and forth from wall to wall like somebody watering a lawn, I can't even imagine.

Demoralized, the poor bastards turned and ran. Scotty immediately signaled us to move up the ramp. We were firing as we went, to keep them moving. After a few yards we came to the bodies that had been scorched. Even through the smoke, you couldn't miss the nauseating stench of burnt flesh. I tried not to breathe or to look, but to keep moving.

The return fire had quieted, but now it started up again. I heard a woman scream. Nancy had been hit. As she went down, Sam One fell too. He and his brother had been carrying the lieutenant. I hesitated, and then Holden yelled, "Let's go, Ricky! Spray 'em! Give 'em a hot shower!" His yelling seemed to touch something off. Scotty started screaming, and all the rest of us did too. I turned on the flamethrower as we advanced, shouting and firing, hoping they'd think it was a regiment. We could see more and more daylight as we went forward and it was a beautiful sight, even through all the smoke.

The two tanks had stopped just inside the tunnel. When we passed them, we were at the very entrance. Though we saw no one, and there was no firing, we didn't dare walk out into the daylight. Thinking I should save as much fuel as I could, I took the canisters off my back and handed the flamethrower to Holden, telling him I was going down to see how Sam One and Nancy were. Sam Two went with me, while the others stayed put. Sam Two stopped at his brother's side, and I kept going until I found Nancy. Lying there, she tried to smile at me, but I saw that she was badly wounded in the hip. I leaned down and picked her up; she was so light that carrying her was no trouble.

"I be fine," she said, adding my name, only it came out "Licky." I smiled down at her, kissed her on the forehead, and started uphill toward the brothers. Sam One had been hit in the legs, but with some help he could walk. Sam Two had picked up a piece of lumber to use as a crutch, and he headed up the ramp on his own feet.

Then we heard Scotty yell, "Get back! Quick!" while he and the others started running toward us. "Planes!" Holden shouted. I heard the sound, and looking back, I saw that two incendiary bombs, possibly napalm, had landed at the entrance to the cave. The angle was such that the flame didn't reach us, and having nothing but concrete to feed on, it didn't last long. A second and then a third plane made passes at the entrance, trying to drop bombs down the ramp, but with no more success. Then each of the planes made a second pass, dropping conventional bombs. The concussion was terrific but the tunnel held and we were far enough down into it to be safe.

When everything was quiet again, the six of us who were still in shape to walk—Scotty, Charlie, Holden, Sam Two, Sally and I—left the lieutenant, Nancy and Sam One where they were, and made our way to the entrance. Smoke was thick around us, but everything was quiet.

"Some of this may be radioactive," Scotty said. I asked what he meant.

"The stuff that's used to make atomic bombs. I think it was in the labs you blew up," he told me. "It said so on the doors. At least I think so. I didn't get to read it very carefully."

"Can you read Chinese?" I asked.

"Oh yes, lad. I've been here seventeen years, you know," he said.

Not having much idea about the danger of radioactivity, I said, "Well, anyhow I got away with it."

He looked at me in a strange way. I don't know whether the material I blew up was radioactive, even now. But ever since I found I had leukemia, I've thought about it a lot.

Right then, I was more worried about getting through the next few days, or even the next few hours. I kept thinking about how, here in Manchuria, I'd been using guns and ammunition from Watertown, Massachusetts, maybe fifteen minutes from my hometown—stuff that had also been used on me!

Holden broke in on my thoughts. "Listen, kid, you did a hell of a job."

"I'm not such a kid," I told him. "I'm nearly eighteen."

He laughed. "How'd an old guy like you get into this assignment?"

When I told him about my asthma, and how I'd volunteered so as not to get thrown out of the Corps, he laughed again. "You got shanghaied, just like I did," he said. "Except that I got caught stealing food in Korea. The army was getting how chow, but our old man, the bastard, decided marines were too rough for that, and fed us nothing but cold K rations. So we decided to get some good food from the army. We drew straws, and I was the one that got the short straw. I got caught, and then they gave me the same kind of choice as you. Volunteer or else. So here we both are. Maybe we should call our congressmen."

Holden told me that Gunny had gotten here the same way. "Punched an officer in Korea because the guy wanted to get his squad wiped out. They put it to him, too, and he had nineteen years in!"

"Those bastards," I said. "I wish we'd get some word from Gunny. I wonder what he's doing."

"What I hope he's doing, lads," Scotty said, "is rounding up friendlies in the countryside to come and get us."

There came the drone of planes again. We backed down the tunnel as fast as we could, dragging the wounded, and hid behind the disabled tanks. We heard the explosion and felt the concussion of more conventional bombs. This round tore up some concrete. There was a silence and Holden and I ran up the ramp to see what was happening. When we saw no sign of anyone, we signaled to the others to move up.

Of the twelve in our group, three were dead; the lieutenant was unconscious, Nancy disabled, Sam One wounded but able to fire, the other six of us in good shape. I wondered again if *they* had any idea how few of us there were. Then I heard Scotty call out, "Hey!" Looking up, I saw a convoy of trucks rolling toward us. Almost at once we heard the report of mortars, and saw the shells exploding. But the trucks were still coming at us.

Scotty shouted, "Let's go for them before they get out of mortar range!" The others of us who could walk began moving forward, firing toward the Communists as they got out of the trucks and advanced toward us, also firing. We dropped to the ground and kept at it. It was soon clear that the Communists were under small-arms fire from our rescue party. The question now was whether we could link up with them in time.

We began edging in the direction of the friendlies, hoping to make it easier, though we didn't know whether we could get to them. I could now see them advancing on the Communist troops in a skirmish line. They were taking heavy casualties, exposing themselves to save us. Realizing I wasn't far from where I'd left the flamethrower, I turned and ran back for it.

Lifting the canisters, I felt totally exhausted. I also knew that if one of those canisters got hit by a bullet it would be the end of me. When I was a little closer, I dropped to the ground and opened up with the flamethrower. It burned everything on the ground in front of the troops, and they broke and ran. By now I must have been really hysterical. I got to my feet and went on firing the thing until it was out of fuel. Once I'd put it down, I picked up a machine gun and started using it—blazing away even when there was no longer any return fire, until the clip was empty.

When we finally reached the boulders where the main body of the friendlies were, Holden really lit into me: "You watch yourself, kid, or you're going to flip. Only a crazy man would run out in the open the way you did!" But if my nerves were shot, I guess probably his were too.

Then I saw Gunny, ran over and put my arms around him in a bear hug. I don't think I was ever so glad to see anyone.

Things looked a little better now, even though we were in the midst of enemy territory, and God knows how many hundreds or thousands of miles from any escape at all.

6

Gunny said they'd heard the explosions and seen the smoke, and that when the soldiers headed down that tunnel, "We figured you'd had it."

"Yeah," I told him. "I guess we thought pretty much the same ourselves."

White and Craig joined up with us as we were walking. Glad as I was to see them, the feeling didn't last long, because I immediately saw some men carrying Lieutenant Damon, who was still unconscious most of the time. He was in bad shape and I wondered how long he could hold on. Nancy, though weak and in pain, was able to smile. She reached out to me and I closed my hands around her tiny ones.

"It's a nice day," she said.

"It's a beautiful day." I knew what she meant—that it was good just to be alive.

I asked Scotty what would happen next.

"We head for another cave about twenty-five miles from here; we've used it often."

"But with Nancy and Sam One and the lieutenant all needing medical attention?"

"When we get there," he said.

"Well then, why don't we move?" I said. "It's going to be dark soon."

It was our fifth day in China. Gunny heard the tension in my voice.

"You been through a lot, kid," he said. Hearing this from a man practically old enough to be my father helped to calm me down.

They'd made stretchers for the three wounded out of branches, rags, vines and I don't know what else. I kept being amazed at the resourcefulness of these people, and began almost to believe they could do anything—these tiny people, some of whom weighed only half what I did, and who carried loads of gear as big as I could manage without ever appearing to get tired.

Right then I was certainly tired. We were moving through rough country, along small paths or no path at all. When at last we got to the cave, its many turns and twists all lit by torches, it was a relief to see the wounded being cared for by people who seemed to know what they were doing.

We hadn't been there long before a group of friendlies came in with what appeared to be prisoners. Some were in the dress of Communist soldiers, but there was one in denims who was much bigger than the others. As he moved closer, it became clear that he was not Chinese. Then Gunny, Holden, White, Craig and I all stared in amazement. He was the same civilian who had put us through our training for this mission, seeming all the while to enjoy watching us suffer!

Scotty hadn't missed our stares. "You lads look like you've seen a ghost. Either that, or you know this man."

"We know him all right," Gunny said with a scowl. At a

signal from Scotty, the civilian was led away from the group. Gunny and I followed him and stood by as Scotty asked, "What are you doing here? With them?"

The civilian looked at him with the same kind of smirk we'd gotten from him while we trained, but he never opened his mouth.

Scotty now explained that when his men had captured one vehicle far behind the convoy that had attacked us, they had found him on board. He hadn't been tied up and hadn't seemed to be a prisoner.

"Somebody should strip him and search him," Gunny said. At an order from Scotty his men undressed him. In his pockets, along with several scraps of paper with notes on them, they found some shipping bills from Lushun—the Chinese name for Port Arthur—and a small blue card that read UNITED STATES OF AMERICA, CENTRAL INTELLIGENCE AGENCY, with the seal of the United States, the man's photo and the name Joseph Roberts.

Would a real CIA man be carrying around an ID card like that? The question occurred to me, too, and to this day I do not know the answer. Could he have been a double agent of some kind? I don't know that either. But anyone who has read about the activities of the CIA during that period will know that some very strange things were being done in 1952.

"What are you doing here?" Scotty asked him once again.

And again Roberts stood there like a sphinx, not saying a word.

Scotty asked Gunny, the ranking American in our party now that the lieutenant was out of action, "Do you want us to try to get some information out of him?"

We all knew what Scotty meant. Gunny said No, and Scotty went off to his men, taking along Roberts's papers. Everybody had questions and no one had any answers. After a while, Scotty came over to tell us he hadn't been able to learn anything new, either from talking to his men or through the radio transmitter he carried.

"I know you lads are tired," he said. "Better get some sleep now. I don't think it will be safe to stay here much longer."

"Where are we going?" I asked.

"A place where we'll be safe," was all he would say.

We'd all learned not to argue, but to grab whatever rest we could. I don't know how long I slept—only that I was groggy when they awakened me. I was still groggy when we got under way. The Chinese people in our party didn't take long to get started—which I suppose was one reason they were still alive.

As we moved out into the night, Holden came up alongside me and Gunny. "I'm worried about the lieutenant," he said.

"Yeah," Gunny said. "But I'm worried more about Scotty. He's nervous, and I haven't seen him that way before. Something must be wrong."

Altogether there were about thirty in the group and Scotty was up front. But this time I decided not to keep my questions to myself. I worked my way forward to ask, "What is happening? Where are we going?"

"To another cave in the mountains, about fifteen miles away." He wouldn't say any more.

I'd been walking in silence for a few minutes more when I heard the sound of planes.

"Probably looking for us," Scotty said before I could say anything. "We're safe in the dark. But we've got to get to the cave before light. They're not going to give up looking."

I began to drift back to the others, passing Roberts and the five Chinese prisoners, all with their hands bound. They were being moved along quickly by their guards, who carried automatic weapons. Though I hadn't got much out of Scotty, I also knew that we owed our lives to him and his men. Clearly our mission had been important to them; but now that it was done, they were protecting us, doing their best to help us get away, simply out of generosity. As for Roberts, how was anyone to know what side he was on? He hadn't given the least sign that he even knew us!

It took us many hours to reach the cave, and once again, while I wanted to do nothing but rest, Scotty and his men were arranging with incredible speed for guards and patrols, and had the transmitter in place. Scotty could work his radio only for very brief intervals, for fear of being picked up by the Communists. After he'd tried for a while and gotten nothing, he came over and said, "Let's talk to Roberts again."

Roberts had now been tied separately from the rest of the prisoners, who had their feet bound and were roped together by the neck at four-foot intervals. Their faces showed no expression, as if they expected nothing but the worst.

We took Roberts deeper into the cave, where Scotty tried a new set of questions, with no more success than before. Once in a while he'd manage that unpleasant smirk, or he'd lick his lips. Though I can't say that I felt sorry for him, I did have a certain respect for the way he clammed up. After a while, at a word from Scotty, one of the guards half led, half dragged Roberts away by the rope around his neck. Then the five of us marines walked over to the fire and sat down, all of us a little stunned at what we'd gotten into. We started talking as a way of comforting ourselves.

Holden said, "Rick and I were shanghaied. And I told Rick about you, Gunny. So that makes three of us."

I looked curiously over toward White and Craig, and White smiled.

"I went over the hill," he said, using marine slang AWOL. "For a girl. I thought I was going to marry her, until one morning I woke up and found the girl and my money gone and the MPs standing there. That's when I got my choice of this or a court-martial."

I looked at Craig. "How about you, Slade?" We'd taken to calling him that, I don't really know why.

"I was a little different," he told us. "I was on the boat to

Korea when they offered me this. I took it. I guess I must have been out of my mind."

"Christ, no," I said. "Could you have had as good a time as this in Korea?" For the first time since we'd all been together, we had a good laugh.

I knew that Nancy's parents had been killed by the Communists. Now I asked Sally about hers.

"They are alive," she answered. "They are fine, I hope. I have not seen them in four years." She paused, dropping her head as if she were ashamed. "They are Communists. My brother, too. But I do not believe in Communism."

I really felt for her—a youngster like that, having made such a decision. "How old are you?" I asked.

"Seventeen. Like you." When I looked at her questioningly, she added, "Seventeen, *almost.*"

I grinned at her and put a hand on her shoulder. The two of us were standing there like that when Scotty came back. He'd been looking at the papers Roberts had with him and that had given him an idea. "I want to talk about it with him here, to see the expression on his face."

The guards brought Roberts to the fire and sat him down. After asking him once again if he had anything to say, Scotty held up the papers. "I have something here I want you all to listen to," he said. While he read we all watched Roberts.

"Six ships sunk. Will not return. They feel the same as most of us. But hung his name on anyway. Sing a song to Jenny next."

At these words Roberts reacted for the first time with an interested, wary look.

"Does that mean anything to you, lads?" Scotty asked.

No one said anything.

"I'll read it again. Listen: *Six ships sunk. Will not return. They feel the same as most of us. But hung his name on anyway. Sing a song to Jenny next.*"

"Who the hell is Jenny?" Holden asked. Instead of answering, Scotty began to talk. "Here is what this *might* mean. The message could be in two parts. The first, *Six ships sunk. Will not return,* could refer to the six of you. As for the second part, I don't know about *They feel the same as most of us,* but the *hung his name* could refer to Hungnam and the *song to Jenny* could be Songjen. They're both in North Korea. They could be talking about real ships sunk at those places or they could be talking about other groups of operatives like you, who will not return."

Watching Roberts, I could see that for the first time he was shaken. He had turned pale and it was costing him some effort to go on looking unconcerned. The message had shaken me a little, too. What did it mean: *Will not return?* That they hadn't made any plan for us to get back? That they didn't *want* us back?

Just then two friendlies came running in and spoke heatedly to Scotty.

He turned to us. "Communist troops are two hours off and headed this way."

"Jesus," Gunny said. "What do we do now?"

Scotty didn't answer immediately, but turned and spoke again to his two men. As they ran off, he said to us, "We have to split into two groups."

"Oh no," Craig said. "Not again!"

"If they catch us together, we're all gone," Scotty reminded him. "If we split up, the pursuit has to divide, and that gives us both a better chance. And if they did catch one group . . ." He shrugged, then went on quickly, "We join up again after we've gone through the mountains."

I asked, "What about the wounded? They're not going to be left?"

"I don't know the answer to that," Scotty replied. "They'll hold us up. It's a decision we've got to make."

"I'm staying with the wounded," I said, and the rest of the marines agreed.

"You can't all stay," Scotty told us.

"I haven't asked anybody for anything yet," I said, "and I won't ask for anything except this. I'm staying with them."

"Okay," Scotty said. "One more can stay. We'll draw lots on it. You know that whoever goes with the wounded travels slowly and has the least chance of getting away."

While we all stood there, he picked up five empty machine-gun shells and a pebble, and handed them to a friendly to whom he spoke in Chinese. "One of the shells has the pebble. The one who gets it goes with Rick and the wounded. Gunny, Holden, White, Craig—and I—will draw."

White was the one who got the shell with the pebble in it. "First time I ever won anything," he said with a grin.

Then Scotty was urging us on. "We don't have much time. Ten men will go with Rick and White and the three stretchers. You have to try to make it over that mountain before dawn. It's going to be a terrible climb in the dark. We'll take the prisoners, try to draw the Communists away from you and then regroup at the fork in the next valley, on the far side of the mountain."

"Do any of the men you're giving us speak English?" I asked Scotty.

"Harry and Joe do. They also know the way over the mountain."

As Gunny, Holden and Craig came up to White and me and reached out to shake our hands, I realized how close we'd all become. Holden said, "Watch it, you guys. Be careful." And Gunny added, "We want to see both of you at the fork."

"We'll be there," White said, and we all shook hands again.

We were getting ready when I noticed Sally and the three other girls standing off to one side, looking tearful. I walked over and put my arms around the four of them—they were tiny enough for that. "Nothing is going to happen," I said. "We'll be together again soon." Then I turned quickly and walked away. I was no better at handling sentiment than they were.

White gave Scotty a wave as our group picked up the stretchers. "See you at the fork," he said.

"Aye, lads." With that we were on our way.

Outside the cave we encountered a strong wind, which made the going over rocks and the steep terrain all the rougher. Nancy and the lieutenant were strapped into their stretchers. Sam One decided he wanted to walk, with the help of his brother. The wind blew still harder and finally it began to rain. In the darkness, the trail became narrower and the rain made the rocks slippery—in places where we knew a slip would have sent you a long way down the mountain.

All at once while Harry and I were carrying Nancy's stretcher, my right leg slid out from under me. I managed not to let go my hold on the stretcher, and Harry immediately lowered his end of it so that Nancy wasn't hurt. But my leg had taken a deep gash as I went down.

"I fix!" Harry had to shout to make himself heard in the wind.

Familiar by now with Chinese home remedies, I yelled back. "Reach into Nancy's pocket. She has some earth in there." Harry found it, wrapped it in a strip of cloth ripped from his own clothes and tied it around my leg. Then we picked up the stretcher and were on our way.

Six hours later, the rain and wind still raged and we were still struggling up the mountain. An hour after that, Joe, who'd gone out in front as point man, came slipping and sliding down to tell us we were only half a mile from the top. I looked at the sky; the rain had slackened, and there was a hint of light overhead.

I asked, "Are we going to make it before daylight?"

Joe shrugged. "We try." Then he turned and started back up again, pulling ahead of us effortlessly. I was exhausted and I could see that White was also gasping for breath. But somehow we plodded on. Encouraged by knowing we were near the top, we could ignore the bruises, the scrapes, and the fatigue. By the time we got there, it was near enough daylight so that we could see into the valley. There was no sign of any human being. In this light the valley below us looked brown, with a thin mist rising.

After that moment's look, we were scrambling downhill, which was at least faster going. But it was also slippery, and all the more dangerous because we were so tired.

I asked Harry whether we could stop for a rest. "No time," he answered. We kept going until all at once we heard the sound of planes. We raced for the shelter of rocks as four fighters came over so low we could have been throwing rocks at them. In the valley they made a U-turn and headed back toward us. I was sure they'd spotted us, but they went right by, up the mountain and over. In a moment or two I could hear the sound of bombs and machine-gun fire, and realized that they were going after Scotty's group. I muttered "Damn it, they're after Scotty," and Harry said, "Lots of caves."

"But if the planes pin them down, troops can catch them."

Harry said nothing. We both sat in silence until the barrage stopped. As soon as the planes were gone, Harry stood up and said, "We must go, we have no time." Once again we picked up the stretcher and were heading down the mountain.

Later we heard the planes again and dove for cover. Apparently we weren't what they were after, since they went for what looked like the same spot as before. It made us feel helpless, not knowing how Scotty's group was making out. But there was nothing to do but go on as soon as the last barrage died away. This time we made it to the bottom. What had looked from above like an open valley was really a series of narrow canyons—just the sort of place to invite an ambush.

I stared at the rock wall ahead of me and asked Harry, trying not to sound nervous, "How do we get around this?"

"Opening in wall," he told me. "We go through, then we rest for minute."

It was a good thing we had someone who knew about the gap in the wall; certainly none of us would ever have spotted it. We clambered through and sat down. Our wounded were either asleep or unconscious; Nancy's color was good, and she appeared to be holding her own. Lieutenant Damon was another story: he looked terribly pale and weak.

Harry hadn't been kidding when he said we'd rest "a minute." We had hardly sat down to rest when he was saying, "We must go."

I gestured toward the lieutenant: "He can't go much further."

Harry only shook his head and said again, "We must go." I was relieved of stretcher duty now, and that made things easier for me.

But not for long. Suddenly there was a burst of machine-gun fire from somewhere near. I looked back and saw the bearers hurrying the stretchers into the protection of the canyon wall.

I yelled to Harry, "Where's it coming from?"

"Not know!" he shouted back. Down behind the rocks, we could see White waving at us, and we started crawling toward him. Our question about where the firing came from was answered as streams of men came at us from both sides of the canyon. We were trapped. And from the look of them, I feared they had more men than we had rounds of ammunition. I was wearing my usual two bandoliers, with a total of maybe a dozen clips in all, each clip holding thirty rounds. I also had one grenade.

I turned to White and asked if he had any grenades.

"No!" he yelled back. I saw sweat pouring down his face, and felt it on mine, from the heat and tension.

I looked over at Harry. "Any grenades?" He put up one finger. That made two, not enough to be worth much. I called out to White and Harry, "You two hit the rear. The friendlies and I will concentrate on the front!" They waved at me and we moved about twenty yards apart. The Communists were firing rifles, machine guns and mortars, heavily and without any direction. We were firing back more carefully, because we had fewer men and a hell of a lot less ammunition. The sound of the mortars got uncomfortably close. I looked around at White and Harry, just as a mortar round hit squarely between them, on the very spot where I'd been maybe thirty seconds before. Seeing neither of them move, I began crawling toward them. I got to Harry first and saw that the back of his head was blown off. I scrambled over to White, praying that he'd be okay. When I reached him I almost choked. Blood was seeping from his mouth, nose and ears. I put an arm under his head, trying to cradle it, but at the same time I could see that he was beyond help—even though his eyes were open and he was staring at me intently. I think he was trying to say something, but all he could do was cough up more blood. Looking down, I saw that his stomach had been blown open. As I met his eyes again, he tried to move his left hand. Then it fell back limp, his head sagged, and I knew he was dead.

Tears sprang to my eyes, and I heard myself saying "Oh God, oh God!" Then my feelings became a blank.

What happened then must happen to a lot of men in battle at those times when they seem not to care about their own lives. I certainly wasn't thinking that now I was going to risk my life, since in my own mind I had no possibility of staying alive. I was already dead; it wasn't as though I risked anything.

I remember to this day the detachment of that moment. There was no heat, no rage, but a kind of icy cold. First I reached down and grabbed White's machine gun. Then I stood up and emptied it. It was hard to fire and not hit someone, because we were in a tiny semicircle with our backs to the canyon wall, and they were all around us.

I tossed White's gun aside, picked up Harry's, stood to my full height, and emptied it. That was a dumb thing to do—except when you think you're already dead and it doesn't matter. But somehow I got away with it. I dropped Harry's gun, picked up my own, and headed toward the stretchers, where I could see Sam One, Sam Two and three other friendlies.

In that very instant, while I moved toward them, both Sams were hit by the same devastating burst of machine-gun fire and blown off their feet. No one could have survived that; I knew without looking. At least the two brothers had been killed together and probably that was what they would have preferred.

Looking down at the stretchers, I saw at once that Damon had been hit by a mortar fragment and was dead. Nancy was unconscious, but from the movement of her eyelids I knew that she was still alive.

Besides the two of us there were three friendlies, who were still firing away. I started firing again, too, as the attackers kept closing in. Their bodies were literally using up our ammunition.

Then, one right after the other, the three Chinese with me got hit. I was the only one firing back. Yet I was aware that the firing was picking up. Why the Communists were bothering at this point I didn't know. I started to grope in my right pants pocket for the little pill in its plastic case. I found it and clutched it, then reached for the knife I carried in my belt. I am about to die, I told myself.

The gunfire increased, and suddenly I realized that it was not being aimed at me! I spotted what seemed to be a squad of Communist soldiers leaving their cover—but instead of running *toward* me, they were running *away!* This new firing, which I had thought was aimed at me, had really been intended for them!

My first thought was that it must be Scotty's group, except that the source sounded like small arms, machine guns and mortars, and there was too much of it to have been coming from them. Then I spotted a whole bunch of new people. Whoever they were, they weren't in uniform: a ragtag bunch, no two dressed alike, wearing odds and ends, including what looked like old American fatigues mixed in with the more usual pajamas. None of them wore hats, but most had headbands—strips of cloth tied around their foreheads. I knew they weren't on the Communists' side, but it still wasn't clear exactly whose side they were on. They waved at me and I waved back. More and more of them kept appearing, until there were about a hundred. I saw someone moving through their ranks —a tiny person, perhaps five feet tall, but with the authority of a leader—who said "Hello."

It was a woman's voice. If I'd been less surprised, I would have said something by way of thanks for saving my life. But all I could manage to say just then was "Oh!"

7

As she came closer, I could see that she was dressed just like the others, in a mixed-up uniform and a headband. She was slender as well as short, weighing probably no more than a hundred pounds. She was also young, and—as became clear at a second glance—very good-looking, with dark eyes, dark shiny hair, and unusually prominent cheekbones. She had a gorgeous smile, and she smiled more openly than the others.

Her English was quite good—fluent, even sophisticated, though you'd never mistake it for American speech. "How are you?" she asked, and when I said "Fine," she said, "You don't look fine."

Now I knew who she looked like. You have to remember that I was just a kid and not much of a reader. But I had read the comic strip "Terry and the Pirates," and to me this amazing woman looked just like the Dragon Lady. When I blurted this out, she asked, looking amused, "Who is the Dragon Lady?"

"You know, in 'Terry and the Pirates.' "

"Who are Terry and the Pirates?"

I must have looked embarrassed, but her smile reassured me. "Oh, it's a long story," I said. "But there's a Dragon Lady in it, and she could be you."

"Dragon Lady. A good name. I like that name." Then her smile went out. I was to learn how quickly she changed from one mood to another, but this time I was startled.

"Are any more of you alive?" she asked.

"This girl is the only one," I told her. "We had two scouts out, but they haven't come back."

The woman was looking down at Nancy. "Who is she?" she asked.

"She was helping me escape from the Communists." I didn't think I should say anything just then about the other group.

"You don't like Communists?" she asked.

"No I don't."

"I don't like them either," she said sharply, making it sound both angry and businesslike. Coolly, she asked, "Where are the others?"

"Dead," I answered, still wary.

"No, I mean the *others.*"

I still hesitated. "Who are *you?*" I asked. "Where do you come from?"

She smiled again. "From these mountains. They are my home. They are *my* mountains."

Since she hadn't said what her name was, I asked, "Is it all right if I call you Dragon Lady?"

She appeared to think for an instant, then nodded briskly. "All right. Dragon Lady." Looking me up and down, she noticed my leg. "Are you hurt?"

"It's all right." Actually the leg was hurting a good deal, but the bleeding seemed to have stopped.

"We'll fix it." She spoke to a couple of men, who sat me down and put a kind of cream on my leg, making it feel moist and cool, and covered it with a bandage. "It will be better," she said. "Now tell me where you are going."

Again I tried to dodge her question with another question of my own. "How did you get here?"

This time she laughed out loud. "I told you. These are my mountains."

"How did you know we were here?"

"We saw you coming over the mountain. Then we saw the Communists attack you."

I would have liked to ask why they hadn't tried to warn us, but I didn't dare. I was, I must admit, a little in awe of this woman.

Then I was distracted by the smell of meat cooking somewhere. "That smells good," I said. She shouted an order, and in a few minutes someone brought me a plateful of meat. It might have been horse, buffalo or snake for all I knew, but it was delicious. I carried the plate over to Nancy. She was lying on her stretcher with her eyes open, and she smiled.

"Want some food?" I pointed to the plate, and she nodded. I tore off a few tiny pieces, propped her head up and fed them to her. She ate slowly, but between us we had soon finished everything on the plate. After that, a man brought a kettle full of hot water, which I used to rinse the bandages on Nancy's hip, and the wound itself. It didn't look red or infected. When I'd retied the bandages, I took off my shirt, wrung it out and bathed myself. By the time I put the shirt back on, several of the Dragon Lady's men were laying out the bodies. I went over and found Damon and White lying side by side. They both looked so terribly pale, these two fellow marines whom I'd never really gotten to know, even though I'd been with them now for something like three weeks. The lieutenant must have been in great pain during that time, but he'd never complained. Much of the time he'd been unconscious—thank God for that. I'd never found out why he'd taken on this mission, or whether he'd been hooked up in any way with Roberts and the other civilian. He'd seemed a decent guy, not a sadist like Roberts. White had been closer to my own age, and less of a riddle. We'd at least had a few laughs together.

When I bent down and went through their pockets for identification, I found nothing except the little pills in their plastic cases. They were now just two corpses, several thousand miles from home, with nothing on them to tell the history of how they'd lived and died.

"We must bury them now, soldier." The Dragon Lady's voice made me jump.

I objected, "There's nothing here but rocks."

"We shall cover them with rocks. We must do it."

I could feel tears rising, and I turned away, embarrassed to be crying in front of this tiny woman. But here were these two men about to be covered with rocks—no coffin, nothing to mark their burial places, no word to their families. I turned away, trying not to shake. But of course she knew I was upset. And now her voice sounded soft. "It's all right. We will take care of it, soldier."

Marines don't use the word *soldier,* and I wanted her to know that. "I'm not a soldier," I said.

"I watched you," she answered. "I saw how you were ready to die."

"Why did you wait the way you did, and then help us?"

"We cannot help everyone," she said. "We cannot fight all the time. There are too many Communists and not enough of us. So we are careful. But we believed we should not let you die." Someone called to her, and she answered and was gone.

I walked over to look at the other bodies: Sam One and Sam Two, both brave men, and Harry, whom I'd just met. How very easy it was to imagine my own body lying beside them!

I heard a commotion, turned and saw why the Dragon Lady had been called away. About twenty captured Communist soldiers had been led into the area, and were now being herded into a circle. The Dragon Lady walked around them and pointed to one who seemed from his uniform to be an officer. She pointed to the rock wall where I had come so near to dying, and the rest of the captives were led there and lined up against it. They all looked petrified with fear. Several dropped to their knees. Now, while I looked on in disbelief and horror, the Dragon Lady walked to one of her men, took his machine gun, and calmly opened fire on the captives. When she had emptied the clip of ammunition, she borrowed a second gun and emptied it. With a third gun, she walked up to the corpses and put a burst of fire into each one.

Her face could have been a mask. Handing the last gun to someone, she approached the officer, now the only survivor. His hands were tied and he had been pushed to his knees, where he huddled with his head bent over. One of the Dragon Lady's men handed her a thick-bladed sword like a machete. She walked up to the officer from behind, lifted the sword into the air, and brought it whistling down, severing the man's neck with one blow.

I had to turn away. When I looked back, her men had made a tripod of three captured rifles, and were putting the head on it. Others were dragging the corpses of the Communists and arranging them around the tripod as though they were spokes in a wheel. The Dragon Lady saw me flinch, and walked over. "You don't like this?"

I shrugged. "It's not up to me. I guess you have to do it."

"You are a *good* soldier."

"I told you I'm *not* a soldier." Somehow, I couldn't quite explain about being a marine.

"You don't like being called that?"

"No, I don't."

"Then I call you . . . " She hesitated. "I call you Khan."

"Khan? What does it mean?"

"Khan is Prince of Princes, someone who deserves respect. A leader."

"I'm not a leader."

She said, smiling, "I watched you. You *are.*" Then came one of her lightning changes. "I think we may be traveling in the same direction, and you can go with us."

I didn't know what to say, because I still wasn't sure whose side she was on. I wondered whether I should lead her right to Scotty's group—if there still was any such group by now.

"Which way are you going?" she asked.

I finally concluded, what the hell, if it hadn't been for her I'd be lying over there on the ground right now. "This valley is supposed to lead to a fork, where we will meet some others."

She nodded. "I know where that is. We will take you." She motioned to two of her men, who picked up Nancy's stretcher. As we moved out, I couldn't help feeling that someone up there must be looking after me. I would have hated to be here with a wounded girl on a stretcher without the Dragon Lady. I thought of the way she'd shot all those soldiers, and of the officer she had decapitated. I supposed she had done that to remind her men of who was in charge; to kill that way took a strong stomach.

I asked, "How long will it take to get to the fork?"

"We will arrive late tonight."

"Thanks—Dragon Lady," I said. And then, "I keep wondering, Dragon Lady, how old you are."

"Very old," she said—though of course she wasn't. "Very old and wise."

"You're all so young, you—" I started to say girls, but stopped myself. "You ladies. My friend Nancy, on the stretcher there, is only sixteen."

By way of reply, she called out something in Chinese. In a few moments two Chinese girls came running up to us. "This one, Lee, is only fourteen. And this one, Sue, is fifteen." They looked no more than twelve—but they were both carrying rifles.

"They're so young to be fighting," I said.

The Dragon Lady replied, "The village they come from

was wiped out by the Communists. They were almost the only ones to escape. After that, they joined us."

I started to say something about the Nationalists, and she looked at me sternly. Then she was silent for so long that I wondered what I'd said that was wrong. "The Nationalists cannot win," she said finally. "They cannot handle the country, they waste many lives."

"But you're not a Communist—" I began, and this time I was sure I had said something wrong.

"No. And I am not Nationalist." After that she said nothing for so long that I decided to drop back with Nancy and her stretcher-bearers, who had fallen behind us. The two girls, Sue and Lee, were walking alongside her.

"These my friends," Nancy said to me. I smiled to see her looking so much better.

"How is your wound?" I asked.

"Much better. They put leaves on it." She gestured toward the stretcher-bearers. I smiled at her again, reaching down to squeeze her hand, and walked beside her for a while. Then I heard the sound of planes. The Dragon Lady was about fifteen yards ahead.

"I hear them," she told me before I could say anything.

"What do we do?"

"We keep going."

"Suppose they spot us?"

"They won't see us. They are jets; they are too high and too fast. The canyons are deep and narrow."

"What do you suppose they're looking for?" I asked her.

"You. Many soldiers are looking for you too, because of what you did."

"What do you mean?"

"At the reservoir. We were near. We followed you, and we saw some of the fighting."

Again, they'd been there and had done nothing! Taking a chance, I said, "We sure could have used some help."

A fierce expression came over her face. "I have my own

people to care for and we do not fight unless we have to. To try to save you there might have cost us more lives than all of you." Then her face softened. "But I saw that you Americans were good fighters."

I had not said anything about being American but had wondered if she knew that I was. Now I shrugged and changed the subject. "So you'd been with us a long time. I thought you said you picked us up when we climbed that mountain."

"We saw you at the reservoir. Then we moved away, and then we saw you again as you came over the mountain."

"And we didn't see you at all."

"Oh no, we know how to follow you so you can't see us."

I had never heard anyone more sure of herself and of what she knew. So I asked, "Are the Communist soldiers following us?"

"Oh yes, they are very close. That must be the reason why your group broke into two parts, I think."

I didn't want to agree. Instead, I asked another question: "Were those the same Communist troops who hit us just now?"

"No. The ones we destroyed were from another division. There are many troops around here. That's why we have to keep moving."

"So the ones who were following us are still following."

"Oh yes."

Again, as if it had been timed, came the drone of planes. This time I could see them, flying at perhaps four thousand feet. I took the Dragon Lady's word for it that they couldn't spot us, and kept moving.

About an hour later, she signaled a stop. "We rest here for a while," she said. "We eat, and you will get to take a real bath —a swim."

We pulled in near the canyon wall. Among the rocks I saw several pools of water. I walked over to one and put my hand in; it had been pleasantly warmed by the sun. I thought of my last "swim" in training, with machine-gun bullets whizzing overhead. What day had that been? Exactly a week had passed since we were dropped into Manchuria. For the two weeks before that we'd been in training, with that daily exercise in the water. Could it have been only three weeks ago that I'd been given the choice of "volunteering" or being discharged for not mentioning my asthma? My God, I thought: the blood, the death, since that day! Three weeks ago who could have dreamed I'd be meeting Scotty, and now this woman? With people I hadn't even known then—Damon, White, Sams One and Two—it was as though I'd already been through a lifetime, and had seen them die!

"You take off your clothes and swim," said the Dragon Lady. "Then I shall bring you clean clothes."

I stood there waiting for her to walk away. Finally I said, feeling awkward, "You must have a lot of work to do."

"First give me your clothes."

I didn't know what to do, except plunge in with my clothes on. The pool was small, maybe ten feet across and four feet deep. A couple of strokes took me to the far side, where I sat down on the edge. The Dragon Lady went on standing where she was, laughing.

"Now give me your clothes," she said.

"First bring me the new ones." I saw Nancy being helped to the pool by the two girls Lee and Sue, I turned around quickly when they began taking her clothes off, and the others started to laugh. After a few moments Nancy said, "It's all right, Ricky, you can turn around now."

I did, and saw her sitting down in the water, with only her head above it, while the other two held onto her. Taking off my shirt and pants, I threw them to the nearest rock, keeping on the underwear I'd been issued in training—something that was a cross between a loincloth and a diaper. I stayed under the water, hearing laughter from the others, until one of the Dragon Lady's men came running up, and what he said brought on another of those sudden changes of mood. The laughter stopped and she hurried off. In a moment, a man brought me some clothes and told me to hurry. When I asked him why, he said "Hurry" again as though it was the only English word he knew. I had started after him when I remembered something. Running over to where my old rags were and reaching into the pocket of the pants, I found my little pill in its tight plastic container and transferred it to the pocket of the new ones. I spotted Nancy limping along, helped by Sue and Lee, and yelled at her, "Get on your stretcher!"

"This is good," she said.

"But you may break that wound open!"

The girls propped her into a sitting position on the stretcher, and I moved on past them to find the Dragon Lady. She told me there were Communist soldiers not far ahead of us. I asked what she was going to do, and she replied, "I am thinking about it. I don't like to go around. We'll see how many there are."

People kept running up to her, shouting, and then running off again. The stretcher-bearers brought Nancy up near me. "They talk about fighting," she explained. "She tells them what to do."

Now the Dragon Lady herself came back to speak to us. "You will not come with us, this is not your fight. I shall leave some men here with you."

I had had enough fighting for the moment and wasn't inclined to argue. I asked, "How far away are the Communists?"

"You see that ridge?" She pointed. "They are just on the other side." She shouted more orders, and four men came up to join us. They nodded and smiled as, with barely a look behind, the Dragon Lady moved away toward her troops. The men began talking to Nancy, who translated for me. "They say they take us to safer place."

"Where?"

"Higher on mountain. They say we have more protection there, can see down below, where is fighting."

The men lifted the stretcher and began moving up the

mountain. After a few hundred yards, they stopped among some huge boulders and one of them handed me a pair of binoculars. Nancy explained, "They are gift from the Dragon Lady to you."

I was going to have Nancy tell them to thank her. Then I thought I would thank her myself, and realized that I might never see her again. It was as though we were living in another century, in this place where killing and getting killed were everyday occurrences that everyone accepted.

Using the binoculars, I spotted the soldiers. "My God," I said to Nancy. "There must be a couple of hundred of them!"

For half an hour we waited with no new developments, until the Dragon Lady's fighters opened up. They'd gotten within fifty feet of the Communists before firing. I could see the Dragon Lady and her people moving out across open ground, with no protection, while the Communists stayed hidden among the rocks. Then, before the Dragon Lady and her force could see them, I spotted four tanks coming from a trail that ran along the canyon, all firing regularly. The Dragon Lady's people in the hills began dropping mortar shells among the Communists, but they did not have the range of the tanks. I was certain now that she would be killed.

Finally a mortar stopped one of the tanks, but there were still the other three. I couldn't stand to watch. Turning to one of our bodyguards, I barked, "Machine gun! Give me machine gun!" He didn't understand, so I turned to Nancy: "Tell him —" She was already explaining. In a moment he had handed me his weapon and I was sliding down the mountain, mostly on my butt, feeling the raspberries form on my skin as I went toward the three tanks. The men in them wouldn't be expecting anything from the rear. Near the bottom, I almost tripped over the bodies of two of the Dragon Lady's men. Seeing that one of them still had four or five hand grenades hooked to his belt, I stopped to grab them. As the last of the tanks moved slowly by, I ran toward it, climbed up the back, and pulled the pin from a grenade. I tossed it into the open turret, jumped, and headed for cover.

There was a loud boom behind me and the third tank stopped dead. I'd had the advantage of surprise, and once the grenade went off, the men inside would have been crushed like chunks of meat in a grinder. When I saw, to my amazement, that the two other tanks hadn't even paused, I went for the second one. Scrambling up onto it, I saw the turret was closed. After puzzling for an instant over what to do, I pounded on the top of the hatch. And damned if the thing didn't open! I flipped the grenade in and then headed for the lead tank. But this time I was out on open ground, and in an instant the tank commander had popped his head up and spotted me while I headed for the nearest cover, which happened to be the tank I'd just stopped. Looking back to see how far away the moving tank was, I saw two of the Dragon Lady's men already on top of it. They dropped their grenades, leaped, and then came the explosion.

Heavy gunfire was now coming from the hills above me. Diving for cover, I looked back and saw what looked like hundreds of the Dragon Lady's men swooping down on the Communist position. It was only then that I realized what her tactics were: she had brought her attack force out into the open, risking all those lives, including her own, to get the Communists to commit themselves. She now had them trapped between her attack force and the reserves in the hills.

I could see they didn't need me anymore—if they ever had!—and I made my way up to Nancy, who asked, "Are you hurt?" I'd forgotten about the raspberries on my rear and on the backs of my legs—until just then, when I tried to sit down. But I answered that I was all right.

Then the Dragon Lady came striding up and stood there looking at me. "You see, you fought like a Khan."

"You fooled me," I told her. "I didn't know you had that reserve force."

"We had to draw them out. In a battle you have to expect

to lose some people. If you do not understand that, you eventually lose *very* many. But the tanks were a surprise. My scouts did not see them. We took care of them—with your help, Khan."

I was embarrassed, but before I could begin to blush the Dragon Lady said, with one of her sudden shifts of mood, "We have much to do," and began issuing orders. The bodyguards picked up Nancy's stretcher and we moved toward the main body of the Dragon Lady's force. Nancy wanted to walk, but one look from the leader kept her from leaving the stretcher.

We went by the shambles left by the fight, passing more corpses. I had seen many by now, but hadn't gotten used to them. Soon we were making our way along a series of narrow passageways in the canyon walls. I was about twenty yards behind the Dragon Lady, and I kept thinking how smart, beautiful and feminine she was, as well as a warrior, leader and strategist. Tough as steel, she could march with the strongest man, she could execute prisoners in cold blood, and then sit and laugh like a girl while I tried to take a bath. And here I was, walking with that long shiny hair, those slim shoulders and boyish hips, right before my eyes.

After about an hour of walking, we came to a low valley. A sickening sight was waiting: bodies, many of them hacked to pieces, lay everywhere.

When I asked what had happened, the Dragon Lady said nothing. Then I could see for myself that these were not the bodies of soldiers. They were civilians, village people. The men had had limbs hacked off. Many of the women had been staked to the ground, spread-eagled, and obviously raped.

It was all I could do not to spill my guts. When I saw the children, I couldn't look any more. I dropped to my knees and started to vomit. They had been tied in bundles and used for target practice. When I saw the Dragon Lady, her face was expressionless. "Why?" I asked her. "Who did this?"

"Probably the Communists," she answered. "Probably it happened this morning, just before we met them."

"But why these innocent people—those children—little babies?"

The Dragon Lady touched me on the shoulder. "They were not on either side. The authorities destroy them to frighten other villages, to say, 'If you do not join *our* side, you see—this is what happens.'"

Men and women were burying the bodies and I knew they needed help, but I also knew I couldn't do anything. I saw that Nancy had been crying, and in a way I was glad. At least I wasn't the only one who was so badly shaken. I took her hand and she gave mine a squeeze. I squeezed hers back, and she started to cry again.

We stood there until the Dragon Lady came up to us and said, "We go now." We traveled for three hours and then stopped for the night on a high ridge. I hadn't eaten since morning, but I had no appetite after what I'd seen. I lay down with Nancy beside me, neither of us saying anything, and looked off through the clear night at the hills in the distance. After a while the Dragon Lady walked up and sat with us. Seeing how shaky I still was, she said, "You must get your mind under control. You must not be weak. Weakness will destroy you."

I raised my head to look at her. "I've been here for about a week," I said, "and I can hardly believe all the things I've seen and that I've done. Nobody in the world would believe me if I told them."

She said again, "You must practice controlling your thoughts."

Nancy, who'd been lying there silently, suddenly said, "Look!" and pointed to the sky. "A star, going very fast."

"We call it a shooting star," I told her. "You should make a wish."

Nancy seemed mystified until I explained, "Where I come from, people believe that if you make a wish when you see a shooting star, it will come true."

Suddenly she sounded like any little girl anywhere. "I wish—"

"You mustn't tell," I said. "Or it won't come true."

When I looked down at Nancy a little later, I saw that she had fallen asleep.

"It is good that she sleeps," the Dragon Lady said. "You should sleep also."

"But my mind keeps racing," I told her, "and I can't."

"First you should close your eyes and think of nothing. Then think of something that is good, and you will sleep."

"The only thing that's been good about all this is the people I've been with," I said.

"Then think of that. Learn to wipe the bad thoughts from your mind. Then you will be in control and you will be strong."

I put my head down on my hands, closed my eyes, and tried to follow her advice. It must have worked; at any rate, the next thing I knew, the Dragon Lady was shaking me awake. She gave me one of her smiles, and then she said, "We must go."

I shoved some dried rice into my mouth. It had been hard to take at first. Back then I guess I hadn't been hungry enough. But by now I was used to it; it's what I had for breakfast and most other meals as well.

We hit the trail, still carrying Nancy on a stretcher, though by now she was more and more eager to walk on her own. The path went uphill and downhill until I wondered once again whether these mountains would ever end. We didn't stop for a rest until three or four hours later, when there was a change of point men, and the ones who were being replaced came to report to the Dragon Lady. After talking with them, she came over to Nancy and me. "We are three hours away from the fork," she said. "We have not yet spotted your men, but we have seen a Communist force. We are watching them, but we have to be careful."

The trail here was even rockier than it had been. We had

gone down into a valley when two scouts came running, and I began to hear what sounded like firecrackers in the distance. The Dragon Lady told me in a moment that the Communist advance guard had made contact with my friends, but that the main force was still two hours behind.

Soon we climbed to the top of a ridge, where it appeared to me from the location of the firing that the Communists had Scotty's group pinned down. I was ready to go, and shouted to the Dragon Lady that we had to do something.

"We wait," she said.

Here was another of those strange twists in the woman's personality. I couldn't understand her not agreeing that we had to do something. "They need help!" I all but screamed.

She said again, "We wait."

This time I was loaded with grenades and clips, and had my own machine gun slung over my shoulder. I yelled, "I'm not waiting for anything!" and went storming down the slope, as fast as I could go on that trail. I knew that by moving a bit to my left it might be possible to surprise part of that Communist force from the rear. It was a foolhardy notion, but I was in no mood to stop and weigh my chances.

The noise of firing made it possible to get within a hundred yards of the Communists without being seen. Four men had their backs toward me. I hit one of them with a burst that bowled him over, then fired at the others as they turned. Now, of course, the advantage of surprise was gone. Before I could decide on my next move, I heard firing from behind me and off to both sides. When I looked around, fearful of being surrounded, I saw the Dragon Lady and her troops. Whatever it was that had made her change her mind so quickly I can't be sure. Had she been waiting to see how brave I would be? Had she planned to be right behind me all the time? Anyhow, it was a relief to see her there; we now had a full-scale attack in progress on the enemy rear.

At the moment, I was not planning tactics. My blood was up, I was in a kind of animal rage. I remember pulling the pin on a grenade and tossing it, and at the same time charging downhill so fast that I got caught in the explosion I'd set off. In fact it knocked me off my feet and left me momentarily dazed. Then I was firing again and I went on until my clip was emptied. As I was looking for a safe spot to change clips, two Communist soldiers stepped out from behind a boulder about three yards from me. Once again I'm sure it was surprise that saved me. If they hadn't been just as startled as I was, they could have cut me down. In the second while they froze, I threw my gun at them. It hit one of them square while the other ducked a little. Then I was simply charging into them. I weighed 190 or 195 pounds, or maybe a little less just then because of my new diet, as compared to their 120 or 130; so for them it was a little like a small American boy being hit by a pro football tackle. I grabbed the knife from my belt and drove it into the neck of one man just above the collarbone, pulled it out, and went for the neck of the other. Then I was on my feet, grabbing one of their guns, firing until it was empty, and lofting it in a high arc toward where I thought the Communists were.

I felt a hand on my arm, and saw one of the Dragon Lady's men. The fighting had stopped, and I didn't even know it. My clothes were drenched with my own sweat and splashed with other people's blood. For the next few minutes I was still too dazed to be quite sure what was happening.

Gunny and Scotty had been there talking to me but I have no recollection of what anybody was saying, and I'd made no move to hug them or show any sign of welcome. I remember seeing Charlie smile at me, and I remember Gunny putting his hand on my shoulder. Then the Dragon Lady was saying, "The main force is not far. They are coming quickly. You people had better go."

Gunny was saying, "We've got a lot to thank you for," and she was answering, "Don't thank me. Thank Khan."

All at once things came together, and I was out of the fog. "Khan!" I said. "That's me, you dumb bastard!"

Gunny grinned and grabbed me, and then Scotty came over and grabbed me too. And Charlie. I looked around for Holden and Craig. "When are the others getting here?" I asked.

Scotty had stopped smiling. "I have some bad news, Rick."

"Bad news," I said, dreading what I would have to hear: Holden killed, and Craig. And Sally. Scotty ended, "And most of my people."

Now I felt myself coming apart—until I looked at the Dragon Lady and felt her staring straight into my eyes. I tried to make my mind a blank, but then Gunny asked, "What about the rest of your group?"

I told him that Nancy and I were the only ones left. "The lieutenant, White, Sam One and Two, Harry, Joe, they all got it." I looked over at the Dragon Lady. "And if it hadn't been for her, we wouldn't be here either. I had my knife at Nancy's throat and the little white pill in my hand when they came along."

Scotty was eyeing her in a very cautious way, and she was looking at him in the same manner. "Do you two know each other?" I said, jumping in as only a kid can. "Scotty, you know the Dragon Lady?"

It was Scotty's turn to be puzzled. "Where did that name come from?"

"It's the name I gave her, from 'Terry and the Pirates.' "

"I don't know who Terry and the Pirates are," he said, "but it's a good name all right."

"Are you two really on different sides?" I asked.

Each looked guardedly at the other, waiting, until finally Scotty spoke. "We follow different paths. Once we tried to get her and her people to join us, but they wouldn't do it."

The Dragon Lady said simply, "We must be leaving. We must say good-bye."

"Where are you going?" I asked, feeling still more shaken.

"Up there." She gestured toward the mountains.

I was realizing for the first time how dependent I'd become. I'd felt safe with her and her people. "Why don't you come with us?" I said.

When Scotty looked at her, the suspicion was gone from his face. "Why don't you?" he asked. "We still would like to have you with us."

She hesitated. "One moment, please," she said, and walked off to confer with three of her men.

His eyes were still on her as Scotty told me, "Lad, you could not have found a better person to help you out of trouble in these mountains."

"Her people saved my life," I said. "They're not bandits, are they?"

"No, lad. They just don't want to choose sides, the way we have chosen ours."

After a couple of minutes, the Dragon Lady beckoned to Scotty, and he sat down cross-legged on the ground next to her for what seemed a long time, but might have been five minutes. At one point I saw him look toward Gunny and me. Finally he signaled to us and to Charlie.

"She says she will go with us," he said. "But there cannot be two leaders. She says she should lead us because she knows the mountains better than I do. And—"

"Wait a minute," Gunny interrupted. "You led us all the way. We can't change that now."

But Scotty held up his hand. "As I was about to say, I agree with her. She does know the mountains better than I do."

Gunny looked toward me. Not wanting to offend Scotty, I said, "She's very smart, she seems to know her way around and I respect her."

Gunny still didn't seem crazy about the idea. "But where's she going to lead us?"

"Get ready for this, lads," Scotty said. "I have a wee surprise for you."

I told him, "I'd like to know what the hell could surprise us now."

"She and I have been going over our plans. Port Arthur is our destination, but it seems to me we cannot head toward it directly because the Communists are looking for us and will be expecting us to go that way. I haven't been able to make contact with people who would help us, so we have to go in another direction. That is why I agree with her plan. It is also why I think she should be the leader. Are there any objections?"

Clearly, any objection now would be from Gunny. We stared at him and waited. He looked unhappy, but he kept quiet.

"It is settled, then," Scotty said, turning to the Dragon Lady. "You are the leader."

She was instantly on her feet. "Excuse me, please," she said, and then whipped around and began to call out orders. In a few seconds six of her men had taken off. Her unquestioned authority still amazed me, and I turned to Scotty to ask, "What in the world did she say to them?"

"She has sent them on ahead to the Great Wall to find a place where we can cross. Once they find it, they'll backtrack and rejoin us."

Mystified by everything, I heard her explain that we would begin by going west to the Changchun. She described this as an open area of low hills and valleys, more fertile than the country we'd been traveling in. We would see trees and fields of wheat. But there would not be the same protection that the mountains had given us.

"Oh great!" Gunny broke in. "So we go off in the opposite direction from where we're heading—and lose our cover to boot."

"And if we do not go in my direction," the Dragon Lady said, with a slashing motion across her own throat, "perhaps we lose our heads."

Gunny hadn't thought she knew enough English to pick up what he'd said and answer it like that. Now, for the first time, he actually nodded and said, "Okay, she wins."

"We have to reach the Khinghan Mountains," she went on. "They are west of here, in Inner Mongolia, near the Russian border."

"The Russian border?" I said. "I don't want to go there!"

"Not *into* Russia," Scotty explained. "We'd be going west, because that is the one direction they would not expect you people to go."

"And so what do we do when we get there?"

"We cross the plain of Changchun, then the Liao River. We stay on the north side of Chihfeng and we go into the Khinghan Mountains, then we turn and head south to the Great Wall, which we cross between Kalgan and Changteh. We stay west of Peking and head toward Chengting. We stay west of that, too, pass it, turn east and go to Laichow Bay. There we try to get a boat to go to Weihai, which is about two hundred miles from Seoul, in Korea."

All this left me in something close to a state of shock, and Gunny looked to be in the same condition.

"It's going to be a long trip, lads," Scotty told us.

"It's already *been* a long trip," Gunny said.

"But not compared with what's ahead."

The Dragon Lady now said, "Across the Changchun plain is three hundred miles. The entire trip might be a thousand miles, but it is probably less."

"A thousand miles—on foot!" Gunny exclaimed.

But the Dragon Lady only shrugged.

"Well," I said finally, "maybe we'll get to see some Cossacks over there."

Scotty laughed. "No, no Cossacks, but you may be seeing Mongolians, and they live about the way they did when Marco Polo went to China."

"No kidding," I said. Gunny said nothing, but he didn't look thrilled.

"We cannot wait," the Dragon Lady told us now. "The Communists are an hour away." She turned to Gunny and me. "Do you come with us?"

"You bet we're coming!" I said.

She gave her orders, two of her men picked up Nancy's stretcher, and we were on the trail again. The rest of her people—there were about a hundred altogether, twenty-five or thirty of them women, I would guess—simply faded into the countryside. Scotty, Gunny and I hit the trail together, and it was a while before I could bring myself to ask what exactly had happened to the others in his group. He told me that they had all died in an attack by fighter planes—the ones we'd heard passing over. "The bastards!" I heard Gunny mutter.

I asked, "What happened to the prisoners?"

"We took care of the Communist soldiers as soon as we left the cave. We couldn't drag them along." Scotty's face left no doubt what he meant. "We kept Roberts with us. In the second attack, the fighters got him."

"Did he ever say anything?"

"Not much. Only something about showing the Chinese we could give them trouble behind their borders."

"But if he was some kind of agent, what was he doing carrying around a card that identified him that way? And what in hell was he doing with Communist Chinese troops?"

Nobody knew the answer then and I don't know it to this day, nearly thirty years later.

But now it was my turn to relive all the deaths I had seen —Damon, White, Sam One and Sam Two and all the others. And then it was time to prepare for what was ahead. Scotty told us that we'd be coming to mountains higher than any we'd yet had to climb, and seeing people who still used bows and arrows. But at least we'd only get into the foothills of those mountains. We wouldn't have to cross them.

Up ahead, the Dragon Lady was waiting for us. She now explained her strategy for eluding the Communist soldiers. "Do you see that mountain?" She pointed ahead of us. "There is a tunnel through it, and that tunnel leads to another tunnel. They will not see us, they will not follow us. After we go through, we shall have a chance to rest."

We arrived at the tunnel entrance while it was still day-light. Inside, we moved through pitch-darkness. For some reason the Dragon Lady said there were to be no torches; instead, we each held onto the belt or sash of the person directly ahead, and groped along in single file. Once our eyes became accustomed to the darkness, it was not as total as it had seemed at first. But it took us two hours to get through, and when we emerged the daylight was almost gone. We came to a stone bridge where the Dragon Lady was waiting. She urged us to hurry.

"It is safer in the second tunnel," she said.

We moved past her, once again in single file, holding onto belts and sashes as before. The Dragon Lady moved past almost at a run, still urging us on: "Move quickly, move quickly." How she could be so surefooted in such dark I had no idea, but by now I was less and less surprised by anything she did. All at once, the leaders brought the column up short. We could hear scraping sounds up ahead.

Curious about what was happening, I slipped from between Gunny and Scotty, linked the two of them up, and worked my way toward the head of the line where I began to see light. I could make out Charlie and the Dragon Lady moving a boulder away from an opening. Pretty soon we were all rushing through a narrow downhill passageway that led outside. I hung back until everyone but Charlie and the Dragon Lady had gone through, since it occurred to me that they could use some help in moving back the boulder; I weighed nearly as much as the two of them put together, after all. But they signaled for me to go ahead. How they got the boulder back into place I don't know. Maybe it had been balanced in such a way that moving it was easy, or maybe they used a chunk of timber as a lever. I'm still not sure.

We had come out into a clear night, and we seemed to be in a bowl-shaped valley, walled in by mountains on every side.

"We stay here for the night," the Dragon Lady said. "No fires."

Once we'd settled down, Gunny, who was trained in first aid, changed the dressing on Nancy's wound. It was looking a lot better, he said. After we'd been sitting for a while, talking of nothing special, Gunny said, as though he couldn't help himself:

"When the planes first attacked, and we started to run for cover, Sally fell—I don't know if she tripped or was hit. Holden ran back to help her and they were both sprayed, cut apart. Craig saw this and just jumped into the open and started firing and running toward the two of them, and the planes tore into him too."

After a pause Scotty said, "Yes indeed, and Gunny here would have done the same foolhardy thing if I hadn't held him down." Scotty was not offering praise, either. "It was stupid," he declared. "Just plain daft. You may be sure you cannot survive long doing that kind of thing."

"But those Chinese," I said, "those friendlies back at the tunnel walked into Communist fire deliberately, for our sake!"

"That was quite different. They were trading their lives for yours, for they felt what you were doing was important. Holden and Craig sacrificed their lives for *nothing*. If Sally had just lain there, she would have had a better chance than she did after Holden drew attention by running to her. The same was true of Craig. He gave his own life without helping the other two at all. If you hope to get home alive, you two had better learn never to do such a thing."

And now it was just us two, Gunny and me, out of the eight who had started training together only a little more than three weeks ago. A little more than a week ago, six of us had made the jump. Now two of us were left to tell the story—if we ever got to tell it. Whether anyone would believe it was something else again.

"Another thing we'd better all do," Scotty said now, "is get our sleep while we can. We have a long way to go."

I woke in the morning to the sounds of the Dragon Lady's

people preparing to hit the trail. Sometimes I wondered if they ever slept; they were still awake when I settled down, and here they were, up before me. I felt stiff and achy, as I did nearly every morning, but I knew that after a little walking I would begin to loosen up and feel better. Dried rice was the menu again. This time we moved so fast that I was shoving it into my mouth as I started along the trail.

After we'd walked for a while I asked Scotty the question that was still puzzling me: "Why isn't the Dragon Lady a Nationalist?"

"She was once," he told me. "But finally she couldn't stand the betrayal, the corruption, everybody stabbing everybody else in the back. She believes, as I do, that the Nationalists would have won if it hadn't been for the black market, the profiteering, all the crookedness that undermined them. Do you remember the weapons we found in the tunnel?"

"With all those 'Made In U.S.A.' signs? You bet I do!"

"There is little doubt about where those weapons came from. Originally they must have been supplied by the United States to the Nationalists."

"And then captured, to be used against us," Gunny said, glowering.

"Captured—or sold," Scotty said, and Gunny's face got even darker.

"I suppose," I said, "the Dragon Lady knows who *we* are."

"You mean that you're Americans?" Scotty laughed. "It would be hard for her not to. As for your status, what branch of the service you're in or if you're in the CIA, that hardly matters. If she wanted to betray you, she could have done it easily and long before this. There's no need to worry about her. Worry about getting through the journey you have ahead of you."

I shook my head. I was worried all right, but what occupied me most right then was wondering if all the canyons were ever going to end. We'd go from one into a valley with a small river running through it, follow the river for a while, and then we'd see the valley deepen, narrow, and turn into still another canyon.

Suddenly, one more time, I heard the sound of planes. Gunny was obviously nervous, but I knew we were deep enough that we couldn't be spotted. The difference between my reaction and Gunny's wasn't really that I was an old pro and he was a rookie, but simply that he'd seen some of his close buddies destroyed by planes right before his eyes only a couple of days ago. When I told him to relax, he looked at me doubtfully, a little annoyed to be given advice by a seventeen-year-old kid, until Scotty backed me up.

"They can't see us," he said. "We've had the good luck that they didn't catch us out in that valley we just went through."

The path began to go uphill, which made it harder on the legs, and for a while we just ramped along without talking. Then Scotty began talking again about the Mongols—their bows and arrows, their huge swords—and about how there were tigers in China.

"Saber-toothed tigers?" I asked, quite seriously.

With a straight face, Scotty said, "Yes, and some dinosaurs too."

At that Gunny burst out laughing, and I said to Scotty, "Well, *you* never heard of 'Terry and the Pirates.'"

He admitted this was so, but before I could fill him in on what it was about, we heard the planes again. Then came the sound of small bombs exploding. It wasn't likely that they could see us, but they were making some very close guesses about where we were! The Dragon Lady signaled with her arms for us to pick up speed and follow her, and we broke into a run. The problem was that in this narrow canyon there was no place to go except along the path. We ran about a hundred yards and then followed the Dragon Lady as she scrambled up rocky ground to a cave in the side of the mountain, where we sat out the barrage.

I called out, "Is Nancy here?"

"Here, Ricky." She was doing a little better on the pronunciation, but it still came out closer to "Licky."

Then I yelled for Scotty and he answered. I asked whether making a light was permitted and was told to go ahead. Like most of the friendlies, I had a cache of my own. I tore a strip off my sleeve, which was too long and baggy anyway, and set it afire. In the moment while it flared, I wished I'd skipped the idea, because of what I saw—bones everywhere, along with dozens of human skulls.

"Did you see that, Scotty?" I said.

"Lots of people in China lived in caves," he told me. "Some still do. This may have been a burial place."

The discovery snuffed out conversation for a while. It wasn't long before the sound of the explosions had stopped, and the Dragon Lady was saying one more time, "Let's go. Quickly."

Almost at once we were on our way out of the cave and scrambling back onto the path. At this point it was rocky, narrow and steep. A few hundred yards farther along, we came to the crest and started down over a stretch that was rougher and more treacherous than anything so far. One side was close against the mountain; on the other there was a steep drop-off. When the front stretcher-bearer stumbled and fell, landing on both knees, my heart all but stopped at the thought of Nancy, stretcher and stretcher-bearers all tumbling down the mountain. But the bearer at the rear dug in his heels and got his end onto the ground quickly enough to keep control of the stretcher. I pushed my way forward, which wasn't easy because the path was so narrow, and could see that Nancy was okay. The knees of the man who'd fallen were badly cut and bruised.

The Dragon Lady came back up the trail as I was helping him up. Her face had a set look, and she wasted no time or sympathy on his injury. I couldn't understand what she was saying, but from the way she gestured, it was clear that she was warning him he would have to do better, or he and the girl would end up at the bottom of the canyon. She shouted up the line, and at once another man appeared to replace the injured one, who hugged the side of the mountain and let people slip past him.

Falling in behind Scotty, I learned that the injured man had simply been sent to the rear of the column, where he could be helped if he needed it.

"It could have happened to anyone," I said.

"But those it happens to don't live very long here," was Scotty's answer. "Because she showed him no sympathy, he'll be a lot more careful from now on."

The Dragon Lady had obviously been living this way for years. I'd been here ten days and considered myself lucky to be alive.

After trudging for a long time in silence, I found that the path was beginning to be less steep. Then we crossed a low ridge, and the Dragon Lady signaled a stop. I could see people, a lot of them, lying on the ground. After an instant I knew that "people" wasn't the right word. Those were corpses.

As we got closer, I could feel my stomach going queasy, and sweat beginning to stand out on my face. There were people who had been staked to the ground. Limbs had been torn off. Women had been raped. I turned away and retched. Nancy, who was now walking part of the time, came over and put a hand on my shoulder. I heard the Dragon Lady asking, "Where are the children?"

A number of her men fanned out to begin a search, while others gathered the bodies so they could be buried. Someone came running to the Dragon Lady, and I hurried after the two of them, though Nancy was calling after me, "You wait."

On the other side of a low rise, the Dragon Lady stood with a couple of her men. Each one was holding a tiny corpse.

"You should not have come," she said.

I asked, "What happened?"

"They were buried alive. They are not alive any longer."

They'd all been thrown into one pit, maybe forty of them. Just to make sure they were dead, her men were uncovering them one by one, and then burying them again. What I couldn't understand was what made people go out of their way to be so cruel, above all to young children. Even Scotty was shaken up, and he'd been fighting here for eighteen years. Nancy was crying—that is, tears were rolling down her cheeks, though she didn't shake or utter a sound. I put an arm around her and said, "It's going to be all right"—not that I had any real reason to think so.

I told Scotty, "I can understand Communists killing Nationalists, and Nationalists killing Communists. But why these villagers?"

"The Communists think they're teaching a lesson to the countryside. Their message is: Don't dare be against us! Be with us, or else!"

"Does it work?"

"People don't want to die. They don't want their children to die. So when they see something like that"—Scotty jerked his head toward where we'd been—"it takes a brave person to dare to fight the Communists."

I thought of *us* here, fighting the Communists, and of the little pill in my pocket. Then once again I heard the drone of planes and there was no time to think about anything.

8

There were two planes, and after one pass they must have spotted us. Now they circled and dived. The Dragon Lady yelled, "Down!"

I heard machine-gun fire. Because we were on the downhill side of their approach, they couldn't get a really good shot at us. After one pass, they had to begin a rapid climb to keep from plowing into the far side of the valley wall. As they pulled out, the Dragon Lady yelled at us to get up and move. With the planes wheeling for an approach from the opposite direction, she sent us running to the other side of the valley, so as to be on the downhill side again.

Twice more we went through the same maneuver, which was just that much more exhausting for me because I was half supporting, half carrying Nancy. Then the Dragon Lady began edging us toward an exit from the valley—a narrow, wooded gulch where we'd be safe from the planes. Once we made it, Gunny declared, "The woman is a genius."

"Now you see what I mean," I said.

Gunny looked at me smiling. "You sound like a proud papa. Or something else."

"Oh, cut it out," I told him, and pretended to take a swing at him. But his remark startled me. I hadn't admitted to thinking of the Dragon Lady in any kind of romantic way, even though she was a young and attractive woman. I'd thought of her as my general, the leader I depended on to stay alive. That was the way things were going to be. The decision I'd made wasn't a conscious one at all. It was just *there*.

She dropped back now to talk briefly with Scotty, who came over to us to report what she had said: "A few miles ahead there are inhabited caves. She knows the people and we're going to be able to stop there and get supplies. The Dragon Lady says you mustn't be surprised when you see the people."

Even though I'd about had my fill of surprises, for the hour or so it took us to reach the caves I found myself wondering what was in store for us. During a pause while the Dragon Lady talked with two of her scouts, Nancy caught up with me. She had been walking pretty well and was looking chipper. Now she took my hand and said, "We run?"

I laughed. "You feel good?"

"Yes."

"Good! All the same, we walk." I gripped her hand strongly as a kind of support and we started forward together. What stopped us before we'd gone a hundred yards was the sight of a group of people dressed in animal skins, as though we'd stepped into prehistoric times! It sounds strange even to speak of cavemen, but that is what they were. We watched while the Dragon Lady spoke with them. Then she turned to us.

"We shall rest here tonight. Inside there is food."

The series of caves we now entered were almost like

rooms, a good deal smaller than the huge caverns where I'd first met Scotty. There must have been fifty or sixty people living in them. Once we'd sat down, they brought us bowls of something thick and hot—a sort of porridge. Whatever was in it, to anyone as hungry as I was it tasted delicious. The main course, as usual, was rice.

After a while the Dragon Lady told us that tomorrow we would begin crossing the plain—and that we would be doing it on horseback.

I had been on a horse once in my life—on a Sunday Boy Scout outing. And one of the things that gave me asthma was horses. When I told Scotty about this, he asked me how bad it was.

"Not so bad. I haven't had it at all lately. But that may be because I've stayed away from animals. I never thought I was enlisting in the cavalry."

Gunny and Scotty both thought this was funny. But the Dragon Lady didn't. She got up and in a few minutes she brought me a small pouch. "Tomorrow, when we ride," she said, "you must take this. Do not eat it, just put some of it under your tongue."

Inside the pouch I found what looked like sand. "I'm not going to put sand in my mouth," I said.

She laughed. "Put a little under your tongue. Just a little. Try it now."

So I stuck a very little of it under my tongue. It had no taste and after a while I forgot it was there; either it dissolved or I had swallowed it. But I was going to need another kind of magic to teach me how to ride!

"Well, how long will it take us to cross this plain?" I asked.

"A few days, perhaps. We shall have to cross the Liao River, and that is perhaps one hundred miles away," she said. At least it wasn't a thousand!

As we talked, a couple of little girls had come up to stare at Scotty and Gunny and me. We were probably the first white men they'd ever seen. While they stood there, shy and hesitant but with no intention of going away, I motioned one to come closer. Then I clapped my hands together, and after a few more motions she got the idea of a game of pattycake. The other kids watched with big eyes, and the grownups all had big grins on their faces.

After I'd played the game with the second child, and then the third, a woman came and said something in a scolding voice, and the kids ran off. Though I didn't know a word of her language, the tone was so familiar that I could almost translate: "Now don't make pests of yourselves, just run off and leave our guests alone!"

I was thinking how wonderful it was that I could play games with these kids even though we came from countries thousands of miles apart and couldn't speak a word to each other. Then all of a sudden fatigue hit me, and I was ready to sack out. We were given some skins to lie on and to cover ourselves with, and in no time I was asleep.

When Scotty woke me the next morning, every muscle ached. There was a strange smell in the air and I saw some men smoking. Though I'd been a smoker—nothing like a pack a day, but regularly—I hadn't had a cigarette since soon after I "volunteered," for the simple reason that there weren't any. I said to Gunny, "Maybe one of those guys would give us a smoke."

"No. You don't smoke," Nancy, who'd been listening, said firmly.

"Why not?"

The Dragon Lady answered. "They smoke opium. If you want a cigarette, I shall find one for you." She waved to one of her men, who walked around a bit, looking for someone in her party to bum a smoke from. In a while he brought me a couple of hand-rolled cigarettes. I gave one to Gunny, and we both lit up. From the first drag I knew this was a mistake. Coughing and gasping, I finally managed to ask, "What the hell was that—rope?"

Scotty told us, chortling, that it was made from the fibers of a plant. "And the Mongols love it!"

The laughter had hardly died down before the Dragon Lady said, "Now we shall go and get the horses." She led us to an open place where a couple of dozen of her men were holding four animals each. Altogether there must have been nearly a hundred—enough for all of us. Where she'd managed to get them, I have no idea even now. But clearly—whether because of fear or love—she was respected in this country, and there hardly seemed to be any limit to what she was capable of. By then, if someone had told me she was going to produce an aircraft carrier on this plain, I guess I would have believed it.

None of the horses had saddles, and the bridle was a single rope around the head. A second circle of rope over the back and behind the front legs served in place of stirrups. One of the Dragon Lady's men walked up to me with a horse that they must have picked for its greatness, though it looked to me like a monster. While I watched, the others began mounting with ease—even little Nancy—and I wondered again how I would ever manage.

Then I saw that Gunny was having trouble too. He'd get his body up but couldn't get a leg over, or else he'd get one leg up and the horse would move a bit and he'd lose his nerve. I laughed out loud and he glared at me. "I don't see you up there either, hot shot," he said.

That stung me. I grabbed the rope in my right hand, tried to get a handful of mane in my left, and with a leap and a pull managed to get my left leg over the horse and my weight on top of him. I was about to say something when my horse fidgeted a little. In a new fit of panic, I clutched at his mane and neck, and barely managed to stay on.

There was laughter all around, but then Gunny had gotten the hang of it too, and we were off—beginning at a slow walk that I suppose was for our benefit.

After watching the way the others hitched their feet into

the ropes and used their heels to make the animal move and the way they handled the reins, I felt more secure. Scotty was staying close to make sure Gunny and I managed. "We're going to be awfully conspicuous, crossing the plain this way with so many people," I told him.

"It's a chance we've got to take. Perhaps we can do it because it's so unexpected." Scotty added that later we would break into smaller groups and begin to ride faster.

I stayed with the Dragon Lady, together with Scotty, Gunny, Nancy and eight or ten others. After a while the Dragon Lady started spurring her horse forward and all the others began to speed up, with Gunny and me doing our best to imitate them. At first I was bouncing with such a jolt that my spine seemed to be forcing itself up through the top of my head. Then Nancy pulled alongside me. "Move with horse," she said. "Like this." I watched the way she rocked, using her legs so that she went up and down along with the motion of the animal and soon—though it was certainly no featherbed up there—I began to feel more comfortable.

We'd ridden about an hour when the Dragon Lady held up her hand and called out the order, which Scotty translated for us, to walk with the horses for a while. This was a great relief to me. After we'd walked for a while, we were told to give the horses some water and then wipe their nostrils with it. For that I used another strip torn from my sleeve. Like the rest, I carried my water in a animal-skin bag, which I refilled wherever I could. The sun was up and it was beginning to be warm; I took a few swallows, but I was careful with my supply. Then I looked around at the countryside—a vast level space with trees here and there, and a few fields of grain.

Still walking our horses, we began moving into a series of low hills, all the time on the watch for planes.

Suddenly I called out to Gunny, "You know what? I've been with this horse for over an hour and my eyes aren't tearing a bit!"

"So the stuff you took must work," he said.

I caught up with the Dragon Lady to ask what the stuff in the pouch had been.

"A certain leaf, ground up. Many among us have this . . . illness that you have. The leaf prevents it. Don't people use something like that where you come from?"

"No. We just have shots." I made the motions of giving an injection to show what I meant, and she nodded to show that she understood.

I thanked her again and dropped back with Gunny and Scotty. Maybe twenty minutes later, the Dragon Lady ordered us to remount and we were off at a full gallop. I was already sore—especially my seat—but the riding was now a lot easier except that the insides of my legs were chafed. Looking around at the others—dozens of Orientals mounted on horses, wearing rags and skins, carrying machine guns and bandoliers— I wondered whether the wild Mongols I'd heard about could have looked much different.

At the top of a hill a rider appeared in the distance. As he headed toward us, I saw him hold up both hands, lower one of them, and then repeat the same signal. The Dragon Lady returned it, and sent four riders ahead to meet him. What a strange sight it was, almost as if we had been on the ocean— the rider appearing at the top of a hill, as if on the crest of a wave, and then sinking out of sight, appearing and disappearing again, until he and his four-man escort wheeled up beside us. The first of the scouts brought his horse alongside the Dragon Lady and the two of them continued at a gallop, talking as they rode. It was at least twenty minutes before she signaled Scotty, Gunny and me to come up, and told us what she had learned: "There is a river ahead and Russians are there." It was a Communist base, she explained, where the Russians were serving as advisers, teaching the Chinese to fly jet planes. When I asked, "What do we do?" she looked at me and said, "We shall see."

After we had ridden a while longer, the chafing along the

insides of my legs worsened. The skin had been rubbed raw by friction. When I told Scotty, he shouted, "You should have wrapped something around them before we started."

Once again it was clear how much I had to learn about taking care of myself in these surroundings. And how lucky I was to have hooked up with these people!

It seemed like hours, though I knew it was no more than a few minutes, before, blessedly, the Dragon Lady signaled for us to dismount and walk our horses again. Soon I spotted a couple of scouts galloping in and, as I feared, our rest came to an end. The scouts rode on either side of the Dragon Lady as the three of them talked. The day had begun to be really hot, and it was a relief when I could stop again and douse my horse's head with water.

Noticing that the Dragon Lady had slowed, I hurried to catch up with her and hear her report of what the scouts had found. There were, she said, six planes, perhaps more, several hangars, several shacks with soldiers in them, a radio station and two buildings that might have trucks in them. "Those," she said, "would be useful to us."

"But how do we get them?" Gunny asked, in the voice of somebody who already half knows the answer, and doesn't like it much.

"We attack," the Dragon Lady said.

Gunny rolled his eyes, but she ignored him. Turning to Scotty, she said simply, "Tonight." The two scouts were already drawing a map in the dirt.

Scotty asked how many Russians there were.

"We do not know precisely but perhaps one hundred people in total." She looked down at the map and studied it for a while in silence. "We shall not try to attack during daylight. So now we travel more slowly and arrive after dark. We hope to strike while they are eating or sleeping. We divide into groups. One attacks radio station and building next to it. This must be done with great speed. Other groups attack planes and the second building and the shacks."

She looked around as though waiting for someone to say something. Finally I asked, "Where are we now?"

"We are north of Port Arthur. And we are going west. We shall cross the river near Tiehling."

"And once we cross the river and get by the airfield, how far is it to the mountains?"

"Two hundred miles." She smiled as she said it.

We went off at a gallop, and traveled for the rest of the afternoon, resting the horses and ourselves periodically. The ground was covered with a low growth that might have been moss. Everything looked green and peaceful, and I thought of what I'd seen in only eleven days in China—the blood, the bodies, the children buried alive. If I ever got married and had children of my own, how could my family have anything to do with the Rick Gardella who had been through all this? Would I ever be able to tell them what I had seen—and what I had done? If I never told, what would it be like to live with that secret for the rest of my life?

I thought of what the Dragon Lady had said about controlling your mind rather than letting it control you. I'd work on that; I'd have to. How else could I handle the memory of those bodies?

"Wait!"

Scotty's voice shocked me out of my trance; they'd all slowed down for a short rest and I'd gone right on. So much for mind control.

The Dragon Lady explained that she was ordering one of her riders out to call together all her leaders. Then we would go over her plans for the airbase. Within half an hour the leaders had arrived. We all sat in one large circle, with the Dragon Lady in the center. She used stones to plot a diagram of the base, describing each group's assignment, going over it repeatedly until she was sure everyone knew exactly what to do. Scotty, Gunny and I were to join her group in attacking the radio station and the buildings adjacent to it.

Each of the group leaders was then given twenty minutes

to rejoin his unit while the rest of us mounted and rode off, walking our horses occasionally but taking no long rests, and eating nothing but a few handfuls of rice while we were on the move. Later in the afternoon the Dragon Lady called in her leaders for another briefing. As we went back to our horses, Gunny said to me, "Kid, when we get there . . . take it easy, will you?"

"What do you mean?"

"I mean, don't lose your head."

"What makes you think I'll do that?"

"Look, kid, all I mean is that you've been through a lot, you've been lucky—*we've* been lucky—and let's not push it."

"Gunny," I said, "let me tell you something. I'm not going to push *anything*. If we could get around that base, I'd skip it gladly."

"Okay," he said. "That's more like it."

A rider was approaching. Since there were always scouts coming and going, I didn't pay much attention to him—until he got close and I saw that it was Charlie.

"Where the hell have you been?" I yelled at him. Though he'd been gone only a short time, it seemed long the way everything did here—a day seemed like a week, a week seemed to go back a year. He grinned at me, pointing to the west. The Dragon Lady, coming up alongside us, said, "He has been to Mongolia, getting ready for our arrival there."

"What did they say when they heard we were coming?" Gunny asked, clowning.

Charlie, clowning back, hunched his shoulders and let out a growl. "They say that," he said, laughing.

"You tell them we said the same," Gunny told him.

As it was getting dark we stopped, and one by one the outlying groups came in. The Dragon Lady's orders were to proceed on horseback the moment it got dark. Fifteen minutes later, all the groups had assembled and stood waiting by their horses—more than a hundred altogether. The Dragon Lady pointed to a hill a couple of hundred yards ahead. Over it and perhaps a hundred yards down the side, she told us, we would find the base that was our objective. We now formed into a skirmish line and when the light was gone from the sky she mounted, as a signal to everyone to do the same. We set off at a gallop. I must admit that I was scared, but also exhilarated.

Once we got over the hill, we were almost on top of the base before we sighted it. We had seen no one and met with no fire when I spotted the radio station and adjoining building that were our targets. As we raced past, people were coming out of another building. My machine gun was off my shoulder almost before I dismounted, heading for the station.

I got through the main door and started up the stairs. By then I was hearing automatic fire outside. Two men stepped out of a doorway on a landing halfway up the stairs; I opened fire and knocked them both down. Stepping over them, I raced for the head of the stairs and kicked open the door I found there, revealing a man at a radio transmitter. I blasted at him and bowled him over. By this time Gunny was directly behind me. He opened fire and hit two men who had just come through a doorway to one side of the transmitter.

I took a deep breath and looked at the three bodies. All of them were Chinese.

We raced through the building, firing at anyone we saw, and finally we shot up the radio transmitter itself. Suddenly all was quiet around us though we could hear firing and explosions outside. Running out, we saw the planes ablaze. The firing stopped entirely. In a matter of ten minutes, the fight was over. We had not suffered a single casualty.

Following the Dragon Lady inside the second building, we found the bodies of ten men, all of them Russians—five officers in black uniforms, five enlisted men whose uniforms were brown. Outside my own group of marines, the only white men I'd seen since I landed in Manchuria had been Scotty, Roberts —and the ten dead Russians. These were the military advisers who had been teaching the Communist Chinese to use the weapons supplied to them by the Soviet Union.

Christ, I thought, we've killed ten Russian soldiers. If it were known, that would be enough to start a world war!

"What about the trucks?" I asked, and the Dragon Lady said, "There they are." I watched as several canvas-covered trucks were being pulled out of the garagelike building and one of the hangars. I could see people already climbing into them. They were small, holding maybe twelve or fifteen people each. The horses were to be left behind.

We lost no time in getting out of there, and were soon crossing a bridge over the Liao. Looking back, I saw the buildings we'd set afire lighting up the sky.

"They could see that all over China," I told Scotty.

"Aye, they might. But by the time they can do anything about it, let's hope we are in the mountains."

We drove without lights, over a road full of bumps and potholes. After an hour or so we stopped short with a screech of brakes, and Gunny and I landed on top of each other in the front of the truck. The reason for the stop, we soon saw, was a couple of Chinese on foot. After speaking with the driver of the lead truck, they came back and got in with us. As we continued our bone-rattling ride, they and the Dragon Lady talked, with Charlie listening and explaining what he heard. The area up ahead was full of Communist troops—and there were also Russians.

"More Russians!" I exclaimed. "Hey! We're not *in* Russia, are we?"

"We're a long way from it," Scotty insisted.

"Then what is it we've gotten into? What's going on?"

Scotty said quietly, "Take it easy, Rick."

"Take it easy, hell!" I shot back. "I'll take it easy if you'll just tell me what's happening, and why we go on running into more troops and more Russians everywhere we go!"

Nancy had come over to sit next to me. Now she put her tiny hand on top of my big paw. I looked at her, felt ashamed and mumbled something about being sorry.

"It's all right, lad," Scotty said. "Just let me tell you what

I can. It appears that the Mongols are upset because of the underground testing that is being done in this area. The men who just spoke to us say those were atomic explosions. We can't be sure of that. The Mongols are saying that animals from their herds are dying and that it's because of the explosions. They are ready to fight."

"And here we are in the middle of it," I said. "It's like the tunnel all over again."

"At least we don't have to worry about being bored." His good-natured tone somehow pacified me, and for a while we jolted along without speaking. With no headlights and no moon, once again it was hard to see the reason when we came to another halt. We got out and people from the other trucks came together in the darkness while the Dragon Lady went into another huddle with her men. Then she came back to tell us that up ahead there was another base, a big one—the headquarters responsible for the underground explosions. "Russians and Communist troops are there," she said.

"So what's the plan?" Gunny wanted to know, while Scotty asked, more diplomatically, "May I speak with you for a moment?"

The Dragon Lady wasn't used to being interrupted. But she went off to confer with Scotty. In a couple of minutes they were back and she announced that we would go around the base.

I was the last one to get back into our truck, and it was starting to move so quickly that I almost didn't make it. When I asked Scotty what he had said to make the Dragon Lady change her mind about the base, he answered, "I told her we'd already attacked one of their bases, and that they had radios and would be after us."

"I wasn't sure she would listen," I said.

"She has an open mind, lad. But you have to understand that every time she comes across a Communist, her instinct is to destroy him. She's got good reason for that—I'll tell you about it sometime—but she also has good sense. She wouldn't have lasted this long if she hadn't. Just now she saw that we'd better bypass that camp."

At that moment we struck something in the road, and Gunny and I were both thrown off-balance again. When we righted ourselves, Scotty was sitting there so coolly that I wondered whether he'd developed some special kind of balance from living the way he did. "What were we talking about?" he asked.

"About *her.*"

"Yes?"

"About what was wrong with her, that you two couldn't get along."

"I didn't say anything was wrong with her, lad. We just didn't see eye to eye."

Again we came to a stop, this time because one of the lead trucks had overheated. Steam was coming from under the hood and the driver was making angry noises like any driver anywhere. In a moment the Dragon Lady had ordered that the truck be left behind. "There is no time to worry about it," she said. "The passengers will be divided among the other trucks."

Her tone was so decisive that I couldn't resist saying, "Aye, aye, sir!"

"You are *sir!*" she told me cheerfully. *"I* am Dragon Lady!"

After we had been riding for a while, I saw that Gunny had somehow fallen asleep. I had actually dozed a little myself even though the road was now bumpier than ever—like driving over a bed of railroad ties. Dawn was coming. As the sky grew light, I saw huge, dark mountain peaks up ahead. I couldn't take my eyes off the scene but stared at it hypnotized until we came to a stop. We all got out and in a little while the Dragon Lady came up, walking with the same swift and erect bearing as always. I wondered if she ever slept at all. She told us that Charlie would lead us to a meeting place that had been set up while she went on ahead. At my questioning glance, she said, "I must meet some people before our group arrives. They do not like to be surprised."

"Didn't Charlie already do that?"

Scotty took hold of my arm and said to her, "We understand."

"What did I say wrong this time?" I asked him.

"Nothing, lad. You just didn't realize that Charlie didn't actually make personal contact with the Mongols. He could not have reached the mountains and returned to us on the other side of the river in two days and a half. That would have meant covering five hundred miles on horseback. Even he couldn't have done that. What he did was to reach the outskirts of Mongol territory and send word on ahead that we would be coming. But she must talk to them herself, the way any ambassador pays respects to the rulers of a nation he is about to enter. It is merely good manners."

Soon we were heading into the mountains, following Charlie in the lead truck. The Dragon Lady had gone off in a different direction. After a while we halted and everyone got out. I watched the trucks being driven off into a gully where they would not be noticeable from the road. "By the time the trucks are found," Charlie told us, "we will be up in mountains."

"And how do we get there?" I asked.

Charlie smiled. "We walk."

I really didn't mind, after all the riding. A good deal of the way I stayed beside Nancy. Her wound had looked bloodier and more dangerous than it actually was, I now realized, but her recovery was still a kind of miracle. "You know, you are a terrific girl," I told her, and she gave me a big grin. "Let's go up and walk with Scotty and Gunny."

"All right," she answered. "I go." Letting go of the hand I'd given her to help her walk, she broke into a run and I began jogging to keep up with her.

"I thought you'd gotten enough running," Gunny said.

"Go to hell," I told him cheerfully.

From then on the four of us kept up a steady pace, though things became more difficult as the path got steeper and the altitude began to be noticeable. The mountains were completely barren, without a tree or shrub. But once I looked off to the right and saw an animal, moving fast.

"A deer!" I shouted.

"A gazelle. Faster than a deer," Scotty corrected me.

It was the first animal of any size that I'd seen roaming wild since we came to China. "Are there any other animals around here?" I asked Scotty.

"You mean besides the saber-toothed tiger?"

I told him to go to hell too.

After a couple of hours Charlie put up his hand to signal a stop. We clambered in among the rocks along the trail and sat down. I was tired yet tense, and it must have shown. When I turned over and lay on my belly, I felt hands rubbing the back of my neck, soothing me. I looked up and saw Nancy. "You sleep," she said.

The next thing I remember was wakening to a rumbling noise that felt to me like thunder. Sitting up, I saw Charlie and Scotty both staring up the mountain. From up there, about fifty horsemen were charging down toward us. My amazement grew as they came closer. They were all huge strapping men. They were armed with swords. And one of them had red hair.

9

"Are those Mongols?" I whispered to Scotty.

"Aye." He said it without moving his lips.

"Then how come the red hair?"

"There are all kinds of Mongols." If he was trying to get me to shut up, it was for some reason I didn't understand.

"All the Chinese—" I persisted.

"Mongols are not Chinese. I'll tell you about it later."

Then I saw the Dragon Lady, who said, "We go with them." Pointing to another group of big men leading extra mounts, she added, "We ride." This time, thinking ahead, I took off the loose skin jacket I'd been given at the caves and put my feet into its sleeves, as if it had been an extra pair of pants, to keep my legs from chafing. The man who came riding up to us now was even bigger than the others, with a voice like a bear growling. There was even something bearlike in the way he looked—huge, powerful and hairy. Neither he nor any of the others had the yellowish skin of a Chinese. Some, like him, were dark; others were as fair as any "white" man, though nearly all had high cheekbones. And they all wore clothing made of animal skins.

"All right, lad," Scotty said. "Move lively now."

I took the reins of an animal near me. As I climbed onto its back, I saw the huge Mongol looking at me, laughing and pointing.

"It's the way you're wearing your jacket," Scotty said. "He thinks it's funny. Easy there, lad," he added—though I knew better than to start anything just then, and anyhow there wasn't time, because we were already moving.

At first there was no trail. We were heading through rough country, over a series of ridges that gave way to gentler slopes and then narrowed into canyons. We did finally come across a trail of sorts, which took us over a slope. On the other side, nestled among the mountains, was the Mongol camp. Looking down on it, I guessed there were two or three hundred inhabitants. When we came to the center of it, the big bearlike man spoke to the Dragon Lady, who turned and motioned for us to dismount.

The Dragon Lady still sat on her horse, face to face with the Mongol leader. They dismounted simultaneously and walked toward each other until they were no more than inches apart. He must have been a foot and a half taller than she was, and probably weighed more than twice as much. What he said to her sounded ferocious. She stood her ground and responded in her high, thin voice, pointing to him, then to the sky, then in the direction we'd come from. It was as though they were carrying on a kind of duel. They went through the whole thing all over again, and then he took a step back and began to laugh, shaking his head up and down. She yelled something and as he stared at her, I could feel those black eyes burning into me. For a moment I actually caught his eye, and I glared right back. Nobody was going to stare me down!

He spoke again to the Dragon Lady in the same laughing half growl, and she pointed to Scotty, Gunny and me as she answered. Finally he motioned for her to sit down, and they went on talking in lower tones.

Looking around the camp, I asked Scotty about the huts the Mongols lived in. "What are they made of? Looks like corn husks to me."

"Aye, lad, it's something of the sort. Here they call it kaoliang, and it has many uses. They build their houses from the husks; they make wine and porridge from it, they use it for fuel, and they feed it to the animals."

"They sure don't waste anything, do they?"

"That's right, lad. There's not much out here for anyone to waste."

I spotted some children clustered together off to one side of the camp, and looked toward Charlie. "Mongol custom," he told me. "When men do business, women and children keep back."

After a while I felt secure enough to drift away from the group and head toward the children. Near them a group of women were silently huddled together. I was within a few yards of the children when I heard a screech behind me, whipped around and saw a huge form coming at me. Without thinking, as a kind of reflex, I swung and caught him right on the jaw—and as any boxer can tell you, that's the worst place to get hit. There he lay, flat on his back, looking like a fallen tree, and in another second or two I was surrounded by Mongols. Then the one I'd hit was on his feet, coming at me again and making threatening noises. It dawned on me what I'd done and how it might affect all of us. While I tried hard not to show my fear, I heard screaming and yelling from the center of the pack of Mongols. It was the Dragon Lady, making her way toward me. Her air of command must have been what got her through to the center of the circle. With the Mongol chief just behind her, she came striding up and stood beside me.

She shook her head and said, sounding almost amused, "You hit his lieutenant! That is not good in this camp."

"I thought he was going to attack me."

"I understand. Still, it is not good." For a moment she seemed to be thinking. Then, with a look straight at the chief, she pointed to me and said, "Khan!"

The chief seemed surprised. He looked at me and then back at her.

"Khan!" she repeated, louder than before.

Again those menacing black eyes of his took me in. This time he strode toward me and brought down his face over mine until we were almost touching. I felt his rotten breath as he growled out something meaningless to me, except that the word *Khan* was in it.

I stood my ground. Part of it was bravado, part of it was feeling the honor of the Marine Corps at stake. The chief reached out his right hand to grab my shoulder. I brushed the hand away. While he glared at me, the Dragon Lady smiled, which made me feel a little surer of myself. When he reached out with both hands, I thought he was going for my throat, and I put my arms between his and knocked them to the side. From his puzzled look, this must not have been what he expected. Then his lieutenant came over, said a word or two, pulled out his knife, and pointed it at me. The chief turned with a growl to the Dragon Lady, looking first at me and then at his lieutenant. Then he began to walk away, with the lieutenant reluctantly following.

By this time Nancy, Gunny, Charlie and Scotty had worked their way through the circle. As the Dragon Lady looked first at them and then at me, she wasn't smiling anymore.

She said, "You have to fight the lieutenant."

I would have my choice of weapons, she went on—either a sword or a bow and arrow.

Trying to keep my voice cool, I said, "I've never used a sword or shot a bow and arrow in my life."

Scotty broke in, "Tell them you'll use a machine gun."

"No guns," the Dragon Lady said.

Then Charlie was explaining, "The Mongols love to wrestle. It is one of their favorite sports."

I looked over to Gunny, who said, "For Christ's sake, knock it off, Rick."

Scotty was looking angry too.

"Hell," I said to both of them, "all I did was go over toward the kids!"

"The Mongols have their own rules, very strict rules," the Dragon Lady said emphatically.

I said I was sorry I'd broken their rules, and asked when the fight was supposed to take place.

"When the sun is high," the Dragon Lady said. Nancy had come and taken hold of my arm. But the Dragon Lady said to her and the others, "Now I talk to the Khan alone, please."

As the four of them walked away, she looked me straight in the eye. "These are hard people. They are part of the Tungus tribe. Most of them live in Siberia, but a few small groups stay here in Mongolia. They are the best hunters in the world."

I understood her to mean that I could never win with a bow and arrow. I said, "What if you told them no weapons, just hands?"

"I shall see what he says." She walked off toward the Mongols, who had moved to a distance of maybe a hundred yards. While I waited, trying not to think at all, I saw a little girl standing no more than ten yards from me. No telling where she had come from, or how she got there. Finally, not knowing what to do, I said "Hi." She didn't answer me, but went on staring and gnawing her knuckle. When I held out my hands to her, she started to reach out, but then drew back. I took a few steps toward her and knelt down. "What's your name?" I asked, hoping she would hear the friendly tone in my voice.

The Dragon Lady had come back. Now she said, "This is my sister."

I stood up. "Your *sister?*"

"Yes. My small sister. Her name is Kim. She is twelve years old."

I knelt down again and said, "Hi, Kim." The Dragon Lady said something in Chinese. Kim took the knuckle out of her mouth, put her hands behind her back and smiled. I put out my hands again and this time, after hesitating, she reached out to catch hold of them.

I moved a little closer to her. "Hi, Kim," I said again.

She looked up at her sister and then smiled again. But she was still too shy to speak.

"Didn't you teach her any English?" I asked the Dragon Lady, who said something to her sister. Then Kim pointed to me and said, "Hi, Khan."

Now, from the Dragon Lady's change of expression, I knew it was time to talk business.

"Soon the sun will be high," she said. "We have to make our plans. You must be careful, for the lieutenant is very strong."

"Have they agreed to hands, no weapons?" I asked.

"Yes. I made them understand that bow and arrow or sword would be unfair."

I thanked her, but her face remained dark. "Do not thank me. He says he will eat you up like a deer."

I glowered at that, and she said, "Now you must listen" —and she told me how to fight. I never doubted for a moment that she knew exactly what I had to do.

"You understand?" she said finally.

"I understand."

There was shouting, and I turned to see the lieutenant storming toward us, followed by what seemed to be everybody in the whole Mongol camp. The lieutenant halted at about thirty yards, and the crowd halted too. He yelled something that ended in a growl, and the Dragon Lady made me understand that he was challenging me. "Now you go to him."

"Okay," I said, and while she followed I walked half of the way toward him. Stopping short, I said, "Now you tell him to come the rest of the way to me. Or . . . or . . . I'll think he's a woman."

"Shall I tell him that?"

"Yeah," I said, surprised to find myself giving her an order. "Tell him that." And she must have done it, because when she had spoken the lieutenant, who'd been standing there with his arms folded, suddenly grew furious. Dropping his arms, he went into a crouch and started toward me, circling to my left. The people behind him let out a kind of gasp, and then screamed.

The lieutenant had come within ten yards and was still circling, getting no closer. As he finished one whole loop around me, the Dragon Lady shouted, "Remember the plan!"

Suddenly he lunged. Remembering, I dropped to the ground, bracing my weight on my left arm and kicking out with both feet. I caught him on the shin and kneecap, feeling the impact all the way up to my hip, and saw him fall. Jumping up, I pounced on him and put my right elbow into his throat. I could tell that he was in pain.

Then I was in pain myself for one excruciating instant before I blacked out completely.

My next memory is of waking up in a hut somewhere, with the worst headache I ever had. Once I got my eyes to focus, I recognized Nancy and then the Dragon Lady, both smiling down at me, then Gunny, Scotty—and the Mongol chief.

"My head," I said. "God, but my head hurts."

Nancy, kneeling beside me, laid her hand on my forehead. "It's all right, Ricky, you be well."

I lay there not saying anything, trying to smile, and after a few minutes things began to be a little less confusing. I discovered that my clothes had been changed, and that I was now dressed in skins, just as the Mongols were.

"Who put me into these?" I asked, and Scotty, looking toward the two women, answered, "They did."

"What?" I stared at them, and it seemed to me that they both blushed. Then I asked, "Whatever hit me?"

Gunny said, "Two buddies of that bastard! When you decked him, one of them came at you with a club."

Whether it was a coincidence or not, just then the chief said something angry to the Dragon Lady, who sounded angry too, and they both went outside. In a moment she was back. "You come," she said to me.

"But my head hurts so—"

She broke in, "Khan, you must come quickly!"

The throbbing in my head seemed to explode when I moved, and for a bit I just stood there, waiting for it to ease, before I got through the doorway.

Outside I saw that it was dark. Several fires were burning, and gathered around them were what once again seemed to be everybody in the village. In front of me stood the chief, with his lieutenant and two other men behind him. "Those are the two guys that hit you," Gunny told me. From the size of them, one would have been more than enough. But I could see now that they weren't about to start a fight. The chief spoke to them and they dropped to their knees. Next the chief spoke to the Dragon Lady and pulled the sword from the scabbard at his waist. The Dragon Lady said, "Now you shall deal out punishment."

"What does he want me to do," I asked. "Cut off their heads?" And I very nearly laughed.

"Yes," she replied. "If you wish."

As though to prove he wasn't kidding, the chief walked up and held out the sword with its handle toward me.

"Take it!" the Dragon Lady said in a loud whisper, as I hesitated. "Don't wait! Take it!"

I reached out and gripped it in one hand. When the chief let go, I had to grab with my other hand to keep from dropping the thing. "What do I do now?" I asked.

"You are to deal out the punishment," she said again.

I turned to Scotty and Gunny, who were no help, and then glanced at the chief. His black eyes blazed as though there were fires inside them, but he stood silently waiting for what I would do.

"Holy Mother of God," I said softly to myself, and took another look at the Dragon Lady and then at Nancy standing near her. Neither gave me any sign. Turning back, I held the sword with both hands and slowly raised it above my head.

The lieutenant and his guards still did not move. Very slowly, I brought the sword down, point first, and drove it into the ground. Then I turned to the chief. "No," I said. "They live."

The chief did not move. While he stood looking at me, I walked over to the three kneeling men, bent over each one and helped him to his feet. I touched each one on the shoulder in turn and then walked up to the chief. When my face was a foot from his, I said, "Friends, friends!" I touched my own chest, pointed to our group and to the three men, and repeated, "Friends, friends!"

Then the Dragon Lady was speaking to the chief, while he stared into my eyes as though he might burn holes in them. Finally he turned to his people, and growled something that ended in a shout of "Khan!" as he pointed to me.

The people all cheered and waved their arms. The chief walked over to where I had driven the sword into the ground. He drew it out with one hand, lifted it over his head, and called out, "Khan, Khan, Khan!" while the people went on cheering and waving. I saw the Dragon Lady and all the others cheering too.

Scotty came over to me and said, "Well, lad, I guess you have them on your side now." And there were a few good-natured digs from Gunny. While the cheering died down, the chief was speaking again to the Dragon Lady. Now she told us that he wanted us to sit at the fire with him and share his food.

When we'd walked over to the fire and I'd started to sit

with the others, the Dragon Lady said, "No. Do not sit here." She pointed to the chief. "You are to sit there. The lieutenant sits on one side of him. He wants you to sit on the other side."

"You see, lad," Scotty said, "you're royalty now."

So I sat next to the chief, who began speaking to me. Not understanding gave me a good excuse to wave to the Dragon Lady to join me. "Tell him I need you here as interpreter."

When she explained, he nodded and said—to my surprise —"Okay." Then he growled out orders to a couple of his men, who brought some chunks of the meat that had been roasting on a spit. This was the first fresh meat I'd eaten since the Dragon Lady rescued us, and it was certainly good. I asked her what it was, and she told me it was antelope.

Once the chief finished eating, he gave another order, spitting out bits of gristle as he spoke. Promptly one of his men brought over some skin bags of the kind we carried water in—but these, the Dragon Lady explained, had wine in them, made from kaoliang. The chief held out one of the bags. I took it in both hands, tilted it back and drank. Though I'd never been much of a wine drinker, it tasted fine. Scotty and Gunny were also being taken care of. Every time I looked, it seemed, Gunny's head would be tilted back with a wineskin above it.

After we'd all gorged ourselves, the dancing began. For a beat, people were pounding the ground or the wineskins with sticks or their bare hands. Before long the Dragon Lady walked to the center of the circle. For some minutes she danced alone, as gracefully as she did everything else. Then Gunny, in his cups by now, got up and staggered toward her. The next thing I knew, she had come over to me, taken me by the arm, and pulled me to the center of the circle. I was sober enough to avoid tripping, and in a couple of minutes I was actually enjoying myself, keeping the beat along with the Dragon Lady. After Gunny fell down and sat laughing, Scotty came forward to help him back to his place. Just as I was beginning to feel winded myself, the Dragon Lady took my arm and led me back to where we'd been sitting. The chief looked at us good-naturedly and said, "Okay!" It may have been the only English word he knew.

Our places in the center were now taken by the lieutenant and his two friends. Watching their movements, which were graceful and energetic, I said to the Dragon Lady, "I've seen that kind of dance before."

"It is a Cossack dance."

"You mean they're *Russian?*"

"Many Cossacks lived in southern Russia, but some lived in Asia also."

"So the same customs just go on for thousands of years?" I said. I felt as though I'd made an amazing discovery.

She nodded. "Many things have stayed the same for longer than that. The Mongols are much the same, as fierce as they were when Genghis Khan was their leader."

"Genghis Khan?"

"He was the great khan who organized the Mongol tribes and trained them to be fine horse soldiers."

"Cavalry?"

"Yes. Perhaps the best cavalry that ever rode horses."

Having seen these men ride, I could easily believe that.

The dancing stopped, and the party began to quiet down. The wine had given me a glow, but my headache hadn't gone away. Now I was tired and beginning to feel cold. When I told the Dragon Lady this, she said, "You stay in my house." After she'd spoken to the chief, he gave some more orders, and at once a couple of men came running with spare clothes—jackets, pants, boots—for all of us.

Once I'd put mine on, I began feeling so drowsy that I could hardly control the urge to sleep. But the Dragon Lady put her hand on my shoulder and said, "You must wait. You must not go until I tell you." She spoke to the chief again. He reached out his greasy hand to pat my back, saying again, "Okay, okay."

"Okay," I said, and gave him a tap on the shoulder.

The Dragon Lady said, "It is all right. You may go. He hopes you sleep well."

Getting up, I waved my hand to the chief as a way of saying "Thanks for everything." Then I smiled at his lieutenant. Smiling too, he stood up and held out his right hand. As I reached for it, he grasped my arm just above the elbow, and I did the same. When I turned to the Dragon Lady, she nodded in confirmation. "It is a sign of friendship."

Then Gunny, Scotty, Nancy, Charlie and I all followed the Dragon Lady into her hut. Like the others, it was made of the husks of kaoliang, and although it didn't look large from the outside, there seemed to be plenty of room in it for all of us. I noticed Kim already sleeping off to one side. The Dragon Lady motioned us to another part of the hut, where she picked up several large skins from a pile and gave each of us one. I rolled up in mine, comfortably warm, and had hardly put my head down before I was asleep.

When I opened my eyes again it was morning. Scotty was already awake. I reached over and poked Gunny, who was still snoring. He blinked and said, "Christ, can't a guy even get any sleep around here?" There was no sign of the others, and I wondered where they had gone. Then I smelled food cooking, and after a couple of minutes the Dragon Lady and Kim came in carrying several skins containing food. I saw something that looked like corn, and asked Scotty about it.

"Aye, lad," he said. "It's what we call maize. It was brought over from America and the Chinese started growing it. They use it for fuel, too, the way they do kaoliang."

"I'm a meat and potatoes man myself," I said as the Dragon Lady brought me a skin filled with corn, meat and kaoliang, "and I was wondering how these Mongols could live on rice and get so big!"

"In China there are potatoes too," the Dragon Lady said. "But not here in the north."

"In the south," Scotty explained, "they grow sweet potatoes, and also peanuts and tobacco. China has more different foods than you might suppose. It also has a huge population to feed. That is the problem."

The Dragon Lady's face had turned serious, even sad. "China must have peace," she said. "When we have peace, we shall grow enough food for all the Chinese people."

I stopped eating to look at her. All I could think of was to reach out my hand and give hers a squeeze. But in an instant her look and mood had changed again. "Today we shall have fun," she said brightly. "There will be games. Mongol games." She got to her feet and went off while we finished our breakfast. I'd been given a lot of food, but it was no more than I could handle. Feeling both well rested and well fed, I got to my feet, pushed aside the skin that covered the entrance to the hut, and peered out.

"Holy God!" I exclaimed. "Am I seeing things, or is that a camel?"

The camel wasn't the only surprise, either. The man riding it was no Mongol. He was white.

10

We stood there dumbfounded while the Dragon Lady ran to greet the new arrival. Behind him were a dozen others, all riding on camels. The leader dismounted and spoke to the Dragon Lady in a language that wasn't English. He looked excited, and so did she.

Then the Dragon Lady was pointing to us, and the two of them were walking toward us as we stood in the doorway of the hut. The stranger might have been in his middle thirties. He was not tall—perhaps five feet eight or nine inches—but broadly built, weighing maybe 180. He wore skins like the Mongols, and as he came closer I could see that he had dark brown hair and that his face was rugged but pleasant. He smiled often as he talked to the Dragon Lady.

They headed for the hut, and he said, "Well, mates, how

goes it?" His accent was not American; he sounded a little like Scotty, but not quite.

Next Scotty was saying, "Glory be! Audy! It's been years!" And the two of them were embracing, while the Dragon Lady stood smiling and Gunny and I stared in bewilderment. Scotty invited the other to sit down and share our meal, and then he said, "Lads, I want you to meet Audy, who's an old friend from Australia." We soon learned that he had been in China since World War II.

"I was a coast watcher during the war," Audy explained. "First in Burma and then in China with two Australian mates. Our job was to keep an eye out for Japanese ships. Both my mates were killed by the Japs and after the war I decided to stay. I feel the same as Scotty does about China. Wouldn't go back home in a million years."

When Scotty asked what he'd been up to, he said, "I've just come from the Gobi, taking care of some business."

Inquisitive as always, I asked, "What's the Gobi?"

"A desert," Scotty explained. "Between Russia and Mongolia."

"I tell you, Scotty," Audy went on, "on my way back, we heard a lot about some group been giving the Commies a hard time. They're in one bloody awful mood down on the plains, especially Manchuria. Don't know what these blokes have done, but the Commies are sore about it."

Scotty grinned at him and then we were all laughing.

"It was you blokes, was it? Been having yourselves some fun?"

The laughter went on for a while before Scotty remembered his manners and introduced Gunny and me by name.

"Pleased to meet you," Audy said, "You chaps American, eh?"

We both hesitated. Then Gunny said "Yup," and I chimed in, "That's right."

Audy laughed. "I fought with you chaps during the war. I'd know a Yank a mile away in the dark."

"Used to see a lot of Audy during the war," Scotty reminisced. "But afterwards he went north into Mongolia, and I lost him."

"I've been up in Mandal," Audy told him. "Then down to Sain Shanda and across the mountains to here. Wanted to see my friends out there."

I couldn't resist saying, "They're sure some friends."

"What do you mean?" Audy asked.

"If you'd been here yesterday, you'd know," Scotty told him. "It's rather a long story. For now I'll just say that we have here with us a young khan." And he pointed to me.

To keep Scotty from going into the embarrassing details, I said, "Oh, it's just a nickname the Dragon Lady gave me."

Audy now looked more confused than ever. "And who, may I ask, is the Dragon Lady?"

"*She* is." I gestured toward her.

"Well, that's a new one on me."

"Rick—Khan, that is—gave her the name," Scotty said. "And that's another story we shan't go into now."

Audy turned to the Dragon Lady and spoke to her in what I suppose was Chinese. She answered in English, "From now on I am Dragon Lady. That is my name. And," she added, pointing to me, "his name is Khan!"

"We're all learning new things," Scotty said. "Until we got here I never knew the Dragon Lady had a sister."

With a cool look, she said, "There are many things about me that you do not know. But there is no time now to tell you everything. Now we shall watch the Mongol sport."

Gunny was up and heading for the door. "I've still got a little of that wine in my system," he said. "I could use some air." He stepped out, but after a second or two he stepped back in.

"My God, they've got *wolves* out there!" he yelled.

The others seemed mildly amused. Going to the entrance, I stuck my head out and saw, sure enough, half a dozen of the snarling animals. Wondering what they thought was funny about that, I said, "Have a look for yourselves!"

"The Mongols keep them as pets, Rick," Scotty told me.

"Wolves? As pets?"

"Aye, lad. They're tame, they're friendly."

"Bullshit!" Gunny said. And when I reached out, intending to pet one of them, he made a lunge for my hand.

"Friendly, huh?"

But the Dragon Lady said, still looking amused, "Come. I shall take you with me."

Following her out, I found there were now no less than a dozen of them, most of them bigger than German shepherds, jumping all around us. The Dragon Lady, who was carrying some of our leftover food, walked calmly up to them, with me still as close behind her as I could manage, while they jumped at her and took the morsels from her hand. The air outside was cool but I was sweating. Looking back at the hut, I saw that Audy, Scotty and Gunny were all staying put. The Dragon Lady dropped to her knees, and the "pets" began licking her hands and face. She said, looking up, "Khan, sit next to me."

Nervous as I was, I found to my surprise that the wolves really were friendly. After they'd licked my hands and I'd begun petting them, out of the corner of my eye I spotted Gunny, moving very slowly in our direction. Several of the wolves turned and snarled at him; but the Dragon Lady spoke to them and they were quiet. She called to Gunny, "You come here, sit with us." Soon he was part of the playful group.

When Audy and Scotty finally sauntered over, I had had all the play I wanted. We strolled about the camp and saw some of the camel riders who'd come in with Audy. In answer to my questions, he told me he was the only Australian in central China—"from Inner Mongolia to the Gobi to the Russian border," as he put it.

"Just as I'm the only Scotsman in Manchuria," Scotty said.

"Do you have your own territories, or something?" I asked.

"It's just where we'd rather be, off by ourselves," Audy said.

"Aye," Scotty agreed. "But we're close, even though we're many miles apart. And we help each other whenever we can."

"Does the Dragon Lady have a territory too?" I asked.

"She's all over China," Scotty responded. "She travels from one end of the country to the other to help people she cares about, and because it is safer for her that way."

"She cares about her country, but she would like to see it without Communists," Audy added.

"Do you think that will ever happen?" I asked. "Nothing seems to go back to the way it was before."

"The Communists won't last long," Audy said. "If they last a hundred years, that is not long as the Confucians see it. What the Chinese have more of than any other people in the world is patience."

"Would you say the Dragon Lady has patience?" I asked.

"Yes, lad," Scotty told me. "A very great deal of patience."

"I wish I knew more about her—where she came from, and about her family. Do you know?"

Audy looked at Scotty, who seemed to hesitate. Then he said, "We can't tell you everything at once, lad. We've got to keep you interested." Before I could press him further, the Mongol lieutenant appeared and he and Audy gripped arms in friendship. When they sat down and began talking in what I suppose was a Mongolian language, I wandered off, found Kim, and was soon showing her and several other children how to shoot baskets, using some makeshift substitutes. In the middle of this, the Dragon Lady came by and led me to where the camels were tied, many of them resting on the ground. In a minute she was showing me how to ride one.

Like the horses, the camels had simple bridles of rope. I took hold of the rope in my left hand and threw a leg between the humps. As soon as I was mounted, the camel got to its feet as though I had given it a signal. The Dragon Lady untied another animal and mounted it gracefully. "You hold on," she said. Then she gave my camel a swat, and we were off, loping along at an easy gait. Its huge stride and deep up-and-down movement made it very different from riding a horse, and of course I was much higher off the ground. It glided through the camp and up a slight rise just outside it, at such a clip now that I didn't suppose any living creature could overtake me—until I caught a glimpse of the Dragon Lady coming up behind me. By then we were a good distance from the camp, and the Dragon Lady turned her mount, calling out that she would race me back. All along the way, I had a feeling that she was going just fast enough to keep up with me.

As we dismounted, I could see a crowd gathering in an open field on the other side of the camp. There were shouts, and as we approached it appeared that an archery contest had begun. Six bowmen were lined up and shooting at targets that seemed hardly visible; they must have been at least two hundred yards away. The Dragon Lady told me that the targets were skin bags filled with water, and that in fact they were about the size of a human head. But the archers seemed to be popping those bags with almost every shot. What astonished me even more was seeing the archers move back another seventy-five or a hundred yards and begin shooting all over again. Though they didn't have quite the same accuracy from that distance, they still hit more often than not.

While I watched, the Mongol lieutenant came up and motioned for me to go with him. When I nodded in agreement, he lifted a thick arm and laid it over my shoulder. I could hear Gunny laughing as we walked off together.

We came to the archers, who stopped shooting when they saw us. One of them handed his bow to the lieutenant, who then gave it to me, along with an arrow. Though I had never fired an arrow before, there was nothing for me to do but fit the arrow to the string and do my best to pull it. The lieutenant, from behind, put his hands over mine and helped me draw. The arrow went off at a crazy angle, and he brought another. This time I managed by myself to draw the bow a couple of inches before I let go. The arrow made a gentle arc and fell with a plop a few yards in front of me.

I said, laughing before anyone else could, "I guess I'm better with a machine gun."

"More is needed than the strength of the body for this," the Dragon Lady told me. "The strength of the mind is also needed. You must concentrate."

After a few more shots with no improvement, I handed the bow back to the lieutenant and grasped him by the arms as a way of thanking him. Then, with smiles all round, I walked back to join Gunny and the others, and we followed the Dragon Lady to a field where riding events were to take place. I was surprised to see that the horses being led out were hardly bigger than ponies. The Dragon Lady, reading my thoughts, said, "Small, but very strong."

Hearing hoofbeats, I turned and saw a new group of ponies being ridden at top speed by children—some of them no more than six or seven years old. The Dragon Lady told us that they had learned to ride almost as soon as they learned to walk.

After the horse races came camel racing. Then there were wrestling matches, and finally Scotty came to tell us that we were invited to a hunt as honored guests; the Mongols would do the actual hunting. We were scattered among twelve small parties, some going after antelope, others after deer or bear. After an hour's ride I waited along with Nancy, absolutely motionless, for what seemed an endless time, until a huge brown shape ambled over the rocks in our direction. We were downwind, so he was nearly upon us when the hunters, all at once, drew their bows, and the arrows went zinging like bees out of a hive. The bear, which must have stood five feet tall, dropped in his tracks. In moments a litter had been made, and the dead bear was being carried back to camp.

While we waited to make a meal of the game that had

been killed, Audy described his adventures in China—how he'd come here as a coast watcher, how his two buddies had died, how he and Scotty had been involved in a savage battle along thirty miles of the Great Wall. When the food arrived, I ate as much as I could hold, stoking up for the days when there wouldn't be any kind of feast. Afterward the chief stood up and led our group into his hut. There, while we all sat in a circle, the chief began to speak, with Scotty translating.

He told us that all along the Khinghan Mountains his people's herds were dying, and some of their horses. They didn't know the reason, but they believed underground explosions were somehow to blame. The people who had set off the explosions had their headquarters at the same base we had gone to such pains to avoid. The Mongols were now so angry, Scotty told us, that they had decided to go to war against the people at the base.

"With bows and arrows?" I wasn't being facetious.

Scotty smiled and shook his head. "Bows and arrows are a part of their tradition, for games and for hunting. But they use more modern weapons, too."

Then I asked whether they had any experience in attacking from an open plain, and the Dragon Lady said bluntly, "No. But still they will do it."

Scotty said quietly, "I think we owe them something, lads. I think we ought to help them."

Without hesitation, Gunny and I agreed.

The Dragon Lady got to her feet and addressed the chief. He smiled as she spoke, looked us over, then spoke to her again. Turning to us, the Dragon Lady said, "We go tonight, and we must go quickly. We must attack and then move south at once."

"All of us?"

"Oh yes," she answered. "The entire village will be moved deeper into the mountains, for once we attack, the Communists will be looking for us." The people of the village were nomads, she explained. "They move all the time. Ten or eleven times a year, they move on again to where the hunting and the grazing are best. Their home is not one place. It is everywhere."

Soon the lieutenant and his two men entered, and the Dragon Lady began laying out a battle plan, while Scotty translated. We would be using horses to approach and to escape afterward. The base, between Chihfeng and the mountains, had its center in one main building; a mile from it was a tunnel leading to the underground testing area. We were to concentrate our attack on the central building.

The Dragon Lady told us that she wanted to take half of our force, but that the chief would not permit this. He said it was his job, that his people would do it. "So there will be just twenty-five of us—the seven who are right here and eighteen others. With his men that will be about one hundred."

I said that was a lot of people.

"It will be a big job to do," she replied. "It will not be as easy as the other base. We had better see to our weapons."

We got our machine guns and bandoliers, and headed back to the chief's hut, where the lieutenant and his two friends were already cleaning their weapons. These were Russian-made, of the same kind as the ones we carried.

The Dragon Lady now went into more detail about the attack. We'd go in from the west, the near side of the camp; as always, she made a sketch in the dirt to show what she meant. "We shall attack from the northwest and the southwest and close them in. A third group in the center will stay back to cover our withdrawal. The Communists will think that we intend to withdraw in the same direction from which we entered, but they will be mistaken."

To attack the main building, she went on, she and Audy would go with the chief in the northwest group; Scotty, Gunny, Charlie, Nancy and I would go with the southwest one. She said, looking at me, "You must keep Charlie close, for he knows this area very well."

I nodded. I had no intention of letting Charlie get far away.

We all walked outside to where the others were mounting up—a motley crew in ragtag uniforms. In addition to their automatic weapons, I saw that several of them were carrying bows and arrows. Of the two groups, the Dragon Lady's moved out ahead of ours, with the backup people in the rear. Riding two abreast, we had soon left the light of the campfires behind us, and found ourselves in total darkness. A now-familiar chill ran through me at the thought of what lay ahead, of how far I was from home. It was a long time before I could shake off the mood.

We came to a stop and Scotty rode forward to learn what was happening. He came back to tell us that this was where the groups were to divide. We started forward again with Charlie leading us off to the right, while the Dragon Lady's people veered off to the left. The icy feeling went through me again as we separated.

After about half an hour, Charlie raised his hand to signal a stop. I watched while he talked with several of the Mongols. Then they dismounted and raced off into the darkness, carrying guns, bows and quivers of arrows. We dismounted too, tied the horses off to one side and sat down in a circle. A chill seemed to have settled into the air, as though my own mood had become a permanent condition. But this wasn't my imagination; by now the night had grown very cold.

"Those who went ahead will open the way for us," Charlie said. "We wait for a time, then we go." He reached into his jacket and pulled out an hourglass. "When all the sand is on the bottom," he told us, "it will be time."

"Suppose the scouts aren't back by then?" I asked.

"We go anyway." Charlie did not sound cheerful when he said that.

But before long the scouts were back, with their quivers

almost empty of arrows. "The way is clear," Charlie said to us. He looked at his timer. We had only a little while longer, perhaps only a few minutes.

"They killed the guards?" I asked Charlie.

"Yes."

"Suppose the bodies are found before we go in?"

Charlie did not answer. Either he wasn't worried or he was being very cool in the face of danger. In a couple of minutes he mounted his horse, the rest of us followed suit and we were off, proceeding down the trail at a walk. When we got to the bottom we fanned out onto the open plain. I took the machine gun off my shoulder, removed one of the clips from the bandolier around my waist and snapped it into the gun, which I cocked and rested on my lap, marveling at how small it was. All the same, I was very nervous and so was everyone else.

A war cry sounded, and we galloped out onto the plain. I wondered that any horse could keep its footing out there, where at first I couldn't see anything at all. Then lights began to appear, more and more of them, until I could make out buildings and people darting between them. Gunfire sounded at a distance off to the left; that, I assumed, was the Dragon Lady's group attacking. I lifted my weapon, positioned it and began firing almost the instant I leaped from my horse. Taking cover as best I could whenever I had to change clips, I headed toward the buildings.

Once again, surprise was on our side. I heard a few explosions off to the left and concluded that the other group must be going for the buildings. About forty yards off I saw two of the Mongols go down, while a group of Communists charged toward them. I sprinted that way too, with Gunny about five strides ahead of me, firing and screaming at the Mongols, "Stay down! Stay down!"—even though they couldn't understand what he was saying.

Then a grenade blast knocked the charging Communists off their feet. It knocked Gunny down as well; he'd fallen within ten yards of the Mongols. I could see, as I hit the dirt beside Gunny, that they were still alive, and I prayed that he would be too. I spoke to him, and for a moment there was no sign of life. Then he said, "Can I open my eyes now? Did you get 'em?" Old fox that he was, he'd decided his best shot at staying alive, alone and out in the open, was to play dead.

Now he yelled, "They can't kill us! We're not human!" To me he said, "I just needed the rest."

Already people were running all over the place again, roused by the explosion, while we lay beside the wounded Mongols, firing at the buildings. Then to our left we saw some of the Dragon Lady's group racing toward them. I concluded that they must be going to set explosive charges, and stopped firing in that direction.

Bodies lay everywhere and some of them were our people.

Charlie came running up with four Mongols, who carried off the wounded men. No more Communist troops were visible, though there was some firing from buildings where they'd taken cover. I saw some of our people running, and then I heard Charlie shouting, "We go! Quick! To horses!"

Sprinting to where a couple of the Mongols were already gathering the mounts, and trying all the while to stay low, I saw that a number of the horses had been hit, and were sprawled out whinnying with pain and terror. This meant that most of us had to ride double. We were a fair distance away from the buildings when the explosion came, rocking the ground under us. That would have been the main building, I knew. But I didn't look back, as we headed for the shelter of the mountains and the Mongol camp. Besides the advantage of surprise and the Dragon Lady's military genius, up to now we had also been just plain lucky. We couldn't afford to gamble on more of the same.

The Dragon Lady's group had been close to us for a long time; but it was not until some time after we linked up, and were deep into the mountains again that we could afford to stop. The Dragon Lady dismounted and walked up to me smiling. She said, "It is done."

"We got the building you wanted?"

"Yes. Now we can go back to the camp."

In another couple of minutes we mounted again, and after maybe half an hour we were at the camp. I was not prepared for what we saw. With the chief growling out orders, everyone was busy getting ready to move on—even the small children had jobs to do. What had been a village of a few hundred people now became a mounted party of the same number, riding along the trail at a slow gallop with patrols out in every direction. The next time we stopped, the chief walked over and began to speak. With the Dragon Lady interpreting, we learned that we had lost forty people in the attack plus about a dozen more wounded, only one of them seriously. The chief was thanking us for our help. He knew we Americans would now be trying to get out of China, and to assist us he was sending thirty or forty men with us on the trip south.

We thanked him but it was hardly possible to say how grateful we were. The Dragon Lady told us what we already knew—that we had to depart as soon as possible. And before we could reach the sea, we had to cross the Great Wall, which Scotty told me was about 150 miles away.

"Will they have planes out looking for us again?" I wondered.

"They will not be able to find us in these mountains," the Dragon Lady answered. And by this time I was ready to believe anything she told me—that she knew everything and could do anything.

We started out with Audy loping alongside me on his camel, which he said he would be leaving with the Mongols until he came back for it.

"What do you mean? Back from where?"

"I mean from the sea, mate," he replied. "Where you and Gunny will be safe."

I turned to him in amazement. "Are you really going all that way with us?"

"Why of course!" He sounded amazed at my supposing it could be any other way.

We stopped after about an hour to rest and water the horses. While we were walking them along the trail again, Gunny came alongside me. I told him how strange it felt to be in a place where you didn't see any other Americans. "Do you suppose we're the only ones in China? Or do you think they dropped a lot of other parties for missions like ours?"

"I wouldn't be surprised," was his answer. "What the hell, it wouldn't cost them much. Drop a few of us in, all over China. If we succeed, fine. If we don't . . . " In the gray light of early morning, I could just make out the hand he ran across his throat.

A few minutes later, we got the signal to mount and ride again. The sun would be coming up soon and I could see an occasional tree and a few patches of grass—a relief from the rocky canyons we'd traveled in so much of the time. I rode along thinking of how these Mongols, people from a world so different, were now my friends—and how a month ago the odds on my ever having met Nancy, who now rode alongside me, would have been one in a million. Now she was someone I'd miss when I was out of China—if I ever got out!

A strange bellowing broke into my thoughts and I looked up to see half a dozen riders approaching. Scotty, when I asked about them, told me they were scouts—the ones the Dragon Lady had sent ahead to the Great Wall. He went on to explain that it was essential for us to cross the wall by dawn on a certain day, which was a holiday when there would be a lot of people congregating there for festivities.

The Dragon Lady rode up now and told us that the scouts, after crossing the wall, had been into Peking which was nearby. Before we crossed it, she added, the Mongols were to leave us. "Then," she said, "we shall split into two groups. My group will go into Peking, and the other will go around it.

Then we shall meet on the south side of the city. We shall be not far from the water then. And we shall go on the water to Weihai, and there we shall try to find a boat that will take you and Gunny out of China."

I asked why her group was going into Peking.

"There is someone I wish to see." From the sound of her voice and the look in her eyes as she said it, I knew there was no use asking anything more.

Now the Dragon Lady told Scotty that one of the men who had ridden with us wanted to talk with him. A young man came up and bowed to Scotty, who bowed in return. After the two of them had sat talking for a while, Scotty came over to tell Gunny and me what he had learned.

"That lad operated a radio transmitter. He was one of three who were trying to help us get away from the tunnel, back there in Manchuria. One radio operator turned out to be a traitor, and all three of those stations were destroyed. Most of the men in them were killed. He is one of the few who escaped." Scotty went on, looking still more somber, "He says that before they were attacked, he had tried to establish radio contact with a station operated by Americans, to tell them about you. He is certain they were able to receive his signal because he could hear them sending. But they wouldn't answer or even acknowledge his message."

Gunny said, "Those rotten sons of bitches. They're throwin' us to the wolves!"

"But Gunny," I said, "suppose they didn't believe the message. Maybe the guy's wrong and they didn't even *get* the message. That's possible, isn't it, Scotty?"

"Aye, it's possible. It surely is." But he didn't sound very sure.

All the same, I kept telling myself it *was* possible. Otherwise I'd have to believe they didn't *want* to rescue us, and maybe wouldn't even let us rescue ourselves.

11

After my own effort to cheer up Scotty, I began to realize how perfectly lousy I felt. "Why would they *not* want to save us?" I asked aloud.

Audy said, "Politics, mate. Ever hear of politics?"

The Dragon Lady broke in, as though she had heard too much griping, "When we cross the Great Wall, Peking will be only thirty-five miles south. I must go there." She stared at me. *"You* will go to the south of it with the other group."

I said without hesitation that I was going to Peking with her, and Gunny did the same.

"No," she said. "It is not your affair."

"But if you hadn't helped us with *our* problems, where do you think we'd be today?"

Again she said No. But this time I was not to be overruled, and after some more sparring I said, "Look. I would just rather be with you than away from you. I feel safer. It's not going to be all that easy for me to leave China; I might not even leave at all." I knew I'd gotten carried away, but just then that was the way I really felt.

"Are you serious, Rick?" Gunny asked. There was a strange look on his face.

"Yeah. I've gotten to feel so much better when I'm with these people, I don't want to go anywhere without them." I wound up, looking straight at the Dragon Lady, "And I am definitely going to Peking!"

"If you feel so strongly," she replied, "I shall not stop you. But you must not go because of feeling that you are in debt to me."

Gunny and I both assured her that that wasn't the reason, and before long we were on the way, with the Dragon Lady in charge as always. The Mongols, she told us, would soon be leaving us. "They will go back toward the mountains, toward the Gobi, until things are quiet again." Since they were nomads, and continually on the move, she told us, the Communists could never be sure where they were. And besides, the Communists preferred not to fight the Mongols so long as the Mongols left them alone.

Nancy had been nearby during the entire conversation. When we were on our way, she rode up alongside me. "Ricky, you say you stay in China?"

Though I'd said it on the spur of the moment, I now found myself thinking about it. "I don't know, Nancy. There is a lot of fighting here, and it's a hard life, but I've found real friends. And I don't know how I could leave you."

"What will your mother and father, your—"

"My family?" I gave the word she had been groping for. "They'd be unhappy, and I'd miss them. I'd miss my home. But the idea of leaving you . . ." It was something I was going to have to figure out—assuming I'd be given any choice in the matter.

A few minutes later we heard bellowing again—and now

I knew that was the signal the scouts gave as they came in. Almost at once, three riders came down the slope on our right. We stopped but didn't dismount while they spoke with the chief and the Dragon Lady. After a couple of minutes Audy said, "There's something funny," and in another minute or two Scotty dug his heels into the flank of his horse and cantered forward to investigate. He and the Dragon Lady came back with grim faces.

"There is a large Communist force on the far side of the mountain," she told us. "They are only three miles from us. They do not know we are here—not yet."

"How many are there?" Gunny asked.

"Perhaps a thousand." She went on, "Although they do not know yet, we do not have much time before they find us. We cannot avoid them unless we go back in the direction we came from, and we do not want to do that. We must get ahead of them, to the west, before we strike. Then, when the chase begins, they will think we are headed further up, toward Mongolia. After that, there is a pass we must reach before they do." She would take a small force of no more than a hundred— enough to hurt and confuse them, while the rest moved ahead to get the soldiers off our trail. We would move while it was still light, so that we would have the dark to escape in.

I turned to Nancy: "This time you stay with the main group."

"Oh no," she said. "I go with you."

The Dragon Lady agreed with me about Nancy. "Charlie will lead the others to safety," she said. "You must stay to help him." She added a few words in Chinese, which made Nancy stare for a moment like a little girl who's been told it's her bedtime. But then she turned to me. "You be careful," she said.

"Don't worry," Gunny told her. "I'll look after him."

Along with Gunny, Audy and Scotty, I moved up to the head of the column. The chief wouldn't be going with the raiding party but his lieutenant would. Moving out, we rode hard for an hour. Then, after pulling up in a cloud of dust, we got down and proceeded on foot. We started up a slope that looked down onto a canyon with a natural bridge over it. Before long, something like seventy-five of us were charging over the bridge, leaving the rest to cover us from behind, and making our way down the side of the mountain to where scrubby trees and rock formations gave us some cover.

When we were about five hundred yards from the bottom, the Dragon Lady signaled a stop. According to my estimate, we had less than two hours of daylight. We had good cover here, but with no weapons heavier than the machine guns we carried, once again we were depending on the element of surprise. Gunny was ten yards to my left, Scotty and Audy were on his far flank, and the Dragon Lady had posted herself about twenty-five yards farther downhill. As time passed and the light faded, I began to fear it would be dark before the soldiers arrived. Then we saw them, less than a quarter of a mile down the trail.

We were to hold our fire until we had a signal from the Dragon Lady. I watched the soldiers and her with my heart pounding as they made their way slowly up the rocky trail. Then they were directly below us. Still no signal. I looked for the end of the column, but it seemed to have none. God, there were a lot of them! They began to go under the natural bridge. Soon it would be dark.

She waved her weapon finally, and we all opened up. Completely surprised, some soldiers dove for cover, some looked up for the attackers. There were so many that they got in each other's way. At last they began trying to climb toward us, firing as they came. But the terrain had been well chosen; it was steep and rocky with some virtual cliffs between them and us.

Now, as suddenly as we'd attacked, we had the signal to withdraw, and we were scrambling back up the mountain, firing as we went. By then it was really dark. As soon as we got to the level of the natural bridge, we stopped firing altogether; the muzzle flashes would have given us away. Staying low, we raced over the bridge. This was all part of the plan— a feinting action to make them think we'd kept going to the top of that mountain and were heading down the other side. And it worked. We crossed without having a shot fired at us. Dark as it was, we ran all the way back to the horses. Though my breath was coming in gasps, I managed to say to Gunny, "Can you keep up, old-timer?"—and he managed to answer, "Screw you!"

After we had leaped onto our mounts and ridden off, I lost sight of Gunny and the others. But the Dragon Lady was directly ahead of me, and I had no intention of losing her. After maybe half an hour we halted, and she rode down the length of our column and back. "We did not lose a single person," she said. "And now I must ride back to make sure the Communists did go the other way."

I told her Gunny and I would go with her, but this time she would not be overruled. "If it is necessary for us to escape quickly," she pointed out, "we may have to separate, and you two do not know these mountains."

"Aye, she is right," Scotty told us, and there was nothing we could say. The Dragon Lady picked twelve men and divided them into two groups—one to go south, the other to ride with her back toward the bridge—while the rest of us, who made up the main group, went in still another direction. After about twenty minutes we were dismounting on a ridge, where we moved our horses in among the boulders. We waited here until two of the scouts came riding back. They raced over to talk to Scotty and Audy, and in an instant the order came to mount again—quickly. Scotty told me, when I asked what was the matter, that there were Communist soldiers twenty minutes away and headed in our direction.

"I thought we'd lost them!" Gunny said.

"We had," Audy replied. "These are others. The ones we attacked may have radioed for help."

We galloped hard for half a hour, I have no idea in what direction. After we had stopped, I asked Scotty how the Dragon Lady would know where we were.

"Don't worry, lad," Scotty told me. "She'll find us. Meanwhile get some rest. We don't know when our next chance for that may be."

I remember trying to settle down—and I must have succeeded, because the next thing I remember is being wakened out of a sound sleep by the noise of horses. Still groggy, I got to my feet and half walked, half stumbled over to where the Dragon Lady stood talking with Scotty and Audy. I wondered again when she ever slept.

The news was that the Communist troops were headed west. We had fooled them. By now they had stopped to wait for the force that put us on the run. We could not wait to see what they did next—whether they would continue west or turn back. We would have to be on our way at once.

We had been on the trail only a little while before two more scouts came in and spoke excitedly to the Dragon Lady. Suddenly we changed direction and were heading up the mountain as fast as we could ride. Five hundred yards farther uphill, we dismounted to walk our horses through a narrow pass. Then we climbed again. We paused at a relatively level spot where there were new orders: about a dozen people, among them Scotty, Audy, Gunny and me, were to follow the Dragon Lady on foot. There was now a moon. After walking awhile we came to a ledge. Looking over, we saw the reason for our change of plans. Down below us were riders, lots of them.

The Dragon Lady whispered, "They are moving toward the pass. They will probably come this way."

Audy asked the question for all of us, and she replied, "We cannot permit them to go through, or they may run into our main force. Some of us will stay and defend the pass. The rest will ride to Charlie and warn him."

Gunny and I volunteered to stay and fight with her, along

with Audy and six others, while Scotty and the rest rode to find Charlie.

"Will the ten of you be enough?" Scotty asked.

"Yes," she told him. "The pass is narrow. Leave our horses back there, we shall be able to get them."

There was nothing more to say. While Scotty took off, we moved toward the pass, keeping down in a half crouch. At a point just above it, we took positions and settled down in the darkness to wait. My heart pounded so that I wondered whether the Communist soldiers could hear it, while time seemed to drag on forever. Then we heard the sound of horses below us. With the moon in and out of clouds, just now we couldn't see much, though we knew the precise location of the pass and how narrow it was. They would be able to get through only one at a time while we might be able to knock them off, almost sight unseen, by firing down into the canyon.

The signal came and we began firing. There were screams and shouts from below. Sometimes the moon would be hidden and sometimes we'd have glimpses of men scurrying like rats down there. I remember hearing the expression, "like shooting fish in a barrel." It seemed that easy.

When the signal to stop firing came, I wanted to go down and see what was happening. But the Dragon Lady said, "No, no, we want to hold them back as long as we can. Then we run."

"Righto!" Audy echoed her. "We run like hell!"

The moon popped out for a few moments, lighting up the scene as if it had been switched on from above—and in those few moments we saw that the soldiers were slipping through the pass and that some were edging up toward us. Once again we began blasting them and hearing the shouts and screams from below. As we fired, the Dragon Lady shouted something in Chinese and two of her men took off to bring the horses closer. In a few minutes we heard bellowing, the signal that the men were back, and she called out the order to move— quickly.

We scrambled up the mountain and, luckily for us, there was no longer any light from the moon. As soon as we reached the horses, two of the men went ahead as scouts, we mounted, and then we were riding, mostly downhill. Once we reached level ground, we were able to pick up speed. But just which way we were going I had no idea. In fact, the way these people got around in the dark, over rough terrain with no clearly marked roads and often not even a trail, remained a mystery. It also made me realize once again how dependent I was on them, how helpless I would have been except for their company.

I lost track of time, too—not having had a watch since our special training began—but we might have ridden fifteen minutes before the scouts came back and reported seeing more troops ahead of us. To elude them, the Dragon Lady had us veer off in a new direction, keeping the same breathless pace. We came to a hillside where there were caves, dismounted and walked our horses in. There were to be no fires. Instead, each of us was to hold onto the tail of the horse just ahead. "Or else you get lost," the Dragon Lady said. "Caves go off in many directions."

One more thing that struck me was the way these people functioned in the dark of a cave—how much better than mine their eyes seemed to be. After a while my own vision improved, and I began to pick up things where there was hardly any light at all. Right then, though, the darkness in the cave seemed total. I could literally not make out my hand in front of my face. As I walked, I sometimes used one hand to feel for walls or ceilings, but even so I sometimes bumped into one or the other.

After a while I heard the Dragon Lady speaking in Chinese, and I could feel scouts brushing past, on their way out. She said to the rest of us, "We stop here. No talking until we find out where the troops are." We stood there in the dark and silence, waiting for I don't know how long. Then came a couple of hoots, followed by a whispered conversation. The orders now were to leave the cave, mount again and ride as fast as we could go.

Once we were out in the open, the moonlight seemed absolutely glaring. We must have ridden for a couple of hours while I wondered how much longer our luck could possibly hold out, even with the Dragon Lady's genius at outwitting her enemies. I had to force myself not to think that way—to make myself believe we'd get through, that *she*'d get us through.

When we stopped for a rest, moving our horses in among the rocks once again, Audy said, "I think we lost them."

"But perhaps not for long," the Dragon Lady replied. She wasn't going to let anyone relax very much. "If they do not bother us, we should make contact with Charlie soon. But we must not lead the Communists to him."

While we sat there resting, I looked over toward the Dragon Lady and saw her looking gloomy. Moving nearer, I asked if anything was wrong.

She said No, and then I asked, "Don't you ever get tired?"

"No," she replied. "I am strong."

I said I didn't mean that; I meant tired of this kind of life, riding, fighting, moving around all the time.

"This is my country," she said. "And in my country there must be fighting—for now."

"Some day soon it will be different, won't it?" I said, not knowing what I was talking about.

She answered, "Not in my lifetime. More time must pass. Blood must be spilled."

How old was she? She might have been twenty-five, though she looked still younger. Back in the States, a woman her age would be either getting married or worried about a job —maybe expecting a first child. This young woman was a military leader, with no sign that she had ever lived any kind of life but this one.

A couple of scouts rode in and she told me with a smile, "We have lost them." Charlie's group was about an hour away;

we would be with them soon after sunrise, but now we would have to go—quickly.

Had there ever been a time when it wasn't necessary to move quickly?

Soon after we started moving, Gunny pulled up beside me. "Well," he said, "I kept my word to Nancy."

"What was that?"

"That I'd look after you."

"Don't be too sure," I said lightly. "We're not back yet." Though I meant it as a joke, the Dragon Lady, overhearing, told him, "The Khan is right. We cannot be sure of anything until we know it is done."

The sun was coming up by then, and though we'd been through a long, hard night, our spirits picked up when two scouts came riding in with a couple of men from Charlie's group and word that everything was all right. It wasn't long before I saw Charlie and Nancy waving at us as we moved down a gentle slope. I galloped toward them, dismounted and gave Nancy a hug.

"I told you it would be all right," I said. I wasn't sure she understood every word unless I spoke carefully, but I knew she knew what I meant.

We learned that the Communist troops had gone off in the wrong direction. But when Scotty spoke of needing sleep, the Dragon Lady's reply was, "That will have to be later." As we moved ahead, walking our horses, Gunny came alongside me again.

"Rick," he said, "were you serious back there, about staying in China?"

"Yes, I was. I feel closer to these people than to anybody I've ever known."

"You're just a kid," he said. "You still haven't given much of a chance to your own country and your own people."

"Yeah, I know you're right," I told him, aware that I hadn't really thought through what I'd said, meaning it without having decided anything. For two nights and a day we'd been on the move, with only one brief rest in the mountains, and I was beginning to feel the effects of fatigue. But we went on pushing ahead, eating and drinking as we rode. Midday came and went before there was an order to halt. Soon after that, I saw the Dragon Lady coming toward us with the Mongol chief and his lieutenant. The chief held out his hands to us, and while I looked up into that fierce face, the Dragon Lady translated what he was saying. "This is where we must part. He wishes to thank you. He hopes that he has shown respect to you for the help you have given him."

Then he went up to Nancy, put his massive hands on her little-girl shoulders, engulfed her in a hug and finally kissed her on the cheek. With each of us, he repeated the farewell ceremony. He had a few extra words for me, the last in the line; "Khan" was one of them.

"He says he is proud of you, and proud to have you in his camp. You are welcome to return any time you wish; you will always be greeted as Khan."

Touched and proud to have this warrior treat me as a brother, I asked the Dragon Lady to tell him I was happy to have his friendship and his good feelings, and grateful for his help. He gave his fierce smile, and again the Dragon Lady translated: "He is sending the lieutenant and forty of his men with us, to protect us. They will go as far as they are needed, even to the sea. The Communists hate the Mongols and are afraid of them."

Then the Dragon Lady brought her little sister Kim to say good-bye. I put my hands on her shoulders and said, "Honey, I'm going to miss you. I love you, I really do." When Kim put her arms around me and squeezed, I felt closer to tears than I had been in a long time. She went on hugging me until I told her softly, "You must be brave like your sister." But she still didn't let go until the Dragon Lady came to lead her away.

"All the women and children are going north," the Dragon Lady told us. "It will be safer for them there."

We spent some time shaking hands with the Mongols who

would be leaving. When they had all mounted and thundered off, we were left once again with about a hundred people, the same number we'd had crossing the Changchun plain. About a dozen had died in combat, and altogether about thirty women and children were leaving, but the forty Mongols who were joining us made up the difference.

Our party mounted and we were on our way again, this time with the Great Wall as our destination. The pace was a little easier than before; we'd trot, walk, then trot again. There was not much talk; everyone, I guess, was busy with thoughts of his or her own. And we were all exhausted. When, around midafternoon, the order came to dismount, I simply slid off my horse.

It started to rain. The air was so cool that I felt chilled almost at once. I put on the few extra clothes I had, but they didn't help for long; the animal skins repelled water only for a while, and as soon as they were soaked they became cold and clammy. The rain had turned into a driving torrent by the time we mounted again, and I felt as though I were freezing. After a while Nancy pulled up alongside me. She must have seen how I was shivering, for she said, "I am cold also. Can I ride with you?" Though she made it sound like a request for a favor, I had a feeling that she was doing it for my benefit. Holding onto her bridle, she nimbly transferred herself to my horse and sat behind me, with her arms around my middle. Though there were so many layers of soggy clothing between us that her nearness didn't help a lot, after a few minutes I did feel a little less miserable.

As it was getting dark, we came to a hillside where there were caves. After the Dragon Lady had sent scouts ahead, she led us deep inside to a huge open cavern where fires were lit. We all sat near them, trying to warm ourselves. I was so tired that the voices of Gunny and Scotty, sitting close beside me, sounded as though they came from a far-off echo chamber. Then Nancy was leaning over me, saying, "What is wrong, Ricky?" But even with her face so near mine, I could barely hear her. Then I couldn't make out anything at all.

The next thing I remember is awakening with bodies piled over me. I was scared when I tried to move and couldn't. Then Nancy and the Dragon Lady, still pressed close against me, were asking if I was all right.

"Yeah, I think so," I stammered, still feeling confused. I discovered now that I was wearing a completely different set of clothes, all of them warm and dry. Then I noticed Scotty, who said, "You had a rough time of it, lad."

"Yeah, you were one shivering son of a bitch," Gunny said. "We were real worried about you."

"How long have I been out?"

"Maybe fifteen, sixteen hours," Gunny said.

"Christ, why did you let me sleep that long?"

"You were one sick bloke," Audy chimed in. "Trembling like a bloody leaf, sweating and screaming. You must had had some bloody awful nightmares."

"How did I get into these clothes?"

"They changed you." Scotty gestured toward Nancy and the Dragon Lady. "That's your third set. You kept sweating right through them."

When I looked at the two women and smiled, they might have been blushing for modesty—except that no one just then had time to be embarrassed.

"They had everybody lying alongside to get some heat into you," Gunny told me.

When I had thanked the Dragon Lady, I asked, "How about the wall? Are we going to get there on time?"

She smiled. "Do not worry. We shall reach it in time."

Then I asked if there was anything to eat. Nancy said, "I get food." Scotty laughed and Gunny teased, "Room service and a pretty waitress. Some guys have all the luck."

Nancy brought some soup with meat in it, which tasted wonderful. While I ate, Scotty explained that the Dragon Lady had gone out to find a certain root, which had been boiled in a soup, and which they had gotten into me somehow while I was lying there, either delirious or dead to the world. Whatever the root had been, it had worked—that and the body heat.

When I'd finished the soup, I asked the Dragon Lady when we would be at the wall.

"We shall rest here today and travel tonight; we shall cross the wall before sunrise." Then she was on her feet again. "I must go and see Charlie and take some food to him. He has been on patrol."

"What a woman!" I said to Scotty, after she left.

"Yes," he answered, "and from a very powerful and highly placed family. She could be living in comfort on Formosa, but she chose to be out here fighting."

When she returned, it was late afternoon outside the cave; the rain had stopped, she told us, and there was no sign of trouble. But she sounded somehow far away as she said it. After she'd stood silent, almost in a trance for a minute or so, she said abruptly, "I think the Communist soldiers have gone the other way." Then came yet another of her abrupt swings of mood. "We had much fun with them, didn't we?"—and her eyes flashed as though she'd been through an exciting game.

"Well, if that was fun," Gunny told her, "I bet we're going to have a lot more fun before we reach the water."

The Dragon Lady was laughing. "They must have tens of thousands of soldiers looking for us."

Gunny rolled his eyes. "I don't see what's so funny about that," he said, and suddenly we were all laughing—though the idea of being chased by an army can't have seemed any funnier to the rest of us than it did to him.

Charlie walked in and told us that it would be dark in one or two hours, and that everything was still quiet. Spotting me, he asked how I felt.

"Never felt better," I told him. And somehow it was true.

He said, smiling, "You did not look better last night."

Then, without any preliminaries except the Dragon Lady's eternal "We must go now," we began to walk our horses out of the cave, moving single file into the evening light. It was cheering to see a little piece of daylight before it faded away.

The main Mongol party had left us a supply of meat, maize and kaoliang for our trek south. Seeing the bundles tied onto the backs of some of the horses, I was reminded that with most of them gone, we were again down a hundred people—not a lot with thousands possibly searching for us. Everyone was silent, probably thinking about the odds just as I was. I began wondering again about the failure of the radio operators to make contact with the Americans who had the transmitter, whoever they were.

As we rode, we descended from the mountains into hill country that made for easier riding. We still saw many caves, and occasionally a patch of land level enough to be used as a rice paddy. Some of the patches were flooded, and after we'd sloshed through one of these we came to a bit of high ground where we stopped to rest.

Sitting next to Scotty, I asked him, "Can you tell me why she wants to go into Peking instead of around it?"

"There is someone there she wants to see, lad."

"Oh? Boyfriend?"

Scotty laughed. "Far from it. The man is a Communist named Sing Yet-soo and he is a former admirer of hers. Three or four years ago she was a Nationalist and had a job in the government. When Sing made a play for her, she snubbed him and he had members of her family killed in retaliation. That is probably why her sister was left with the Mongols—to keep her safe. The Dragon Lady has been waiting patiently for a chance to avenge her family, and now she sees it."

"So she really is not a Nationalist anymore?"

"No, lad. She should never have been in the government. She couldn't function in a bureaucracy, I'm sure you can see that. Whenever she saw corruption—and there was much of it to see—she spoke up. When she didn't like what the Americans were doing, she did the same. Of course that just wouldn't work and eventually, since she didn't get on with them, she simply quit and went her own way. Now she fights for herself and her people, *against* the Communists, but not *for* the Nationalists. I think that is a mistake, and I have told her so. I stayed a Nationalist even though I saw so much that was wrong. That's what brought us to a parting of the ways."

Now, of course, I understood why this amazing woman wanted us to stay out of her mission to Peking.

We mounted again, and hadn't been riding long when Charlie dropped back to say that we were about a mile from the wall.

One mile from the Great Wall! As I write this, I recall having read that the Great Wall of China is the only manmade object visible to the naked eye from the moon. I didn't know that at the time, of course. But what I would soon be seeing by the clear light of the moon was to me a schoolboy's dream.

As I rode, I tried ticking off the days, though I couldn't be sure anymore that I knew which one it was. I knew we'd made our drop into Manchuria on May 9 and as nearly as I could calculate, a little more than two weeks had gone by since then. That would make it either the twenty-fourth or the twenty-fifth. I supposed that none of the people who'd sent us had expected us to last this long—but then how could I know? There was so much I didn't know. How could anyone have predicted that this was where the expedition would take us? Who could predict how it would end?

Scouts were riding up to report and then going off again, and I could feel a kind of buzz around me, as though the others also thought of reaching the wall as a milestone.

We rode to the top of a rise and there it was.

12

The wall went off in both directions, over hills and valleys, for as far as I could see. A minute after we'd sighted it, we broke into a gallop. We were out in the open, where we could be spotted from a long way off, so we had no time to waste. As we got closer, I could begin to make out some details. It was maybe three stories high and wide enough on top to be used as a road. Every couple of hundred yards, a watchtower rose one story above the wall itself.

"It's fifteen hundred miles long, lad," Scotty told me, "and it begins at the sea."

I asked him, "Is there anyone in those towers?"

"Let's hope not, lad!"

We pounded toward a spot about fifty yards from one of the towers, where we reined in. From there I could see that the construction was of earth and boulders, which in one spot had simply crumbled apart. Several of the Dragon Lady's men had managed to roll away some of the bigger stones from what I could now clearly see was a breach in the wall.

Dismounting and leading our horses carefully, we picked our way through the opening. As I led my mount through, I looked up and around me with an eerie feeling. I was looking up at a wall that ran fifteen hundred miles and was God knows how many hundreds of years old!

But there was little time to be marveling over how old it was. As soon as we were all through, we had mounted again and were on our way. The Communists might not be in every tower, but we had to suppose they'd be sending out patrols.

As we left the wall behind, I had to turn back for one more look, wondering as I did so whether I'd ever see such a spectacle again. After about five miles we halted, and the Dragon Lady brought us several bundles that her men had been carrying. She said, "This is the clothing for the six of us who go into Peking, so that we will look the same as the population. When we get to the outskirts of the city, the others will take our horses. They will circle around Peking to the south and then go east. We shall meet them on the North China Plain."

While I wondered exactly where on the North China Plain we would meet—though I was sure she'd arrange that —she told us that the plain, in contrast to where we'd come from, was heavily populated and would be the most dangerous part of our journey. Besides Gunny and me—she referred to me as Khan—she would be taking the Mongol lieutenant and two of his men with her while the others, led by Charlie, made their circuit of Peking.

The Dragon Lady told Gunny and me, as she handed us the clothes we were to wear, "The hats you will pull down so that your hair and your faces will not show. You decidedly do *not* look Chinese," she added with a smile.

"But with our size—" I began.

"There are all sizes of Chinese. Some who live in the north are tall, as tall as you. Not only the Mongols, but people from all over China come to Peking. It is a very big city. It will be all right, if you keep your hats low. We shall enter in daylight."

"In daylight?" It slipped out, even though I'd resolved to keep my mouth shut.

"Yes, in daylight. But there is a holiday," she went on, "and Peking will be empty. The people will go to the Great Wall to hear Mao Zedong make a speech. But I am told that the man I seek will remain in Peking because he has much work to do. He works very hard. He is a very ambitious man."

The moment came to split up. We shook hands and said our good-byes. I hugged Nancy, and she said, "You be careful." Then they were gone.

There were now ten in our party, including the four who would take our horses with them to wait at our rendezvous. The clothes we put on were standard Communist dress: high-necked tunic jackets, wide baggy trousers and huge hats, worn low as the Dragon Lady had instructed. Light was appearing in the east as we rode over rolling hills toward the city. Soon we came to a rise from which we could see it in the distance. Then we dismounted and turned our horses over to the four, and they rode off.

On foot now, we went in single file at a steady pace, each carrying a basket of gear. I wish that I could describe the city of Peking as it looked to us, but the truth is that I had my broad-brimmed hat so low that I saw nothing but a narrow circle of ground, with no more than a glimpse of the buildings we were approaching. I've read that the outskirts of the city have since filled up with schools and housing for workers. But this was 1952, before the Communist government had done much building, and the population was only two and a half million rather than the nearly eight million it is today.

As we got closer, more and more people came into my range of vision, all of them headed out of the city. Many were carrying flags and banners; some were playing flutelike instruments; a few were on bicycles. No one paid any attention to us.

The baskets we carried looked innocent enough from the outside, though they actually held weapons and bandoliers under a layer of kaoliang and maize. They were large enough, in fact, to hold the hunting bows and arrows the Mongols had brought with them.

The numbers of people became first a wave and then a flood of humanity, all in high spirits because of the holiday. In the midst of all this the Dragon Lady spotted a group of bicycles and one tricycle with a cargo platform, which she somehow managed to commandeer. In a moment we had fastened our baskets to the tricycle platform and were pedaling into Peking. I still kept my hat so far down and my head so low that I saw little except the wheels in front of me. Out of a corner of my eye, as we moved from the outskirts toward the inner city, I could see that the bases of the buildings were becoming grander and more elaborate. Once again I was scared and at the same time oddly exhilarated by the notion that with all those thousands of Communists out looking for us, we were cycling straight into their capital.

I saw an imposing stone wall to my left and I sneaked a glimpse of a huge stone lion in front of a wall, confirming my impression that we were now in an older, grander part of the city. The wheels ahead of me finally came to a stop before an old stone building, where we pulled the bikes off to one side and waited with them while the Dragon Lady and the lieutenant knocked at the front door. An old woman opened it and the Dragon Lady motioned for us to enter—quickly, as always.

In a darkened room we were greeted by six other people, each one of whom the Dragon Lady embraced, smiling, and to whom she then introduced us. Our baskets had been retrieved by the two Mongols, and we now each took out our weapons and put them all into a single basket. Meanwhile the Dragon Lady was speaking rapidly and quietly with two of the older people in the house, while the Mongols posted themselves at the windows to watch the street.

The Dragon Lady now told Gunny and me that her

"friend" was in the city, and that she knew where to find him. "So we shall go," she said.

The Mongols secured the loaded basket to the tricycle, we got onto our bikes again and rode until we came to a wall. Here, after we had parked the bikes, we took our weapons from the basket and concealed them inside the baggy pants and tunics we wore. This was not difficult, since the Russian guns were so light and small—only about three feet long, or the same length as the Mongols' hunting bows.

Cautiously, we began walking along the wall. After we'd gone about three hundred yards, we came to an arched opening that might have been eight feet high. First the Dragon Lady motioned the two Mongols to go through; she followed and then she beckoned to us. We made our way past four buildings; then we came to a fifth and went in. It was an immense structure that might have been a shrine or a museum, with many statues and carvings of marble and jade.

As we entered, the Dragon Lady hurried to a window on the far side of the building. She peered through it and then waved Gunny and me over to her. She said, pointing to a building directly across the way, "My 'friend' is there. We shall wait."

We sat and watched, not talking, for what seemed like hours. Then, all at once, the Dragon Lady's entire body came to an alert, and in the same instant I saw two men emerge from the building we had under observation and head straight toward us.

The Dragon Lady signaled to one of the Mongols, who handed her his bow and an arrow. She fitted the arrow to the bow and moved toward the nearby door while the Mongol lieutenant, with bow and arrow likewise ready, stationed himself on the other side of the door. The Dragon Lady motioned us into a small room off the main chamber while she and the lieutenant waited, partially hidden by the statues that guarded the entrance.

The two men were talking as they strode into the building

and past the statues where the Dragon Lady and the lieutenant had concealed themselves. They passed into an adjoining room, and the Dragon Lady and the Mongol lieutenant immediately stationed themselves on either side of the door leading into it. Within a few moments the two men reappeared, still engrossed in conversation, and the Dragon Lady spat out a curse as they passed. They looked up simultaneously; one froze in his tracks, and the other wheeled, intending to flee. Instead, he caught an arrow in the throat.

The two Mongols, Gunny and I now ran out to seize and gag the other man. His face had a look of utter terror and hopelessness; shaking with fear, he sagged as though about to collapse, until a blow from the Dragon Lady's open hand straightened him again. "Khan and Gunny do not have to watch what will happen," she said, never once taking her eyes off the man. "This is something I must do." Then, when we didn't move, she said, "I do not wish you to see me like this."

Gunny clutched my arm. "Come on, Khan, let's wait," he said, and I followed him into another room. We could hear the stifled sound of the man's voice, and then a scuffling noise. Gunny nudged me and pointed to the window. Looking out, I saw four men headed our way, and raced for the other room. What I saw there stopped me short.

The body of the Dragon Lady's "friend" hung naked from the outstretched arms of a statue—all except for the head, which had been placed neatly in the cupped hands of another statue.

While I blurted, "There's someone coming!" I saw that the body had been castrated. The marble floor was slippery with blood. I turned away and saw the Dragon Lady and the Mongols making for the entrance. They took up positions just inside it and Gunny and I joined them.

We could hear voices outside, where the men had stopped to talk about what I could only suppose was the life-or-death decision of whether or not to go in. One man hesitated and then withdrew, while the other three entered. The Mongols were at them instantly—a hand clapped over the face of each, one man and one knife at the throat of each. The only noise any of them made was a sort of strangled gurgle.

While the Mongols were dragging the three bodies across the bloody marble of the floor to a smaller room, two more men came in through the door. Without batting an eyelash, the Dragon Lady spoke to them, and whatever she said was funny enough that one of them laughed. As if on cue, she and the lieutenant went to work with their knives; quickly and quietly, the two had been finished off, and more blood was spreading on the surface of the marble floor.

At a shout from one of the Mongols, the Dragon Lady held up her hand. "Guards are coming," she said. "In here, quickly." She and the Mongols had already taken up their positions at the entrance, with their knives out. I took mine from my belt; I saw that Gunny had his ready too. Outside we could hear the guards talking. There were five of them and the same tactics served us as before.

Gunny said, "We better get the hell out of here," and with the Dragon Lady in the lead, we headed for the exit. I did a quick calculation. We'd come to Peking for one killing and we'd ended up with twelve. I asked, pointing to the corpses, "What do we do with those?"

"We leave them," she said. "We shall go and meet Charlie now." And she led us to the spot where we'd left the bikes, which for some reason she now decided to abandon. We stuffed our weapons back into the basket and set out on foot. A couple of times I reached up to pull my hat down low, although there was no one else around to see me.

After passing between two buildings, we came to a road, which led to a square enclosed by massive buildings. Here again, the place was empty of people. But as we crossed it I heard a sound—and that sound led to one of the most bizarre events of the entire adventure in China. What I heard was a kind of screech from the direction of a building on the far side of the square. As we walked, I saw alongside the building what I soon made out as a row of about half a dozen cages.

Without thinking, without asking, I went closer, until I could see that the cages were hardly more than three feet square and three feet high and made of strong wood. And I now realized that the screeching sounds were made not by animals but by human beings—men down on all fours in a space too small to let them stand!

Even though I didn't want to see any more, I couldn't help going closer. What I saw then were men in rags, so filthy that you could hardly see the color of their skin. Yet not only were they human beings; I now saw unmistakably that they were white! "White" is hardly an accurate word, since they were so dirty; gray would be more like it. Still I was certain that their features were Caucasian.

One of these men was reaching an emaciated gray arm through the bars and pawing the ground in front of him. Then I realized that food had been dropped on the ground—just out of his reach. He raised his head to stare at me—a creature close to starvation, with a gaunt, bearded face. But what struck me most was his blue eyes and his long, matted hair, which had once been blond. Our two stares met and locked. Finally he managed a word—drawn out and hesitant, as if he hadn't used it in a very long time. But there was no question that the word was "American."

American. A chill ran all through my body, and I began to shake. Crouching down, I reached out toward his arm. His bony hand, with almost no flesh on it, plucked at my arm, desperately but with no strength whatever.

"American?" I repeated, feeling stupid, but not knowing what to say. "You're American?"

He opened his mouth, but whatever he was trying to say came out as a sort of croak.

"I'm American too," I said, pointing to myself with my free hand while he still held onto the other.

Then, in the same drawn-out croak, he said other words,

which I am certain were, "Loo ... ten ... ant ... com ... mand ... er ... U ... nited ... States ... Na ... vy."

At that I pretty nearly went crazy. Leaping to my feet, I started tearing at the bars with my hands. The wood frame of the cage and the bars themselves, which seemed each to measure two by two inches, were hard as iron. I pulled out my knife and started to hack at it, shaking the cage with one hand as I slashed with the other. Then two figures came at me from the other side of the cages, shouting and waving what I guess must have been sticks or clubs. They wore high-necked tunics and red armbands. In my furious excitement I ignored them, and went on slashing at the bars. Before they quite got to me, a couple of arrows whizzed in my direction. Then the Dragon Lady was tugging at my arm, and the prisoners in the other cages had begun screaming. "We must go, Khan!" she kept saying. "We must *go!*"—while I went on with my slashing.

I remember hearing her give a shout in a language I didn't understand. Then came a blow on the back of my head that knocked me unconscious.

I woke to find myself tied to the platform of the tricycle, with the Mongol lieutenant pedaling, while the rest rode ahead on bicycles. For some time my aching head kept me from thinking clearly of anything. But then the men in the cages came back to me.

Were they all American? I couldn't be sure, but it seemed likely. And I knew that one of them was. "Loo ... ten ... ant ... com ... mand ... er ... U ... nited ... States ... Na ... vy." I couldn't get the sound of that out of my mind then and I still can't, to this day.

While all this came running back into my mind, we had reached the outskirts of the city. There we left the bikes and headed south on foot, carrying the basket with the weapons. Even then I was moving as though in a trance. How did those men get there? Were they prisoners of war taken in Korea? But prisoners of war, as any boot is taught, are supposed to be treated according to the Geneva Convention.

One thing I had learned: the Chinese were brutal to their enemies. The Dragon Lady had shown little mercy to her captives. She had decapitated two men and castrated one of them. Mercy appeared to be a luxury nobody in this place and at this time could afford.

I kept going over and over what I could have done to help that caged American. The little capsule in its plastic case leaped to mind, a thought that startled me into realizing that I'd lost track of it somewhere and left it in one of the many changes of clothes while I was cold, sick or unconscious. What had I done to help those men in the cages, except maybe raise a little glimmer of hope—which was probably worse than nothing?

Another thing I'd never be able to get out of my head was how many men I'd gunned down, or knifed or blown up. Sure, I had reasons—but those reasons didn't change what I'd done, or keep me from remembering.

As we moved along, I wondered whether Gunny was thinking the same kind of thoughts, blaming himself in the way I was. He had kept silent all this while, and when I looked over to him he would not meet my eyes.

As we left the city, we began to encounter hordes of people returning from the holiday celebration. More times than I could count, I tugged my hat down over my eyes again. I have no idea how far we had trudged when we reached the top of a small hill and caught sight of the four Mongols with the horses.

Soon we had mounted and were heading south toward the main group, going from a walk to a gallop. We were all glad to put some distance between us and Peking, knowing what we'd left behind us. No one was gladder than I was, now that I had a picture of what had been done to a captured American. When I gave the question a little more thought, I realized that no one would suffer more on being captured than the Dragon Lady. I shuddered every time I thought of it.

13

Crossing the plain, we began to see walled villages with the dark rich green of fields and trees around them. Great numbers of people were hard at work, paying us only casual notice as we galloped past.

Finally we came in sight of our main group. The reunion with them didn't last long; soon the order came to split up into two groups. "We are too many, too noticeable," the Dragon Lady told Scotty. "You and Charlie will take one group. I shall take another."

Gunny, Audy, Nancy and I were to go with her; we'd take some of her people and half the Mongols, to make up a force of fifty. Scotty and Charlie were to form an equal force out of the other twenty Mongols and the rest of the Dragon Lady's people. She explained to Scotty and Charlie where we'd meet again, outlining what she thought was the best route to follow.

Looking over my shoulder as we took off, I could see the others disappear into the haze and I had to wonder whether I'd see them again. After a few miles, there were new orders. "We shall be passing many people," the Dragon Lady said. "We shall travel in single file, keeping twenty yards between. Do not pay any special notice to the people you pass. Act as if you were one of them. If anyone questions you, don't answer. Just keep your head down. I or one of the others will answer for you."

Though this was the country with the largest population in the world, we hadn't seen very many people thus far. But the more of them we met now, the greater the chance that something could go wrong and interfere with our chances of reaching the coast. We were proceeding slowly, and although I could understand why we didn't dare act like fugitives on the run, the pretending to be casual, with the hat kept low over my face, was beginning to be a strain. I couldn't help thinking about what would happen if anyone got a close look at the blond, blue-eyed boy from Massachusetts underneath the disguise. I tried to hypnotize myself into staying calm by concentrating on the steps of my horse.

People and wagons were all around us now. The rice paddies appeared more frequently and often we would cross a bridge over one of the streams that watered them. Suddenly we were being led off toward a village with a high stone wall around it. When we reached the gate, the Dragon Lady spoke to an old man who was acting as a sort of gatekeeper and he motioned for us to go in. As we filed through, what struck me was the number of people swarming inside those walls. After we had dismounted, the Dragon Lady spoke with a villager and then said to Gunny and me, "Go with him. You will change clothes, then we shall have to leave. Quickly."

In answer to a question from Gunny, she explained, "You are wearing *Communist* clothes. I don't like to wear those. Do you?"

"No sir!" Gunny said. "I mean, no ma'am!"

Her face eased into a grin. "Five minutes."

Following the villager into a hut, Gunny and I were given clothes in the Mongolian style, though less heavy than the ones we'd seen in the north. We got into them quickly. Outside we found the Dragon Lady, who had also changed her clothes, already mounted and waiting for us. "Why have you taken so long?" she asked good-naturedly, and we had been so tense until then that we all laughed.

Once we were on the road again, I noticed that the people who passed would glance at us and then look away quickly. The Dragon Lady told us that all the Chinese, whether Communist or non-Communist, were afraid of the Mongols, and I could believe that it must be so.

By now we were continually crossing bridges, many of them spanning canals with dikes on each side. The plain was so low that without the dikes it would have been flooded. After we had been traveling for a while, we came to a halt. Up ahead, a group of Communist soldiers appeared to have gotten out of a truck and rounded up a group of about fifty people. When the Dragon Lady started around the truck, a soldier who looked like an officer shouted something to her. She answered and waited calmly as he approached, with a kind of leer on his face. After another exchange, he reached out to touch her arm, and now his grin was really ugly. She pulled back her arm as she answered him, and in the same moment the Mongol lieutenant pulled up alongside her at an angle that allowed me to see what happened next, though I was twenty yards away. The Mongol riveted the soldier with his powerful stare, whose effect I knew about from my own experience. I watched the soldier's hand fall away from the Dragon Lady's arm as he took a step back. Then, calling out something harsh, as though to save face, he waved us on. We passed the soldiers one by one, looking straight ahead. I was so anxious that it wasn't until we'd gone a hundred yards that I risked a peek over my shoulder to make sure we'd all been allowed to pass.

Some time later, the Dragon Lady dropped back alongside

me to say that we would soon be stopping at a village and that she thought we would leave the horses there. When I asked why, she said, "They make us too noticeable. But there is a chance we can keep them. We shall see later."

"Do you know people there?" I asked. She said she did, and I asked, "How is it you know everybody everywhere? You seem so young to have met so many people!"

She shrugged, and I said, "How old *are* you?"

She gave me a stare that ended in a smile. "I told you. Very old and wise."

"Okay," I said. "But let me ask you something else. In Peking—those prisoners—"

"Yes. Those prisoners were American, and we could understand the way you felt. But you were putting all of us in danger. So—" She gestured with her head toward the Mongol lieutenant. *"He* hit you. I told him to do it."

I nodded, but I must have looked as unhappy as I felt, because she now went on, "You must understand that he has vowed to protect you with his life, to make sure you reach the water and then go to an American ship. He made a promise, Khan, and he will keep it."

She pointed to the right. "We must go that way, across the fields there. The village is not far now." We left the road, and were soon moving at a fast pace between rice fields, where people were at work. The stone wall of the village came into view, and then we were reining up at the entrance. While we dismounted, a group of people came out to meet us. After the Dragon Lady had spoken with them briefly, several of them took our horses and we went in on foot. Once again I was struck by the density of the population. The whole area was small but with hundreds of people packed into it.

"Are the villages always this crowded?" I asked her.

"Yes, all very crowded," she replied. At a word from her the Mongol lieutenant spoke to his men, and in a moment they had fanned out and were mingling with the villagers. A figure now came toward us who had the look of a head man if I ever saw one. After a few words with the Dragon Lady, who pointed to Gunny and me as she answered him, the man strode up and made us welcome. Our little party—the Dragon Lady, Nancy, Gunny, Audy and I—followed him to the far side of the village, where he led us to a house that I suppose was his. It had just three rooms, and in one of them at least fifteen people sat in a circle. They had been eating, but now they all got to their feet and bowed to us. We bowed back, and then the head man motioned for us to sit down with them. We were given rice and maize, which we ate without speaking while the chief and the Dragon Lady talked quietly.

When the food was gone, the people all bowed their heads and began a kind of mumble. I looked over at Gunny and saw that he was just as puzzled as I—until the Dragon Lady caught my eye and then bowed her own head. I realized then that the mumbling was a prayer. As Gunny and I sat there with our heads bowed, nobody had more to pray for than we did.

After that, the Chinese people began chatting among themselves. One young fellow, who must have been about my own age, insisted on talking to me. The Dragon Lady, noticing, slid closer and explained, "He wants to know if you are American."

"What will you tell him?"

"What do you want me to tell him?"

"Do you trust him?"

"He is my cousin, and I trust him."

She turned and addressed the young man, who was still looking at Gunny and me as though we were the main attraction in a museum. He went on talking with the Dragon Lady but every now and then he would begin looking at us again.

Soon I could hardly hold my head up, and I asked Gunny if he was as tired as I was.

"More so," he said.

I turned to the Dragon Lady, with a motion to let her see how sleepy I was. "You come with me," she said, and walked us all to another room where there were several mats on the floor. "You sleep here," she said.

"Don't say another word," Gunny told her, and in an instant he had flopped down on a mat.

I looked at Nancy, thinking she would be sent to another room to sleep. But she declared, "I sleep here."

"How about you?" I asked the Dragon Lady.

"I shall sleep here, too."

Audy said with a laugh, "And I'll sleep here *too!*"

I suppose the Dragon Lady was still amused by my modesty. But what was really on my mind just then was how five of us would find floor space in a room that must have been no more than six by four feet. I didn't wait to learn how it could be done; I was so exhausted that I was no sooner on a mat than I was sound asleep.

I woke in the dark, to a faint flicker of light from the fire in the next room. Nancy and Audy were still asleep, but I found Gunny and the Dragon Lady sitting by the fire in the other room, eating rice and talking.

They looked up as I came in, and I asked what time it was.

"The middle of the night," the Dragon Lady said.

"What are you two talking about?" I asked them, and Gunny said, "Business." I thought he looked a little uncomfortable.

"What kind of business could that be?" I said. "In the middle of the night?"

"Well, mainly what's going to happen in the future."

I said, "What future is that? Is there anything to make you think there even is a future for guys like you and me?"

The Dragon Lady said, "You should not think that way."

"I'll tell you what I think," I burst out. "I think my future ended back in that tunnel. Back there, I had no thought of ever getting out alive. From then on, every minute I've lived has been a bonus—one minute more that I didn't dare expect."

Gunny nodded, looking somber. But then he said, "Well, dammit, you did get out of there. That's what counts now."

"No," I said. "What counts is that when I was in that tunnel, I wrote myself off as dead. Something came over me that made me lose all fear. It wasn't that I suddenly became a hero, or felt like Superman—nothing like that. It's just that every minute, every day I get now is extra. So I have *not* been making any long-range plans for any future!"

I was a little surprised at hearing myself say all this, and I halfway wondered whether I really meant it. But it was true that for days now I hadn't once seen myself back in America. The place known as the future was nothing but a blank screen with nobody looking at it.

Gunny said, "For Christ's sake, smarten up, kid. You're gonna get out of here—that is, unless you go on thinking like that!"

"Gunny is right, Khan," the Dragon Lady said. "You must not think that way. We all care for you too much."

I shook my head and then I shrugged. "If there is a future for me, I won't throw it away." Then I said, "But you never did say what the business was that *you* were talking about."

He laughed, and then said, "Seriously—"

"Seriously?" I grinned at him. "You don't know what the word is. But don't get me wrong, Gunny. I think you're one hell of a guy." Once again, what I was saying surprised me—but this time I knew I meant every word of it. "Back in the States, if you were a senior NCO and I was a snuff, you might have treated me like shit. All I know is that here, you've never pulled rank on me. A lot of people would have." I stopped, feeling a little embarrassed by all that I felt. The experiences we'd shared had brought us closer than anything else ever could have. Those experiences weren't over yet, and who knew where they would finally take us?

Gunny said, "Well, Rick, I'm pulling rank on you right now. Rack out. We got a long way to go tomorrow and we got to be off early. I'm going back to sleep." And he got to his feet and headed back to his mat.

"What about that business?" I said again.

"I'll tell you. Only not now. Now let's get some sleep."

In no time I'd dropped off again, and when I woke next it was daylight. Nancy appeared with plates of food for Gunny and Audy and me, and we'd just begun eating when the Dragon Lady came in. I knew this meant there wasn't much time to finish our meal. As soon as we had, we went with her into the room where the Mongol lieutenant was sitting with two of his men. They left after she'd talked with them briefly, and then she said to us, "We shall take the horses. We do not yet have to leave them."

Just then there was a commotion outside the door. We heard Audy's voice, and he came in in a rush, bringing Kim with him.

While the Dragon Lady spoke excitedly with her sister, Audy explained, "She came with some important news." The two of them talked for some time, and it seemed to me that I had never seen the Dragon Lady as she was now—almost rigid with anger.

"It seems that some of the people we killed in Peking were high government officials," she told us finally. "Very high government officials." She paused. Then she said to me, "Do you remember the man who came to the door with three others, the one who did not enter with them?"

Yes, I remembered. I'd seen how one man hesitated and then walked off—the decision that had saved his life.

She said, glaring at me, "That man was Mao."

"Mao?" I repeated. "Mao *Zedong?*"

"Yes!" She was almost spitting with rage.

I said, "I never really looked at him."

"And neither did I!" She was almost shrieking. "But if I had, I would have given *anything*—I would even have spared Sing Yet-soo—to put an arrow into him! *Anything!* And now I shall never be so close again!"

I couldn't think of anything to say.

Getting back her self-control, she went on, "As you can imagine, they are furious in Peking. They are sending out troops over all the area to look for us. But luckily they do not know which way we went. So those troops must go in every direction." She seemed to take some satisfaction in giving them that much trouble.

"But we're still in the middle of it," Gunny said.

"Yes," the Dragon Lady told him. "That is why we must head south. We must now split up."

"We're already split up," I reminded her.

"Not split enough," she said. "We must now form at least *six* groups. We shall head toward Loshan, where I have friends, and cross the Grand Canal. We shall pass many, many people, so we must be careful. Until we meet at Loshan, our six groups will be near each other. But I must warn you: we may have to change our direction at any time. So the groups will be close enough that we can speak with each other every day."

I asked, "What about Scotty and his people?"

Before answering, the Dragon Lady spoke to the Mongol lieutenant, who nodded and went out. Then she turned to Gunny and me. "The lieutenant will send two men to warn Scotty and tell him to detour to meet us at Loshan. If we can all reach that place safely, we shall have a choice of routes to follow. But I must warn you," she said again, and her face and voice were as grave as I'd ever seen them. "We can trust no one. The Communists are determined to capture us. Their spies are everywhere. They have offered a large reward to anyone who captures us. The trip to Loshan will be very dangerous."

"They can't outfox the fox," I said, trying to sound as though I believed it.

She did not smile at being called a fox, but answered with a shrug, "We shall see. Once we reach Loshan, our chances will improve."

"Let's say we get to Loshan," I began. "And let's say we make it from there to the coast. How are we going to contact the Americans?"

"We must find a transmitter. I think we shall do that without much difficulty."

I had one more question: "What happens to Kim?"

After a word to her young sister, with both of them glancing at me, the Dragon Lady said, "She goes with us." Then as though anticipating what I was thinking about the danger, she went on, "When I was her age, I wanted the same thing—not to be left out."

Kim said something now, and the Dragon Lady translated: "She has something to give you—something that belonged to our parents. She wants you to have it." While I stared, Kim put into my hand a set of rosary beads, made of greenish jade, with a hand-carved ivory cross.

"They're beautiful!" I said, putting my arms around Kim. She reached up and kissed me on the cheek, and when I saw tears welling in her eyes I had to turn away or I would have been crying too. I saw the Dragon Lady watching with a soft look that made her a totally different person from the one she had been only a few minutes before. Now I put one arm around Kim and the other around the Dragon Lady, and hugged them both at once.

But in a moment the thought of the commander came back into the Dragon Lady's face, and I heard it in her voice: "Now we shall divide into groups. It would be best for you Americans to go separately. So if one is caught, the other will have a chance to get to the sea."

It was a sobering idea, and I hated having to think of it. I said, looking at Gunny, "We're the only two left."

"Yeah," he said. "But she's right, Rick." He turned to the Dragon Lady. "Okay, so we split."

"Khan, Nancy, Kim, the lieutenant and one other Mongol will go with me. Audy and Gunny will go with three Mongols. Do not worry, Gunny. You will be in good hands."

"I'm not worried about *me,*" he said, staring in my direction. "Take care of the girls, and don't go gung-ho on us. Play it safe."

"Right," I said. "I'll take care of them. And no gung-ho."

Then the Dragon Lady began outlining our trip. "From

here we travel south. We do not divide into groups until we reach the meeting of the Grand Canal and the Hwang Ho."

I asked how long it would take us to reach Loshan, and she said, "Perhaps two days, perhaps a week." She turned abruptly and shouted an order to someone, who disappeared and came back with a leather bag. From it the Dragon Lady pulled out two sets of binoculars—one for Gunny and one for me. The first set she'd given me had been lost in the fighting.

Gunny already had his up and was scanning the distance.

"A good thing that," Audy said. "With the land so flat, you can see a long way. Spot a Commie from miles off."

"There is also another enemy out there," the Dragon Lady said. "This is the season of floods."

Audy confirmed this: "The whole bloody area can go under water."

"But also the floods might work for us," she said. "Now we go. They are searching for us every minute."

Outside all of our people were waiting. A number of villagers were standing by. When the Dragon Lady said something to them, Audy explained, "She's telling them we are heading east."

"But aren't we heading south?"

"Quiet there, mate," he warned. We mounted, and we did start by heading east. When we were a mile or so from the village, two scouts dropped back as rear guards. After we had passed a few more villages, we took a route through the rice paddies that veered slightly to the south. There was a halt when we reached a kind of basin, where we waited for the scouts to appear.

"It is all right," the Dragon Lady told us finally. "We are not being followed." She appeared to read my thoughts about the friendly villagers. "There are spies and informers—eyes and ears everywhere. We cannot be too careful. Soon there may be planes looking for us. Now we must get back on the road and mingle with other people. You two must keep your hats down low."

After riding due south for less than half a mile, we came to a road that was simply a river of people—so many of them that we had to ride alongside. After a while we dismounted and walked our horses, with the Dragon Lady in the lead. I was right behind her; then came Kim, Nancy and the others, strung out in a long line, our weapons hidden in baskets that had been secured to the backs of the horses.

Before long we began to see Communist soldiers standing by the road, keeping a close watch on the people going in both directions. The farther we went, the more of them there were, and the closer together what seemed to be checkpoints. But the guards were only watching, not stopping anyone.

Out of the corner of my eye I saw Nancy working her way up to me. "More Communists as we go south," she whispered.

"I can see," I told her, doing my best to keep my head down. "You must get back in line." I smiled from underneath the hat, and could see her smile as she dropped behind me.

Over the next few miles there must have been a hundred soldiers stationed along the road. They made me feel like a hunted animal. While I tried to sneak past, unarmed, right under their noses, my heart pounded so hard that I halfway believed they would hear it.

It was midmorning by now, and the flow of people along the road was thicker than ever. I was surprised to see one of the Mongols mount his horse and leave the road, heading off toward a rice paddy. Seeing that we were near a checkpoint, I lowered my head. Then I heard a commotion, and up ahead I could just make out that the Mongol was being stopped by three soldiers, who had begun interrogating him. As I got closer I could hear the threat in their voices. But the Mongol went on sitting astride his horse with his hands folded, not saying a word. I didn't know whether they thought he couldn't understand them, or were afraid of him or just baffled. But finally, looking annoyed, they waved him on.

My spirits had risen briefly at seeing the giant outwit the soldiers, but now they fell again at the thought of how noticeable the Mongols were; it seemed to me that the Communists had to connect them with our raids. How many Mongols could there be in China at the moment who were giving trouble to the authorities?

As we rode, I noticed that the soil was darker and richer than before. This was river-bottom country, with canals everywhere, all of them held in their channels by high dikes. Toward early afternoon a light rain started to fall. At the same time, the weather was so much warmer that I took off all my extra clothes, keeping on a long-sleeved shirt to hide the color of my skin. I'd smeared dirt on my hands, neck and face. But what mainly helped me at times when soldiers were within a couple of feet of me, was simply the unbelievable numbers of people crowded along the roads—literally thousands of them. It must have been that after a while anyone trying to watch would be hypnotized by the sight of so many people passing.

Again and again I made out the walls of a village off to the side of the road with hundreds of people at work in the fields around it. The rain became heavier and it felt so good that I would have loved to throw my head back and let it wash the grime and sweat from my face. But of course I didn't do any such thing.

The checkpoints now seemed farther apart, and after a while the Dragon Lady dropped back to tell Nancy and me, "After the next checkpoint, we shall leave the road. There is a village nearby where we can stop and rest for a time." She veered off the road a little later and after riding less than a quarter of a mile we were in the midst of a huge, soggy rice field. Keeping clear of the green rows while we sloshed through water, we made our way across it and uphill onto a plain. After a mile or so we came in sight of a village. Before we got to the wall surrounding it, the Dragon Lady signaled us to stop while she rode on ahead. Hundreds of men, women and children were working in the fields, and they gave us a curious glance now and then while we waited, not moving. It must have been nearly an hour before she returned and signaled for us to enter. During those final few hundred yards the wind was blowing and it began raining harder, so I was all the happier at the thought of shelter.

The houses of the village, as those in the others we'd seen, were small and primitive—and just as packed with people. I wondered how they could live jammed together that way. Some of the Mongols took our horses and we went in on foot —Gunny and I still keeping our hats pulled low. After what the Dragon Lady had told us about spies, we could hardly feel relaxed. The Mongols, always a little remote and wary, stayed outside the village with the horses, and didn't mingle at all with the people of the village, while we were led into a low-ceilinged hut and given food.

From the beginning, though, there had been some uneasiness in the air. After a few moments I saw that the Dragon Lady and Audy were both agitated and soon she was saying that we must leave.

I asked what was the matter.

Audy answered my question. "The Communists have been really butchering people. It's no good here. The villagers are too bloody upset."

So we went out into the downpour. Just as we were mounted and about to start off, three figures on horseback appeared in the distance, heading straight for us. They were all riding like madmen. As they got closer, I could see that one of them was a white man. When he leaped from his horse, he turned out to be at least as big as the Mongol lieutenant— maybe six feet six, and weighing as much as 250 pounds.

Two smaller figures, wearing robes that covered them from head to toe, sat on their horses while the big man walked toward us. He was black-haired, with dark eyes. "And are you just going to sit there and stare all the day?" he asked, with a grin that showed a lot of very white teeth. I guessed from his accent that he must be an Irishman—not Boston Irish but the real thing. An M-1 rifle was slung over his shoulder, and he carried two knives on his belt.

The Dragon Lady dismounted to meet him, and several of the villagers came outside the walls again. As soon as they headed back inside, she was motioning for Gunny and me to follow her, and soon we were back in the same hut as before.

The black-haired giant looked around and grinned again. "O'Malley's the name, John O'Malley. And whose company do I have the pleasure of on this hell of a fine day?"

We introduced ourselves, and I went on wondering about his two small companions. They were still engulfed in the robes they wore, though they looked as though they must be soaked through. Finally, with a glance at them, O'Malley said, "We have a bit of a problem." When the two figures finally shed those wet outer clothes, I saw what it was. They were both women, Caucasian, and dressed in the garb of nuns.

While they stood there quietly shivering, O'Malley said, "The Communists seem to have gone quite daft. These two sisters are from a little church on the other side of the Grand Canal, four miles to the south. A force of Communist soldiers came up the road, shooting everything and everyone in sight. They walked straight into the church, firing. I was in the back with a priest and the sisters. When the priest ran out into the sanctuary, they shot him. I gathered up the two sisters here, got them onto horses, and off we rode. As we were leaving, the soldiers were setting the church afire."

A couple of the villagers now took the nuns aside and gave them food. They were Belgian, O'Malley told us; whether they didn't know English at all, or were under some kind of vow of silence, or were just in a state of shock, I never found out. For a moment the rest of us simply stood there, no one saying anything, until I thought to ask O'Malley where he had come from.

It was a second or two, while he looked at me as though it was none of my business, before he answered, "Burma."

"That is a very long way," the Dragon Lady said. "What is your destination?"

O'Malley glared at her for a second. Then he said, "You're a tiny thing. If you stood sideways, I might not even see you."

Though he sounded genial, it was a brush-off and the Dragon Lady knew it. "But I am *not* standing sideways," she retorted. "I am asking your destination."

He let out a big laugh. "No, you're not standing sideways, and I *can* see you. Very well. I am heading for Indochina."

"Are you lost, perhaps?" she asked. "You are a very great distance out of your way."

He said, laughing even louder, "I came up here to go to *church!*" Then he added, "No, I have to meet some friends first. Then we will go south again. To help my countrymen in the fighting in Indochina."

The Dragon Lady stared. "I did not know the *Irish* were fighting in Indochina!"

This time he nearly exploded with laughter. "Sure, and you'd be deaf not to hear the Irish in my voice. But I was in the French foreign legion for fifteen years, and now I'm heading for where the fighting is."

"And what about *them?*" I nodded toward the nuns. They now sat in a corner eating rice, looking nowhere but down into their bowls.

"Oh, I'll manage. We're only three, and we should be able to slip through. The soldiers are busy looking for someone else." He seemed to be thinking, and his stare moved from the Dragon Lady to each one of us.

"It wouldn't be yourselves, I suppose?" he said then.

The Dragon Lady answered with another question. "Have you seen many Communist soldiers?"

"Many? The whole road is a nest of them!"

Audy was now looking alarmed. "What road did you say you were on?"

"I didn't," O'Malley said, still parrying. Again he seemed to be thinking before he replied, "Just south of Tungping."

"That's the very same bloody road Scotty would be on," Audy said.

"If you have a friend on that road," O'Malley told him, "he'll be overrun."

The Dragon Lady now said, "Our schedule must be changed."

"Then you'd best hurry!" O'Malley told her. "You've a long way to go, and the mud will be so deep that horses will be of no use."

"Perhaps Scotty and his people will not be stopped," the Dragon Lady said quickly. "We passed many Communist soldiers and we were not taken. Scotty may not have been so lucky. But if he has been taken, we must try to help him. With surprise and the weather, even a small strike force, one of our size, could perhaps succeed. If necessary, we must be ready to try."

Audy, Gunny and I all readily agreed—though I couldn't help adding to myself, "But how?"

Then O'Malley said, with a look at us, "I may as well go too."

"You have the sisters to care for," the Dragon Lady reminded him.

"Ah, then, if I'm killed," the big Irishman said, "you must agree to look after the sisters."

"Agreed," the Dragon Lady said.

O'Malley gave his flashing grin, shook hands with all of us, and then reached into his pocket like a magician about to perform a trick. What he brought out was an old, battered tin flask. Unscrewing the top, he held it up and called out, "A toast for the battle to come!" After a healthy swig he said "Ahhh," and passed the flask to Gunny.

"Whiskey?" Gunny asked.

"Homemade."

"It's been a long time," Gunny said, and took a mouthful. He swallowed, gasped, and held out the flask to Audy, who declined it. Then he offered it to me.

Although my experience with drinking was close to nil, I filled my mouth with the fiery stuff. That was my first mistake.

Trying to swallow it all was my second. I choked, gagged and spat all over the place, trying to catch my breath while the whiskey made its way through my insides, burning all the way.

"Have another, son," O'Malley said, while Gunny tried to keep a straight face. "Half of that one went on the floor."

When the laughter died down, the Dragon Lady got back to business with a question to O'Malley. "Tell us about the condition of the terrain between here and Tungping."

"Mud, as I said. Getting worse all the time. We hardly made it ourselves. I was sure our horses would break a leg. Now it will be impossible; you'll not be riding there."

"How can we make any time without horses?" Gunny asked.

"I made it all the way from Burma without one," O'Malley told him.

Gunny said, taking on the challenge, "Well, hell, we came all the way from Manchuria, and half of that was on foot!"

"Ah, saints preserve us, so you *are* the ones the Communists are after!" O'Malley declared.

I said to Gunny, "You sure know how to keep a secret!"

"Never mind, lad," O'Malley told me. "It's hard to keep that kind of secret. There are only a few of us foreigners in China, and when you hear about a group of them causing trouble, it's not too hard to figure out who it might be. Believe me, your secret is safe with me!"

The Dragon Lady had been talking with several of the villagers, who now brought out some skins. "Get your weapons," she said, "and wrap them in these to keep them dry."

We went outside to follow her instructions, and found a gale blowing. Huts were swaying; here and there a roof had been torn off, and the rain seemed to be driving at a forty-five-degree angle to the ground. Following the Mongols outside the village walls to where the horses were, we retrieved our weapons from the baskets and took them back to the hut. We found the nuns kneeling in prayer. Almost without thinking, I put down my machine gun and bandoliers and knelt down myself.

"The Lord is my shepherd, I shall not want . . . " I hardly knew where the words came from, but there they were. When I looked around, the Dragon Lady, Gunny, Audy, Nancy and Kim were all kneeling too.

I had always believed in God, and right now the time had come when it was comforting just to ask for a little outside help.

We got up and no one said anything for a moment or two. Then, as if there had been a signal, we were all moving. I slung the bandoliers and the binoculars over my shoulder again, checked my weapon, and wrapped it in the skins I'd been given.

The Dragon Lady was saying, "Nancy, I should like you to take Kim, the two sisters and some of our men to a place where we shall meet you. It will be difficult, for you will not be able to travel on the roads; you will have to cross the plain, which is like a marsh in this weather. You will have to take great care."

She paused and looked for a second at Nancy. "If we are late," she said, "—if we do not come to the place by the right time, then the Mongols will lead you back to the mountains. You must not wait longer than the time I shall tell you."

"No!" Nancy said. It was as though the word leaped out of her. "We wait. We do not leave without you."

"Nancy!" the Dragon Lady answered sternly. "You will not wait one minute past the time I tell you. Every minute is a danger to the people with you. You must promise!"

Tears broke from the girl's eyes and rolled down her face. She stared at the Dragon Lady and then at me. I walked over to her, put my hands on her fragile shoulders, and said gently, "We're going to be there, don't worry. But you must promise."

She went on looking at the two of us. At last she said, "I promise," and added, "Please be there!"

I could hardly keep the tears out of my own eyes. While I turned and walked away, the Dragon Lady put an arm around Nancy and walked with her, telling her in Chinese exactly where and when we were to meet. And then, once again, it was time to go.

In a couple of minutes we stood outside the village wall, in the pelting rain, watching while Nancy and her group veered off to the right and vanished into the storm. Then we had to concentrate on our own journey. The mud gave us trouble almost from the first step. At best it didn't quite reach our ankles; at worst, we were sucked in up to the knees, all the time struggling to keep upright in the face of the wind. Adding to our exhaustion was the fact that it was now getting dark. Soon the mud was an intimate addition to our clothes, and it kept working its way through to the skin. I'd wrapped my machine gun as carefully as possible, but I worried about how I was going to check it before firing, if I ever had to.

Darkness came fast and we slogged on, bunched close together so as not to lose each other. There was almost no visibility. Even in all that rain, I was sweating like a pig. Whenever I stopped for a drink of water, I got a dose of mud along with it. Finally the Dragon Lady held up her hand for a stop and we gathered into a single group. There were about thirty of us now. She told us that the Grand Canal was just ahead. "Scotty had to cross the canal here," she told us, "where it meets the Hwang Ho. So we shall cross. We shall take the road he took, and we shall catch his group very soon, I hope."

We resumed our plodding for about half a mile. Then we were at the canal, and again she was signaling a stop. She and the Mongol lieutenant went off to make a reconnaissance, leaving the rest of us there to rest. I looked over at O'Malley, who was so quiet that he might have been in a trance. Gunny, noticing it too, shook him and said, "Hey Irish, snap out of it!"

But O'Malley only said, "Things are not going right. When they are, I'll be the first to tell you. But now they're not."

Gunny asked what he was talking about, and after another couple of moments his eyes seemed to focus.

"Now," I said, "tell us what the hell you were talking about."

"Talking? Was I talking? What did I say?" O'Malley asked.

"A lot of bullshit," Gunny told him.

"So I was. So I was, I suppose," O'Malley said. None of us was satisfied with that, but we all settled down to wait for the Dragon Lady. About ten minutes later she was back.

"There is a big bridge up ahead," she told us, "But it is guarded. So we shall walk under it."

Gunny asked how we were going to do that—by walking on water? I was glad he had begun asking the dumb questions.

"Yes," she answered with a laugh. "You will see. There is a footbridge along the abutments, at the level of the water. We shall walk on that."

What she called a footbridge was hardly even that. It had no rail, it was narrow and slippery, and in places it was actually under the water of the canal, which was turbulent with flooding from the storm. But there was nothing to do except follow her, watching our footing as we moved in single file along those swaying planks, with nothing to hold onto except the pilings of the bridge. These were spaced about ten feet apart, and what made things worse was the way the planks kept moving away from the pilings and then drifting back with the movement of the water. That meant having to dash from one piling to the next while the planks were up against it, and then squatting down on the boards to hold on as as it moved away again—then another dash, another squat. The footbridge was held together with rope, but didn't seem to be attached to the main bridge. I don't know what kept it suspended.

When I finally set foot on land, the Dragon Lady was waiting, moving each one of us along while she watched to see that everyone had made it. We waited while she took a final count. It appeared that no one was missing.

Then we were moving through the mud again for another

half hour, until we came to a road. The storm had left it deserted. After the packed roads we'd traveled in daylight, the emptiness seemed strange. There was a delay while the Dragon Lady sent out scouts. The road, once we started forward again, was so muddy that it was very little better than trudging across the plain had been.

Some figures up ahead meant another halt, and this time the Dragon Lady ordered us to get down. Staying at a half crouch in mud and water left our clothes and skin in worse condition than ever, but we hid until it was clear that the people coming were our own scouts. The Dragon Lady talked with them for a while and then came over to report.

"The Communists have camped about a quarter of a mile ahead. In a field just across from them they have shot about two hundred people."

I suppose the same thought went through all our minds. Audy was the one who voiced it: "What about Scotty and Charlie?"

"The scouts do not know. We shall move up as close as we can and see what we can find out."

We trudged forward through the mud, and again the signal came to halt. I said, "Why not hit them now, while they're asleep?"

"No," she replied. "We shall wait for the scouts to come back again." And she told us to check our weapons.

Glad for a chance to do this, I unwrapped my machine gun, and found that it wasn't quite as filthy as I'd feared. I did the best I could to clean it in that weather, squeezed out the water from the skins and rewrapped it.

Half an hour must have passed before the scouts returned once again with their report. Now she told us, "We are thirty yards from the bodies of the prisoners they killed. The Communists are right across the road. We shall get into their camp to see if any prisoners are alive. If there are not—" She paused. "Then that will mean that Scotty and Charlie escaped, or else they are out in the field . . . with the other bodies."

14

O'Malley was the one who finally broke the silence.

"I've got a plan," he said. "But it depends on the weather."

While Gunny and I looked at him in surprise—we'd gotten used to expecting nobody but the Dragon Lady to offer any plans—she said, "I would like to hear it. But with any plan, we must finish off all the Communists and get away quickly. And there must be no survivors who might send out a message."

O'Malley began, "You may think I'm daft. But first hear me out. You know how afraid they are of ghosts." Gunny was giving him a hard look. But the Dragon Lady put up her hand to give O'Malley a chance. "If we could spook them," he went on, "scare the hell out of them, and then have people hit them from the rear . . . "

While Audy made a gesture toward his head that showed what he thought, the Dragon Lady was saying, "It might work."

O'Malley then explained his plan in detail. He wanted some of us to rise from the midst of the field where the bodies were, as though we were ghosts, and walk straight into the Communist camp. Covered with mud, we'd certainly look like corpses just risen from out there. But the rain would have to have stopped, giving some visibility, before it would work.

"Yes," the Dragon Lady agreed, "they do frighten easily. And that would perhaps distract them long enough for us to attack and finish every one of them off. Remember: No one must be left alive to send out any warnings."

Since she thought it had a chance to work, all at once it became our plan. She got everyone together and then divided us into five groups. Four would attack from the sides of the camp and the fifth would play the challenging and dangerous role of the dead who had been raised. The Dragon Lady, Gunny, Audy, O'Malley, the lieutenant and I, along with several others, made up this group. The Dragon Lady was to fire the first shot to signal the attack.

We moved out, with the wind and rain driving as hard as ever. Crouching low, wading through mud and water, we sloshed into the field, where I tried not to look at the corpses. Covered with mud until they were partly submerged, many revealed neither sex nor age, except for the very young ones. The size of the children made them unmistakable; those tiny bodies made me so angry that as at no other time, I actually wanted to kill the soldiers who had been responsible. And if O'Malley's crazy plan worked, my chance to do it might come.

When we'd moved about ten yards in from the road, our group spread out and we lay down in the mud and water, waiting for dawn and a break in the weather. The dawn we were sure of; the weather we could only pray for.

After we'd waited for what seemed to be hours, light finally appeared in the east. As I looked around me, the first thing I could see was the outline of the body nearest me. I closed my eyes, not wanting to look. Opening them again, I realized that the wind and rain had both died down, as though approving of our scheme.

While I slowly turned my head to peer across the road at the Communist camp, the Dragon Lady came crawling toward me through the mud. Speaking softly, she told me that Scotty and Charlie were prisoners. For a second I was relieved just to hear that they were alive. Then I began to remember the kind of thing that was done here to prisoners of whatever side. Still lying motionless, she whispered, "We must continue with our plan."

The forms of the Communist sentries were now becoming visible only yards away. There would have been no way to hide there if the fields hadn't been strewn with corpses. As I tried to erase the image of them from my mind, I heard voices. Lying there afraid to move, with our weapons wrapped, we were never more powerless than at that moment.

The pounding of my heart brought a new wave of terror as I heard the voices growing louder. What now came into view was a group of what appeared to be farmers, perhaps thirty or forty of them, all ragged and muddy, with their hands bound behind their backs, being herded in our direction by Communist soldiers. I scanned the group for any sight of Scotty or Charlie, but didn't see either of them. A soldier who seemed to be an officer was shouting orders to the others. Obviously this was the field of execution.

With a sudden, deliberate and yet fluid motion, the Dragon Lady stood up. Holding her weapon behind her, she gave a low moan. Then the rest of us, our weapons hidden, rose likewise and moved slowly toward the road, moaning as we went. Through the morning mist, I saw that I was part of a skirmish line, an assault carried out by ghosts—and that we had scared the hell out of those soldiers. As they panicked and ran screaming, a few of them dropped their weapons. The prisoners were every bit as frightened, and their flight added to the confusion. The terror was catching; soldiers pouring out of their tents were in a panic even before they saw us.

From the size of the bivouac and the number of men I'd seen running, I guessed there were about a hundred soldiers. Thus far, not one had turned to look at us. Then an officer appeared to have grasped the situation. From a distance of about twenty-five yards, he began to bark orders, drawing his pistol meanwhile.

From the speed of her response, it was clear that the Dragon Lady had been watching for this moment. Tossing away the wrappings from her weapon, she let loose a burst of gunfire that knocked him off his feet.

At that the rest of us began firing. In the slaughter that followed, we had not only surprise and superstition on our side, but also confusion as the farmers started running for freedom. Now the four other groups of our force caught the Communists in a crossfire that finished them in a few minutes.

Audy was the first to reach Scotty and Charlie; he was untying them when I got there. I could see that they were alive and in fair shape, though Scotty had been slashed badly and Charlie had a deep, ugly wound in his scalp.

"For a while, lads," Scotty told us, "you had me pretty frightened too. I really thought the dead had come to life."

O'Malley, coming up behind me, roared at that. We explained, as we introduced him to Scotty, that it had been his idea. Now Gunny and I helped Scotty to his feet.

"Can you make it?" I asked.

"Aye. I've been worse. I've also been better." He turned to O'Malley. "And thanks for your help."

"I'd do it any time," he replied. "But now I believe we're going in different directions. So I'll be saying good-bye." And he shook hands all round.

"If you have trouble, try to get word to us," the Dragon Lady said. "You know our direction."

"You're a remarkable woman," he told her, "and I thank

you for your offer. But John O'Malley has been looking after himself for quite a while now. Got to be moving on."

After one more round of good-byes, O'Malley was off down the road, alone and on foot, a stranger in a dangerous country. I've thought many times since about how China had its way of converting the likes of O'Malley, Audy, Scotty, maybe even myself. To what? Different customs, a different way of life, a new way of seeing the important things? I'm still not sure.

When he was about twenty-five yards from us, O'Malley halted, turned, waved and shouted, "God bless you all!"

As we waved back, I couldn't help saying softly, "God bless you too, John O'Malley!"

Then the Dragon Lady was assembling us once more. Once we had picked up as many of the slain Communists' weapons as we could carry, we were off. We saw no one—the weather had taken care of that. The road was muddy, but easier going than the land around it would have been. From it we had a broad view of the field where the slaughter had taken place. I stood there sickened yet hypnotized until Gunny slapped me on the shoulder to get me moving.

Seeing that Charlie needed help, I pulled up alongside him and lifted his arm around my own shoulders so that we could walk together. Though Charlie was still a little dazed, Scotty seemed to be in good shape. We'd lost only one man in rescuing the two of them. As I looked around at our group, faces splattered, hair matted, clothes caked with mud, I could understand how O'Malley's trick had succeeded.

We were marching into a fresh wind. Before us I could see the canal. Then the Dragon Lady signaled a halt. She conferred for at least fifteen minutes with a scout who had just returned—which meant, I could be pretty sure, that a new plan was being hatched. By now I'd lost track of the number of changes of plan, and I wasn't surprised to hear her announce, "We have a boat but we shall not go to the Grand Canal. We shall go on the Hwang Ho instead—and it will take us to Laichow Bay. That is near Weihai."

"And Weihai," I exclaimed, "is where we get the boat to Seoul!"

She nodded and all at once what had been a kind of dream seemed close—a thing that was possible, that could really happen. And knowing that brought a new kind of uneasiness. What had kept me going up to now was *lack* of hope—not giving a damn. I didn't want to change that, all of a sudden; it would make a nervous wreck of me.

I tried not to think of all this, to force my mind in other directions as we trudged on. The sun had come out and the wind was drying the mud that still covered most of me. When I began to brush it from my clothes, the Dragon Lady cautioned, "Don't clean up too well. You should look like a farmer or a Mongol."

After twenty minutes or so we met two more of the Dragon Lady's scouts. They told her the Hwang Ho was only a mile away, and that there was a boat waiting for us. "The owner of the boat is a friend of mine," she said, "and he will take us to Laichow Bay. Also he has a radio."

A radio meant contact with Americans—another sign of how close we were. Once again I tried not to think about what it meant. The Dragon Lady ordered us to leave the road and to form into two columns, one on either side of the road. We moved like this for so long that I lost all sense of time. Finally, as we descended a slight hill, two large expanses of water lay before us: the canal on one side, the Hwang Ho on the other. Several junks were tied up at piers on the river, and the Dragon Lady headed for one of these with her usual sureness, as if it were something she did every day of her life. People at work on the piers or repairing boats in the water glanced at us, but didn't seem concerned.

Following her cue, we went aboard. She pointed to a cabin, told us to go inside, and then leaped back onto the pier. Inside the cabin, which was dark and stuffy, we found three men, to whom I nodded, not knowing what else to do. They nodded back with no sign that they were either startled or worried at seeing us. Audy explained presently that there were to be two boats and that the Dragon Lady was dividing up our people between them.

Soon the Mongol lieutenant was aboard, along with the others assigned to our junk. I could hear the crew preparing to cast off, with still no sign of the Dragon Lady. I was beginning to be nervous and at seeing from the cabin porthole that the lines were cast off, my heart started to pound. Then out of nowhere, she came into the cabin. She had been on board, up front, the whole time. She told us now, "You must stay away from windows and doorways, out of sight. Before long, if all goes well, we shall be at Laichow Bay."

In a couple of minutes we were under sail, out on the river and moving swiftly with the current. The Dragon Lady motioned for Gunny and me to follow her. "We shall try the radio," she explained as she led us into a smaller cabin just behind the other.

"What is your call sign—your call letters?" she asked.

Gunny and I stared at each other, looking blank. "Christ, I don't know," he said.

"Do you remember if Lieutenant Damon said anything about a frequency?" I asked him.

"No, dammit! We were none of us briefed about any such thing. Now what a time to think about it!"

The Dragon Lady spoke to the captain, who started fiddling with the transmitter, tuning in on various frequencies. We could hear the static and voices fading in and out. Then, after some time, we heard an American voice.

"Eagle One to all eagles. Return to nest. Return to nest. Acknowledge. Over."

"Jeez, Gunny!" I said.

Sounding as excited as I was, he said, "How do you work this?"

"Press it to talk," the Dragon Lady said. "Release it to listen."

Pressing the button with his thumb, Gunny said, "Eagle

One, Eagle One. Can you hear me? Can you hear me?" He released the button and waited. There was no answer. He pressed the button and spoke into the mike again. "Eagle One, I'm an American. Can you hear me? Come in! For God's sake! I don't have a call sign! I'm an American. Come in!"

Again he released the button, we waited, and again there was nothing.

"Dammit!" Gunny barked. "Why don't they answer?"

"They do not know who you are," the Dragon Lady said quietly. "And they do not want to give their position away. Neither do we. So we must stop now, so as not to give it away."

Scotty had walked into the room, and when we told him what had been happening, he said, "You need some sort of code word, lads, so your own people will know who you are."

"Code," I said. "Wait a minute! When we landed in Manchuria, what was the password the lieutenant used with Yen?"

Gunny looked at me, trying to remember. Meanwhile the boat captain had been fiddling with the radio. Frantic, I said, "What's he doing? He'll lose them!"

"He has to remain in contact with his friends," the Dragon Lady told me. "They are watching the Communists for us."

"But hell," I insisted, "we'll *lose* them!" But behind the angry annoyance, my mind was searching for the password. I paced up and down, groping; then I shouted, "Quick! Sand! *Quicksand!*"

The operator went on fiddling with the radio.

"I remembered the password!" I shouted. "So let's send it, let's see what happens!"

But when the Dragon Lady looked up, it was with bad news. "The Communists have gunboats at the mouth of the river, in Laichow Bay. We must go ashore."

"Can't we try the password once?"

She spoke to the captain, then told us firmly, "No. Not now. They are too close, they might pick up our position. We shall have to wait."

"But where will we get another radio?"

"As soon as we leave, the captain will call someone—someone on shore who has a radio. We can try to send the message from there."

I asked how long it would take us to reach Weihai.

"A few days—if all goes well," she said. Then she stared at me and asked, as though out of nowhere, "Have you decided now what you will do?"

It took me a second or two to realize what she meant. Then I remembered that I had said I wanted to stay. I hadn't thought about it in any systematic way but now that we were so close to actually being at the sea, I knew where my wishes were aimed.

"I think I'm going to go," I said. "I'll miss you, and I'll miss Nancy and Kim. But at least I'll see them once more."

The Dragon Lady replied softly, "You will not see Nancy and Kim again."

"What do you mean? Why not?" Suddenly I was upset, and surprised at the emotion that surged through me.

"They have started back to Inner Mongolia, where they will be safer. Our journey has become dangerous, with so many people. So I had to send them back." She looked at me, and I saw her eyes go soft, as they rarely did. "Please do not feel you were deceived. I know you cared for them. But it had to be done, and quickly. It is better this way."

I said soberly, "I know you did what you thought was right."

Just then we felt the boat bump gently alongside the pier. I welcomed the interruption. The thought of not seeing Nancy or Kim had brought me closer to what I dreaded even more— the thought of not seeing *her* again either.

Out on deck the captain gave us baskets to hide our weapons in. The day was warm and pleasant, the water was bright in the sunshine. We were all smeared and caked with mud— a total mess. Without hesitating, I took a flying leap and landed in the water.

"Come on in," I yelled, and in a minute they had joined

me—Gunny, Scotty, the Dragon Lady, even Charlie—for a leisurely bath before we waded ashore. Our skins and our clothes were now a couple of shades lighter. Feeling the water run from my sopping hair on my face, I asked Gunny if he had a comb.

"Got something on the line?" he teased, and I gave him a shove that sent him back into the river. While we were still splashing and shoving each other, the Dragon Lady was assembling her people from the second boat. We would be bidding good-bye to most of them before they began the long trek back to Mongolia. In no time they were on their way, leaving only a small group of us to head for the sea: the Dragon Lady, Gunny and I, Scotty, Audy, Charlie, the Mongol lieutenant and three of his men.

Staring at the backs of the departing group, I felt a tense sadness. This was the end of something. I didn't know what might be beginning, but the long journey with them was over.

Then almost at once, we were also moving on.

The ocean of mud left by the storm was already draining and beginning to dry out. Now there would be only an occasional slight dip in the terrain. Altogether it was as flat as anything I'd ever seen. After we'd gone a mile or so, a village came into view and we headed toward it. The place seemed strangely solitary. Not many people were working the land around it and inside the walls I saw no more than fifty people, with perhaps half a dozen huts. We were led by a villager to one of these. Audy told us, after listening to what he was telling the Dragon Lady, that this was the shack with the radio.

Though I was eager to try it, the Dragon Lady said, "No, we shall eat first. The villagers suggest caution because the Communists are near. If we have to flee, I should like to do it with full stomachs."

While we ate, Scotty told us what had happened to him. He and the others had been passing some soldiers on the road when suddenly they found themselves in a fire fight, for no reason that they could see. "They had the jump on us," he said. "Some of our people got away; most were cut down. They overpowered Charlie and me and wanted to shoot him on the spot. But I told them he was too important, their superiors would be angry." He smiled. "I believe they thought *we* were *you.*" He looked at Gunny and me. "Good thing we weren't, lads, or you wouldn't have come to rescue us."

When the meal had ended, the radio was brought from its hiding place somewhere within the hut. The Dragon Lady began tuning carefully, and while we listened an American voice broke through.

"It would be good if we had some sort of call sign," she said.

I urged, "Try Quicksand."

"But that was only a password and countersign," Scotty told me. "Something to use in the field. Not the same thing at all."

"All the same," I persisted, "what have we got to lose?"

The Dragon Lady pressed the button to transmit and spoke into the mike. "Quicksand, this is Quicksand. Come in."

We waited. All we heard was a crackle of static. We waited again. Still nothing but the crackle.

Scotty said, "Let me try. Maybe the accent is scaring them off." While he picked up the mike, the villager who had come in with us spoke to the Dragon Lady, and she explained, "He is afraid that if we transmit for too long, they will know our location. Then the whole village may be in danger."

"Maybe they're not hearing us," I said, feeling depressed.

Audy put a hand on my shoulder. "It's the right frequency. They're just not answering."

The Dragon Lady went on conferring with the villager— asking him, Scotty explained, about another transmitter somewhere out on the road. "In an hour we can try again," she said. If that failed, she went on, we had two choices. One was to go to the coast, to Laiyang, where we might find someone with a portable transmitter we could use. Then we could travel south along the coast, sending messages as we went.

"That'll be bloody dangerous," Audy interjected. "We'll be trapped with our backs to the water, with nowhere to go if we're found out." And Scotty agreed.

The Dragon Lady nodded silently. Then she said, "The other choice is to head back to Mongolia."

We all groaned. Then I said, "You people have got to get back there whether we get out or not. And how many times can you roll the dice without crapping out?" I said it as much to myself as to anyone else.

The Dragon Lady looked mystified, and Gunny started to chuckle. "It means rolling the dice many times and being lucky, and then finally not being lucky," he explained.

"Oh," she said earnestly. "I shall remember that"—and we all laughed.

But Gunny had turned sober again. "Suppose we go to the coast," he said. "What are our chances?"

The Dragon Lady said, "They will depend on whether we can make radio contact and get help before we are found. If they find us first, we shall not have much room to move, and there will not be many of us to fight . . ." Her voice trailed off. Then she brightened. "We roll the dice," she said. "But we shall be lucky."

"I never won anything in my life," I told her, trying a feeble joke. "But I'm willing to bet on you."

All business again, she said, "We must have some sort of code, a signal for the radio. Something so that the Americans will need to talk to us. Something . . ."

We all sat puzzling over the problem until Scotty jumped to his feet. "The message Roberts had on him! Do you remember how it went?"

While I tried, still drawing a blank, Gunny slapped his hands together. "Get that radio working!" he shouted.

The villager ran up the antenna again and Gunny said, "I'm going to send this message, and then we run like hell for the coast!" He picked up the mike.

"Command post," he said, "this is Quicksand. Roberts. Roberts. Six ships sunk. Will not return. They feel the same as most of us. But hung his name on anyway. Sing a song to Jenny next. Quicksand, Quicksand, can you hear me? Over."

The son of a bitch had remembered every word!

While we listened, Gunny repeated the message, this time pacing his words, taking care to pronounce each syllable. Again there was no answer.

After he'd tried one more time, still with no response, Scotty said, "They're bringing the brass in on this one. Give them five minutes. Then try again."

The villager was beginning to look concerned and the wait seemed to go on forever before Gunny said, "Let's have a go at it."

And this time the answer came!

"Quicksand. Quicksand. This is Spec One. Do you read me? Over."

I slapped Gunny on the back. He ignored me. "Spec One, this is Quicksand. Affirmative, we read you. Over."

"Quicksand, this is Spec One. What is your approximate location? Over."

Gunny stared at all of us for a second. Then he spoke into the mike again. "Spec One. This is Quicksand. We are near onion. We are near onion. Over."

"We read you. Can you stand by? I say again, Can you stand by?"

"Negative, we cannot stand by," Gunny answered. "I say again, we cannot stand by. We are moving. Will call you tomorrow morning. Tomorrow morning. Do you read us, Spec One? Over."

"We read you, Quicksand, loud and clear. We have your approximate location. We will wait for your call tomorrow morning. Over."

"This is Quicksand. Affirmative. Tomorrow morning. Out."

Ecstatic, we broke into a cheer. "I kept it short," Gunny

explained, "because I figured we were being monitored. Give 'em time, and they could triangulate our position."

"Tell me one thing, Gunny," I said. "What in hell is *onion?*"

"Hold on a minute and I'll tell you," he said. "I remember when I was in Korea, I was looking at a map of China. I saw this place, L-i-e-n-y-u-n, and I pointed to it and asked one of my buddies how it was pronounced. Lienyun. Sounded to me just like *onion.* Throwing that at them, I figured we'd be close, but not *too* close."

I said, "Too close to what?"

The Dragon Lady said, quick as always, "He means that the Americans will not be the only ones plotting our location. We cannot even be sure those are real Americans we spoke to. They could be defectors, in the pay of the Communists. What is good is that we are not really close to Lienyun. Not close enough to be there by tomorrow morning."

"You're some shrewd son of a bitch," I told Gunny admiringly.

He said, pretending to be hurt, "Took you a while to find out! But now we've got to be cutting out of here. They'll be looking for us."

While we got ourselves ready, the Dragon Lady was having a lively conversation with the villager. After the rest of us had gotten our gear together and gone outside, she and Audy came out carrying a large basket. When I asked what was in it, she said, "The transmitter. The owner has made us a gift of it. But it is better for him too not to have it any longer." While I peered inside the basket at the portable radio with its hand-powered generator, I saw Charlie waiting with an expression that made me uneasy.

"Now I must say good-bye," he told us. "My injury is not all healed. You will be traveling fast. I will only slow you down. Instead I will prepare for our trip back to Mongolia. That way, I can do more good."

Charlie's words gave me another jolt. I thought of Nancy

and Kim. Every time I left someone now, it was for the last time. I went over and gave Charlie a bear hug, and once again I had to turn and walk away so as not to be seen with tears in my eyes. I had been through more with him in a few weeks than I would in a lifetime with most people. While the others made their farewells, I realized that what I felt about Charlie I also felt about everyone else in this strange, exotic crew. When—*if*—Gunny and I ever got out of here, I knew I'd be leaving a sort of family behind.

We marched off at top speed. From our full strength of a hundred, now we were down to just nine—the Dragon Lady, Scotty, Audy, the four Mongols, Gunny and I. The afternoon was warm, and as our clothes dried out completely, I began to feel parched; but we traveled without stopping for a drink. I thought how strange it was—drowning in water one day, thirsting for it the next; one day nothing but mud, the next day nothing but dust.

We cut across country, keeping to narrow footpaths, avoiding main roads. We now saw few people. Fatigue was already creeping up on me, and Scotty had told us it would take two days to reach Lienyun—*if* we didn't run into any trouble. It was a relief when, with darkness approaching, the Dragon Lady signaled a stop. But it was only to tell us that we would not get there in time unless we traveled faster. Now, she said, we were going to run.

She turned and broke into a trot. We all followed and to my surprise, though my legs had been bothering me, with the change of pace they actually began to feel better. But it wasn't long before I was sweating heavily and feeling limp. We jogged for at least an hour before the next stop came. I sank to my knees, sucking in deep breaths, feeling drained of strength, breath and water. "Don't drink too much," she cautioned. "Just moisten your lips and take a sip. We shall rest five minutes. Then we run again."

The five minutes passed quickly. I saw that Gunny was exhausted too; so was everyone. But once again when the

Dragon Lady was on her feet we all managed to follow somehow.

As I ran, my mind slipped into a kind of trance. I recalled incidents from my childhood, the sports I'd taken part in, the training for this mission, all the running we'd done then. And now an odd thing happened. With my mind wandering off, I'd ceased to keep an eye on the Dragon Lady and wasn't ready when she stopped short. There I was, charging into her like a runaway buffalo, knocking her down and falling over her.

We'd all been in such close quarters for so long that the physical contact in itself was nothing new. What happened now was that I realized in a way I hadn't before that she was a woman. Slowly I began pulling myself off her and at the same time helping her up, with my hands underneath her shoulders. I had never been quite that close to her before, or touched her body in quite that way. Our eyes met and stayed locked in the same steady gaze.

I heard Scotty saying, "Why don't we all take a breather?"

Her shoulders felt strong and wiry yet delicate under my grasp. "Are you all right?" I finally asked.

"Yes," she answered. "Are you?" I'd never heard quite that sound in her voice before.

"Yes, I'm all right."

"Soon you will be going home," she whispered.

"Yes," I said. "I guess so. It won't be easy." Then I leaned down and kissed her gently on the lips. I hadn't had much experience as a ladies' man, and God knows I hadn't planned this. We just stood and looked at each other again until she dropped her hands from my shoulders and we pulled apart.

After a minute she had the old amused look. "Shall we run all night, or shall we rest?" she said.

"I think we should follow Scotty's recommendation."

"Then let's tell them." We walked over to where Scotty, Gunny and Audy were sitting. The Mongols, as usual, had moved off by themselves. By now it was dark. I took out a skin bag of water, and we each had a long swig. We hadn't sat there long before the Dragon Lady was asking whether we had the strength to go on running through the night. There were hills ahead of us, she said. Also, we could not run during the day without arousing suspicion.

Though no one was eager to run again, we all agreed that we had to do it. This time, as I ran, my thoughts were all of the Dragon Lady and the way she'd looked and sounded. I wondered how I could want to leave whatever it was that *she* was to me. I asked myself what there was at home. My emotions were so confused that I all but broke out laughing at the thought of us nine, taking such incredible chances to reach the sea—for the sake of somebody who couldn't even be sure he wanted to go!

But also, as we ran, I loosened up and began to appreciate the task we'd undertaken. There was a moon now and I could see the terrain getting hillier. The ups and downs put a strain on my wind as well as my legs. The next time the Dragon Lady signaled a stop, I took a sip of water that went down the wrong way. I started coughing and for some moments I couldn't stop. The Mongol lieutenant came over, looking worried, and put a hand on my shoulder. He said something to Audy, who explained, "He's offered to carry you."

"No thanks," I told him as soon as I could speak. "Tell him I'm okay." I was embarrassed, all the more because there was no doubt in my mind that he could have done it. The Mongols were carrying the food, water, radio and weapons, but in all our running they never broke stride or asked for a rest.

As we resumed our run, I found myself worrying about the next message we sent. Each time we transmitted, the Communists would be one step closer to locating us. We took one more break just before sunup. With the first light of dawn I felt a little safer; all through the night, in the back of my mind there had been the fear that we might stumble onto an encampment of soldiers. With light showing in the east, the Dragon Lady quickened the pace for one last sprint before the cover of darkness was gone.

Once the sun came up, my aches turned into pains. I wondered about Scotty, Gunny and Audy, all of them a good deal older than I was. When it was full daylight, we paused on the side of a hill near a clump of trees. I saw the Dragon Lady standing there, her hair blown by the breeze, the rags she wore outlining the shape of her body. I was looking at her in an entirely new way now and I told myself I'd better stop it.

While the rest of us slumped to the ground, grateful for the rest, the Mongols stationed themselves a little apart from the line of trees. One of them had taken my binoculars for the first watch. After a silence, the Dragon Lady turned to Gunny and me. "When you first sent the message, you used a name—"

"Quicksand," I said.

"No, no. It was a man's name."

"Roberts," Gunny said.

"Yes, yes, that's it. Roberts. Who is he?"

"He was a CIA agent from the States. Or anyhow that's what I think he was."

She thought for a moment. "So they think you are this agent, this Roberts, calling."

"Well, if they do, they're in for some surprise," I said. The more I thought about this, the less I liked it. But I was too exhausted to brood for long. In a minute or two I was sound asleep.

The voices of Gunny, Audy and Scotty woke me. My legs ached. When I asked how long I'd been asleep, Scotty answered, "A couple of hours."

The Dragon Lady had been off talking to the Mongol lieutenant. Now she was beside me.

"How far to onion, or whatever it is?" I asked.

She said, "We could reach it by tomorrow morning."

"Only we told them *this* morning," I pointed out.

"They will wait."

"Because they think we're Roberts?"

She did not answer. Anyhow, we had enough other things to worry about—such as the message we were going to transmit right now.

Soon the radio picked up the American voice: "Quicksand, Quicksand, this is Spec One. Do you read? Over."

Scotty flipped the switch to send. "Spec One, this is Quicksand. Read you loud and clear. Over."

"Quicksand, have you reached destination? I say again, have you reached destination? Over."

"Spec One, this is Quicksand. We need another day. I say again, another day to reach destination. Over."

"Affirmative, Quicksand. Will look for you same time tomorrow. Be as quick as you can. The business is over. Be as quick as you can. Over."

Scotty flipped the switch again. "Spec One, this is Quicksand. We have a man ready for the world. We need shipment. We need shipment. Do you read? Over."

The voice came: "Loud and clear, Quicksand. One package for shipment. One package for shipment. Over."

"Spec One, will be at destination tomorrow morning. Need shipment quickly. Cannot wait. Need instructions. Over."

"Hold on that last interrogatory, Quicksand. Can you call back after dark? Say again, can you call back tonight? We will have orders. Over."

"Wilco, Spec One. Will call back after dark. Out."

Scotty snapped off the radio and turned to us with elation in his face. We all began to cheer, hug and pound each other on the back.

Then for a second or two the Dragon Lady clung to me.

I said, softly now, "I may really be leaving soon."

"Are you happy?" she asked.

"I don't know," I said. "Part of me wants the trip to start all over again. I know that's selfish but it's true."

"Yes, I know," she said. We strolled away from the others, full of things we wanted to say but couldn't and after a moment we reluctantly returned.

"The package ready for shipment," Audy announced.

"The *battered* package ready for shipment would be more like it," I told him. "Or rather, *two* battered packages." I looked toward Gunny, waiting for the laughter to begin. Instead there was an embarrassed silence.

Then Gunny said, "No, Rick, I'm not going."

"What?"

"That's right, Rick. I'm not going back."

Looking around, I could see that the others already knew. What I couldn't take in, what I couldn't handle just then, was that everybody had known but me. "Since when is all this?" I blurted out.

There was another pause. Then Gunny said, "Rick, I'm no traitor, you know that. And I'm no coward."

"But you don't want to go home."

"That's right. I never had a home, Rick, except the Corps. And after what happened to us, and what I've seen here, I'm staying."

"But in less than a year you'll have twenty, and you can retire!"

"Ricky, you've seen the way the government treated us. They couldn't care less. They'd find a way to screw me out of my pension too."

"Gunny, that wasn't the *government!*" I was beginning to yell.

Then Gunny was yelling too. "Wake up, kid. The government is supposed to know what its forces are up to. If it doesn't even do that—then God help us all! And even if I did get the pension," he went on in a tone that was quieter but grimmer, "could I retire on two hundred a month? I'm thirty-six years old, and I've been in the Marine Corps for nineteen of those —more than half my life. What am I supposed to do with myself now? I'd been in two wars, and still that bastard CO in Korea was all set to have me court-martialed. I can do without that bullshit!"

"And here you'll be in the middle of a war that goes on all the time," I said.

"So that's what I know how to do anyhow. I got nothing back in the States, no friends, no family, no job. So I'm staying."

I asked, "Then why did you keep it a secret from me?"

"I wasn't going to change *your* mind about going back. Once we got close to the water, I knew you'd have to change it again."

"I don't know how you can be so sure."

"You've got your whole life ahead of you, kid. You've got family. Also, you've got to go back and tell the story of what we did."

I looked around me, angry with everybody. "First you sneak Nancy and Kim away," I said, glaring at the Dragon Lady. "And now this."

It shook me to see her look at me the way she did then—as though I'd actually hurt her. I'd never seen this steely woman so near to crying. She said, "I didn't want them here because I was afraid you would decide to stay. That was part. Part was that I was also afraid for them, that they would not be safe."

Now I was unhappy with everything, including myself. But I said, "I understand," and then, "I'm sorry."

She shook her head as though she didn't think I understood at all. Tears rolled down her cheeks. "You fought here with us, Khan. You are a brave man. But now you must go home. Let me say to you what my father told me once. He was a wise man and he told me, 'Life is a beautiful miracle and it is given only once. The choice you make can never be made a second time. Enjoy what you have chosen. Never look back. Look forward and live the miracle.'"

It took several minutes for what she had been saying to sink in. Finally I said, "I'll always remember what you told me." And I've never forgotten.

Then she said something else I've never forgotten.

"Khan, although you have fought bravely here, your fight is not over. You may have another war to fight when you are at home."

When I asked what she meant, it was Scotty who answered. "Your group was sent over on a mission. It seems clear to me, lad, that you were never supposed to go back. Now, after you've done what you've done, seen what you've seen—now there may be people who will not *want* you back, not want you to tell your story."

He was saying things that I'd been afraid to think through.

Gunny joined in then, "Because maybe no one is supposed to know about our mission. Maybe they don't want anyone around to tell about it. Remember, it's most likely *Roberts* they're expecting to pick up. They may be in for one hell of a surprise, don't forget."

By then I couldn't think of anything to say.

"We shall speak about this again later," the Dragon Lady said, and soon we were hitting the road again—walking fast now rather than running, passing many people at work in the rice paddies. All the while, my mind was racing. Gunny would stay in China—alive and by choice. The bodies of Damon, Craig, Holden and White would all remain. Sally and Yen had died, but at least on the soil of their own country. I thought of them and of all the bodies I'd left behind—scores of them, the Chinese and the Russians I'd killed. Could I justify all that killing, even in a country where killing was a way of life?

I found the Dragon Lady walking beside me, looking up at me. I wondered whether I'd been talking to myself. She asked, "Are you all right?"

I smiled and said yes. I reached out to take her hand, and held it for a while before I let it go, thinking again about whether I really wanted to go back. The Dragon Lady had probably been right about sending Nancy and Kim away. I'd come to feel very close to them both, partly because they were young like me. And they might have influenced me to stay if they'd been with us now. But no, I'd made up my mind; the thing was decided, for a lot of good reasons. Well then, why did I seem to keep forgetting what those reasons were?

The day had become hot and sticky, and when we came to a stream I was happy to jump in for a quick wash. But the Dragon Lady had warned that we were in a dangerous area and would have to keep on moving. Everywhere people were working in the rice fields. Though we skirted them wherever we could, while holding a direct route to Lienyun, we often wound up sloshing through the wet fields as a shortcut. Though wading slowed us down and was hard on the legs, after a while, once again, I could feel my legs loosening up.

As the day ended, we went even faster. Clouds partly covered the moon but there was enough light for us to see where we were going. As I adapted to the pace, it began to seem almost comfortable. At the same time I was becoming rather lightheaded, and it didn't seem long before we were stopping for a rest.

Once we were on the move again, I felt a strange tension growing among us. Like a scene in a Grade B movie, it seemed quiet—too quiet. And that I didn't like it. The small group drew in closer together, at the risk of losing its scouts—the Mongols, carrying our gear, now close to us instead of moving in isolation.

Near the top of a hill we stopped. While the Mongols fanned out again as security, we set up the radio. Establishing contact this time was not so easy. I had almost fallen asleep when I heard, "Quicksand, Quicksand, this is Spec One. This is Spec One. Do you read? Over."

What made this so crucial an exchange was not having any code; instructions for the pickup would have to be given in the open. Spec One's information was as guarded as possible: Pier Number Four at first light tomorrow, with no mention of Lienyun itself.

Almost immediately one of the Mongols came in, and after a frantic exchange with the Dragon Lady he raced off again into the darkness. He had learned, she told us, that a large group of people, perhaps fifty or more, were coming toward us. Whether they were soldiers or not, she did not yet know.

While the Mongols patrolled, the five of us who were left took out our weapons and waited, staying low. When the Mongols finally emerged from the darkness, they brought with them two men who looked distraught. They had come, the Dragon Lady explained, from a village about a mile off, where Communist soldiers were torturing and killing people—especially children. "We have a decision to make," she said.

"Decision?" I hefted my machine gun and said, "Let's go."

The Mongols sped into the darkness and we followed, running. Almost immediately I began to sweat. My heart was pounding. How much longer could our luck hold out?

We could hear the crackle of gunfire, muffled at first by a fold of the hills. As we got closer, a glow appeared in the sky; racing between two hills, we found the village on fire, and now we could hear both the shots and the screams of people in pain.

The Dragon Lady signaled a halt. "We cannot run in blindly," she said. "We must see what is happening." As we dropped to our knees and positioned our binoculars, the Mongols appeared on the slope and spoke quickly to her. "They are killing everyone," she told us. "They have gotten the children together and put them in the school."

We spread out; then, at her arm signal, we sprinted in a skirmish line toward the village. My thoughts as we careened down the hill were more confused than they had ever been—and yet it was all so simple. We were close to the sea. If we got through this, I was thinking, this would be the last combat for me. If we didn't, it would still be my last combat.

I brought my machine gun to the ready as I ran.

15

At the edge of the village, bodies were strewn about. No one had seen us yet, and the Dragon Lady and I crouched together, out of sight of the others among the buildings. Four soldiers stepped around a hut that was perhaps twenty yards away, spotted us and pointed. When I raised my weapon they merely stared—and then, for reasons I'll never understand, they burst out laughing. For an instant I froze; but in what would otherwise have been a fatal moment, the Dragon Lady fired a burst that knocked down the four of them before they could get off a shot.

The firing was ricocheting all around us. I fired back in the direction it seemed to be coming from, and we ducked between two huts. But soon it was apparent that the soldiers weren't shooting at anything in particular. They might almost have been drunk, and they were in as much danger of hitting each other as they were likely to hit us, because there were so many more of them. While I watched, in fact, that was actually what happened, as the rain of bullets continued and the Dragon Lady went on firing.

Now I could see Gunny across the road, firing from behind some sort of cover, while the Dragon Lady was leading the way to the school. Running, we kept low, using the huts for cover, and waved for Gunny to join us. We stopped firing as we moved through the village, and the soldiers' shots tapered off as well. Thinking of the soldiers who had laughed, I wondered whether everyone hadn't gone crazy.

"The school," the Dragon Lady said, pointing to a large building, and we headed for it. Gunny and Scotty had caught up with us. Gunny kicked in the door, and the Dragon Lady and I went inside.

Years later, that scene would come to me as one of the worst of my bad dreams. In a far corner, half a dozen kids huddled together crying. Almost a hundred others had been butchered. I was all the more shaken because of the Dragon Lady's reaction. Her hold on her machine gun tightened until I could see it quiver. Then she turned and would have run out —except that I reached out and stopped her, just as Scotty pushed through the doorway and had his first glimpse of the slaughterhouse.

Looking around, we counted five living, whimpering children—the oldest possibly three years old, the others hardly more than infants. Why they had been spared, there was no telling. The others ranged in age all the way from babies to teenagers. The walls were sprayed and splotched with what looked like red paint but wasn't; it was blood. I turned away myself and the Dragon Lady said, "We must see if any of them are still alive." Then Gunny, Scotty and I began going from one child to another, picking up one body and then laying it down again next to the others. Halfway through, Scotty had to go outside; I could barely control my own stomach, and as soon as I got outside I heaved my guts. The final count was ninety-eight bodies.

What had become of the soldiers wasn't clear. Meanwhile, the Dragon Lady told us to consolidate and get to high ground before a counterattack took place. Scotty and I each lifted two of the surviving children, and Gunny grabbed the fifth. We got out quickly, making our way to a ridge beyond the town from which we looked down over the burning houses. Suddenly the Dragon Lady asked, "Where is Audy?" While the rest of us stared, she was saying, "You wait here!" and had taken off down the hill. Realizing that it was too late for any word of protest, I quickly put the two children on the ground and started after her. "Be right back!" I called out.

The four Mongols, who had covered our withdrawal and were now making their way uphill, likewise turned and followed as we tried to retrace our steps among the huts, but without finding any trace of Audy. Then the Dragon Lady sent the Mongols to comb the outlying areas, while she and I waited in the doorway of a hut. I wondered how long we could wait, not knowing how many soldiers were left alive or where they might have gone. It seemed that the town had been deserted, though, until a squad of soldiers dashed by. We were concealed and held our fire. Then the Mongol lieutenant came striding toward us with Audy over his shoulder, two of his men following. They paused among the huts to reconnoiter before making a dash across the open space that separated them from us. All this happened very fast. I saw that Audy's back was covered with blood, and then the Dragon Lady was signaling to the Mongols to keep on moving.

After I'd gestured to the lieutenant that I'd carry Audy for a while, and been waved off, I ran back with the Dragon Lady toward the high ground. The lieutenant was close behind us while two of the Mongols again covered our withdrawal. I asked the Dragon Lady where the other Mongol was and she replied, "Do not worry about him. He will get away."

We had no sooner reached Gunny, Scotty and the five children than the Dragon Lady ordered us to pick up the children and be on our way.

Keeping to the line of the ridge, we moved off even though the fourth Mongol had still not appeared. With Audy hanging like a sack over the lieutenant's shoulder, there was still no telling whether he was more than barely alive. One of the kids I was carrying had fallen asleep. The other had discovered my ear and was busy playing with it. There was a sudden halt as the Dragon Lady discovered that the radio had been left behind. While two of the Mongol lieutenant's men went back for it, we had a chance to lay Audy on the ground and see how he was. I was relieved that there was no blood coming from his nose, mouth or ears, though he'd been hit twice in the back and had lost a lot of blood. As Gunny and I were leaning over him, he opened his eyes briefly and looked as though he might be trying to say something; but all he could do was cough.

"Easy buddy, easy," Gunny said, and Audy managed a smile. His breathing was hard, with a rasp. We all looked at each other with the same worried question, and then Scotty said, "Let me look after him for a while. You three go and get some rest."

The Dragon Lady, putting one hand on my back and one on Gunny's, led us off into the darkness. We'd sat there for a while, none of us saying anything, before I finally asked the Dragon Lady, "What was going on with those soldiers that made them so crazy?"

"Like a bunch of zombies," Gunny said, and I agreed. Only zombies could have done what they did in that schoolhouse. Thinking all over again about the frightful bloodbath we'd seen there, I couldn't handle it anymore. Trying to control myself only made it worse. I threw myself face down, landed my forehead on my machine gun and lay there shaking.

I could feel Gunny and the Dragon Lady both leaning over me, and Gunny was saying, just as he had to Audy a little while before, "Easy, buddy, take it easy."

Once I'd gotten a grip on myself, I felt a bit ashamed. Why the hell was I feeling so sorry for myself when we had those five children to worry about? "The kids," I said. "Is anybody looking after them?"

"They're all sleeping," Gunny said, and for some reason I started to cry again.

"We shall have to take them somewhere that is safe," the Dragon Lady said. "You know that now we cannot reach our destination by morning."

"Who cares?" I yelled. "I don't give a damn when we get there!" Then a kind of stupor came over me, and for a while no one said anything. "But about those soldiers," I asked finally. "No one normal would act that way."

"They were not normal," the Dragon Lady said. "They were machines. Before a battle they are given a drug in their food or their drink or else they smoke it, so that when they fight they do not know what they are doing. It makes them unafraid."

There was silence again until Scotty walked over to us. He took a deep breath and said, "Audy is not doing well. I've stopped the bleeding, but he had already lost a good deal. The bullets went straight through him. I tried to close everything up as best I could. But . . . " He took another breath. "I had to push things back into place . . . " He dropped his head, looking exhausted. When the Dragon Lady asked if we could help, he only shook his head and went back to watch over his old friend.

Then came the bellow that was the Mongols' signal, and in a couple of minutes the lieutenant and his men were back, bringing the basket with the radio in it. With that worry disposed of, our main concerns now were Audy and the children, and after that the question of the delay in our schedule.

In answer to the first, the Dragon Lady said, "There is a village near called Kenyu, where I have friends. We can leave Audy and the children there to be cared for. But we shall not be able to reach Lienyun by the morning."

"Will we make it by tomorrow night?" I asked, and when she said yes, I was suddenly struck by an idea: we could radio to ask for a twenty-four-hour delay, which meant we'd have twelve hours' leeway—time to look things over instead of just walking in.

Gunny asked, "Will they wait another twenty-four hours?"

"I think so," the Dragon Lady said. "It is a good idea, Khan. We shall do it. Now we must get started."

We picked up our burdens and took off at a fast trot in the moonlight. Soon, from a ridge, we could spot the village. The lieutenant put Audy down gently; we did the same with the kids, who were drunk with sleep, and the Dragon Lady and two Mongols went down to negotiate. Before long everything had been cleared, and with a reminder from the Dragon Lady that we must slip in and out quickly, we had entered the town and were following her into a hut. A group of women were already waiting there to take the children, and in another room others immediately started tending Audy.

After one long look at the man and the children I'd never see again, I made my way with the others back to the high ground. The pace became more exhausting as the ground got hillier and steeper. Nobody was talking. I kept thinking about Audy and about the third Mongol. It now seemed clear that he would not meet us—which meant that he must be either dead or captured. After a while we stopped to bivouac and set up the radio. While I sat with my back propped against a rock, resting, Gunny came over and joined me. I said, "You know, I'm going to miss you, you son of a bitch."

I could see his grin in the moonlight but his voice when he spoke was serious. "Same here, kid. I never really had a friend in my life before. But you, Ricky—you're a friend. I figure if you have one friend in your whole life, then you're ahead of the game. If I ever have a kid, I hope he'll be like you."

I was so touched that I could only growl a little. And I knew he was just as uncomfortable with so much emotion. "So now, kid," he said, "I'm going to find myself a place to sack out. See you in the morning." He got up and walked off a little way.

The Mongols were out there somewhere in the darkness, and Scotty—who could fall asleep faster than anybody I ever met—was around on the other side of the rocks. I slid down and stretched out on the ground right where I was. In a couple of minutes, just as I was beginning to doze off, I realized that the Dragon Lady was sitting next to me.

"Now it is very peaceful," she said. "And soon, Ricky, you will be gone."

"Ricky?" I said, a little scared at hearing her call me that. "No more Khan?"

She had propped her head on her hand, and she lay there looking at me in the moonlight. "You are not Khan the warrior now. You are Ricky."

I said, "Maybe some day I can come back." I didn't quite know what I was saying, but I meant every word when I whispered, "I'll never meet anyone like you."

She put up her hand and touched my face. "You do not have to tell me anything," she said. Her face was close now, and I leaned over and kissed her.

Then I put my hand on her hair.

Then I ran my hand down her back.

Then I pressed her slim little body against mine. I could feel every inch of her, from her face down to her toes, responding.

We were together when I woke. She was still asleep—the first time I had ever seen her sleeping. I didn't want to wake her but neither did I want to be seen with her like this. When I tried disentangling my arm from her, she woke.

She gave me a smile, raised her hand and ran it over my face. Then abruptly she sat up. "We must get on the radio."

We found Gunny and Scotty already fiddling with it. Had they seen us together? One look at their faces was all I needed to know that they had. But there were no remarks from anybody.

Scotty said, "Shall we try?"—and at a nod from the Dragon Lady he began fiddling with the transmitter again.

"Spec One, Spec One, this is Quicksand, this is Quicksand. Do you read us? Over."

He had to repeat it twice more—while we all got more and more jittery—before the answer came.

"We have a delay," Scotty told them. "We cannot make destination on time. I repeat, we have a delay. Do you read?"

"Loud and clear," the answer came back. "Interrogatory. What is the cause of the delay?"

Scotty ignored the interrogatory. "We have a twenty-four-hour delay. We need twenty-four hours. Over."

"We will give you twenty-four hours. No longer. Say again. Twenty-four hours, but no longer."

"Loud and clear," Scotty replied. "Rendezvous in twenty-four hours. Out."

The Dragon Lady told us now that it would take only two or three hours to reach Lienyun. "We shall wait so that we arrive in darkness."

"What the hell are we going to do all day?" Gunny asked.

The Dragon Lady smiled. "Rest."

And that is what we did. We lay around all day in the warm sun, with the Mongols patrolling, as seemed to be their nature, until the shadows began to lengthen. That was our signal to be on our way—to whom or whatever it was that would be waiting.

The last thing we did was to hide the radio among the rocks. It was an unnecessary weight now that we didn't need it anymore. Then we were off and in less than three hours we came in sight of the South China Sea. It glistened in the moonlight as we made our way down to the beach, where we huddled together on the sand while the Dragon Lady sketched out the area. The fourth pier, our place of rendezvous, was perhaps half a mile away.

The four of us were to approach it through the water, armed with knives, while the Mongols wrapped the rest of our weapons and carried them overland to meet us. It was less likely that they would be stopped, and they would be nearby to act as a support once we'd boarded the boat.

After we'd left the weapons and bandoliers with them, there was a brief rehearsal and then we headed into the water, holding our footing as long as we could and then swimming parallel to the beach. Soon we could make out the piers in the darkness. The moon disappeared behind the clouds and that was a good sign. While the Dragon Lady swam in an arc to find the right pier and then the boat, I followed with a slow breast-stroke. Finally, treading water, she pointed to a large, two-masted junk among the pilings.

The whole ocean seemed to be at our backs as we closed in. I could make out a figure walking along the deck; then it disappeared through a hatchway. We found a ladder near the stern. The Dragon Lady signaled silence with a finger to her lips; then, with her knife's blade clenched between her teeth, she positioned herself to climb aboard. I lunged, intending to go ahead of her, and clamped my hand above hers on the ladder. Though she shook her head, I insisted and finally she moved aside for me. With both hands on the ladder, I listened a moment or two and then carefully and quietly pulled myself up out of the water, moving slowly to avoid the least splash. Moments later, with my head at deck level, I could take in the entire boat from one end to the other.

Though the moon was out, luckily our side of the boat was in shadow. Seeing no one, I hoisted myself onto the deck and darted for the cabin door. Glancing back, I saw the Dragon Lady's head appear; I waved her aboard, and she glided toward me like a cat, with Scotty and Gunny behind her.

As we positioned ourselves on both sides of the cabin hatchway and I reached for the knob, we heard a man's laughter inside, and then the sound of a second and a third voice.

We stepped back into the shadows, and I whispered, "The weapons!"

The Dragon Lady vanished into the darkness; then she was back with the three Mongols and our guns. Armed with those, we moved back to the hatchway.

She whispered, "We go on the count of three. Do not shoot unless it is necessary."

She held up one finger. With my machine gun gripped firmly in my left hand, I unsheathed my knife with my right and held it at the ready. Two fingers. Then three. Gunny threw open the hatch, slamming it against the bulkhead, and we bolted through, down two steps and into the cabin's interior before fanning out while the Mongols covered our rear. My wildest imaginings could not have prepared me for the shock that would come in an instant.

A few feet away three men sat at a table, with filled glasses before them. Caught by total surprise, they sat frozen in place for several seconds while we stared at them and they stared back at us. It was a deadly silence. Then Gunny broke the quiet, "Holy Mother of God!" He spoke for me as well because I saw the terrible truth.

Of the three Americans or whatever they were, I recognized one at once. A rage came over me—over all of us—that I've lived with ever since. A calculated breaking of faith by our own people had caused the deaths of our comrades. We were trained, sent on a mission, and abandoned—purposely.

The man turned white. Then he blurted, "You're—how in hell . . . ?"

"You know him?" Scotty asked.

"We know him."

"Watch this," said Gunny quickly. "Spec One, this is Quicksand. Do you read? Over."

"You worthless bastards!" snarled one of the others. Then quickly assuming an air of command, he spoke to me, "Stand at attention. Where's Roberts?"

But my eyes never left those of the one man I knew had

betrayed us. "We know him." I was in a cold fury. "Just like we knew that bastard Roberts. This is the other one who trained us. And threw us to the wolves."

It was all in the open now and both sides knew it. The countless nights I've lain awake thinking about what happened next have all ended in a question: Could it have been different? Conditioning by teamwork and unrelenting fighting over the last three weeks had accounted for our survival. Killing the enemy was the important goal if you survived. And here was the enemy.

Suddenly it happened, so quickly that our response together was reflexive. Out of the corner of my eye I saw the third man lunge for a weapon leaning against a nearby bulkhead, and that triggered the two others to do likewise. Diving across the table, I drove my knife into the body of the man who had trained and betrayed us. The blade entered where the chest merges with the throat and when I pulled it out, he was dead. Quickly I turned to see that Gunny and Scotty had made quick work of the two others while the Dragon Lady and the Mongols looked on. No shots were fired: it was silent work with cold steel, done according to the law we'd lived under in China: Kill or be killed.

As I looked at the bodies, the reality of what we'd done for revenge and survival hit me. We had killed three Americans.

I felt Gunny's hand on my shoulder, trying to steady me as he said firmly, "Three Americans, Ricky, but not *our people.*" In a frenzy, I shook his hand off. I turned over the table, I punched at bulkheads, all the while screaming at the top of my lungs. Gunny, Scotty and the Dragon Lady had to wrestle me down. The Mongols who had come rushing in, now stood over me with expressionless faces. At a word from the Dragon Lady, they and then Scotty left the cabin. In a few minutes I could feel the boat underway. Calmed by exhaustion, I tried to get my thinking clear again.

Finally I asked, "Where are we going?"

"Out to sea," the Dragon Lady said.

I stared at the bodies on the floor. "You see what we did." I said it to no one in particular.

Gunny said, "We killed three bastards. They were playing games with us, and the last one they played, they lost."

I sat there stupefied, wondering what we could do now. "We can't just go out to sea," I said. "Between the Communists and the Americans, we'll get cut to pieces."

The Dragon Lady answered, "We must get out, away from here. Then we can use the radio. We shall keep moving, to make it harder for anyone to find us."

"They'll find us," Gunny said.

"Yes," she agreed. "They will find us. But now search through those men's pockets. Perhaps you will find something to help with the radio."

It was a while before I could bring myself to go and help Gunny. When I did, I found in the pockets of the man who'd trained us a wallet containing an ID card with a photograph. It read, UNITED STATES GOVERNMENT, CENTRAL INTELLIGENCE AGENCY. The name on it was James Strong. Again the bewilderment. Why would an American intelligence agent carry ID papers? What was going on?

While I stared at it, Gunny was saying, "Tell me, kid, do you still want to go back?"

The question stung like a whip. "I've got to find out," I said. "Do they think *we're* traitors? I've got to find out."

Gunny gazed at me. "You don't think you'll get a straight answer, do you?" While I stared back, he said, "Rick, you're not going to be able to get them. I can smell it now."

Pointing a finger at him, I said slowly, "We'll see about that. And I'll tell you one thing more: they're going to know I'm back, they're not just going to write me off!"

Gunny's face changed. He nodded slowly. "I know what you mean. And you're right." He turned to the Dragon Lady. "The question is, can he get back? Can we stay close enough

to shore to broadcast and beach the junk if something happens
—and then run like hell back across China?"

"Yes," she answered. "We can."

"Well," he told her, "it's a long shot. But we don't have
much choice." He looked at me hard. "She said a few days ago
that once you made up your mind, you wouldn't change it."

"That's right," I said. "I did choose to go back. And by all
that's holy, that's what I'm going to do. Whether they like it
or not."

The Dragon Lady said there was something she must do
and hurried from the cabin. That left the two of us with the
corpses.

"Better search these other two and get it over with,"
Gunny said. It wasn't a pleasant assignment, and my own
search turned up nothing. But then Gunny was shouting,
"Look at this!"

He held up a card.

Turning it to the light, I read out loud, "United States
Foreign Service. Aleksei Kutuzov."

I was just saying, "What would that be, German?" when
the Dragon Lady came back into the cabin. She said quickly
that it was a Russian name.

While we both stared, she added, "Perhaps he is one who
works for both sides."

To this day, I have no clearer idea than I had then about
who trained us or where their orders came from.

"Whoever they are," I said then, "the question is, what
the hell are we going to do with them?"

Gunny said without hesitation, "Feed 'em to the fishes.
Like any other garbage."

The Dragon Lady concurred. She shouted a command
through the hatchway, and in a few moments the two Mongols
had come in and were dragging the bodies out. "We shall feed
them to the fishes," she said. "To the fishes who swim down
deep!"

Gunny said, "Okay, now we send a message." We headed for the radio room where in a couple of moments we were joined by Scotty and the Dragon Lady. "Well, here goes," Gunny announced. "Either we make contact real quick or we start running like hell back to Mongolia."

He pressed the button to send. "This is Quicksand, this is Quicksand. We are Americans. This is urgent, I will not say again. If I don't get acknowledgment, we'll defect, we go straight to the Commies. We'll go straight to Mao if we have to. Will tell everything. Everything. Acknowledge loud and clear—or God help you and everyone. We're standing by. Over."

We waited. The radio operator was obviously calling in the communications officer. In a couple of minutes we had an answer.

"Quicksand, who are you, mister? We're in dark here. Need specifics. Give more identification. Over."

Gunny replied, "This is Quicksand. We are Americans waiting for a pickup off the mainland. Strong and Roberts are gone. That is all I can tell you. Say Wilco or we return to mainland . . . and God help us all. Give me a call sign. Over."

The answer came. "Quicksand, interrogatory. Can you tell us the star of *The Outlaw?* Say again, who is the star of *The Outlaw?* Over."

Gunny looked at me, puzzled. "Jane Russell," I told him, and he transmitted it.

The reply came back at once. "This is Eagles Nest, Quicksand. Correct on interrogatory. Need coordinates. Say again, your location. Over."

Gunny looked at me. "If we give a location from the charts, we're dead ducks." He hesitated. "I'll try onion," he told me. "Strong understood that one. Let's hope these guys will too."

He sent the message: "Eagles Nest, this is Quicksand. We are two miles east of onion. Repeat, we are two miles due east of onion. Over."

Christ, I said to myself, how many times before the Communists know we're at Lienyun? But Eagles Nest, apparently not understanding right away, asked us to stand by. While we did, I wondered about Eagles Nest. Wasn't this the command post for those same bastards, Roberts and Strong?

We waited, getting more and more nervous. Then the answer came. "Quicksand, this is Eagles Nest. We have your approximate location as two miles due east of onion. Hope we understand you. Can you head due east from your present location? Over."

"This is Quicksand. Wilco. Due east. How long to pickup? Over."

"Less than two hours," was the answer. Then Eagles Nest said, "We hope you're authentic. If you're not, the devil take you."

Gunny was running with sweat as he spoke, but what he said was simply, "Likewise. No sweat. Out." Then he put down the mike. "Well, it's done."

"What happens now?" With all the doubts I had about Eagles Nest, I couldn't help shaking at the thought that I would soon be on my own.

It was Scotty who answered. "We're taking the small boat to shore. You're staying aboard this one. The currents will take you east without power; you can't risk running a motor. Then, lad, you're on your own."

The leavetaking I hadn't dared imagine was quick. It was also emotional and my tears flowed freely: Gunny throwing his arms around me, then Scotty embracing me, the Mongol guards clasping my arms and their lieutenant with his right hand on my left shoulder, repeating the only English word he knew, a word he'd first heard after I fought him: "Friend." Seeing how shaken I was, Scotty cut in to lead me to the wheel. "It's a calm sea, lad. You shouldn't have much trouble." Then he climbed down into the small boat, which now rode free in the water. The Mongols were already waiting, steadying the boat by grasping the ladder.

Before he finally climbed down, Gunny handed me a folded piece of paper. "Keep it with you," he said. "It's for you to read—you and the people who pick you up." Then he turned and jumped into the small boat, without looking back.

I felt the Dragon Lady's arms around my waist. Turning to receive her head against my chest, I realized what I'd already forgotten, how tiny she was. Leaning down, I put my arms around her, lifted her until her face was even with mine, and kissed her on the lips. "I love you."

"I love *you*."

She climbed down the ladder, quickly. Through the darkness, I watched them cast off and then wave. After a while they were barely visible. Then there was nothing.

Alone, I found myself clutching the rail, as though for support. Then I reached up to finger the rosary beads I'd worn about my neck ever since Kim gave them to me. I wept long and hard. I watched the water as the boat cut cleanly through it. A sudden chill seized me; rushing to the cabin, I retrieved my machine gun and took it with me to the bow.

Remembering the note Gunny had given me, I reached into the pocket of my tattered pants, unfolded and read it.

Dear Rick,
First, I hope you understand why I'm staying—because I found what I wanted, just like Scotty did. But the important thing is that I have found out from the Dragon Lady a way to check and make sure that you are safely back in the States. Sometimes when you pick up the telephone and it's a salesman, just listen. Then you can tell him to bug off. Through friends, we can check and see if they are leaving you alone. If at anytime something happens to you, we will take matters into our own hands even if it means going to the Communists. I don't think the bastards will want that, so they better lay off you.
Don't think every telephone call you get is going to be from

her friends. It won't. You won't even know, neither will the bastards.
So long and God bless you. We all love you.

Gunnery Sgt. Robert Masters, USMC
Special Force Group One, China

The moon had gone behind clouds, it was dark, and there was no one now to see me shivering in my wet clothes, lost and crying. What had I lost? What was I gaining? What lay ahead? A thousand miles in twenty-two violent days through the heart of China with death stalking us every step of the way to the southeastern coast and now waiting for a rendezvous with my people. *My* people? Hadn't I just left *my* people? Your *other* people, a voice seemed to say to me. Why was I crying? Because I had been involved in so much killing? You'll just have to live with that. Can I? You'll have to. I'm afraid now. Afraid of what? Of what they'll do to me. You've got another responsibility now. I know that. But there's something else. Like what? I've learned something. What? I don't know how to say it: a sort of discovery. Mine. But I'm not sure what it is. What *is* it? I'm not sure. Try. I can't. Yes you can, name it. I'm not very good with words, I'm seventeen, I . . . *Name* it. It's just that I've learned so much in the last three weeks. Enough to last a lifetime. In a way it has been a lifetime. Before words like *brotherhood, compassion, love,* were only words. Now I think I know what they mean. Not bad. What's the matter with that? But not just because the Dragon Lady and I . . . I know. It's more than that: there are Kim and Nancy and the baby I rescued. Anybody else? Gunny, Scotty, Audy, Charlie and John O'Malley. And many others. So what's the matter with that? I can't stop crying. Why bother? It can be good sometimes. You know, all these things I have trouble finding the words for, I learned from a strange people. I had come as a stranger and was made welcome. You are very fortunate: for that reason if for no other. Let not thy heart be troubled. The ancient comforting words. Touching the rosary. Sobbing softly now. Remember the miracle. I could almost hear her speak those words by which I would live. A sudden breeze chilled me, and then as quickly as it came, it died. Then there was no sound but the waves against the side of the boat as the current carried me to my mission's end.

I don't know how long it was before a powerful thrust upward broke the surface less than fifty yards off. Moments later, along the starboard side, I could make out the conning tower of a submarine.

Clutching my machine gun, I watched for the next several minutes as a small, dark shape bobbed its way toward me; and when it appeared alongside, I saw it was a manned rubber raft. Then through the darkness I heard a crisp American command: "Ahoy topside. Show yourself."

Aboard the submarine no one said a word. and I was hustled into a cabin. I saw a clean bed and a sink—everything spotless and in order. After a minute there was a rap on the hatch, and three men came in. One of them was an officer. I smiled at them. Nobody smiled back.

The officer asked, "Who are you?"

"I am PFC Lawrence Gardella, Special Force Group One, United States Marine Corps."

It's no wonder he stared at me, I suppose—ragged and bruised, with a string of green jade rosary beads around my neck.

"And just where did you come from?"

I'd been ready for that. "I'm sorry, sir," I told him. "I cannot say any more than that."

"Who else was with you?"

"I can't say that either, sir."

After staring for a second or two longer, he turned to one of the men with him. "Get this individual a bath and some chow. And some decent clothes."

Glaring at me now, he said, "I'll talk to you later." He

wheeled and made his exit. The hatch closed behind him.

A couple of minutes later another sailor appeared.

"First a shower," he said. "Then some chow." He actually smiled; he seemed the friendliest of the lot. But I wasn't exactly getting a hero's welcome.

After my first shower in a month, I put on the clothes they'd left for me. They weren't a perfect fit but they were an improvement on what I'd been wearing. The same sailor was waiting to lead me back to the cabin, where I found a tray with soup, coffee and pudding on it. As soon as I'd finished everything, I slept—I don't know for how long. When I woke I couldn't remember where I was. As soon as I did, I stepped outside the cabin. Two sailors intercepted me. I said something about wanting to take a walk, and one of them said, pleasantly enough, "Sorry. This is a submarine, not an aircraft carrier."

"Okay then, how about some more chow?"

"Right away," he said. He seemed a nice enough guy. I went back into the cabin, sat down on the rack, started to doze and was almost asleep again when the food arrived: bacon and eggs, ham, pudding, coffee, milk and juice! I was halfway through when a couple of corpsmen in white coats walked in. One had a tray with some medical paraphernalia on it.

"Time for your shots," he said. "We don't know what you might be carrying."

I held out my arm for him to swab. They gave me the shots and were gone. The last thing I remember of my stay aboard the submarine is the sight of their white coats framed by the hatchway. From May 30, 1952, through the entire month of June, I was pretty much out of it, although I remember the voices I heard now and then. In particular, I remember a meeting with someone—someone very special. Before I put down what I remember of that, though, there are a few things I should tell you about the rest of my life.

16

My adventure in China lasted from May 9, 1952, when we were dropped in, until May 30, when I was picked up by the submarine—just three weeks. After three weeks of living so fully, it might seem that the rest of my life—twenty-eight years of it as I write this—has been dull by comparison. I think it's more accurate to say that I've lived two lives, almost as though I'd been two different people. My life since I left China has been enough like the lives of most people that a few pages are all I need to tell you about it.

On July 5, 1952, my mother came to visit me at the U. S. Naval Hospital in Annapolis, Maryland. She found me with my arms and legs bandaged, and was told that I had been hospitalized because of a severe allergic reaction to poison ivy in the field. This was, of course, not true. What those bandages covered, if they covered anything, were the various bruises, scrapes and scratches I'd acquired on the other side of the world.

About ten days after that visit, I was dismissed from the hospital. After another ten days, on July 24, I was honorably discharged from the Marine Corps. When my mother met me at South Station in Boston, she was clearly upset by the way I looked. And for a long time my refusal to talk about my experience in the Corps was both a mystery and a source of anxiety to her.

I didn't know what I was going to do with the rest of my life. I tried reenlisting as a marine and was rejected. I lived with my parents in Allston, about a mile from Harvard Stadium, and for months I kept to myself, drank a lot and worked at odd jobs now and then.

In the spring of 1953 I met Marie, who brought me back from the hell my life had become. I stopped drinking and found steady work. On November 21 of that year, when Marie was still only sixteen and I was one day short of my nineteenth birthday, we got married.

In 1955, the year I went into construction work, our first daughter, Susan Marie, was born. Our second, Janet Muriel, arrived three years later.

In 1958 I began moonlighting as a cab driver in Boston, working from five to midnight after an eight-to-four day in construction. I kept that up for years. I got my first assignment as a construction foreman in 1960, and by 1963 I was a general foreman—the youngest in our area, so far as I know.

Our grandson, Robert Edmund Storme, was born in 1974.

It was in 1977 that I found I had leukemia and decided to put the story of my China mission in writing. On May 31, 1979, just two weeks after the manuscript was sent to a publisher, I returned home from work to find my wife had been beaten, left bloody and dazed as though she'd been drugged. Nothing had been taken—none of Marie's jewelry and none of my collection of guns. The local police kept an eye on her all that summer.

On July 13, 1979, I had the encounter in Harvard Stadium with which this book begins.

Three weeks later, on August 7, our apartment was broken into and ransacked, though once again nothing was taken. In our bedroom we discovered several peculiar and frightening things. Marie's coat had been laid on our bed with the stuffing from a pillow inside the hood to suggest the shape of a human head, and with the right sleeve folded across the chest. My pistol had been placed where the hand would have been. The fabric of the coat had been ripped with a knife. And in a picture on the wall, a circle had been drawn around Marie's head.

Around this time Marie received a number of mysterious telephone calls.

I am as certain as I can be of anything, as I write this, that these incidents add up to deliberate terrorization with the purpose of scaring me out of having my story published. Just who was responsible, of course, I do not know.

Now let me go back twenty-eight years, to just after I left China.

17

On May 30, 1952, before I could finish the American meal I'd been served aboard the submarine, I was given a shot that left me drugged. I woke dazed and groggy. Again I didn't know where I was. When I tried to get up, I found that I was strapped to the bed, across my legs, waist, arms and chest. As my vision cleared, I saw the total whiteness of a hospital room. To this day, I don't know where that room was. It couldn't have been aboard the sub—the quarters were too spacious for that. Was I in the naval hospital at Annapolis or somewhere en route? Hospital rooms everywhere look pretty much alike. The two figures in white who were present were not the two corpsmen who had given me the shot.

One of them asked how I was feeling.

I said, "I've felt better. What's going on?"

"Take it easy," he said.

I noticed a pole with a bottle attached, and a tube from it leading to my arm. Never having seen such an apparatus before, I asked what the hell it was. The corpsman explained that I was being fed intravenously, because I'd been sick and in shock.

Then the second corpsman asked me a question: "How about the others?"

I looked at him. "What others?"

"Don't play games," he said disagreeably. "The others in your group."

I answered, "I'm not playing games. Find out for yourself."

While the men looked at each other, I began to wonder whether they were doctors at all. One of them came toward me with a syringe, and injected something into the tube leading to my arm. I remember that a kind of whistling went through my head. After that I lost track of things again.

Other things were happening as I drifted in and out of consciousness. Once I awoke and heard voices through a slightly opened door.

"How are they going to list the others?"

"Missing in action."

"The poor son of a bitch in there," the first voice said. "He should get a medal. Instead, he'll get nothing but a hard time."

"You think it's all true?"

"After what we've been giving him, it's got to be. It's a wonder he's even alive."

"That's for sure."

"The letter we found on him is probably what did it."

"Yeah. The blackmailing son of a bitch!"

I managed a hoarse yell, "They're not missing in action, they're dead! They're dead, you bastards!"

The two men came in, and I heard one of them mutter. Then I went under again.

I remember, another time, seeing three men standing

over me while I tried to bring my eyes into focus and hearing one of them ask how I felt.

"A little bit groggy," I told them. "But okay."

"You've been through a lot," the same voice said. "Can you hear me? Can you understand me?"

I said, "Yeah."

"We want to send you somewhere. Somewhere in Asia."

I said, "Yeah, where?"

"Indochina."

"So I can be missing in action?" And they put me under again.

Then I remember waking in another hospital room. This time I wasn't strapped down. The sheets were crisp and smooth, and I was dressed in pajamas. I had a radio by my bed and there were flowers on the window sill. I swung my legs over the side of the bed and tried to sit up. Immediately I felt dizzy and my head began throbbing. A second later, the door opened and two civilians came in. One of them spoke softly. "You'd better get dressed. There's someone upstairs waiting to see you." He pointed to a corner of the room, where a set of marine tropicals was hanging.

I stood up slowly and carefully and managed to get into the uniform while the two men watched. I felt like an old man —weak and stiff and tired. The corridor into which I followed the two men was thronged with people in white. At least I really was in a hospital this time.

We got onto an elevator, and when its door opened we walked through a doorway and into a room with the shades drawn, with almost no light coming through. As my eyes became adjusted to the dark, I saw that several people were waiting.

A voice came from the far end of the room: "Son—"

Someone interrupted,

"John, leave this to me. Those —— have gotten us into this. Now let's see if I can get us out of it." The voice was snappy, and somehow it struck me as familiar.

"Son, we are . . . awfully sorry for what happened. Awfully sorry. May God help us all." The voice paused again, as though saying a prayer. "We know everything now, son. I didn't know before. I'm sorry I didn't."

"Didn't know?" I asked. *"Who* didn't—"

One of the others said, "Keep your voice down. Do you know who—"

The snappy voice with the familiar twang intervened again. "John, I told you to keep quiet!" Then, more calmly, "Son, there's nothing you or I can do about it now. It's too late. If you talk about what happened, what you did, you could start a war. You've got to keep your mouth shut."

As my eyes grew more accustomed to the semidarkness, I could see that the figure was short and blocky, and wore a square-cut, double-breasted jacket. As he moved, even in the dim light, there was the tiny glint of a reflection from his glasses.

The voice softened. "You deserve a lot but this country can't give it to you. It can't give you any medals, because all of this is going to be forgotten. None of it will be in the records. None of it will have happened. I'm not asking you to forgive *me,* I'm asking you to forgive our country. I found out about all this only by the grace of God. But I can make you a promise. This happened. It won't happen again. That's my promise. You have to make one in return."

"Yes, sir?"

"You must remain silent. Tell no one. I'm asking you to promise that for your country."

"Yes sir, I promise," I said. Then I asked, "Sir, what happens to me now?"

"You will be discharged for medical reasons. I understand you have a history of asthma."

"Sir, I have a favor to ask you," I began. Though what I really wanted to ask was to get back into the marines, I also knew there was no point in asking for that. So I said, "When

I was picked up, I had on a set of rosary beads. They were very special. I'd like to have them back."

"John—" the short man said. He didn't have to say any more. He sounded very much the boss.

The man who had left the room was soon back. He handed something to the short man, who now walked toward me. The rosary beads were in his hand. I took them and thanked him.

Then one of the others drew up a shade, and there was no longer any doubt in my mind about who the speaker was.

"Son," he said, "I'd like to shake your hand."

The hand he held out was small but strong.

Before I let it go, I asked, "Sir, where am I and what day is it?"

"This is the U. S. Naval Hospital at Annapolis, Maryland, and it is June 28, 1952." Then, abruptly, President Harry S. Truman released my hand, wheeled about and walked smartly out of the room, with the others close behind him.

Two weeks later I walked out of the hospital, with the rosary beads in my hand.

Epilogue

Not all the questions you must have about the story I have told can be answered. For some of them, the reason is simply that I don't know the answer. For others, to give it would endanger the lives of others. But there are a few things that I can at least try to clear up, though they will raise further questions.

Why did I go back on the promise I made, never to tell the story? There are several reasons. One is that it was an old promise and the world has changed. I believe my experience has something to say to policymakers. And I now know that the government never really kept the promise that was made to that seventeen-year-old kid. My illness, my wife, my priest —all of them gave me the same message: that it was right to tell the truth about what I knew, regardless of how awful it might seem.

Where was President Truman on June 28, 1952? Could he have been talking to me in the hospital that day? A journalist who checked his schedule for that day found that he was in Washington and that no appointments were listed on his calendar. Annapolis, Maryland, is thirty-five miles from Washington, no more than an hour's drive away.

What do Marine Corps records say about me and the special force? That I never left the States, that the medical records of my stay in the naval hospital were destroyed by fire, and that there are no records that any of the men with me—Damon, Masters, Holden, White or Craig—was ever in the Corps.

What happened to my friends in China?

I'm happy to be able to say that as of the time I write this, Gunny, Charlie, Kim and the Mongol lieutenant are alive and well.

Audy is also alive, but has never really recovered from the wounds he suffered when we rescued the children from the village near Kenyu.

Nancy and Scotty are dead. Nancy was killed in a battle in 1954. Scotty, after surviving forty years of combat, died of natural causes in 1977.

God only knows where John O'Malley is.

I've also learned the Dragon Lady is alive, and has twin sons—*our* sons. They are big and blond, and as of the time I write this, they are twenty-seven years old. Some day before I die, I am going to see them.

May God give me strength, whatever happens.

PUBLISHER'S NOTE:

Lawrence Gardella died on Monday, February 16, 1981, as this book was going into production.